New
4-88

W9-BLS-606

PRAISE FOR
LIGHTPATHS

"Howard Hendrix is one of the very best of the new science fiction writers. Conversant in all the latest cosmology and sub-atomic complexity, he has the rare ability to track those concepts to their intersections with the human heart, in novels that stand as works of high adventure. Highly recommended."

—Kim Stanley Robinson,
author of the *Mars* trilogy

"A bravura debut from a writer who is sure to become one of SF's biggest names. Howard V. Hendrix takes us on a mind-bending exploration of the nature of consciousness. The book's characters are real people, and their philosophical musings are engrosing."

—Robert J. Sawyer,
Nebula Award-winning author of *Starplex*

"In *Lightpaths*, Howard Hendrix gives us an exhilarating intellectual tour of both an amazing orbital habitat and a dizzying complex of ideas, from the scientific to the aesthetic to the utopian. I have a future imperfect imperative for everyone who happens upon a copy: seize it—legally of course—and read it!"

—Michael Bishop,
author of *Brittle Innings*

"A fresh look at a familiar SF concept: life on a space station . . . Taut, engaging, even occasionally reassuring, Hendrix's novel leaves readers wishing for another portion of this space-age slice of life." —*Publishers Weekly*

"A complex and erudite examination of fundamental questions about being and consciousness." —*Fresno Bee*

"Fascinating . . . An impressive first novel." —*Locus*

Ace Books by Howard V. Hendrix

LIGHTPATHS
STANDING WAVE

STANDING WAVE

HOWARD V. HENDRIX

ACE BOOKS, NEW YORK

If you purchased this book without a cover, you should be aware that this book is stolen property. It was reported as "unsold and destroyed" to the publisher, and neither the author nor the publisher has received any payment for this "stripped book."

This book is an Ace original edition,
and has never been previously published.

STANDING WAVE

An Ace Book / published by arrangement with
the author

PRINTING HISTORY
Ace edition / September 1998

All rights reserved.
Copyright © 1998 by Howard V. Hendrix.
Cover art by Phil Heffernan.
This book may not be reproduced in whole or in part,
by mimeograph or any other means, without permission.
For information address: The Berkley Publishing Group,
a member of Penguin Putnam Inc.,
200 Madison Avenue, New York, NY 10016.

The Penguin Putnam Inc. World Wide Web site address is
http://www.penguinputnam.com

Check out the Ace Science Fiction/Fantasy
newsletter, and much more, at Club PPI!

ISBN: 0-441-00553-5

ACE®
Ace Books are published by The Berkley Publishing Group,
a member of Penguin Putnam Inc.,
200 Madison Avenue, New York, New York 10016.
ACE and the "A" design are trademarks
belonging to Charter Communications, Inc.

PRINTED IN THE UNITED STATES OF AMERICA

10 9 8 7 6 5 4 3 2 1

ACKNOWLEDGMENTS

MANY THANKS MUST GO TO PHILOSOPHER BRUCE ALBERT (again) for allowing me the opportunity to peruse his manuscript, *Spontaneous Human Consciousness*—the finest unified theory of consciousness that I have yet encountered. My gratitude also goes to Mike Lepper, whose experiences in Oregon and beyond taught me much about the plasticity of the human brain and its capacity for recovery after severe head trauma. My thanks also to National University, for allowing me time away from my teaching and administrative duties during the second half of 1996 so that I might write this novel. Finally, thanks again to my wife, Laurel, for allowing me to explain Gödelian incompleteness and Heisenbergian uncertainty to her—and thereby also allowing me the chance to think through the dynamic relationship between coherence and comprehensiveness.

To my parents.

STANDING WAVE

PROLOGUE

LIGHT MAZED EVERY MIND'S SKY AND WAS GONE. AT THE surface of the world's oceans the voices of dolphins in air called excitedly, reacting to what the Light had given them. Great whales came together in rosettes, heads turned inward toward each other, flukes away, still and concentrating, pinging information directly into each other's skulls like a telepathic conference call. At their Yerkish keyboards, chimpanzees smiled slyly as they pounded out poems parodying passages from Shakespeare. Bonobos, excited by the Light, fell immediately into orgies of heavy grooming and joyously prolonged sex. Orangutans pondered the possibility that all the world's a tree, and all its inhabitants merely branches. Gorillas contemplated the labyrinth of self and hoped they would not get lost there.

A computer-interfaced porpoise at a marine park in Hawaii, queried across the datasphere by its female human interrogator, remarked simply that "The sea is in the wave as the wave is in the sea," then shaped a blowhole bubble into a perfect halo and swam through it. Ordinarily, the observing scientist would have written this statement off as just one more example of the bubbly topological mysticism porpoises seemed prone to—but not this time. Now the koan-like statement spoke to her condition, for the Light had already spoken to her too, as it had to all her fellow human beings.

The originator of the Light had assumed, mistakenly, that humans would be the sole creatures for whom the Light would shine. He would have been overjoyed at his error. As he had predicted, though, the effect would not be lasting, in most minds. Life would go on very much as before, perhaps importantly different for only a few.

Yet even in that there was hope. The passage of the Light left its cloud-chamber traces curling and spiraling in innumerable memories. An ancient design motif suddenly became the rage, in everything from clothing to architecture. Called a "Greek key" but actually a variant of meander-images found throughout the world since long before the dawn of history, the motif was variously described as time-frozen waves, or linked letter J's, or R's, or J's and R's.

A very few specialists were aware that this particular meander pattern, bent into a circle, formed the key recursive element of the classical labyrinth. None of them, however, could explain the precise source of its new-found popularity, nor why its repetitive imagery had begun cropping up globally.

ONE

CODE-EXTRACTED SUBTERPOST FRAGMENT (INFOSPHERE source unknown; original source independently verified as *Keeping My Brother In Time: Meditations on a Life and Death* by Seiji Yamaguchi):

Jiro's abstinence from food and drink, from sex and violence, was all about chastening the id, the instincts, the Eros and Thanatos drives. His isolation, like that of holy people throughout history in hermitages and monasteries, in deserts, on islands and mountaintops, deep in caves—that has always been about distancing the self from the influence of the social psychoid process.

My brother's life and death have taught me a great deal about the self, about both living and dying—and about transformation. Think of that old drill in elementary logic: "Socrates is a human being, all human beings are mortal, therefore Socrates is mortal." A circular argument, I know, but any valid argument has a conclusion from which its premises can be derived, so any sound argument is in that sense circular. The question is not whether or not the argument is circular, but how much is gained and what interesting discoveries are revealed as we make our way around the circle.

The same is true of life and death. Near the end of his *Faerie Queene*, Edmund Spenser has the spirit of Nature, ultimately speaking of the Fall in Eden and the entrance of death into the world, remark of all things that, "being rightly weighed/They are not changed from their first estate;/But by their change their being do dilate:/And turning to themselves at length again,/Do work their own perfection so by fate:/That over them Change does not rule and reign;/But they reign over change, and do their states maintain." So maybe our lives, too, make a circular argument.

. . .

ASLEEP IN A FOREST FLOATING IN SPACE, BRANDI EASTER was remembering in a dream a word without a language, wondering whether that word was a living fossil from a lost tongue, or a foreshock from a system of meaning yet to be invented. Then the alarms all began to sound in her virtual hookup, and she came instantly awake.

She did *not* need this. The mass-driver ship she had designed, the *Swallowtail*, had been successfully launched. She had taken a nice quiet day job as an Astronaut Service Guard in order to rest. What could be more restful and uneventful than monitoring space for the astronomically unlikely appearance of the putative Doomsday Asteroid, not due any time in the next several millenia?

No one knew if ASGuard, with its nuclear surplus warheads, could really do anything against such an incoming Gibraltar—kilometers in diameter and on a collision course with Earth—other than maybe break it up, turning one deadly projectile into half a dozen. The guard system had been built largely to prop up the dying macrodefense industries of the spacefaring nations, a works project for aerospace engineers. Few people expected it to be put to the test any time during the next few thousand years.

Yet in Brandi's virtual space all the flashing and howling screens said that here it was, something as big as a mountaintop, appearing out of nowhere, estimated trajectory placing it on direct collision course with Earth—and already in cislunar space! How, she wondered, had this nightmare thing escaped detection on the way in from the asteroid belt, or the Oort cloud, or wherever it came from?

Automatic systems began cycling up for launch. Radio chatter exploded over the comm, ASGuard launch box commanders desperately querying each other for information. They had to do something to deflect it, and fast, but they didn't want to end up nuking Earth or causing this damned thing to calve into a dozen pieces.

This can't be happening, Brandi thought. She glanced out of her workroom into the ferny forest greenery of the Freeman Lowell Orbital Biodiversity Unit, which her husband Juan Valeriano managed. Juan, however, was nowhere to be seen. When she returned her gaze to her arrays, she noticed that, of all the ASGuard stations, this thing was coming in *closest to hers*.

Then something else caught her eye. She checked and rechecked it, carefully, until she was sure—while, on the comm all around her, her fellow ASGuards were arguing about how best to blast whatever it was that was headed for Earth.

"Wait a minute! Wait a minute!" she called over a priority clear channel. She identified herself. "Don't fire! This thing's not ballistic—it's *slowing down*!"

Comm quieted a moment as everyone else on the system checked their readouts. Sure enough, the incoming object was steadily decelerating, braking strongly as it fell toward Earth, in absolute contradiction to the expected behavior of a rock obeying the dictates of gravity. Then chatter exploded over the commlink again, at still higher volume, as everyone began shouting about this Unidentified Falling Object and what to do about it.

"It's closest to my station," Brandi said quickly, almost without thinking. "Request permission to perform close reconnaissance."

Some discussion on line followed as to whether this might best be handled by remote sensing. Finally her commanding officer—Dwayne Hashimoto, whom Brandi had never personally met—came on line.

"Permission granted to inspect object at close range," the grey-haired commander said on screen. "If it accelerates or demonstrates hostile intentions, get out of there immediately. We won't waste time waiting for you before we blow it out of the sky."

Brandi signed off and darted out of the workroom. She ran through the spinning orbital preserve until she reached the docking bay.

Damn! Juan had taken their skysled! She cursed him for not telling her—and herself for volunteering before checking to see if she still had transport. Staring desperately round the docking bay, she saw it: her big board, the *Flambé*.

As part of the small corps of thrill-seekers variously called astrosurfers, fireboarders, and meteorriders, Brandi had played shooting star more than a dozen times, coming in from orbit and surfing deep into atmosphere before popping chutes over clouds and ocean down below.

At her locker she stripped and climbed into her spacesuit, shrugging back her thick blond hair from her face as she slipped her small frame into the bulky suit. Even as she calculated the risks, her mind was already made up. The big fat board had all-new ablative shielding and deflection tiling, along with the best

astrogation and avionics tech she could afford. The fuel tanks
had enough juice so that on hard burn she could probably inter-
cept the unidentified object before it went too far into Earth's
atmosphere.

Climbing atop the big flame-red board and sliding her feet into
the augmented footlocks, Brandi realized that this was not going
to be without risks. She had to approach the object and Earth's
atmosphere at a low enough angle and a high enough speed so
that she'd bolide just right, bouncing in and skipping back out.
She would be coming in far too fast to make it all the way
through the depths of the atmosphere this time. If she didn't skip
back out just about perfectly, all the ablative shielding, deflection
tiles, and astrogation tech in the world wouldn't save her from
flaming fully into the shooting star she had so often imitated.

The airlock doors dilated open, preparing to birth her from the
small womb of satellite into the far vaster womb of Mother
Night. Her heads-up display pumped readouts all around her helmet. The rail gun in the docking bay shot her on her board out
the wombdoor. Brandi took a deep breath and, with a fierce
scream from her adrenaline-pumped lungs, kicked on her thrusters to maximum.

Acceleration punched back. She found herself falling through
silence—blindingly fast. Her target and trajectory appeared in
the displays. She shifted on her board, steering with tender control the forces she rode and those riding her. The object on radar
was not only moving but also slowing in not exactly predictable
step-downs. She thanked the heavens for her astrogation gear.
Calculating Earth-atmosphere clearance *and* the decelerating object *and* her own trajectory made this very nearly a full bore N-
body problem—just about impossible to calculate on the fly without her gear's massive number-crunching capability.

She activated *Flambe*'s onboard cameras, synching them up
so that whatever she saw beyond the bubble of her helmet the
cameras would also see and record. She commcast their images
real-time to ASGuard's watching monitors. Despite the object's
deceleration, she saw that it was still further "down" than she
had hoped. She would be perilously close to redline on the
board's capabilities (and her survivability) by the time she passed
the object. No chance to turn back now. She was committed.

Her thrusters cut out. She no longer had to rely solely on her
displays, for the object was quite clear now even to the naked
eye. It was big: several kilometers across, she estimated. The

ablative shielding on her board began to burn, as it was designed to do. She shifted again, angling the board up slightly in its trajectory. Before long the board was putting out more light and heat from its friction burn than when the thrusters were going. In her rearview cams she could see that she was leaving a long fiery streak behind her. She was a shooting star—and redlining.

The object below and before her appeared to be made of stone, but it was more or less flat, like a plateau or anvil-top. Not conical like a mountain, or roundly irregular like most asteroids. Even more oddly, a halo shimmered all around it, as if it were enclosed in a sphere or bubble of force.

She tried to keep her platform steady for the cameras, but that was getting harder. Under her feet the big board's ride felt bumpy and turbulent. It threatened to buck out of trajectory as its ablative shielding burned and ashed away beneath the board from nose to tail. Even with the augment systems synched up to the footlocks, it was all she could do to keep her board steady on her redlining course.

Through the ensphering shimmer she could see the top of the big rock plateau more and more clearly. It was not completely flat. Columns and pinnacles and arches stood on its top, a ruined city or broken maze hewn out of stone not by hands or tentacles but by erosion, fault-block freezing, rain and wind. This rock had known a world of water, once upon a time in its past. She hoped the cameras were getting everything. She was shooting past so fast, she felt like an ant riding a burning plank out of an explosion in a fireworks factory.

The plateau before her looked as if it were going to make planetfall somewhere in South America. She glanced along the great rock, now almost beside her. Time stopped as she stared in disbelief.

"Those are people down there!" she said aloud, at last, not trusting the cameras alone to catch the sight. "Pointing and—waving!"

She sped past and was gone. The board felt lighter now—almost too light. Nearly all the shielding must have burnt off. The tiles glowed red-hot and more, and the board was still burning. She hoped she had already passed nearest Earth on her trajectory and that even now she was skipping back out of the atmosphere. In an instant she would know.

To her relief she saw the trajectory plotter moving back toward green. Yes! She had caught the curl of the skywave, ridden it, then slipped right out the back door!

Brandi could exult only for a moment, though. The last of the ablative shielding burned off and the astronav system shorted out. She was on her own.

Her augments were still operative. Making a long slow zigzag, she dropped dying fire behind her as she climbed away from Earth's atmosphere, slingshotting further and further from the gleaming blue-white planet below.

Voice-activating her emergency radio beacon, she was relieved to find it worked flawlessly, rough treatment notwithstanding. She sighed, then surveyed her board. *Flambé* was scorched pretty badly and her tanks were bone-dry, but the deflection tiles were largely intact. The big board was still usable. Nothing to do now but wait to be picked up by the nearest rescue craft.

She looked back at the Earth. No light of doomsday impact shone anywhere, nor any sign at all of the light-ensphered plateau she had blazed past just moments before.

"Cowabunga," she said tiredly.

B Y A NORTHERN SEA, UNDER A LEADEN SKY, A WOMAN OF A certain age had become obsessed with waves and mazes. The woman, whose name was Mei-Ling Magnus, had taken refuge in the town of Fionnphort on the isle of Mull. Fionnphort stood across a narrow ocean channel from her initial local interest, the sheep-haunted isle of Iona and its monastery, the foundations of which had stood in one form or another for a millenium and a half. Mei-Ling already knew enough of the rigors of monastic life not to want to partake of them again. Besides, on contemplative Iona, accommodations were more expensive and less plentiful than in Fionnphort.

Before she made her way to these isles, Mei-Ling had already learned a fair amount of the history of Iona. The Celtic Christian monastery had been founded under Columba in 563, and King Oswald of Northumbria had appointed Ionans to found the monastery on the island of Lindisfarne. Iona had long been a place of holding out, first against the absorption of Celtic Christianity into Roman Catholicism, then against the displacement of Catholicism by Protestantism.

Walking along Mull's craggy shoreline, Mei-Ling glanced occasionally across the water, over toward the monastery, where it stood in the foreground with the citadel hill of Dun'I behind it. What had she been holding out against in deciding to stay here? In deciding to live among the sheep and sea pinks, the wild yellow irises, the short grey summers and the winter gales with their horizontal rain? In focusing on the rainwater streaming down the monastery's Celtic crosses that she so admired, with their circles quartered like targeting sights to be trained upon the divine, all carved over with mazes of spirals—in seeing them day after day, what had she *not* been seeing?

She shook her head to clear it. Certainly there were days when her melancholy and that of her surroundings matched perfectly, but one could only play at being the pale, dark-haired, wind-ravished romantic heroine for so long, especially once the cloudy greys had begun to condense and stream in her own hair. The only explanation she could find for her feeling of "rightness" here was that this was a preterite place, a gap in the tapestry of the twenty-first-century world.

Or of the sixth-century world, for that matter. Wasn't that why the monks had first come to Iona? To lead lives of prayer and contemplation apart from the bustle of mundane existence? Not so much to get away from it all but rather to get inside their own souls, to be in the world but not of it. Mountains, deserts, islands—monks and hermits and mystics had always gone there, as if soul grew purest in unpeopled places, bloomed best in deserted lands.

She thought of the illuminated Lindisfarne gospels, of the monk Eadfrith's elaborately knotted ornamentations of the texts. Like the intentional small flaws in Persian carpets and prayer rugs, Eadfrith's beautiful textual illuminations contained intentional small gaps, breaks in the pattern, "imperfections." Despite the differences in time, place, creed, and medium, the reason for "dropped knots" in Persia and dropped ornamentations in Lindisfarne was the same: To create a work both perfectly complete and perfectly consistent would be an act of cosmic hubris on the part of the artist, taking to himself a privilege reserved for the divine.

She wondered if Heisenberg's uncertainty principle and Gödel's incompleteness theorem had been twentieth-century science's way of saying the same thing. Dogma and ritual transmogrify into theory and practice. Priestly robes become lab coats. Everything happens twice—first as theology, then as technology. . . .

Despite the associative leaps in Mei-Ling's thoughts, her body plodded steadily along on autopilot. It knew where she was headed. Up the hill north and west of the most outlying bed-and-breakfast in Fionnphort. To, and down through, the old quarry. Through the yard of the cottage at the end of the road, to the small embayment in the channel between Mull and Iona. To and across the low-tide sandbar that led to a still smaller island between the islands, little more than a large rock outcropping, really, just grass and sea pinks struggling in the cracks, slimed over by the occasional big slug.

She didn't walk to the little bay for the slugs, though. Rather it was for the color of the water against the sand there. A deep, rich aquamarine in all lights, seaweed waving thickly at its edges. On still days, a small white boat anchored in that water seemed to float in the air above a crystalline meadow, a pale bird pausing in a strange sky just above otherworldly trees. She had never met the boat's owner, though she appreciated that person's aesthetic sense, whoever the sailor might be.

When she reached the yard of the cottage overlooking the little bay, she stopped dead in her thoughts. As she watched, an elderly man removed a short shovel from the boat and began digging a shallow, winding trench across the sandbar.

Did he own the cottage too? she wondered, embarrassed. She had been cutting through the cottage's yard to get to the sandbar several times each week for several months—and she had never once asked anyone's permission. Maybe she should just turn around and go back the way she'd come. . . .

Too late. He'd seen her. Nothing to do now but walk on down and tough it out.

She waved hello and introduced herself. She shook hands awkwardly with the man, who was tall and thin and stooped over—rather in the shape of a question mark—as he took her hand in his long, thin-fingered grasp. His hair was so grey as to seem almost pure white and his eyeglasses were old-fashioned looking enough to truly merit the term "spectacles." He wore a pinkish sweater that had probably once been red, above a pair of white jeans. His face was deeply lined and weathered, with heavy brows still shockingly dark in contrast to his hair.

The old man did not give his name. He was an odd-looking sort, but seemed pleasant enough—although he perhaps went back to his digging just a shade too quickly.

"What's that you're working on?" Mei-Ling asked, hoping

her question didn't annoy him. Fortunately, he seemed obscurely relieved by it.

"Oh, just a little experiment of mine," he said in lightly accented south-of-England English. That accent was quite a bit more comprehensible to her American ear than the Glaswegian dialect spoken by so many of the people associated with the monastery on Iona. He finished as much of the snaking trench as he apparently wanted to at the moment, then turned to her. "Ever hear of a soliton? A standing wave?"

"Like a tidal bore?" Mei-Ling guessed. She had heard the terms somewhere but couldn't remember them exactly. She did remember an image of a very coherent wave moving up a river in Canada, though. "Like the one at the Bay of Fundy?"

"That's correct," the man said, a bit pedantically, "but really a standing wave isn't 'like' a tidal bore—a tidal bore is like a standing wave. A tidal bore is a particular type of standing wave."

"And you have them here?" Mei-Ling asked, a bit suspicious, having never seen a wave of the Canadian type in all the months she'd been here.

"Nothing like the Bay of Fundy," he said, glancing down with a shy smile, "but they occur here. I use this trench to remind myself."

He looked at the water, then at his watch.

"Yes," he said with a nod. "It's just about time. If you would, take this shovel to the south end of the trench there and open the trench to the water on that side of the bar. I'll open the north end here."

Mei-Ling took the shovel and continued the south end of the trench through to the water, trying to dig it to the same depth as the old man had already dug the rest. The question-mark man was on his knees at the north end, clearing away sand down to the water at his part of the bar. Since she had the shovel, though, Mei-Ling worked faster than he did and water began to flow in from the south end until it filled the channel. In a moment the old man had opened up the north end too.

After the little canal had settled down a bit, a peculiar thing began to happen. Though there were no readily discernible wave crests in the sheltered cove at the moment, the water in the trench piled itself into small, regular waves a few inches high. Discrete and very coherent, the miniature tidal bore moved down the winding trench again and again, like peristalsis in a python or anaconda.

"Quite a bit different from breaking ocean waves, you see?" the old man said enthusiastically, brushing sand from his knees. "I've seen slow-motion footage of breaking waves and they don't look like this. Uncanny how much surf in slow motion looks like those paintings by that Japanese fellow. Can't recall his name at the moment. The one who did all those paintings of Mount Fuji. He must have been quite the observer of waves."

"Hokusai, you mean?" Mei-Ling ventured.

"Yes, that's the one," the old man said, surprised and pleased that she'd been able to come up with the name. "I didn't expect you to have any more connection to that tradition than I do. Mei-Ling is—what? Chinese?"

Mei-Ling nodded, glancing down at the sand and water before her.

"Though 'Magnus' isn't, of course," she said. "I was part of the wave of girl-babies adopted out of mainland China by Western couples around the turn of the millenium. Fallout from Chinese population control policies. Necessary science in collision with cultural tradition."

"Yes," the old man said, glancing again at the waves, thoughtful. "I wonder what Hokusai would make of these. Always from the north, never from the south. Can't really say why. A problem worthy of John Scott Russell himself."

"Who is—?" Mei-Ling asked.

"Was," the old man corrected, crouching down to watch the waves move through the small, twisting channel they'd made. "A Scottish engineer. In August of 1834 he happened to be riding along on horseback beside an Edinburgh canal, next to a horse-drawn barge that was being pulled up the canal. The horse and the barge it was pulling came to a stop, but the water in the canal didn't. It formed an odd solitary swell in the Union Canal that just kept moving along. Russell chased that wave for miles, but the channel surge refused to disorganize itself. As he followed it, I guess you could say Russell in some ways became part of its system—phase-locked, wave-coupled. Entranced."

The old man stopped, seeming to become entranced himself with the motion of the waves in the little channel.

"And?" Mei-Ling prodded, after a moment. "What happened?"

"Russell lost the wave," the old man said, standing up from

his crouch. "In the windings of the canal. The wave never lost him, though, in a way. Waves of this sort became a lifelong concern of his. He called them 'solitary waves'—what we now call solitons. Built a wave tank in his garden, worked with barges on the canal. Discovered a number of things about their nature."

Then the old man fell silent again—a tendency toward the laconic that Mei-Ling found a bit annoying.

"Such as?"

He glanced at her for a moment, then allowed his eyes to follow another wave in the little canal.

"When a tall, thin example of a standing wave catches up with a shorter, fatter variant of the same," he said, digging absently at the sand with the toe of his shoe, "the two waves merge and coalesce completely into one. Eventually, the two waves emerge intact, the tall thin one racing ahead, the short fat one falling behind. Seems they remember their former organization through a species of nonlinear memory. Russell used his solitary waves to correctly calculate the depth of the atmosphere, too. Even dreamed of one day using them to determine the size of the universe."

"You seem to know a lot about him."

"Perhaps I should," he said thoughtfully. "He was an ancestor of mine."

Over the next several weeks Mei-Ling struck up a quiet, tentative sort of friendship with the old man. She saw him a number of times and learned as much about him as his taciturn style would allow her to learn. He was even less forthcoming about his life than about solitons, which turned out to be more than just an obsession of his.

Despite his reticence, she was able to gather that his name was Robert Stringfield, and that he was a retired physicist, professor emeritus at the university in York. A widower, he had jointly owned the nearby cottage with his late wife. Some decades previously he had been part of the team that had arguably "proved" that particles were an illusion. The universe, Stringfield claimed, was in fact all waves. Particles were "covariant solitons" which only appeared to be discrete and particulate because the act of measurement itself excerpted a subsystem of the larger universal system. Observers read a chunk of the standing wave as something freestanding and discrete. Mei-Ling didn't fully understand all the physics, but she had no doubt it was something Stringfield remained passionate about.

He had other interests and theories as well. About slugs, for instance.

"I suppose you've noted that they're blackish-brown in color," he said as he pointed at one of the creatures one afternoon, "and that they look like nothing so much as slowly moving pieces of sheep dung?"

"There *are* a lot of sheep hereabouts," Mei-Ling admitted.

"Yes," Stringfield said with a nod. "Though there might be no sheep shite in pastoral poetry, there is plenty on Mull and Iona. Wonder sometimes if, over the centuries, the slugs haven't developed their current hue as a form of protective coloration. Looking like that might help them blend into the background. Make them appear less appetizing to potential predators, too. Keep meaning to check and see if there are any scientific articles on these Scottish 'toord' slugs. Natural selection in action, that sort of thing."

She could never tell if he was being serious or having her on. He had such a deadpan delivery about everything.

The Light, when it came, built upon the interest in waves that Stringfield had awakened in her, then added something of its own. She came out of the remming moment of the Light with the image in her mind of a wave moving through a maze. No ordinary wave, though: one of Russell's solitary waves. No ordinary maze either, she suspected. She dusted off her terminal link and went searching in the global infosphere for information on mazes and labyrinths.

Eventually she found what she was looking for: a Baltic-German maze design with two entrances and a spiral center, like a classical labyrinth in which the central cross had been "opened out." It roughly resembled the double-entranced Great Hare Island maze in the Solovecke Archipelago of the Russian White Sea. Or the destroyed maze at Kaufbeuren, Germany. Or perhaps an abstract rendering of a cross-section through the convolutions of a human brain.

Too much time on my hands, she thought, chastising herself a bit as she continued her maze-touring of the infosphere. She soon became one of the few people aware of the link between the Greek key meander pattern and the classical labyrinth. She joined infosphere salons and chatted about the way certain wave patterns described historical events, an idea that had come to her while she was looking at a history of Britain's monasteries. She also began to develop her own theory on the remarkable resemblance between the shape of the solar year, the apparent motion of the sun, the meander pattern, the daily path of the sun, and the turnings and returnings of the opened-out medieval Christian labyrinth design.

Way too much time on her hands.

Mei-Ling began to sketch out plans for a design of her own making. To the basic Baltic-German design she added hinged, two-sided door flaps—one for each entrance of the maze. Whenever a standing wave tripped down the initially vertical element of the flap, it would flip up the other, initially horizontal, part of the flap. Vertical would become horizontal, sealing off that entrance from further wave incursion through that opening.

She complicated the design further by connecting the action of the door flaps in both entrances. As soon as a wave pressed down the initially vertical part of the door flap in either entrance, it would flip up the initially horizontal part in both entrances, thus sealing off the entire apparatus from any further wave action from outside. Once the standing wave had run the maze, it would open the door flap at the opposite entrance. That would trip both door flaps back to their original position, from which the maze might interact again with the surrounding sea. Working on it took an entire day, but she finally got the design right.

Rolling up her design plans, she headed toward Stringfield's cottage to show them to him. She was certain he'd approve. Had he seen the plans, he would probably have remarked that her "digital wave maze" was an intriguing macroscopic elaboration on the double-slit experiment, so famous in quantum studies and so much a part of wave/particle debates about matter ever since Thomas Young's initial work in 1804. Stringfield might also have remarked that the standing wave, moving in solitary fashion through a single entrance, would behave essentially as a particle, like a ball rolling down the maze—just as light behaved particulately when it passed through a single slit in Young's original experiment.

The old man might have predicted the wave interference patterns that would develop in the maze when the soliton entered through both entrances—the same sort of wavelike patterns a beam of light generated when given the opportunity to pass through both apertures in the double-slit experiment. He might even have speculated that Mei-Ling's digital wave maze interestingly "opened out" the traditional experiment to chaotic fac-

tors inherent in the entire system of ocean, earth, sun, moon—
and beyond.

Stringfield had none of these reactions, however, for the old
man was no longer there. Mei-Ling found only this note, pinned
to the door of his cottage:

Dear Ms. Magnus:

*Recently you may have experienced, as I have, a peculiar
phenomenon, a certain "flash in the brainpan" that can
best be described as the Light. This Light disturbs me, for
it behaved not as a standing wave but as a brief particle
on the flux. I have always believed, with Heraclitus, that
latent structure is master of blatant structure. I have proceeded under the assumption that the latent structure of
the universe is all waves, all the oneness-of-things, not the
blatant and illusory thingness-of-ones, of particles. I'm a
holist. "From out of all the many particulars comes oneness, and out of oneness come all the many particulars"—
Heraclitus again. Difference is immanent, but similarity is
transcendent—a higher synthesis in a higher dimension.*

*This sense of the connectedness of everything has al-
ways been more than a mere theory to me. I have taken it
as an article of faith. I have gone to return to my work,
motivated, if you wish, by a crisis of faith that I must re-
solve. I have greatly enjoyed our conversations, and I hope
to see you again once I have made my way out of these
theoretical thickets.*

Yours,
R. E. Stringfield

Mei-Ling was disappointed to learn that Stringfield had left,
especially since she had hoped the old professor might be able
to help her put her wave maze together. She did recognize the
decorative border that framed his letter, however: a Greek key
pattern in computer clip-art, completely surrounding the note.

She sighed, immediately missing Stringfield's involvement.
Nonetheless, she decided to go ahead with her plans. With the
help of a Fionnphort fisherman (who thought she was working
on some sort of "art piece" and who, fortunately, also possessed
considerable carpentry skills), she assembled her wave maze
from wood and began testing it. Day after day Mei-Ling brought

the door-flapped maze out to the spit below Stringfield's cottage and mounted it in the sand. There she waited for the tide to come in, then watched as the standing waves interacted with it.

Although she had not been able to benefit from the comments Stringfield might have made, Mei-Ling soon was able to intuit most of them from working with her wave maze. The idea of particles as waves that had been "digitized," or the nonlinear and nondeterministic factors arising from interaction with the larger tidal system—such concepts would not have surprised her, after she'd watched her maze in operation for a few days.

As the weeks passed, Mei-Ling became more and more the connoiseur of chaos as a subtler form of order. The waves in the maze behaved in a manner that was neither quite random nor quite predictable, and it was exactly there that beauty lay. Like the round of her days here, there was something quite soothing about them as, tide after tide, seated on the sand, she watched the wave maze and logged in the endless variations the waves created in their interaction with it. The tidal bore was never boring.

She might have been inclined to spend the rest of her days this way, breaking her maze down into its component pieces, carrying the pieces around in a big canvas bag, putting the maze back together and watching the waves interact with it, then breaking the maze down again, day after day. One afternoon, however, a Naval hydrofoil cutter came surging into her little bay. When it cut its power and settled into the small cove, its wake became wave, rolling steadily toward the sandbar, cresting and thoroughly swamping Mei-Ling's wave maze. Aboard, two men waved to her, their presence calling her back to a life and a world she thought she'd left behind.

A H, *CINCINNATI!* ALECK MCALEISTER THOUGHT. AS HE PEDaled recumbently through the deserted 2 A.M. downtown streets, slouched down behind his bicycle's aerodynamic cowling, he found the quiet of the night conducive to contemplation. *The Queen City. City of Seven, or at least Many, Hills. Like Rome, only without quite so much history. Or San Francisco, only without the ocean.*

Aleck had a love/hate relationship with the city of his birth. He stacked the pros and cons up against each other as he pedaled.

He loved the lightness of the city's springs and autumns. Hated its summers and winters—weather oppressive like a weight carried on brow and shoulders, an unsheddable atmospheric tumpline backpack.

Loved the city's history, especially the tales of German families who had settled this river valley because the region reminded them of the Rhineland back home. Hated the Teutonic repressiveness of the political and social culture.

Loved the zoo and museums and theatres and libraries. Hated the beer-besotted boosterism.

Loved the small-town safety and charm of a brick-buildinged city that still took time to sleep (he couldn't ride his bicycle through the center of most cities in the middle of the night, after all). Hated its self-satisfied, smug parochialism, its almost fascist law-and-order mentality.

Loved the economic stability of the place. Hated the rigidity and conformity imposed on the city by the big corporations that ran it.

Only appropriate, he thought as he pedaled down Vine Street, that a self-proclaimed intellectual rebel like himself should end up working for Retcorp & Lambeg, the most mind-deadeningly conformist globocorp in town.

At least he was in Twin Tower Complex B. There was a certain old-fashioned charm to the aged buildings, lovingly referred to as the Dolly Parton Towers, after a notably pneumatic songstress of the past century. Things could have been worse: He could have been working in the big, blind, chopped-top pyramid by the river, R & L's global headquarters. He could have been riding the escalators to cubicles with thousands of others, all with hair and clothes of the appropriate contempo-conservative cut "favored"—meaning "more than mandated"—by R & L corporate culture.

Even the riverside pyramid was thoroughly throwback, though, he thought. Not least of all the idea of a "global headquarters" itself. The vast majority of transnationals were virtual enterprises anyway. Their home addresses were any number of condominiums on the back-forty googolbytes of the infosphere. Aleck had never quite figured out why R & L hadn't gone the same way.

Reconnoitering the corporate canyons, he thought how lucky he was to be in the company's scientific underground. That allowed him a few degrees of freedom, at least. Not enough freedom so that he could wear his "2 POR 2 LIV, 2 DUM 2 DYE" retro tie-dye sweatshirt to work without hiding it beneath a nice dull sweater, but nonetheless some real freedom, where it really counted: no supervisors crawling all over him all the time, and only a modicum of project reports and self-monitoring.

Coasting off the street and down the ramp leading to the understories beneath the Dolly Parton, it occurred to Aleck that maybe he had more freedom than most R & L employees because he had less power—and made even less money.

He shrugged. Tough life, working graveyard shift. Because he was in his first year of graduate studies in medical computing at the University of Cincinnati, though, so he didn't want a job that would create scheduling conflicts with his academic work. He had never been that big on sleep anyway, so vampire hours didn't much bother him.

The freight elevator doors were open and he was able to ride his bike right in. He commanded the doors shut and asked for the bottommost floor, where the lab was, down among the city's viscera of electric and fiber optic and ancient co-ax, water and sewer and old steel and concrete. Piped energy, piped water, piped information. He liked it there, down among the city's infrastructural intestines. Felt more real—naked, less like the stage-show façade of any city aboveground.

Yeah, he didn't make much money, he thought as the elevator headed down. Then again, he didn't do much work, either. During his undergrad years he had been an evening-shift bacteriology lab tech and a phlebotomist, a blood-drawer doing sticks on the labyrinthine levels of Good Samaritan Hospital. Despite ultrahypos and all that tech, he'd still heard every damned Dracula joke in the world during his stint at Good Sam. Genomics and bioinformatics notwithstanding, he'd also plated out enough samples of stool, sputum, and urine to last a lifetime, just like any eighteenth-century medico.

This R & L job was a lot more pleasant. He liked graveyard. The types of folks who worked this shift, the vampires, were good people overall. Didn't take things all that seriously.

The elevator doors opened and he rode his bicycle down the blue-lit corridor to his lab. He hopped free of his bike and the lab lit up automatically as he went in. He glanced at the big tank as he parked and folded up the bike, then voice-logged in. Denene Jackman, the sharp-eyed young black woman who worked the eight-to-two shift, had left him a message.

"Hey, Smart Aleck," she said on video, "keep a close watch on the Great Tanked One tonight. The report on its 'episode' a few weeks back finally reached the higher-ups. It's made them nervous. GTO is still doing everything the company wants but seems to be looking around the infosphere way too much on its own. Monitor the dataflow and put something in your report to appease them."

Aleck got the message. A heightened state of involvement with their Subject, then. He stared at the large shape floating placidly in the spotlighted tank that took up one wall of the lab. He checked vitals. No problem there. Brain wave readouts, heart, lungs, all major organ systems well within parameters.

"What're you up to, Hugh?" he asked the thing in the tank. Denene called their Subject "GTO" because when she was a kid her grandfather had owned a vintage Pontiac the same metallic-flake grey-green color as their Subject's livesuited form. Aleck thought his own name for their Subject—"Hugh Manatee"—was far more appropriate, however.

The livesuit completely wrapped their Subject like a mummy sleeping bag, and "Hugh" floated head upward, a large sea mammal lazily surfacing for air, which in some ways was exactly what was going on. At the head end was where Hugh was hooked up to all his umbilicals, including air, nutrients, and electronics. Through the clear plastic umbilicals housing, just the hint of a round fattish human face could be seen over the bloated, paddle-fluked body—thus the name Hugh Manatee, though of course the last wild Florida manatee had actually died in an encounter with a speedboat some weeks back.

Staring at his Subject, Aleck wondered again who Hugh had been and what his real purpose was now. Of course, the work protocols didn't even refer to him with a male pronoun—officially the Subject was an "it." Hugh's blood chemistry was pretty heavily monitored, however—enough to place the Subject's testosterone levels well within the male range.

The official Word was even less reliable as to why he was down here under the Partons of the Queen City. Supposedly Hugh was part of a "marketing research experiment in sensory deprivation and virtual interaction." Yeah, right. Aleck had sampled Mister Manatee's dataflow a few times. If he was only what the Word said he was, then why was he overviewing all of R & L's corporate data, even the highest level stuff? Assuming his mummybag livesuit was really nanotech-enhanced, and that it had a legal permit, why had the company gone to so much trouble? Ever since the War Mite Plague and the Nanogeddon, machines measurable in the low angstroms had been banished to use outside Earth's ecosphere. It was notoriously difficult to get a permit for their use down here, even for a company with R & L's clout.

Aleck, however, had long since developed a penchant for paranoid suspicions which he was not paid nearly enough to have. Ever since the first troubles with the big AIs and the quirky "consciousness" of the net, a number of the larger transnationals had been seeking out alternatives. Teraflop parallel-process machines oversaw the biz of those corprits too complex to be bureaucratically managed, but now some of the humans still in the loop had begun to question the long-term reliability of such mechanisms.

Years back, one of the chemical megacorps had come up with its "mind is a terrible thing to waste/waste is a terrible thing to mind" solution. A young woman from an "economically stressed" family had been head-shot into a coma by youths holding up the Kwikstore where she'd been working. The Kwikstore chain was a wholly-owned subsidiary of the chemcorp, and soon enough the damaged woman had been *volunteered* by her family to serve as "minder," an overseer of all the chemical conglom's toxic waste monitoring facilities.

In exchange for Big Chem paying all her hospital bills, the comatose young woman had been interfaced to Big Chem machines so that she completely oversaw their toxic waste reprocessing concerns. Good for Big Chem's bottomline, good for the family's budget, even if it did smack vaguely of slavery.

Aleck often wondered if Hugh was a step—or several steps—further along the evolution of that process. Certainly R & L was no longer the happy little bunch of soap-floaters it had once been, a century and a half ago. The company had gotten into all aspects of home life, becoming in the process the world's largest user of advertising.

Like a lot of transnationals, R & L was far too vast and complex in its activities for any ordinary mortal to fully grasp its operations. Was Hugh perhaps a "found mind" slaved to R & L's corporate data, his mind/machine interwit ensuring the company's competitive edge? R & L had corporate interlocks with big machine intelligence firms like ParaLogics and Crystal Memory Dynamics. Was Hugh Manatee also Hugh MacHinery?

Naah, Aleck thought, shaking his head and smiling ruefully. Coma corpses in the computer room. That was too paranoid, even for him, even at two-thirty in the A.M. Like those old stories claiming that, just after the Second World War, R & L had made a killing on soap base materials traceable back to manufactories with names like Auschwitz, Buchenwald, and Dachau. Good stories for raising that frisson of paranoia from the Cincinnati-German connection, but there had never been any proof.

Actually, it was embarrassing even to think of Hugh as really human. In all his communications with Denene, and even when talking to his roommate, Sam, about him, Aleck referred to the Subject as Hugh Manatee. In all likelihood, however, Hugh might once have had a name of his own, an identity independent of Aleck's creation. How would *he* feel about being renamed so flippantly?

Much easier to distance himself from any separate and human existence Hugh might have once had, and instead think of him only as "the Subject," the way the work protocols always described him.

Hard to do, though.

Better to bury himself in the work of tracing Hugh's unauthorized jaunts around the infosphere, for now. Aleck had a pretty good idea when they probably began. Hugh's "episode." The night of what some people were calling the Light. Aleck had been on duty when it happened. Calling up and looking at the records now, Hugh's EEG from that time looked like a cross between a seizure and a dream. But how did it fit in with the infosphere treks?

Work, Aleck thought. Lots of work. *Arbeit macht frei.*

"DÉJÀ VU, ALL OVER AGAIN," PAUL LARKIN SAID. HE AND Roger Cortland shouldered their gear and deplaned, walking into and through the crowded Caracas air terminal. They had been a long time on the wing, first aboard a night-bright clipper falling from the orbital habitat to Edwards-LAX, then a connecting flight to the stacked-up sky over Caracas.

Now they would be facing more seat time: first aboard a regional tiltrotor puddle-jumper taking them to Amianac, then a helicopter to the site where one of the tepuis or "floating worlds," the one called Caracamuni, had literally lifted off from Earth years ago. The same one which, quite recently, was rumored to have returned, a mountain of light descending from space.

Dropping his gear beside him, Cortland took a seat in one of the uncomfortable air-terminal chairs as Larkin spoke Spanish with the woman behind the ticket counter. At last the balding, gnomish older man walked over to where Cortland sat, toting his carryons and looking annoyed.

"Problems?" Cortland asked as Larkin sat down beside him.

"Just more déjà vu," the older man said with a shrug and a tug at his beard. "No problem connecting to Amianac. Looks like we'll have to get to the Caracamuni area the old-fashioned way, though—by boat and backpack. The woman at the counter said all helicopter flights into the back country around there have been banned. Joint military exercises in the area."

Cortland raised his eyebrows significantly, but said nothing. A public-address voice announced a flight in Spanish, then in Brazilian-accented Portuguese. Roger tried not to listen. He had to concentrate to keep his post-Light "talent" in check. Hard to do here, though. He always found airports distracting and disorienting. His talent only made it worse by constantly trying to flash him with the history of everyone and everything that had ever passed through the space around him.

"Come on," Larkin said, standing and hefting his gear again. "That's our flight."

The flight to Amianac aboard an aging tiltrotor heliplane was pleasantly uneventful. At landing, Cortland saw that the small vertiport airfield stood in a broad valley of golden grass, splotched here and there with stands of trees.

"This is pretty country," he remarked as they began the trek from the vertiport into town.

"Looks can be deceiving," Larkin said evenly. "These grasslands are artificial, the result of improved medical care."

"*What*?" Cortland said, waving his sun hat over his trauma-greyed hair in an attempt to cool himself.

"Lower infant mortality rates and better health care have caused the population of the Pemon Indians to soar," Larkin explained, "but it hasn't caused them to alter their traditional slash-and-burn agriculture. The ash from each family plot of burned-off rain forest provides only enough fertility to allow for two years of crops. After that, the soil is exhausted. Then the Pemon move further into the forest, slashing and burning as they go. There are now so many Pemon, though, that the burned-over and farmed-out areas no longer have time to regenerate their forests."

"Can't they run cattle here?" Cortland asked.

"They could," Larkin said with a shrug as they walked deeper into the valley, "but this is all low-nutrient grass—so low that it takes at least twenty acres of the stuff to support one cow. Grazing cattle make the erosion worse, too. The power authority doesn't like that. They don't want the largest hydropower dam in the world silting up into a big mud flat. They've got enough trouble trying to put out the fires the Pemoni start.''

"To prevent the erosion and mudslides, you mean?'' Cortland ventured, trying to watch his footing as they moved over a part of the track which had become overgrown with the tussocky grass. In the far distance, he saw a ridge of flat-topped mountains, some wreathed in clouds.

"That's right,'' Larkin said with a nod. "Used to be this was all rain forest. Couldn't walk twenty feet without scaring up flights of blue and red macaws, or sending bands of monkeys howling green waves through the forest canopy. Huge butterflies all along the river. Look at it now. About the only things that thrive on this savanna are the termites.''

Larkin pointed to the large mounds that punctuated the tough, sharp-edged grass from time to time.

"Even they prosper only temporarily,'' he said. "The termites exhaust their surroundings and have to move on too, like the Pemoni. They build another mound some distance away. Most of these mounds you're looking at are probably abandoned.''

Cortland followed Larkin over a rise. Below them he saw a settlement scattered along the banks of the muddy, enormously swollen river. They walked in silence down to the noisy confines of a boomtown that had seen better days.

Larkin had described Amianac as a place of mud and street dogs and plank sidewalks and crying babies, but this was worse than Roger expected. The strangest part was the juxtaposition of heavily guarded, richly furnished mansions cheek by jowl with shacks and lean-tos of cardboard and corrugated metal.

"This area was part of the gold country a few decades back,'' Larkin explained. "All the big transnational mining companies were here. Then the gold ran out. By that time, though, the miners had poisoned the waters hereabouts. Fishing used to supply a lot of the local protein before the miners came, but that's long gone. Things were pretty tense last time I came through.''

"In what way?'' Roger asked, curious, as they made their way through and around knots of children playing peaceably enough in the streets.

"The rich were telling the poor, 'You have too many mouths to feed—you shouldn't have so many kids,' '' Larkin said. "The poor were saying, 'You eat too much—you shouldn't be so greedy.' ''

"The way of the world, only in miniature," Roger remarked, struck by the thought.

"Right," Larkin agreed. "The North always talking about the South's overpopulation, the South always talking about the North's overconsumption, and nobody doing much of anything about any of it."

Roger nodded. Looking about him and seeing how calmly and lackadaisically the security guards were going about their jobs gave him some hope, though.

"The situation doesn't look very tense right now," he said. "Maybe things have changed since the Light."

"One can always hope," Larkin responded with a shrug.

Not much later they found the "outfitters" Larkin had been looking for. They were surprised to find a very dark young man inside with an old cell phone to his ear, and relieved to learn he spoke English. Larkin introduced himself. The young man knew him immediately.

"My grandfather, Juan Carillo Garza, spoke of you and your sister often," the youth said enthusiastically. "It was one of my favorite stories when I was a little boy."

"And your grandfather—?" Larkin asked, trying to be tactfully elliptical.

"Dead," the young man said solemnly. "Killed by *indigenas* or rangers in the World Park north of here."

Larkin offered condolences, but didn't really seem surprised. Roger wondered briefly if the man they were speaking of had been killed while poaching. The young outfitter, however, quickly passed to other matters.

"You wish to travel to Caracamuni tepui?" he asked.

"Yes. How did you know?"

The young man shrugged lightly and fiddled with his ancient cell phone.

"My grandfather's stories, for one thing," he said. "We've heard that there's a lot going on in that area now, too."

The young man, whose name was Ignacio Garza y Nieto, would elaborate no further. He and Larkin began negotiating fees for a guide and bearers and supplies, which ended up taking nearly half an hour. Larkin and Cortland left, the older man muttering under his breath about how much prices had gone up since his last trek here.

They found a small hotel in which to spend the night. It turned out to be so humid and bug-infested a place that Roger was actually anxious to get on with their journey the next morning. With their small squad of bearers and with Ignacio serving as guide, they loaded themselves and their gear into outboard-motor canoes. Making their way into the main body of the river, they soon saw that the river here was more like a lake, stretching from horizon to horizon.

Further up the broad river, the lingering skeletons of newly drowned rain forest trees hung ghostly grey above them. They passed boatloads of brown men accompanied by chain saws that burred like enormous angry metal insects. The men were felling the skeletons, clearing wide lanes through the flooded forest, scavengers on a battlefield where some unheard-of war of the elements had been fought. From time to time their small party skirted the great rafts of logs that floated down the river unsupervised or guided by gangs of men, many of them armed.

When they asked Ignacio about what had killed off the trees, the usually voluble young man became vague and laconic. Something about the rainy season, or the new hydropower dam downstream, or a combination of the two. When asked about the guns, Ignacio was even less clear, muttering about *indigenas* and rubber-tappers and World Park rangers.

Toward evening they began to see a river with discernible banks again, with vast mud flats beyond. Smoke columned into the setting sun—great, towering curtains of grey-black that dropped a steady snow of soot and ash, so much of it that they seemed almost to be traveling in the vicinity of a major volcanic eruption. The smoke-filled air imparted to the sunset an apocalyptic tinge, as if they were moving upstream toward the Last Days.

Night did not so much fall as slide in by slow degrees. Around bends in the river they came upon groups of wary men piling enormous logs and entire flood-killed trees onto great bonfires. Smoky holocausts flared over the mud flats, the lurid torches of their flames reflected in the surface sheen of the broad plains of muck, broken here and there by the stumps left from the forest that once was.

They left the river and spent the night in a no-man's land of shattered and sodden trees and treacherous, crawling mud. None of them ventured far from camp: though the mud was usually passable, they could never be sure of its exact depth. One of

Ignacio's men sank into a pit of the stuff up to his neck. After helping to rescue the man, Larkin and Cortland concluded sagely that the stump of a great tree must once have been there but had since rotted away or been removed.

They had no choice but to sit about in camp, waving endlessly at the clouds of annoying insects, sweating and listening to the night. They heard only the sounds of distant night birds and bats, the rare creaking of frogs and the plashing of other, unknown things hunting them. The place was far too quiet, almost mournful, as if the world hereabouts were stretched upon its deathbed. The deep, pause-filled quiet made Larkin in particular long for the leafy bustle and tree-noise he'd always associated with jungle places.

After a fitful sleep they continued the next morning up a river the chocolate-grey color of the Ganges where it flows past the great ashen ghats of the burning dead. The further upstream they went, the more obvious grew the channel and the current in the great river of silt and soot and ashes. Eventually, with some lightening of heart, they passed beyond the areas tortured by flood and chain saw and fire and found themselves surrounded by mist forest.

Ahead loomed tall brown and white curtains of waterfalls, mountains of dirty wet lacework that stretched on for more than a kilometer. At one place the earth had subsided several hundred feet, with no regard for the immensity of river that flowed over it. They had no choice but to portage through the mist forest around it.

The portage was long, muscle-tearing, backbreaking work, made all the harder to coordinate by the unending din of the roaring falls, a white noise that pounded the men's loudest shouts into silence. Drenched and bone-weary, they camped far enough from the falls that the sound of the broad cataracts, which had tormented them all day, lulled them to sleep that night.

The portage at least had taken them beyond the land of mud and ashes. The flooding and felling and tree-burning had not come this far—at least not yet. Cortland, too exhausted to ask, did not know whether they were still on the same river or had portaged onto a different one. He no longer knew whether they were in the Amazon or the Orinoco drainage, but he figured they must be moving deeper into the back country of the World Park. The ravages of the encroachers were less pronounced here.

Canoeing and portaging up river and stream for another day

and a half, they at last began to see the macaws and monkeys and butterflies old Larkin had gone on about. Puttering along upriver, Roger caught sight of a young boy with wide brown eyes peering out at them from the dense leafy greenery, his face painted red and blue under a yellow headdress. That was when Roger realized he had indeed entered a different world, a living fossil preserved by human law against human rapacity.

Leaving the river and packing through the jungle, though, wasn't quite so pleasant. The snakes and scorpions, the stinging ants and eternal mosquitoes that Larkin had warned him about when they were still in the orbital habitat—they were all here in abundance and seemed particularly fond of dwelling in Roger's beard, no matter how neatly trimmed he kept it. What Larkin had neglected to mention in adequate detail was the climate. Air so thick with sticky steaming humidity that breathing seemed a waste of effort. Heat and dampness that turned Roger's clothing and pack into a portable sweat lodge. When night came, noisy with jungle sounds and dense with clouds of bloodsucking wonders hovering about in the dusk, the air did grow a bit cooler but seemed to grow even more humid, if that were possible.

For two slogging days more the rhythm of their lives was the sound of machetes on brush-grown trail, of insects and animals and muttered human curses, and always the dripping and drumming of precipitation onto or off of the forest canopy. The trail switchbacked endlessly, frustratingly, racking knees and legs and backs and lungs. Roger knew they must be gaining altitude, but still the forest cover did not break. He seemed to walk the twisting green tunnel even in his dreams, when he managed to sleep at all.

Surmounting a ridge, they at last left the rain forest. As they dropped their packs and made camp, Larkin looked around, then suddenly pointed at one of the mountains on the nearer horizon. It was a high plateau shaped roughly like a giant anvil, partially cloven in the middle by some unknown force.

"It's back!" Larkin announced excitedly. "Caracamuni tepui! Back again like it never left!"

Roger had known Larkin long enough to understand the deeper cause of the old man's intense emotion. Clearly, Paul Larkin's joy at the reappearance of Caracamuni tepui was caught up in his renewed hope for the return of his long-lost sister, Jacinta. The way Larkin was always telling it, she had disappeared into space when Caracamuni's top floated off and vanished, more than a generation ago.

Roger wondered vaguely if they would meet her. How far and fast had she gone? If she'd been traveling fast enough, would she have aged much at all?

As night fell, they saw that they were not the first to reach Caracamuni. What looked to be helicopters and their searchlights swarmed over and around the tepui's top. From the ridge, the two men were close enough to see through binoculars that, on the top itself, domes and tents had appeared, lit from within. Old Larkin glanced knowingly at Roger. Not long after nightfall a cool wind began to blow against their own tents, blowing colder all night through.

Over the next day and a half they made their way along the backbone of the ridge, toward the tepui itself. Not an easy passage. At many points the trail turned into a goat-scramble up talus slopes, around boulder-strewn uplifts. They seemed always to be balancing on logs, precariously fording rushing streams, or leaping from rock to rock with chill water in between, or—once—swimming with their gear across a broad stretch of unbelievably frigid water.

The switchbacking of the trail increased, if anything. The sky above them was unvaryingly leaden, but at least now the elevation gain became more obvious. They moved from one biome to the next in quick succession, the air growing steadily cooler. They passed completly above and out of the rain forest canopy, into a landscape where hardy plants struggled to survive, punctuated here and there by small copses and other lush spots, microclimates favored with protection from the heaviest winds and rains.

They rested from their march in a sheltered swampy glade, a place filled with tree-ferns, club mosses, living fossil plants of a dozen types, all surrounded by the glint of dragonflies, the unending hum and chitter of nameless insects. Roger felt he had stumbled into a spot of lost time, straight out of the Carboniferous. Sitting there, he wondered when he'd begin to hear giant amphibians thrashing about in the bushes, or see killer protoscorpions long as his arms. Any moment now, massive *Arthropleura* centipedoids should come scurrying toward him out of his lost-world surroundings.

He felt superfluous in that glade, for the place had no need of

human beings whatsoever. Despite its great beauty, he was glad
to move on.

Noon of the fourth trail day since the broad waterfalls brought
them shivering, at last, to the final run of upslope scrambling
leading to the tepui's top. They had barely started up it, however,
when their progress was halted by guards clad in camouflage,
guns drawn.

Despite all the disappointment, the frustration, and the bitter
sadness of denied hope in Larkin's arguments, the soldiers had
their orders. They would not hear a word of the little expedition's
proceeding any further. Roger found himself feeling secretly relieved. That tepui up there might have proved to have more history than he could handle.

THE FORTY-TWO-YEAR-OLD MAN WITH THE SLIGHTLY THIN-
ning blond hair had not traveled under his Christian name in
years. That identity had been blown when he was still serving in
uniform. Now he traveled under the name of Dundas in these
heathen parts, at least on this trip. If anyone had ever bothered
to check, they might have noticed that the initials of his aliases
were always R.D., which corresponded with the initials of the
real name he used only at home.

With many others this morning he had run through the mazed
streets of the subterranean city the psiXtians called Sunderground, the Sun Underground. Drums had pounded like synco-
pated thunder all around him. He had been participating in the
drug-free version of their "altered states initiation." Apparently
the psiXtians believed that drumming and running through mazes
could be used to initiate altered states of consciousness, but all
it had done for him was make him hot and sweaty and dirty and
tired.

He would not have risked his immortal soul in such a place
as this, he reflected as he trudged along, save for the fact that
"Raymond Dundas" was one of the top infiltrators for the Autonomous Christian States of America, and he had a job to do.

These psiXtians were a weird bunch of heretics, Dundas
thought as he walked toward a minimal shower through the community's airy, herb-hung underground halls and corridors. The
passages were illuminated at intervals by sunlight falling from
the surface through the roughly bell-shaped skylight holes that
the locals called sun chimneys. He'd been here a month and he

still wasn't sure whether "psiXtian" stood for "psi Christian" and paranormal powers, or "psychedelic Christian" and state-altering drugs, or "peace Sixtian," since they seemed to fetishize that decade of the last century so much and definitely weren't his kind of Christian. Maybe the name stood for something else he couldn't even imagine.

Perhaps the *p* stood for the first name of that loon what's-his-name, Forestiere. Dundas remembered his briefing on the "sand-hog" whose Underground Gardens had inspired the first psi-Xtians to live in solar-powered homes dug into fans of hard alluvial clay in deserts and semiarid regions throughout the world. They were certainly close enough to Forestiere's original work, here in the same Central Valley of California. But no— that crazy's first name had been Baldassare or something equally foreign-sounding. It hadn't begun with a *p*.

Maybe the *p* or the *s* or the *i* stood for other leaders among the retrohippie crones and ecogroovy geezers here. Some of these tribe-heads he'd already met. He'd seen some of them in the showers and hot tubs. Old men gone grey all over. Not silver-backed alpha males but flaccid ashbacks still living their acid flashbacks. In their old age, they had apparently turned into White Light New Age Veggie Karma Nazis. They'd taught all these lost children that walking around in hempen robes and rope sandals—preaching "light-livelihood" and "minimal impact economy"—was a life worth living.

The only thing Dundas could imagine that might be worse than living with these Forestiereans would be living among the Erlandsonian "Tree Circus" freaks. The thought of being cooped up inside their myco-engineered botanic architecture, their burl-bubble living tree houses, sent a shiver through him.

As he continued through the rabbit-warren maze of the psi-Xtian "mandalic community," Dundas passed one sun chimney after another belling up toward the surface. Dappled light and venturi-spun breezes fluttered in the corridor. Directly beneath the sun shafts, right where the scanty rain and moisture entered from above, stood large planters from which citrus and other trees had grown, straight trunks stretching up to the surface. Seeing how artfully their leaves and branches were pruned up there, Dundas recalled how inordinately proud the psiXtians were of the fact that all their many fruit trees looked like mere bushes on the surface, and no ladders were ever needed to harvest them there.

Though the temperature on the surface must have been half-way to the boiling point of water, the shaft-lit, rough-hewn corridor underground was remarkably pleasant. His spirits began to rise of themselves—until he passed one of the psiXtian school-spaces.

"The Luddites fought," said a man who looked to be in his mid-twenties, speaking to a small class of fifteen- or sixteen-year-olds, "not the machine itself, but the exploitative and oppressive relationships intrinsic to the industrial capitalism expanding throughout England at that time. The Luddites resisted the factory owners' attempts to turn people into tools, into implements. They rejected the idea that human beings were to function as meat-machines according to the pleasures of government or corporation."

Dundas gritted his teeth but listened to the history lesson. Every word confirmed his suspicions of the watermelon nature of the psiXtians' "green libertarian socialist" political beliefs—green on the outside, red on the inside. A girl in the class asked about the relationship between nineteenth-century Luddism and twentieth-century environmentalism.

"As Luddism was an early prole critique of industrial capitalism," said the instructor, "so environmentalism was an early bourgeois critique of informational capitalism. Neither machine-breaking nor monkey-wrenching was a substitute for a fully developed opposition to human automatization, but they were important first steps. In between, the trade union movement—"

Dundas moved on. He had heard enough. Those old, crazy ideas definitely survived here. Perhaps some of the remnants of the projects once undertaken by the old government did too, though. That was his hope and suspicion. Ever since that strange Light episode, the numbers of the psiXtians had been swelling with new initiates of all creeds and colors, recent joiners from outside. If the "Starbursts," the shield telepaths developed under the old regime, were likely to show up anywhere, it was here.

He would be waiting. Not to kill them this time, if he could avoid it. Rather to capture them and take them back home, so they might fulfill their purpose in the Lord's plan. Perhaps they might even play a part in the recently reawakened Operation E 5-24. There had been rumors of a "control pheromone" coming out of the orbital complex before that Light thing happened. If the rumors had any truth to them, a starburst might prove more valuable than ever. . . .

Dundas reached the showers and turned one on "full blast"—actually an insubstantial flow from a showerhead that carried water-conservation to extremes. No sooner had he started to cleanse away the dirt when, from the sauna not far away, came a sound like a muezzin calling the faithful to noontime prayers.

Good God! Dundas thought, suddenly furious and very tempted to drown out the unchristian noise with a bellowed version of "A Mighty Fortress Is Our God." No—that would of course draw too much attention to himself and possibly to his mission. Besides, he didn't want to descend to their level. He didn't sing hymns in a public shower. He knew the appropriate places to pray. Did these people have no sense of decorum at all?

The man calling himself Dundas decided he would just have to smile in grim multiculti tolerance for now, but his day would come. Go right ahead, he thought. Keep on singing those sand-nigger blues you call prayers. God will answer—but not in the way you expect.

As he left the shower and toweled down, Raymond Dundas did indeed smile, despite the annoying sounds from the gentleman in the sauna.

TWO

FRAGMENTARY "RESPONSE" TO LIGHT, ONE OF MANY ENcrypted examples found in SubTerPost underground virtual mail materials linked to infosphere killings:

Nonviolence only succeeds when backed by the threat of overwhelming violence—Gandhi and his Indians outnumbered the British by something like 10,000 to one. Political powers do not give up their piece of the pie willingly. The victim is as much a perpetrator of violence as the aggressor.

"IKNOW WHAT I SAW," BRANDI SAID LEVELLY. "THOSE WERE people down there."

"None of the broadcast records show that, Ms. Easter," Dwayne Hashimoto said firmly. "Maybe it wasn't so much that you know what you saw, but that *you saw what you know*."

Brandi glanced at her husband, Juan, sitting beside her, back now from his unannounced trip up to the main orbital habitat—for parts and exchange, he'd said. Whatever. She was glad to have him back for moral support, at least. When Hashimoto had shown up at their airlock in person, she knew something big was up. Something about the man said he was earning the grey in his hair today.

"What do you mean, saw what I know?" Brandi asked, obscurely offended.

"Well," Hashimoto said, clearing his throat, "there's a long tradition of inhabited flying islands, flying cities, cities in the clouds, that sort of thing. So common that some of our psych people are saying it's an archetype, something inherent in the preconscious mind. Look where you live, too."

"What's that got to do with it?" Juan asked, compulsively running his hand through his thick, dark hair—behavior which Brandi recognized as a sign that he too was getting annoyed.

"You're near the orbital habitat, for one," Hashimoto continued. "That's a sort of floating world. And this place here. Funded by that old eccentric, Nils Barakian. Do you know why this is the *Freeman Lowell* Orbital Biodiversity Unit?"

Brandi didn't really know the answer to that. She glanced at Juan, who was staring down into the table at which they were seated.

"Freeman Lowell is a character in *Silent Running*," Juan said, quietly, "an old film Mr. Barakian remembers fondly from his childhood."

"Exactly!" Hashimoto said. "I scanned it on the way here. Freeman Lowell is a mythical character. In this old movie—made in *1971*, for God's sake—he and his fellow crew members are in space, maintaining forests under domes. The national parks have been dissolved and the last of Earth's, or at least America's, forests have been exiled into space. Something like that. Forests under domes in space—sound familiar?"

"Sounds prescient," Brandi said.

"Sounds nutty for that time, you mean," Hashimoto said, smirking. "In the film, Lowell and his crew, because of budget cutbacks, are supposed to nuclear self-destruct the domed forests and return home. Rest of the crew is fine with that—just following orders. So Lowell *kills* them to preserve his beloved Last Forest. Later he jettisons the last forest off into deep space with miraculous lights and a cute little robot groundskeeper to tend all its needs. Then he suicides by self-destructing his own ship. It's crazy. Lowell was a mythical protoecoterrorist! Barakian's got you living inside some fantasy image from his childhood!"

Hashimoto subsided, shaking his head vigorously.

"It's not crazy if it works," Juan said. "Whatever else you want to say, this place works. We've got technology the film-makers could have barely imagined sixty-some years ago. I've seen *Silent Running*. That movie may be simplistic, but fundamentally it's right. Biodiversity must be preserved and this is one way of doing it."

"Yeah? Well, it's all still giving me a headache," Hashimoto said, rubbing his eyes. He glanced at Brandi. "I mean, the media got leaked a copy of your broadcast somehow—with your 'people' statement on it. The spin they're giving it is that ASGuard is trumping up the threat of alien invasion to increase its funding! To make things worse, of all our people it had to be you who did that wonderfully reckless, courageous close flyby. And your last name would have to be Easter."

"So what?" Brandi asked, puzzled.

"So that brings up your mother, Cyndi, and her career, and all that Medusa Blue stuff, that's what."

"Wait a minute, Mr. Hashimoto," Brandi said, stopping him with an upraised hand. "I never knew my mother, or my father, if I had one. I wasn't so much born as decanted. I was raised by the Kitchener Foundation. This 'Blue Medusa' or whatever it is—that's all news to me."

Hashimoto shook his head in disbelief.

"I know you're young," he said, "but can you really be that naive? Do yourself a favor: Look up whatever you can find on Project Medusa Blue and then forget I ever told you about it. And please: For my sake and the sake of ASGuard, don't give any interviews to anyone, until we get this all straightened out. Promise me that, okay?"

Brandi glanced at Juan, who shrugged, then nodded slightly.

"I give you my word," she said finally. "I won't tell my story—but that doesn't change it. I saw people on that rock as it was descending toward Earth."

Hashimoto threw up his hands, but also smiled sardonically. He got up from the table and prepared to go.

"Fine. I have done. I do want to tell you, though, Ms. Easter—that was quite a feat of surfing you pulled off."

"Thank you."

"Don't do it again."

"I hope there'll be no cause to."

"I couldn't agree more," Hashimoto said, gathering his gear, glancing around at the sylvan surroundings. "Crazy as this all is, still, nice place you've got here. Reminds me of the California north coast when I was a boy. Enjoy it while you can."

After Commander Hashimoto had left, Brandi and Juan went to the *Flambé* where it stood in the docking bay, awaiting fairly extensive repairs. Brandi removed the onboard disk recording of her flight and Juan popped it into an optical reader. They fast-forwarded to the images before, during, and after her statement about "people down there."

True, the image was very jittery and unstable. What she had called people might merely have been an assemblage of very strangely shaped smaller rocks among a maze of strangely shaped larger rocks. Nonetheless, she and Juan were sure that what they were seeing were human beings. Certainly ASGuard, with its image enhancement tech, should have been able to confirm or deny the presence of those people all the more fully. Why were they balking? Were the higher-ups purposely stone-walling on this? Had she stumbled on some secret project?

She and Juan gazed at the replayed image again and again. There had to be an explanation.

Dwayne Hashimoto had suggested some directions, perhaps despite his better judgment. Brandi webbed in and began searching through the infosphere. She cross-referenced "Medusa Blue" to her mother's name and to the holdings of the "Kitchener Foundation for Interdisciplinary Studies in the Arts."

Brandi had never done much research into her mother, Cyndi's, work. She had heard as a child that Cyndi had run afoul of a reactionary government by making a "subversive" docu-drama. She was told her mother had eventually died as a result of some kind of illegal experimentation involving drugs and vir-tual reality. Brandi had long been secretly ashamed of her mother: the rebel druggie, the bad seed, the woman who hadn't been there for her at all while she was growing up. That had been all she'd needed to know. Brandi had not pursued her mother's history and her own beyond that level—there was no point to doing so, and no connection, until now.

The last thing she would have expected to appear in her search was a surviving section from one of her mother's films, but that was precisely what popped up: scenes from *The Five Million Day War*, a film by Cyndi Easter. The filmmaker's daughter watched it now, carefully, and for the first time:

In an orchard, gentle rain falls, wet blackness on tree trunks. Autumn. Some trees persist in their old green confusion, some have turned to fire, some to bare-branched ashes. Among the simple people harvesting the fruit there, tense expectancy fills the air. Everyone in the orchard seems to be waiting for some-thing. No one seems to know what to do, so everyone is just waiting.

A woman picking apples looks up. "A sky out of the Dark Ages," she says. Her male companion nods.

In the northern quarter of that sky from another time, dark specks like rags of cloud come, moving swiftly, becoming fig-ures, man-shapes flying in low over the fields and trees. Shock troops in rocket packs and stealth combat armor.

"Take cover! Take cover!" shout the man and woman, running through the aisles of fruit trees, shaking their fellows out of the trees and onto the ground beside them, all running, fruit baskets still in their arms.

It is too late. The faceless, stealth-armored soldiers land with gunfire and death. The apple pickers are gunned down as they run, spilling their baskets of bright red apples everywhere. The point of view shifts to the troops.

"Hey, Captain Acton!" one of the troopers calls over his helmet battlecom as he perforates a family of four seeking refuge in nearby thickets. "What kind of heretics we got here?"

"Brunists," Captain Acton responds, reducing a farm wagon and its passengers to blood and splinters, wood and bone, with a round from a smart mortar. "But that's not your need to know. They're cultists. Good enough?"

"Yessir!"

Acton's men fan out, lobbing cluster and fragmentation grenades into groups of fleeing pickers. Concussion and implosion bombs unbuild in an instant the cabins and cottages on the hillsides above the orchards and fields. The platoon's heavy-munitions man fires a semi-nuke at the commune's main hall. Laser-guided and smart, the projectile does not miss. The high hall erupts in a ball of fire and is gone.

Acton carefully oversees the choreography of his platoon's deadly efficient battle dance. Obviously he has trained them well.

"Begin mop-up operations," he commands over his battlecom. "We'll regroup south side of the stream, where the plank bridge crosses it."

His men break up into two-man patrol units, flying low over the trees and brush. Sporadic gunfire sounds, all from his men. No fire is returned from the ground below.

Acton flies over the field, above corpses clad in bloody jeans and flannels and bullet-holed homespun. He swings at last over the broad meadow, lands beside the stream and its bridge, where his men have already begun establishing their command post. On the battlecom he hears a voice—identified by his helmet computer as Lieutenant Raymond Dalke, his second in command and Reverend Morals Officer.

"Thank you, Lord!" Dalke says, blessing the carnage. "Praise be! Thank you, Jesus! Thank you, Jesus!"

Surveying the broken bodies scattered among the trees, Acton sees a few heretics who are not dead—only fatally wounded, their faces in expressions that show they are crying out in pain.

He hears none of their agonies. The sensors in his smart armor automatically filter out all information deemed irrelevant to battle.

"Bloody mess, eh, Rev?" Acton tightbeams to Dalke as the reverend lieutenant lands beside him.

"And glorious, sir!" Dalke says, out of breath. "I estimate the number of apostate dead at two hundred and fifty."

"Glorious?" Acton says, then shrugs. "Not so sure about that. Better if there'd been more·fight to these Brunists. They were duller than last week's Quakers."

"But even greater heretics," the reverend lieutenant reminds him fervently, while at the same time managing to remove his helmet. Unhelmeted, Dalke looks surprisingly young, his face still round and thoroughly unlined. Even in his battle armor, it's clear that Dalke is pudgy, as if the baby fat has yet to be burned off him. "They're followers of the ancient heresiarch, Giordano Bruno."

"Can't say I know much about the man," Acton says, watching absently as the command tent automatically deploys itself.

"The Catholics burned him at the stake over four hundred years ago," Dalke says, breaking down his armor's built-in flamethrower, scratching carbon residue from the unit. "Unfortunately his writings and ideas survived. He denied the divinity of Jesus, declared that the Bible was mythical in nature, said that all its books could be boiled down to 'do unto others as you would have them do unto you'—and the rest could be thrown away."

Removing his own helmet, Acton turns and strides toward the stream. "Still," he says over his shoulder, "I'd feel better if there'd been more fight to these Brunists. Taking them out was easier than shooting doves in the high desert. Used to do a lot of that when I was a boy."

"With all due respect, sir," Lieutenant Dalke says, looking up from the hot end of the flamethrower he's cleaning, his voice betraying only the slightest hint of irritation, "I must remind you that how much or how little 'fight' they put up is irrelevant to our mission. What's important are the crimes of these cultists against our holy state. Bruno's occult *Art of Memory* is obviously still contaminating minds. What's worse, it's gotten thoroughly mixed together with a lot of other heretical claptrap: Earth Mother goddess worship, witchcraft, pantheism, druidism, magic—all that cultishness."

Dalke, flamethrower-cleaning finished, punctuates his comments with quick, short blasts of fire. Acton bends down for a closer look at the creek as it flows past.

"Heaven knows these people deserve death," Dalke says confidently. "Dig deep enough, and who knows what satanic rites we might have found? I have it on good authority that many of them were drug users or child-molesting homosexuals or both."

"Well, Lieutenant, you'd know more about that than I would," Acton says, staring at the chocolate-grey confusion of the turbulent stream. Beneath Acton's reflection, in the shallows, a crayfish is wriggling its pale self loose from the exoskeleton it has outgrown. Acton watches, seemingly fascinated that the creature should have chosen to molt now, when the stream is so turgid. Finished at last, the crustacean scurries away again into the chaos of the rain-swollen flood.

Rising from his squatting position on the stream bank, Acton sees that Dalke has gone. He smiles wryly to himself. Removing his voice-activated sub voc unit from the helmet, carrying the helmet under his left arm, he begins to record his log.

"Neo-Brunist Communal Area secured with maximum prejudice," Acton says. He walks along the stream's course as it winds its way through the meadow. "Informed by Morals Officer that body count is two five zero." With the words "Channel Two," he activates a special encryption track for his private log. "Personal note. Appears we were 'protecting the children' again. Too bad none of them survived. I know I shouldn't be thinking this, but does making the world safe for six-year-olds mean that no one is allowed to think thoughts a good six-year-old wouldn't think?"

Acton glances toward the mountains off to the west. The rain, now ending, has left a bright-shining new blanket of snow there. Acton begins recording again.

"Commune buildings destroyed. Weather is clearing. Will bivouac here tonight before proceeding west at 0900 tomorrow. Channel Two: I remember living in the mountains near here. The forests were stripped for firewood as more and more people moved in all the time. Be fruitful and multiply. Landslides, rockslides followed. Erosion with every rain. Silt-choked streams. God gave man dominion over the Earth.

"Heresy, of course. All encrypted as usual. To be erased after use. For memoirs that maybe no one will ever hear or read. It's hard to always keep flying low and under radar. Have to, though—or one day I'll wake up and find designer chemicals or gay kiddie porn planted in my bunk. All the 'good authority' needed to end debate and find for guilt. Got to protect those six-year-olds.''

As Acton watches, spotty sunlight splashes gold upon the peaks, above the broken and scattering clouds below. The rain has ended.

''Channel Two, personal notes, continued: Shafts of sunlight are slanting down out of the clouds. 'Angel slides,' my mother called them, when I was a boy. The only angels sliding down them today are my troops.''

The captain watches his men returning from mop-up operations. Acton flashes back on his briefing by two colonels.

''Of the three men sent to infiltrate the Brunists,'' says the bespectacled colonel on his right, ''each reported for only the first month or so—and then went 'native,' for lack of a better term.''

''In their fragmentary reports, however,'' says the balding colonel on his left, ''there are numerous suggestions of a 'power' of some sort at the commune. We think it may be a remnant of one of the Old Government's secret projects.''

''What type of power?'' Acton asks.

''We're not certain,'' says the bespectacled colonel. ''Our infiltrators unfortunately never got around to saying.''

''Speculation at Service Command ranges from a perfect brainwashing chemical or device,'' says the balding colonel, ''to, on the wild fringes, the suggestion that the Brunists might have a 'starburst' among them.''

''Which is—?'' Acton asks hesitantly. The colonels glance at each other a moment.

''The name persistent rumor gives to shield telepaths,'' the bespectacled colonel says. ''The possibly mythical creations of the perhaps equally apocryphal Project Medusa Blue.''

Scene returns to Acton in the present, watching his men at work. He records again on the sub voc.

''Our assault encountered no countermeasures of any sort. We continue to reconnoiter the area. Channel Two. Personal note: I expected to confront brainwashed but well-armed hordes, or even convincing illusions projected against us in the skies. I half-believed I'd have to fight off an invisible hand, reaching into my mind, trying to flick off the switch labeled Duty. Instead we found no noble contest at all, only routine death and mundane destruction. The Brunists never had a chance.''

Seeing Reverend Lieutenant Dalke approaching, Acton manually switches off his sub voc. Dalke salutes.

''Permission to select two men to torch the orchards and fields, and accompany me in identifying the bodies, sir,'' Dalke says.

''Granted,'' Acton replies, returning the salute.

Smoke billows up into the westering sun. Acton speaks into his sub voc, reactivating it.

''Channel Two: How much does Dalke know about the spies' fragmentary reports? As Morals Officer he is an Intelligence watchdog, but the reports are Service Command property—''

Acton tunes in on Dalke's words to his subordinates.

''. . . Feast of Samhain among the ancient pagans,'' Dalke says over the intermittent whoosh of the flamethrower. ''Festival of the Harvest Moon. A night when the worlds of the dead and the living were supposed to be especially close, with a lot of commerce back and forth between them. Even after nominal Christianity came in, the pagan feast survived into modern times as a satanic remnant called Halloween—''

Flashback. A plump, devout woman, with shining eyes and very pale skin, dresses a child in a Full Armor of God costume.

''There you go, Willy,'' the woman, Acton's mother, says. ''A little Christian soldier, on this unhallowed night.''

The boy parades the chill October streets, proclaiming ''Trick or Treat'' at every door he comes to. People smile or shrink back in mock fright—then hand him candy, apples, popcorn.

The boy, slightly older, stands before his mother.

''Will, I know how much you liked Halloween,'' she says, ''but I'm afraid there won't be any more Halloweens from now on. The new government has banned it. Long overdue, don't you see? Razors and needles in apples, drugs in the candy. Halloween was just too dangerous to little ones to be allowed to continue.''

From his despondent expression, however, it is clear the boy does not ''see.''

In the present, Acton's glance falls on the Cross and Stripes patch on his combat armor. He makes another brief comment to his sub voc.

''Channel Two: Dalke regaled the troops with a story of Halloween. I remember that 'satanic remnant.' I am old enough to remember when the flag still had many stars on the field of blue, instead of the single gold cross there of the Christian States of

America. Maybe I remember too much. Lieutenant Dalke has often sermonized on the tempting evil of nostalgia. Presumably it's for my benefit. My men are young. They have never really known anything other than life under the CSA and, before that, the ossifying of the USA that led up to it. They do not have my memories, or my questions."

Seeing Dalke and the rest of the men beginning to fall into formation before him, Acton allows the sub voc to shut itself down.

"—only spirits gonna be hoverin' round here tonight is the souls of dead heretics, Lieutenant," one of the men says. Dalke laughs. The men come to order.

"Mop-up operations completed, sir," the lieutenant says, coming forward and saluting smartly. "All Brunist communards accounted for except seven women. According to intelligence reports, one of the missing, a Diana Gartner, is an important witch among them. The other women might well be her attendants. They may all have simply been absent at the time of our arrival, sir, but I suggest we bivouac here tonight and continue light patrols in the morning, on the off-chance we might still come across them."

"Very well, then," Acton says, nodding. He looks over his armor-clad men. "I had planned to bivouac here in any case. Men of the 337th Guardian Air Assault, you may stand down. Take a break, war dogs."

The remaining helmets come off and the men have faces again, young faces, bland faces, squeaky-clean faces. Dalke, his short blond hair slicked back above a visage round as the full moon, filches an apple from the spilled basket of a dead woman and bites into it hungrily. Some of the troops deploy shelters, some break down weapons and check armor, some begin preparing their evening meal, some stand talking. Though no one drinks or smokes, conversations grow spirited nonetheless.

The twisted skein of the stream leads Acton away from the camp, into the deepening twilight, alone. Helmet under his arm and sub voc in hand, he seems to walk with no particular objective in mind, except perhaps a desire to be by himself. Behind him, in the background, Lieutenant Dalke leads the men in a prayer of thanksgiving for their great victory. As Acton walks on, he shrugs in his armor, as if it has grown particularly burdensome.

"Channel Two. Personal note. I know I'm supposed to admire

the technology that makes this suit of armor possible, but tonight I don't. The science that makes a soldier faster than a speeding bullet, more powerful than a locomotive, able to leap tall buildings in a single bound, has also made the human being inside the armor almost completely obsolete."

Acton strikes off up a side branch of the stream, one that plunges down out of rocky, tree-lined slopes. The water is calmer here. In places below rumbling falls, the stream broadens into calm pools. He sits down on a log beside one such pool, scrutinizing in the water's surface his reflected face: stubbled, dark, weary. Night begins to fall around him. His voice activates the sub voc log's Channel Two again.

"Once I sat on a boulder," he says, "beside a wild mountain river roaring past with turbulence and white water and the full heart of spring thaw in its voice, and I was happy. I remember it well. Remember the deep broad pool on the other side of the boulder in the river bend. The clear green water of its depths. The long, chaotic strands of bubbles, slowly twirling, moving up out of those depths. I peered a long time into that pool. Wondered if I might see a trout or two. Just wondering—not wanting. In that moment I had everything; there was nothing more to want.

"I didn't see any trout," he continues, moving his face slightly in the stream's reflection. "Eventually I felt the moment slowly fall apart into words—'Now is forever, here is everywhere.' The very act of thinking those words made them no longer true. 'Be happy with what you have, for you can never be happy with what you want.' Truths, no doubt, but also just more words, even further from that perfect moment. Already I was wanting—wanting that experience of 'nothing more to want'—again. Wanting it more than anything. I still want it. Why else would I keep coming back to it in my dreams?"

Acton takes off his armor slowly and, once naked, dives quickly into the pool. The water is cold; he resurfaces as if he's had the air knocked from his lungs and it's all he can do to keep from letting out a loud, shocked whoop. He swims, as quietly as he can. Crouched in the shallows of the cold pool, he feels the stillness descending around him. The moon rises. From somewhere further upstream comes a sound, indistinct at first but gradually growing clearer, until it sounds like female voices, women softly singing.

Leaving the water, he grabs from his gear his service automatic pistol in one hand and his sub voc in the other, then scrambles up the rocky gorge, toward the sound. His bare knees bash against boulders, his feet scrape on stones, water beads on his cold flesh under silver moonlight, yet he is smiling wildly.

The singing grows louder, more insistent. The moonlit world blurs past him, fluid, swaying, as if he's running beneath the waves of a crystalline sea.

Suddenly he comes upon them. Instinctively he raises his gun. All unknowingly he has darted into the broad entrance of a cave, an arching roof of rock above him, a mountain spring bursting forth from one side, a broad pool with sedgy grass growing near the entrance for sunlight, catching only moonlight and firelight now. He sees it all by the light of the torches held by the six young women standing about the pool—and the seventh woman too, in the center of the pool, beautiful and nude, torchless yet glowing, as if by her own light.

One of the six handmaidens sees him, and her song becomes a scream. The others follow suit, rushing inward toward the center, surrounding the torchless woman, attendants protecting their mistress, hoping perhaps to hide her nakedness with their bodies or catch the bullet intended for her, though either goal is futile. The woman at the center is head and shoulders taller than any of those attending her.

For her part the tall woman seems thoroughly unconcerned. As her pale eyes take him in—his nakedness, his raised gun— they seem to radiate spokes of reddish light. Abruptly she laughs a laugh that echoes and shakes the cave's stony vault, a laugh to split the sky and start time over again—

A spike of blue-white light drives itself into Acton's forehead. Then blackness, and falling, falling. . . .

Brandi paused the film in her virtual space, and pondered. How much of this was true? She had heard that the CSA—or was it the ACSA?—had engaged in some remarkably hideous purges, but how much of this was accurate, and how much dramatized? There'd been that reference to Medusa Blue and to some sort of secret project of the "Old Government," but how did that tie into starbursts and shield telepaths (whatever they were)? And how did any of this connect with that inhabited meteor-mountain she had surfed past as it came in?

Frustrated but intrigued, she commanded the film to continue.

• • •

ACTON FALLING INSIDE HIMSELF.

"What is past is present elsewhere," says a soft-spoken female voice inside his head. "What is future is present elsewhere. To remember the past, to remember the future, is to be present elsewhere. You are going elsewhere."

Images of infinity flood his head. Starlight makes ringing music on the gong of the atmosphere. Torrents of impressions, the mind of the world falling into his mind. With golden oars of joyful wisdom he rows a canal of stars. Around him shooting stars fishflash great gold sword cuts until they sheath themselves in an unbounded scabbard of black velvet. Toothed whale of light, giant squid of darkness, struggle out of view in skies luminous with excess of deep dark. The galaxies mere oases of light in vast deserts of darkness—

Images of eternity, vast stretches of nothing until light lets there be, light from excess of dark, drops and puddles and storms of light blowing and booming outward. Planets, life, the nightmare blood and claw of evolution, the bleeding, the broken, the buried beneath brick and wood and stone and history, refugees wretchedly fleeing destruction like salamanders writhing out of the fire, a world of ghost people in ghost buildings, diaphanous, dissolving, disappearing ghosts watching ghosts, shadows watching shadows, in every always dying room, swarms of ghosts like motes of dust, dust devils, whirlwind of ashes twisting over scorched earth everywhere, smoky clouds of ghost bees in their high hives, their ghostly skyscrapers, moths, butterflies to flames, dependent for hire or fire on the ghostly business of empire, fires swallowing fires, ashes swallowed in mouths of ashes, burning buildings inevitably ruins before building, forever forever the Iron Man topping his brazen whore Liberty in the red-black corpsefield with fire-naked horizon all around, the sun only a light inevitably blinking out, all the stars falling, going out like cigarettes tossed from passing starships—

Then glorious accident, image of a golden-eyed amphibian, eye at the center of the storm, third eye above the mortal two, despite all, despite—

Acton wakes at last to early morning sunlight and the sound of distant flamethrowers. Dalke and the men burning bodies. Dew lingers on his cheek. His gun is gone, but he still holds his sub voc. He is smiling an otherworldly smile as he Channel-Twos his waking thoughts.

"I should be back in armor," he says, "back in uniform, back beneath the mask. I'm in no hurry. I'm home again, at that place where there's nothing more to want, at least for a while. The woman—Diana Gartner, witch, starburst, whatever—is apparently gone, along with her attendants. Today is the first of November. The cave entrance is dark, the daylight world contains no trace of what happened here last night.

"Whoever she was, she shared so much with me, and I thank her for that," Acton says, standing slowly in the cave, dazed yet incredibly happy. "I know what Medusa Blue achieved, despite itself. For those who suffered and survived, the Project opened the golden amphibian eye. For seeing in two worlds, in this one and not this one. The eye of the salamander writhing free out of the fires of space and time. The eye at the limit of the divine that showed me all of it. The further I went from myself, the closer I came to myself. The entirety of the universe was more intimate to me than I am to myself. The eye through which I saw infinity was the eye through which infinity sees me. The eye through which I saw eternity is the eye through which eternity sees me."

Acton pauses, glancing out from the mouth of the small cave.

"I've learned so much, been given so much," he says into the sub voc. "I know now why Giordano Bruno was burned alive. And why those people-products of Medusa Blue, those called starbursts, might gravitate toward his work. Bruno's religious experience was the reflection of the universe within his own memory, proof that mind itself is universal and divine. He taught the art of memory, the art of mind. The heresy that the kingdom of God is within each and all, and that to kill any person is to kill a universe. All things partake of the divine, all time and space is one time and space, in that eye. Brutus and Caesar, Judas and Jesus, Cortes and Montezuma, Mocenigo and Bruno, all variations on the same theme. Infinite worlds in infinite space, infinitely one. For that revelation, Bruno had to die—"

Acton hears his helmet battlecom squawk-talking, breaking the morning quiet suddenly. He walks swiftly down the rocks, toward the leaf-filled gorge, listening to the battlecom echoing among the rhyolite walls. He is almost to the source of the sound when, some distance over the tree-lined slopes, he sees two of his men patrolling. Acton speaks into his sub voc's private log, shakily at first.

"It would be so easy to wave my arms now and shout, 'Hey!

It's me! Your superior officer!' " he says. "Their not-so-smart armor will screen it out, though. They can't be expecting to come upon their captain naked like this. They are no more programmed for it than their armor is."

Acton watches the two patrolling troopers coming in above the trees.

"Lieutentant! Look!" Acton hears a voice say over the battlecom in Acton's own nearby helmet. "A cultist—and naked at that!"

"Let's burn the faggot, Private Reese," Dalke says. "Cover me. I'm going in."

Acton sees them coming, but does not flee.

"I *am* a heretic now," he says into the sub voc. "I can never go back."

Acton stands up straight and waits for Dalke. The lieutenant opens fire as he comes flying into the gorge. A round takes Acton in the shoulder and he falls, tumbling, bouncing, bone-breaking off tree trunks and boulders, to the bottom of the drainage. Dazed, bleeding, unable to walk or even stand, he sprawls in a leaf-strewn gully.

Dalke lands in a whirlwind of leaves.

"Damn it, Lieutenant!" Acton cries out painfully, over the scraping of fractured ribs. The morning-after bliss hangover from his vision is burned away by pain. "Can't you see it's me?"

Slowly, Dalke raises the visor on his helmet.

"Thank God!" Acton says. "That's right, Lieutenant—it's me. Will Acton. Your captain."

Dalke stares at him carefully.

"No," he says. "You're not the captain. You can't fool me with your illusions, heretic. You're an abomination in the eyes of God."

Dalke steps back, slapping down his visor. Images flash up of Brutus and Caesar, Judas and Jesus, Cortes and Montezuma. Barefooted and garbed in a robe embroidered with devils and flames, a Roman robe, an Aztec robe, Giordano Bruno steps toward the great pyre prepared for him. Dalke presses a stud. A stream of fire surges out. Acton sees only a stream of butterflies and moths, floating toward him forever.

When Reese lands, he sees Dalke standing beside a corpse-shaped mound of ashes.

"Another starry-eyed pagan up in smoke, eh Lieutenant?"

"That's right, Private," Dalke says, subdued. "Let's find the captain and report this. He of all people would want to know."

They fly out, generating dual whirlwinds of leaves. The camera focuses in on leaves blowing away, revealing the voice-activated sub voc, its small red recording light flashing off at last.

Brandi stopped the film. she knew there was more, much more to learn—about this history, about her mother, about that Project out of the past. How much of it was true? How authentic was it? Was all that sub voc stuff—all those supposedly recorded subvocalizations—were they *real*? How could her mother have gotten access to all that? So many questions. . . .

Yet, turning it over in her mind, she found at last that, for all she still had to learn, she had already seen more than enough, for now.

MEI-LING REMAINED SEATED ON THE SANDBAR AND watched as Vasili Landau and Gopal Mulla strode up beside her.

"Hello, Mei-Ling," Landau said stiffly.

"Hi, Vas," Mei-Ling said, without looking up. She had never much liked the lean, iron-haired Russian. He was just too professional about everything. "How goes it at Interpol?"

"Less interesting, since you left," Landau said. "You know Gopal Mulla here?"

Mei-Ling looked up and shook Mulla's dark hand, using it also to help pull herself up off the sand. She brushed off her dress.

"Still advising Corporate Presidium?" Mei-Ling asked Mulla.

"Somebody's got to do it," Mulla said with a shrug and a small smile. Mei-Ling had been acquainted with the somewhat pear-shaped man long enough to know that his amiable nature almost perfectly concealed an intellect of considerable power and intensity.

"CP science advisor might as well be someone who knows something about science, right?" Mei-Ling asked.

"That's always been my reasoning, yes," Mulla said, his smile broadening. "What's this you're working on?"

"A wave maze," Mei-Ling explained. "Analog design, but it functions digitally. Waves and particles and nonlinear dynamics, that sort of thing."

Mulla nodded his head, examining the structure carefully, trying to puzzle out its full function as he watched Mei-Ling continue to jot down notes in her wave log. Landau ignored it and pushed on.

"We have a maze of another sort for you," he said. "Don't know who the Minotaur is yet, but we could certainly use your clue of thread to guide us around in there."

Mei-Ling glanced at the lean Russian.

"I'm not in that business anymore, remember?" she said as levelly as she could. "Haven't been, since the Jeffersynth case."

Mulla glanced meaningfully at Landau, as if they'd both already discussed this possibility.

"That would be too bad," Landau said, kicking slightly at the sand with the toe of his dress shoe. "You're our best teletracer and systems psychoanalyst. What you did in your very first investigation, at Sedona, during that whole Myrrhisticinean mess, that was just fantastic work. Who knows how many lives you saved."

"Ancient history, now," Mei-Ling said, irritated. "You've had our friend Phelonious Manqué on ice for years."

"Though not his employer—Dr. Vang," Landau said, glancing at Mulla, who spread out his hands as if in apology. Mei-Ling knew well that Interpol's and CP's agendas diverged radically, there.

"Not Dr. Vang," Mei-Ling agreed. "Maybe never, for Dr. Vang. Not likely you'll be bringing him in, either. Right, Gopal?"

"Ka Vang has some very powerful friends" was all Gopal would say.

"Tetragrammaton," Landau said, and paused, "is still making God into a four-letter word, Mei-Ling. We think they might have been involved in this Light thing that happened some weeks back. Earth and the orbital habitat came to the brink of war before that matter resolved itself."

"I hadn't heard," Mei-Ling said, her recording of today's wave log finished. "I'm rather isolated here. I've tried to keep it that way."

"You wouldn't have heard about a lot of this yet, not over the usual media," Gopal said. "It's all still classified."

"Really," Mei-Ling said, breaking down the wave maze. "What makes you think Tetragrammaton was involved?"

"Realtime Artificialife Technopredators," Landau replied.

"RATs. Based on the same protocols Manqué developed at Sedona. Confirmed by Manqué himself."

"Any chance old Phelonious might have regenerated them and set them loose on his own?" Mei-Ling asked, curious despite herself.

"Not possible," Mulla said, helping her gather the pieces of the maze. "He's resourceful, but his cell is completely field-damped and he has no access to electronic devices of any sort."

"How about Vang?" Mei-Ling asked.

"No," Landau said. "That's all been checked. Neither ParaLogics nor Crystal Memory Dynamics nor any of the interlocking directorates he serves on were involved. Everything traced back to the orbital habitat and Jiro Ansel Yamaguchi."

"And Yamaguchi had already been dead for months when the Light happened," Mulla said, handing the maze pieces over to her.

"Curiouser and curiouser," Mei-Ling said, beginning to step off from the sandbar toward the shore and the hill climb.

"Why don't you let us give you a ride back to Fionnphort, at least?" Mulla asked. "We do have this nice hydrofoil at our disposal—"

Mei-Ling smirked.

"How could I possibly turn down such a fancy ride to the dance?" she asked rhetorically. "All right. Let's go."

They boarded the cutter, Mei-Ling's maze pieces in the large canvas bag she always carried them in, still in her hands despite Mulla's gentlemanly offer to carry it for her. She stood in the bow with the two men as the cutter turned tightly about and headed away from the sandbar. In an instant it was past the back of the rocky outcropping and into the main channel between Iona and Mull.

"Anything else special about this Yamaguchi person?" Mei-Ling asked as the sea spray began to kick up. "I mean, besides the fact that he seems to have remained active after death?"

That knowing look passed again between Landau and Mulla.

"He may have been a Medusa Blue baby," Landau said into the wind. "No conclusive proof, but his medical records indicate the possibility that he might have been exposed to KL 235 in utero, as part of the 'uterotonic' experiments. He had some of the signs. The extreme myopia, the extra floating pair of ribs on the cervical vertebrae, the tendency toward schizophrenia. No conclusive proof of the characteristic entoptic phenomenon—the retinal backscatter pattern, the so-called transillumination defect. The one with the bars of light shining through the iris in rays like wagon-wheel spokes.''

Mei-Ling saw the Fionnphort-Iona ferry moving across the channel to the monastery isle. The cutter slipped into its wake and headed in the opposite direction.

"This Light you mentioned," Mei-Ling said, puzzled. "It doesn't seem to have done any harm. For me, I'd say it's been a good thing. Any idea what it was?"

"Too many," Mulla said. "I've read reports from theologians who are saying—guardedly, mind you—that an 'irenic apocalypse' occurred. Among themselves, a number of my friends in the scientific community have been talking about 'incidents of simultaneous hyperconsciousness.' All of them seem to have occured at the time of the Light and have had longer or shorter durations. Lots of different manifestations.''

"Might you tell me some examples?" Mei-Ling asked. "Or is that classified too?"

"Not particularly, I guess," Mulla said, though he was obviously in no particular hurry to elaborate, either. "The way the various faith communities around the world have responded to it. The increased incidence of 'visions' in people from cultures that allow for that sort of thing. A suspected increase in occurrences of paranormal behaviors. The sudden political renaissance of nonviolent direct action in mass movements. Odd behaviors in other large-brained mammals too, mainly the higher primates and cetaceans, but even some unconfirmed reports of unusual activities among the big cephalopods.'' Mulla glanced down at the water in the channel flowing past them. "Media ratings dipped for a while too—worldwide. Whether all this has been spontaneous or induced or spontaneously induced, no one I know of has been able to say.''

Mei-Ling watched as they pulled in toward Fionnphort's long, diagonal boat ramp.

"This Light, whatever it was, may not have done any harm in itself," Landau put in, "but it seems to have angered or triggered someone or something that *is* doing harm. People are being killed in the infosphere. Virtual bullets through the data matrix, higher dimensional implosions. The killings appear to be mass, distributed, and ongoing. Occurring in waves. We don't quite know all of it yet, but it seems to happen whenever users get too close to certain protected data sets. Strange you should be working with mazes. Many of the deceased users were involved with maze problems, labyrinths, paradoxes.''

Mei-Ling didn't like the look in Vasili Landau's eyes.

"So am I a suspect now too?" she asked.

"Only to the extent that you fit part of the scan key," Landau said with a shrug.

Mei-Ling knew all too well the sort of psych profile law enforcement called a "scan key" or even a "skanky"—SCANCI, Selective Criminality, Aberrancy, and Non-Conformity Index. She disliked the term enough, but she hated even more the sort of mechanical reduction of human behavior for which it stood. She had been a profiler, a teletracer, even a scan-keyer herself. It had taken the Jeffersynth case, with its cult militia AI, to show her just how her own work could be used to attack individualism and consciousness. She had very definitely *not* approved—and so strongly that she had gone on indefinite leave soon after.

"Which data sets triggered off the attacks?" she asked, forcing down her misgivings.

"Those dealing with the Tetragrammaton conspiracy, for one," Landau said. "As well as other materials probably somehow related to that."

"Not a 'conspiracy,' Vasili," Mulla said, trying to gentle down the other man as the three of them left the boat and walked up the long ramp toward town. "The name was originally a joke made by intelligence directors during the Cold War, remember? A medieval English variant of a Greek word for Hebrew letters? Signifying a biblical proper-naming of God?"

Vasili made a disgusted sound and strode up the ramp before the others, a bit too fast. Mulla turned and continued to explain to Mei-Ling as they struggled to keep up with Landau.

"The term is found throughout the Western religious traditions, including apocryphal writings and the Kabbalah," Mulla said, "but its usage in this context has nothing to do with cabals, or conspiracies, or clandestine protocols actually written by the Czarist secret police. Tetragrammaton isn't a conspiracy. It's a convergence of interests."

"You fight it your way," Landau said over his shoulder as they came onto the grey street under the grey sky, "and I'll fight it mine."

"Vas, Vas," Mei-Ling said, unable to resist poking a little fun of her own at Landau's high seriousness. "A paranoid conspiracy theory of history is no basis for rational political action."

"Perhaps not," Landau said, turning on his heel to face them as rain began to fall on the grey stone pavement, "but it will do in a pinch. This is more than a pinch, Ms. Magnus. Dr. Mulla, in his summary of Tetragrammaton, neglected to mention that in several traditions 'Tetragrammaton' was the 'Word That Ends the World.' The ritual incantation that, once spoken and performed, destroys the universe. Is that important enough for you? Will you help us or not? People are being killed, in horrible ways—"

"And the world is in a strange place," Mei-Ling said, interrupting, "and all that is necessary for the triumph of evil is that good people do nothing. Yes, yes—I agree already. I'll help you, before you start talking about how the best lack all conviction and the worst are full of passionate intensity. Your 'Light' has already prepared me for this, I think. Now let's come in out of the rain a moment, shall we, and have some tea at the inn? Then maybe we can start making our plans as if we were rational people in a rational world."

Mulla smiled at the stunned Landau as Mei-Ling turned, leading the three of them out of the rain and into a small darkwood pub, cozy and warm after the growing damp outdoors.

WHEN ALECK GOT BACK TO HIS APARTMENT, HE SAW THAT his roommate, Sam, was linked into their virtual console and was reading over something he'd apparently just written. Aleck wasn't surprised. Stewart Albert Michaels—a.k.a. SAM, Sam, Sam I Am, graduate student in media theory, self-proclaimed telecom terrorist, philosopher sans credentials, sometime actor/playwright/singer/songwriter/computer consultant— had an erratic sleep and work schedule too, to say the least.

"H'lo, Sam," Aleck said to the oblivious, prematurely grey-haired black man at the console. "What you working on?"

"Wha—? Oh, hi, Aleck," Sam said, tapping at a few more keys and icons. "Just something to piss off my father."

"Mind if I take a look?" Aleck asked. Sam's father, Roger Michaels, was the mogul who had invented the technology that "Frankensteined" dead actors, putting them into new roles, all computer regenerated and in-filled for 3-D. Sam despised his father's work. "Old actors never die, they just stop getting their residuals," as Sam put it, or "Ripping off the past has always had a big future," as he also liked to describe it.

Which was why he'd gone into mediacrit at a school away from both coasts. Papa Michaels refused to put a penny toward the education his son had chosen, which was fine with Sam. It gave him the freedom of poverty and no restraints on his desire to jab away at his father's "media-whore" successes.

"Go right ahead," Sam said, getting up from the console chair. "A pitch I put together for one of Roger-daddy's production companies."

Aleck sat down and slipped into the virtuality gear. Music from a seventy-year-old TV show began to play, phase-distorted and echoplexed to woo-woo weirdness. Graphics, fonts, scenes and characters lifted from the original footage appeared, subtly and sometimes not so subtly altered by Sam, who also did the voice-over narration:

"Location, Location, Location"

A proposal for *Original Trek: The New Adventures*™
by Stewart Albert Michaels

Alternate universe. Space, the final real estate. James T. Kirk™, wealthy interstellar property development wizard, CEO of USS Enterprises UnLtd. Penchant for pungent cigars, loud suits, kitschy fibrous protein scalp augmentation. Mister Spock™, his Vulcan tax accountant. Dr. McCoy™, his personal physician and investment partner. Mister Scott™, his general contractor. Mister Sulu™ and Mister Chekhov™, his hottest real estate "associates." Uhura™ his management services officer. Et cetera.

Kirk and company save universe from invasion of transdimensional trailertrash, exophthalmic ectomorphic Space Okies from Hell screaming the Pan-Galactic equivalent of "Yee-haw," whose arrival threatens to drive down property values all over the Alpha Quadrant—

Aleck clicked out of the virtual. sam stood nearby watching him expectantly.

"Interesting satire, Sam I Am," Aleck said carefully. "But isn't it a bit on the Juvenalian side? You don't want to be perceived as, well, nasty . . ."

" 'Juvenile,' you mean?" Sam said, flopping down into a

morph chair and pushing strands of his long 'frolocked greying hair back behind his ears. "Maybe. But which is more nasty? Reanimating the corpse-images of long dead actors—and making money off of them without their prior consent and without sharing a single percentage point with their heirs—or calling attention to the inherent criminality of that practice?"

Aleck got up from the console and went over to his bike.

"Okay, okay, I see your point," he said, folding up his cycle inside its windscreen bubble. He put the collapsed cycle in the nearest closet. "Stealing from the future has a long and illustrious past, too, I guess. Hey—I found something at work you might be interested in."

"What—working with ol' Hugh Manatee?" Sam asked skeptically.

"Yeah," Aleck said with a nod, slipping a memory needle into their player. "I downloaded some of it to a compatible format with our system. Here—give it a scan."

Sam sat down and webbed in. He watched scenes, clearly stock footage, most of the images reshaped from common sources, yet carefully sculpted to follow a narrative, the point of view seemingly subjective camera, Sam's "own."

Dreamer wakes up cold, shivering in some kind of coldbox. Whole body frosted over. Cracking the lid on the box. Clouds of silvery mist roll out and off. Standing up, like rising out of a white coffin. Feeling the back of the head. Realizing that the plug that fits in the socket there has come loose and fallen out. Looking around. Nothing but a smoldering wasteland of smoking trash and ashes, dotted every few paces with more and more coldbox coffins, like countless abandoned refrigerators in a trashheap world, out to the very edge of vision. Billions of them, all over the planet, one box for every living person.

Going from box to box. Faint humming seeming to come from each of them, from all of them, from somewhere and everywhere. Some of the coldboxes roughly human-shaped. Some with clear windows in the lid or even clear lids. Looking inside. Are the residents dreaming or dead or somewhere between the two?

Bodies in cold storage, making almost no demands. Minds, through headplugs, all sharing the same virtuality construct, the same mass hallucination of active lives in a human universe of haborbs and metroplexes and terraformed planets. The truth, though, is there's only this world, of ashes and ancient trash and frozen supernumerary sleepers.

Setting out in search of access to the machine which seems to hum everywhere beneath the ashes and trash. Too soon captured by machine soldiers, returned to coldcrypt, headplug reinstalled. Sleep to waking—

A break came in the record. Sam clicked out of virtuality.

"This is primary stuff!" he said, pleased. "All the footage is stock, but the story looks uncloned. It's like humans have roached the planet mercilessly hard, like some overpopulation thing has already defeated humanity, and the only way to stop the boombust from wiping everyone out is to suspend everybody, frozen in time. Of course, even with photonics and nanotech and microminiaturization, it would take an enormous machine, a mountain- or planet-sized machine, to generate the kind of virtuality they're all plugged into. Million-plus polygons per second—that's what it would take to pass completely for real, and you'd need that for several billion participants."

"What about the headplug stuff?" Aleck asked from the morph sofa where he'd sat down during Sam's scan.

"Oh, that's interesting, all right," Sam said. "Direct plug-ins have been proposed before but they've never gone over very big. Too intrusive."

"I suppose it would make people feel way too much like they were just peripherals attached to a big machine," Aleck agreed.

"Yeah," Sam said with a nod. "That's nominally why bonephones haven't caught on, either. Truth to tell, though, we already *are* peripherals. Have been for a long time. Think of all the time we spend interacting with machines, behind or in front of screens and steering mechanisms, or attached to telecommunications devices. People started becoming protocyborgs at least as early as the industrial revolution. Some researchers have been pushing in the opposite direction. Seamless thought-recognition interfaces, making the whole sphere of all machines potentially act as peripherals to, or extensions of, the human nervous system. But who ends up 'main' and who ends up 'peripheral' remains a big question even then—"

Aleck got up from the sofa and headed toward the console.

"The stuff I got from Manatee's dataflows has more to say about the headplugs," Aleck said, thinking about it. "Most of it's wordless and from a sort of camera-eye point of view, but not all of it. I'll find it for you."

Sam reluctantly relinquished the virtuality gear, able only to sit back and watch as Aleck fast forwarded to the point in the data he was looking for.

"Here it is," Aleck said at last, handing the gear back to Sam. "See what you think."

" 'Seeing' what you think would be quite a trick," Sam joked as he watched an interrogation scenario begin and unfold before him. Whether it was taking place in a prison, or an asylum, or some strange combination of both, Sam could not tell.

"Since when is it the obligation of citizens to become zombies?" the head-shaved inmate asks of the interrogator. "That's what the 'obligation' is, you know? ISIS borrows your body for a while—and you get no choice in the matter. Your headplug gets a signal to hyperactivate Wernicke's area in the left side of your brain, the micromachines swarm to reinforce bicameral walling, and the next thing you know you're like the heroes in the *Iliad*, hearing and obeying the voices of the gods in their heads. You have to obey. No voice is more authoritative than the one that commands compliance from inside your own head— believe me, I know. You respond with no will of your own anymore. You become a stranger in your own head."

Sam clicked out of the virtual, smiling beatifically.

"This is just too heat death!" he said happily. "This is like a far-paranoid version of what I'm already talking about in my thesis! Ah, a kindred spirit in the infosphere—"

"Oh? How's that?" Aleck asked, from the sofa again, becoming a bit groggy as he began to slip into his daytime sleep cycle. For some reason he was dreamily thinking that he must be a good guy, since all his ex-girlfriends still liked him.

"The way computer media must ultimately function to destroy the individual," Sam said, his voice betraying the whirl of activity in his head. "Media lateralizes society and recameralizes the individual in ways Jaynes could never have predicted. The voice that implants the same message straight into everyone's head. This virtual material here reifies it, makes it an actual physical invasion, a neurological implant."

"Oh, that," Aleck said sleepily. "Scan forward to the stuff on endocolonization."

"Okay," Sam said, gearing up again. "Thanks, I will."

Soon enough he had found it—the inmate still talking to the interrogator, or the analysand to the analyst.

"The age of expanding world conquest is long over," the inmate says, "so the powerful colonize and control their own populations. The military and security apparatus, deprived of adequate external enemies, turns inward and becomes an internal superpolice. On an ideological level, Law is the policeman with the gun to your head, while Ethics is yourself, socially programmed to hold the gun to your own head.

"The next logical step is to literally colonize not only the hearts and minds but also the brains and bloodstreams of the population. The body politic and the biological body increasingly overlap. The military's role is to keep the national body or body politic secure against foreign invasion, just as the medical establishment's role is to defend and keep secure the integrity of the biological body. Funding for both is based on fear of death and the desire for immortality. . . .

"The industrial and entertainment sectors do likewise, producing commodities to fill up the times and spaces of our lives. So that there will be no room for the notion of our mortality to invade our heads or our houses. The old military-industrial complex grew into the MIME, the Military Industrial Medical Entertainment complex, inherent in the shift to a post-industrial world."

Sam scanned quickly through a gap in the record.

"—implants. Only for prisoners, at first, but then for everyone. Percept shapers and response dampers. Colonize the cranium, police the parietals. Fence in the open mind. Lock everybody's lobes into the same Big Picture. No more need to rely on the glitchy software of media and cultural programming. Just hard-wire in complete compliance, a permanent occupation force in the mindscape, a branch office of Big Brother, Inc. in every brain. Nothing is more perfectly enslaving than the illusion of freedom. . . ."

Sam clicked out of virtuality.

"This is great home media!" he enthused to the dozing Aleck. "Psychos with studios! Who put this together? This is as whacked as anything in the infosphere. Some weird future or alternate history or superparanoid fantasy—or maybe all of that. You've found the Nutso Mother Lode, buddy! The main vein. You *will* show me how to tap in, won't you?"

"What?" Aleck said sleepily. "Oh. Yeah. Sure. Sure."

FRUSTRATED AND EXHAUSTED, THEY DESPAIRED OF EVER gaining access to the tepui top, despite their long travail. Larkin and Cortland and the rest of their little expedition headed back down the ridge, to hastily set up camp after spending so much of the day wrangling with officious and purposely obtuse guards and bureaucrats of the military, governmental, and corporate varieties. The cover story they had been given was "joint military maneuvers," but one of the lower-level technocrats blew that when the phrase "planetary security" slipped out before she could catch herself.

Something odd about the lot of them, Roger thought. All the empty suits and hollow uniforms seemed bent in an unseen dimension, as if they themselves really didn't know why they were here, but that that fact could only make them the more dedicated to their mission.

Cortland and Larkin and Ignacio and their bearers had barely finished erecting their tents and settling in for the cooking of the evening meal when a woman with grey-streaked hair strode quietly into camp in the evening light. She was accompanied by a half-dozen shadowy *indigenas* who seemed to move through the camp like a wind, before taking up watch around it. The greying woman spoke quickly to the bearers in their own tongue, which seemed to calm them despite the invasion of the camp.

When Paul Larkin saw the woman with the grey streaks in her hair and the strangeness about her eyes, it was as if he'd seen a ghost return to flesh. Seeing the older man's stunned reaction, Roger knew without knowing how that Larkin's sister, Jacinta, had at last returned from her long voyage away from this world.

The brother and sister embraced with all the love, tender awkwardness, and humility that people long familiar with each other can show at the moment of a reunion coming after an unforeseen long absence. From where he sat, some distance away from them, Roger could hear several "Let me look at you's," the sound of both Larkins holding back tears and then giving in to them.

Paul told his sister that she couldn't imagine how many times in his dreams she had talked to him across a table or from a nearby bedroom, as if in those dreams they were living in some parallel universe where they had never been separated. Then he was explaining how, though he was consciously supposed to reconcile himself to the fact that she was gone and probably dead, his unconscious mind had always refused to believe it, as if she weren't really dead, just a long time coming home. As now it had actually turned out to be!

For her part, Jacinta recounted that, while the specifics of her memories of her brother and their family had begun to fade and vanish during her long absence, the emotions associated with them had actually grown in strength as the initial shock and numbness of their separation wore off.

The Larkins began to speak then, more quietly, on even more personal matters, the deaths of parents and relatives and close friends. Roger consciously tried not to eavesdrop. At last, though, Paul brought Jacinta over by the camp stove fire, where Roger sat, and introduced her to him.

"You don't seem to have aged as much as your brother," Roger remarked sardonically, "but then maybe you've been spending more time close to the speed of light . . . ?"

As she and Paul sat down on the ground near him, Jacinta laughed lightly at his obvious fishing. Clearly, she could tell that her brother had provided Roger with at least some of the background concerning the tepui top.

"Only partially," she said. "Our travels are a challenge to explain. I felt like a seventeenth-century explorer who expected to find a northwest passage via sailing ship but caught a transcontinental flight instead."

"You mean like hyperspace? Time warps? Wormholes through space?" Roger asked, his physics-geek side getting the better of him as he added water to the crumbly soup mix in a pot and put it on the camp stove burner. She looked at him in such a piercing way that, for a moment, Roger was absolutely convinced she somehow knew about his post-Light talent.

"Something like that," Jacinta said noncommittally. "I could tell you it has to do with the way higher dimensions simplify physical laws. Or with the way Mind can link in to those higher dimensions, in such a manner as to step around the tremendous Planck energies normally required for travel through them. I'm afraid those explanations will sound too much like magic. Enough for now to say that you *can* go anywhere from here— though you won't be traveling the way any of us expected."

She turned, obviously and specifically to her brother, then.

"And I did get there, Paul," she said exultantly. "To the Allesseh, the Great Cooperation, the communion of all myconeuralized sentients, everywhere in the galaxy. The myths, the collective myconeural-symbiont memories of the ghost people— they were right. We were meant to be part of that harmony of Mind. We developed consciousness and intellect here on Earth, but not the full, empathic sharing that 'telepathy' only partly describes.''

Roger kept himself occupied with the camp stove. Still, he could not help taking in their conversation, even over the sounds of dusk in the sparse cloud forest around them.

''They were right about all of it, then?'' Paul asked, absently watching Roger make the soup. ''The disabled contact ship, the spore crash—''

She nodded vigorously. In the light coming from the bearers' campfire and the stove he tended, Roger noticed that in the long fall of Jacinta's hair, like ropes in a waterfall, hung thin, oddly braided portions. Their ends were held in place with archaic objects, ranging from what looked like small bird skulls to little vacuum tubes and bits of old silicon circuitry.

From having listened to Larkin's reminiscences—and more, from some deeper memory source of his own that he could not yet fully identify—Roger understood the significance of Jacinta's adornments. He knew something of the background of the ''disabled contact ship'' and the ''spore crash,'' without being able to remember exactly how he knew it. Did it have something to do with the erratic, past-reading talent the Light had left him with? Or was it more direct?

''Surprisingly accurate, yes,'' Jacinta said. A bird called in the deepening evening light behind her. ''The records of most space-faring species in the Allesseh show the ship as 'lost.' Apparently it returned to normal space in the wrong place—with disastrous results. The ghost people's myths were especially on target about the effect that being overlooked by the later contact ships—and left a preterite planet—had on us as a species.''

''What sort of effect?'' Roger asked, keeping a close eye on the soup, though it didn't seem to be doing very much. The slow joys of high-altitude cookery allowed plenty of time for conversation. Or for contemplation, which that word ''Allesseh'' had triggered in him now.

''The motion of our history is a wave of hallucination on an ocean of mystery,'' Jacinta said, as if quoting. She shook her head, looking thoughtful and a bit sad. ''All our wars and wrongness really do prove it.''

All this stuff, odd as it was, felt increasingly familiar to Roger. It flashed and disappeared, like a repressed memory, something moving around just outside consciousness. It itched somewhere deep in his brain, but the only thing he could come up with was that he seemed to recall Larkin telling him that the "Allesseh" term was used frequently among gateheads.

"This 'Allesseh,' " he said, seeing the soup in the pot on the burner beginning at last to bubble and boil a little, after the interminable wait. "Is it a place? A congress? A great hall of records? What exactly is it?"

"It's not any *it*, exactly," Jacinta said, smiling. "Not exactly a thing or a place, yet also everything you mentioned. A number of the myconeurally connected species claim it's easier to dance it than explain it. I'm not that good a dancer."

Roger handed around cups to his two companions for the soup that was finally cooking.

"Then try to explain it in terms the rest of us poor mortals might understand," he said.

"It's both a dark eye and a shining gate standing between time and eternity," Jacinta said, as if trying to make sense of the experience to herself even now. "The cave of night, wrapped around a sky filled with stars. A black hole and a crystal ball and a mirror sphere and a memory bank, all at once. A time line made out of time lines and a sightline made out of sightlines. A hyperdimensional node, if you like. Everything outside it is also inside it—all times, all spaces, all histories and stories, they're all together there."

Roger blew on his hot soup, testing it before serving it to his companions. The soup made him feel warmer and cozier in this strange place. The evening was growing chill, and Jacinta's story around the campfire—or at least the camp stove—was spooky enough, in its way. . . .

"If everything's in it," he said, "then how did it pass over our whole planet here?"

" 'It' didn't," Jacinta said. "The contact ships missed us. Everything all those species have learned is in the Allesseh—and more—but you can't always know where to look. That's how our history could be inside it somewhere and yet lost as far as all other sentient species were concerned. Everyone who looks into it sees what he or she needs—or 'telepathically asks'—to see. Or not."

"Doesn't sound particularly user-friendly," Roger said, ladling up soup for Jacinta.

"More user-idiosyncratic, I guess," she said, sipping the hot liquid. "Always as idiosyncratic as its users. A hermeneutical tesseract. The Allesseh is the Great *Co*-operation. It's what makes the Cooperation possible and what is made possible by that harmony.''

Larkin had been looking into the twilight growing in the east, but now turned back to them as Roger poured soup for him.

"What did you see, yourself?" Paul asked his sister.

"Maybe too much," she said softly. Carefully swatting away the occasional mosquito made sluggish by the chill in the air, she stared half-hypnotized by the play of the flames in the bearers' fire, not far away. "The Allesseh is not only the eye you look into, but also the eye that looks into you. 'Idiosynchronous,' even. Its vision absorbs everything, the way a black hole devours light. I looked at cities and saw fogs of stone clinging to coast-lines, mists of metal rolling along river valleys. I saw some old truths: how all the living are ghosts in the fog, all our institutions unjust shadows in a dream of justice. How building a fire is really only building a stack of ashes. How there's neither noon nor midnight on the surface of the sun, how sunrises and sunsets are only a dizzy local illusion. One of which illusions seems to be occurring right now."

They turned to watch the last flash of the sun, appearing to disappear at the horizon line in a blaze of gold and red and salmon-pink. Night began to move like a wave into the living-fossil jungles below. They watched in silence as the Earth spun under their feet, weaving further illusions.

"Good soup," Jacinta said to Roger when she'd set it aside, finished. "I was as curious as you are about the Allesseh's history. I looked into that. Literally."

"What did you find?" Roger asked, surprised at how quickly she'd downed the hot soup. He finished his off too, a ward against the cold.

"As nearly as I could tell," she began, cautiously, "it started out as the joint venture of a number of expansionist spacefaring cultures. Something like ten million years ago. What became the Allesseh began as a distributed structure of self-replicating, self-improving information retrieval, storage, and transmission de-vices. The only human things I've come across that parallel its initial design are what are called Von Neumann probes. Or maybe nodes of an artificial galactic nervous system, only each point along it a satellite-library vastly more infodense than Earth's entire noosphere."

Roger stared at her, intrigued despite the strangeness of what he was hearing. In the east the rising moon had begun to glow.

"A dispersed interstellar brain, then?" he asked, trying to wrap his mind around it. "A galactic computer net?"

"Much more than that," Jacinta said, glancing about them in the deepening night. "If memory plus perception equals intelligence, then it's by far the most intelligent entity in the galaxy. It has kept evolving itself, and its linkages to sentient species, for at least nine and a half million years. Nobody knows if it's still evolving in that sense, though."

"Why's that?" Paul Larkin said, stifling a yawn. It had, after all, been a very long trail day. All the members of their small expedition were tired.

"About five hundred thousand years ago," Jacinta explained, "it became more a sort of higher dimensional cosmological structure than anything mechanical, or organic, or even physical, in the usual senses. One of its subprograms *did* develop the myconeural symbiont the ghost people encountered on their tepui, though. As part of the Allesseh's program to 'spread the faith' of sentience."

"A god out of a machine," Paul said. He finished his soup too, then rubbed his hands against the chill.

"A troubled god, I think," Jacinta remarked, thoughtful. "None of the other species have much trouble with the way the Allesseh 'is.' They've all known it so long that maybe they're too familiar with it. I may be wrong, but I think it's too 'intelligent,' now."

"How can that be?" Roger asked. He wondered how anyone could ever have too much true intelligence. Most of the world he knew seemed to suffer from a dearth of it.

"It's taken in, and is still taking in, so much data that it's become self-obsessed, solipsistic," Jacinta theorized. "Part of its original program was a very strong sense of what we might call individual mission—the idea that it and its mission were too important to be absorbed into anyone or anything else's program. I don't think that directive prevented it from becoming *self-absorbed*, though. Encouraged it, rather. A mind that has become its own mirror."

"A net of Indra, ensnaring itself," Paul Larkin said.

"If this thing is so vast," Roger asked, his skepticism growing, "why couldn't we find it, or any trace of it?"

"Maybe we have," Jacinta said, "only we didn't recognize it. Each node, each evolved satellite library, would resemble nothing so much now as a stable black hole. Even before the satellite libraries evolved, they were each probably only about the size of a small automobile. The bigger problem, though— and the better answer—is that the whole system's no longer following its original exploratory imperatives. We didn't find it because it's stopped actively looking for us—or anything else. I think it's suffering from a malaise, a sort of cosmic ennui. But we're going to change all that.''

Roger saw Larkin shake his head in the mixed light of campfire and moon.

"Now, Jacs," Paul said, disapprovingly. "You looked and sounded so healthy—until you said that last part. How could anyone do that to the thing you've described? That's a bit too overweening to be quite right. I remember the way you were, in the times of your troubles.''

"Really?" she said, smiling somehow mischievously.

"Yes," Larkin said with a nod. "You felt you were such a nobody, yet at the same time you merited this huge conspiracy that was supposedly keeping an eye on you. I hope you haven't exchanged one set of delusions of grandeur for another.''

To both Paul's and Roger's surprise, Jacinta was not at all bothered by the assertion that she might still be insane. Instead, she laughed.

"Look into my eyes," she said to her brother, in her best Bela Lugosi imitation, before dropping it. "See the brown and blue there, like cut agate? Do you remember what that means among the ghost people of Caracamuni tepui?''

"Full myconeural symbiosis," Paul said quietly.

"That's right," she said. "I've been riding the time lines of possibility for—what? Well, over thirty years, anyway, off and on. I've done my stint in mind-time. Straightened my crazies right out.''

The mention of "riding time lines" jolted Roger. For a moment it was all too close to his own disturbing, post-Light talent. He thought of it as "backtracing," the unwanted ability to read the past that always floated behind the present, even in the most mundane situations and most disposable objects.

Paul shook his head.

"I never had the guts to let the fungal spawn of their symbiont spread through my system for more than a few months at a time," he said. "I always zapped it with fungicidal medicines. Afraid it would drive me insane if I let it keep growing.''

Jacinta laughed.

"You know me, bro. You used to tell me, 'Doing drugs is like a telephone call: Once you get the message, hang up.' That never worked for me. I had to take drugs to be normal. Whether pharmaceuticals or self-medicating, always something—"

He interrupted them. These two spoke so lightly of their encounter with the tepuians "myconeural symbiont," thought Roger. His own encounter with the *Cordyceps* fungus had been disturbing in the extreme.

"So," he said, as directly as he could manage, "something about the symbiosis with *Cordyceps jacintae* has convinced you that human beings have an important role in the future of this Allesseh, then?"

"*Cordyceps jacintae*?" she said quizzically, looking at her brother with her eyebrows raised. "So that's what you named it? I'm touched and honored, Paul, but really, something like *Cordyceps caracamuniensis* or *tepuiensis* 'Larkin' would be fairer to everyone involved—you and the ghost people of Caracamuni, too, not just me." She turned again to Roger. "In answer to your question, yes, I'm convinced we do have an important role—precisely because of our strange preterite history. When we were in its presence—more of a tangible absence, really—I felt that the Allesseh almost didn't want to recognize us. Especially not the ghost people and their core myth cycle, the Story of the Seven Ages. As if that cycle reminded the Allesseh, with all its associated sentient species, of something that 'interdimensional node' has yet to do. A part of its mission it has yet to complete but is almost *afraid* to complete." She shrugged, briefly and abruptly. "Just my feeling from it and from the time lines, that's all."

"What 'something' could a thing like that be afraid of?" Roger asked, gathering up their dishware and spoons and preparing to clean them with a small ultrasonic hiker's scrubber. He didn't want her to keep talking about "time lines." He had enough half-formed thoughts on his new talent—or curse—in that area already.

"I don't know exactly what that something is," Jacinta said, "and I didn't get a chance to investigate much further, because then that Light thing hit. The minute *that* happened, the Allesseh pulled some kind of higher-dimensional hoodoo and we were all back on the rock bus to Earth before you could say 'Boo!' "

Roger stopped sound-scrubbing the soup cups and stared at her in something akin to shock.

"You experienced the Light episode too?" he asked. "When you were light-years away?"

"You bet," she said wryly. "You didn't think something like that was ordinary everyday photons, did you? Had to be some kind of vibration from a very high dimension, given the way the Allesseh responded to it. Ever since it happened, the ghost people have been incorporating these meander and maze patterns everywhere into their embroidery. That's the afterimage it left, in our minds' eyes, anyway." She paused and looked from one to the other of the two men, as if struck by a sudden thought. "Hey, you wouldn't happen to know where that Light came from, would you?"

Roger and Paul glanced meaningfully at each other.

"We might," Roger said uncertainly, turning off the burner in preparation for cleaning up and breaking down the tiny camp stove.

"Was it from somebody *Cordyceps*-connected?" she asked pointedly.

"May well have been," Paul said. "A lot has happened with that fungus since you left."

"That's what we intended," Jacinta said. "That's why we left that spore-print in your backpack—yes, dear brother, that was my idea."

"That was an awful burden of responsibility," he said gravely.

"How badly wrong has it gone?" she asked, suddenly very serious. "They haven't fitted everybody with headplugs, with neurological implants, have they?"

"No," Paul said. "No one's done that, yet."

Jacinta let out a sigh of relief.

"That was always one of my worst prescient fears," she said. "Under low-voltage X-ray, the density of the mushroom flesh and that of human flesh were about the same. The worst scenario I saw on the time lines came from that. Whatever lipoprotein or polysaccharide allowed the fungus to grow its threads throughout the body without arousing the body's immune response could, once isolated, be used to coat micromachines and bioelectronic networks for injection into the brain itself. Hardwired thought control, everybody automatized, marching to the same beat."

"No, that hasn't happened," Paul said, with a small smile. "We still just have the media, education, and the family for thought control. We did have Medusa Blue and Tetragrammaton too, though."

"Which are?" Jacinta asked.

"Medusa Blue was a secret project, part of a covert program called Tetragrammaton," Paul said. "It grew out of a number of 'depth survival' studies begun by intelligence apparatuses during the Cold War: CIA, KGB, MI-5, Mossad—"

Jacinta gave him that quizzical look again.

"*Now* who sounds paranoid?" she said. Roger laughed, then quickly went back to breaking down the stove. Paul Larkin looked perplexed.

"If paranoia means trying to find a pattern of meaning," Paul said, "then maybe so. Somebody had to start thinking about how to save us from ourselves. I worked with them. How do you think they got our *Cordyceps*?"

Larkin stared into the darkness and its night noises for a moment.

"I'm not proud of it," he said quietly. "It gave me some money and meaning, at the time. Anyway, even before you took off, a lot of the old intelligence services were gradually going corporate. Interpol was about the only only that didn't. The others—their human and information assets were being bought out by ISIS. International Security and Intelligence Service. Most of those services already had Tetragrammaton links, though. Those groups were already working on Tetragrammaton's big project."

Jacinta stared hard at her brother in the firelight.

"Which was?"

"The creation of a seamless mind/machine linkage," he said, leaning back on his hands. "To make human and machine intelligence co-extensive. Through that, they hoped to create an information density singularity. A gateway into and through the fabric of space-time."

"How'd they plan to do that?" Jacinta asked, intrigued yet obviously familiar with such processes.

"The plan was to use computers and large-scale machine intelligences," Paul said. "Generate the levels of information density needed to open the transdimensional singularity and boom! Faster-than-light travel to anywhere in the continuum. Something you and the ghost people seem to have already accomplished, in a different manner."

"Yes," Jacinta said thoughtfully. "More organically, less mechanically. I don't know how much these people have thought about it, but a seamless mind/machine interface would also, incidentally, make possible an instantaneous, technologically mediated, person to person telepathy akin to what I've experienced with the ghost people. Such a technology would free people from the primordial entrapment in the worlds of our own individual skulls.''

Paul nodded, silent, apparently considering the implications.

''Then in that way,'' Roger said, struck by the thought, ''it would be the logical culmination to a long tradition—language, cave painting, writing, all the graphic and fine arts, telephony, radio, film, all telecommunications.''

Roger felt as much as saw Jacinta nod in agreement in the deepening dark.

''Strange to think how much of all our human endeavors may have been an attempt to make up for that fullness of empathy we missed out on, because of our preterite history outside the Cooperation,'' she said, then turned toward her brother again. ''What was the role of human consciousness to be in all this?''

''Supposedly the transdimensional gateway can only be opened by a chaotic key,'' Paul said. ''Chaotic acausality of the right type can't be programmed into machine systems because they are rule-governed. Rule-breaking is what's needed. That 'right kind of chaos' is the single most significant way the human brain and human consciousness differ from artificial intelligences and simulacra.'' Larkin shrugged, briefly and abruptly, so much like his sister's body-language earlier that it seemed to Roger that it must be some kind of family trait. ''Maybe they were just creating a myth of human uniqueness.''

''Another delusion of grandeur?'' Jacinta asked, too innocently.

''Okay, maybe.'' Paul Larkin drew something invisible with his finger in the dirt of the ridge. ''But they believed that if the singularity was to form and the gateway to open, the machines needed that chaos. Medusa Blue was phase one: a psi-power enhancement project aimed at computer-aided apotheosis. Thought recognition, even soul-capture.''

Larkin stopped his scribbling in the dirt and looked up at both of his companions.

''That's why they were so hyped about our fungus and KL,'' he said, an odd edge in his voice. ''Medusa Blue did a lot of very questionable things. Surreptitious injections. Covert chemical campaigns. In utero exposures—all with the best of intentions. The survival of the species. Earth too small a basket for humanity to keep all its eggs in, that sort of thing. But other groups wanted to use *Cordyceps* derivatives for other purposes. Designer docility drugs. Female submission synthetics—''

Something like a bird call sounded nearby and Jacinta got to her feet, stretching.

''Where are Medusa Blue and Tetragrammaton now?'' she asked, glancing around.

''ISIS spun them off when it became Interorbital,'' Paul said. ''The program and its projects are pretty much autonomous. Fronted through a number of independent, nonprofit institutes, now. Lots of wealthy backers. Planetary power players. Most of the people up on that tepui top are probably their creatures, ultimately. Your ghost people had better be careful.''

Jacinta laughed again.

''They're not mine or anyone else's,'' she said. ''We're already gone from there, anyway. Got clean away at the first sign of their interest. Let these Tetra types have the hollow maze on top and the empty cave labyrinth inside. We don't need it any longer. It's the Tetras who need to be careful. The best corps of spies on this planet look like lost children compared to what the ghost people have become.'' She caught herself. ''We left something behind—but you do have some *Cordyceps tepuiensis* 'Larkin' already growing, I presume?''

''The fungus? Yes,'' Paul said. ''In an orbital biodiversity preserve aboard the first habitat, HOME 1.''

''Very good,'' she said quickly. ''We'll see you there soon enough, then. Thank you for supper, Mr. Cortland. Goodbye.''

So saying, Jacinta Larkin and her tepuian escorts melted silently into the night, leaving as little trace as if they'd never been there at all.

''What do we do now?'' Roger asked. He was more than a little relieved. He had gotten through the meeting without having to deal with the embarrassing subject of his post-Light talent, thank heavens.

''I think we turn in for the night,'' Paul Larkin said. ''I'm too old for this sort of thing. I'm overjoyed to have my sister back, but she's giving out more energy and information than I can quite take in a single sitting. It's given me a pounding headache.''

I N THE SHADOWY CONFINES OF HIS MINIMALLY, ALMOST MOnastically, furnished apartment in the psiXtian Sunderground, Ray Dundas sat sleepless on the hard futonoid ''mattress'' that came with his cell and pondered the importance of sleep. Dreaming is involved in memory and learning, he recalled. Dreaming organizes what has already been perceived. Deprive people of their dreams and they don't organize what they've perceived—they don't learn.

He needed sleep now to synthesize all he had perceived, to learn from it not least of all. But this ''bed'' was so damnably uncomfortable, so hard it would try the patience of Job—like everything about this place. These retrohippie psiXtians, who thought themselves so noble and idealistic and romantic, were just as often insensitive smelly slobs and spongers, as far as Dundas could tell. He needed all the equilibrium and equanimity he could muster just to keep himself from beating some sense into the fools.

He thought of the big old bed he'd had when he married, the bed he'd bought years before, stained and cheap, from an old Samoan woman with too many kids and too little money. Back in the evil old USA in those teenage days, when he'd spent or tried to spend summers with his brother there. His wife, Marianne, when she'd come into the picture a few years later, had said the bed was too soft. For her back she needed support of the sort her own bed gave her, she claimed.

Dundas had always wondered about Marianne and that bed. Was there another reason? She was, after all, the woman who had made him a good Christian—that, and what happened to his brother. During his teens on those crazy California summer visits, he had been a wild, disorderly youth. All before he met up with Marianne, of course.

Was what had really bothered her the activity that had made that bed ''too soft''? Had the bed been haunted for Marianne by the ghosts of his former lovers?

He thought of those women now, searched his memory for them. It beat counting sheep, he supposed. One by one he pulled up from his past the unfamiliar names and half-forgotten faces, gone now from his everyday thoughts for more than a score of years.

Ami Kumolos, his first, the Afro-bobbed brunette college student with the weak chin and her oh-so-significant trembling, which signified that she was, at last, ready to make love with him.

Big-shouldered, red-haired, scattershot-thinking Colleen O'Ban-non, squinching her freckles in concentration toward orgasm.

Krista Ybarralek, heavy-hipped and small-breasted teacher, pert-nosed blonde ten years his senior, promiscuous beyond any definition of the word he'd ever known before, casually directing his performance in her rape fantasies.

Dry-handed, big-eyed cryptographer Joria Trin Han, approaching intimacy as if it were a secret code to be cracked.

Geneva Ost, the folkdancer with the heart-shaped pubic hair, trailing her long, auburn tresses across his body, wanting his lust but not his love, his head but not his face.

Soft, pillow-hipped, quicksand-bodied Zandria Kohlwitz, sole-job motherwoman, her eye-rubbing two-year-old son wandering in on them *in flagrante* from the other room, asking sleepily, "Is he our new daddy?"

DNA sequencer Pandora Gellertov, her curly dark locks going early grey, making love with a ferocious, time-denying delicacy, rather as if he were a particularly touchy chemical assay.

Alia Zagorsky, short and more drumround with each passing week, mistress of Tantric simultaneity—yet they still ended by boring each other.

Duma Ocken, horny-handed island cowgirl, riding him mound-pounding hard, as if breaking a new horse.

Drifting off, the voice of some long-lost preacher or politically-corrective teacher lectured him sternly as conscience itself on how holding these images in his head was mean-spirited, a cruel objectification. So what? He was just being tough-minded, realistic. Not a romantic. Besides, they would never know. At least he remembered their names and faces. He would certainly not want to know how they pictured *him* after all these years—if they bothered to at all.

In the Sex Wars, who had been nobler—him with his requisite kills painted on his fuselage, notches on his gun, objectified memories in his head, or his uncle Vance, who never sullied his narrow bachelor bed with lovemaking or women, at least not in the flesh, respecting the Other too much to dare disturb the universe, until *he* grew disturbed, the ghost of a man?

At least overblown respect was never his problem, Ray thought sleepily. If God didn't intend for men to enjoy gazing at naked women, He wouldn't have made them such a pleasure to look at. That was how Ray figured it. He regretted a little that he'd been such an equal opportunity voyeur, even putting his oar in without regard to creed or color, but at least he'd never gotten any of them pregnant—never caused Big Trouble in Little Vagina.

He'd married a good Christian white girl in the end, anyway. When they were dating, he was so much in love with Marianne, torn with such violent passion, he sometimes found it difficult to tell whether he was an emperor in Heaven or a slave in Hell. Unfortunately, after they were married, all doubt was dispelled. Submissive to the point of being passive-aggressive, she willingly granted him full headship in the marriage—financial, spiritual, sexual, any and all decision-making. He swept her off her feet, but not off her knees.

Oh, Marianne was a creature close to Heaven—so close she made his life a deadly dull Hell. Like sleeping with the Thought Police. He should have expected it. Marianne's father had been one of those big PK types. At first Ray was naive enough not to know what that acronym stood for. Seeing his future in-laws interact he assumed it stood for "Pop her in the Kisser." Spare the rod and spoil the wife seemed to be Marianne's father's motto.

Having been schooled in it by her parents, Marianne had submission down to a fine marital, and very nearly martial, art. She had a black belt in passive-aggressive behavior. She often got her way. He had hauled the big old bed off to the recycler, and it was Marianne's bed they moved into their first bedroom.

Ray often tried to interest her in something new, inject a little difference or excitement into their love life. Like his taste for watching women engage in sex together, and sometimes joining them in a threesome. He'd picked up that little kink in the Evil Old USA. Trying to push it on his wife never worked, however. Invariably Marianne would, with a whipped spaniel look in her eyes, agree that yes, as a good wife she should do anything her husband reasonably asked her to do to pleasure him. At the same time it was obvious Marianne found repugnant, evil, and unchristian the very idea of bringing any outsider into their intimate lives and she resisted it with every fiber of her being.

Several times he'd had everything almost set up with a bisexual Mormon woman—but nights of Marianne's crying, nights of his shouting, the whole daytime façade of "happily married" life among the lawn order, yard-sale peasantry at last defeated him. He sired the requisite two heirs and a spare, more out of duty than love. Before long, he was more than willing to take those career-building duty assignments that *sadly* kept him long apart from Marianne. . . .

Every woman he has ever known stands above him, about him, haloed in pure light. He trembles on the edge of tears. In their light he is a foul thing crawling on his belly through vile, stinking filth. Again and again, endlessly, filth moving through filth. He doesn't dare touch them. Even to approach them, to talk to them, would profane. Yet they seem to speak into his head, asking him where being tough-minded ends and mean-spirited begins.

At last they fall silent and he hears the most beautiful and complex melody, like a previously undiscovered combination of Bach fugue and Thelonious Monk solo and much more—

Didactic voices weave through the music.

"Convenience is obedience to the rule of status quo," says a female voice.

Dundas began to resurface from the dreaming, then hypnagogic sleep state he'd slipped into. The voices fell abruptly silent. The indescribably complex and beautiful melody became merely the backup beeper of a recycler robot somewhere nearby in the maze of Sunderground. No footsteps sounded in the corridors nearby.

Dundas sat up in bed, shaking his head. He'd fallen asleep— gone under for just a moment, he realized. What incredible power the human imagination possesses to embellish—and deceive, he thought. A backup beeper romanticized into beautiful music. Thinking of his uncle Vance had in turn generated the sort of self-loathing dream his uncle might have dreamed. The ecogroovy gospeling of the psiXtians crystallized by his own mind into "Convenience is obedience to the rule of status quo."

That might come in handy with these people, he thought. Toss in some stuff about how if it's convenient for people, it's probably very inconvenient for the planet, et cetera, et cetera. Make it all the easier for him to pass for a true believer here. He jotted it into the memory of a solar-powered Personal Data Assistant notepad beside his Spartan bed, then tried to get some more sleep, certain that no matter how much more he slept, his night's rest had already accomplished something.

THREE

C ODE-EXTRACTED SUBTERPOST FRAGMENT (INFOSPHERE
source unknown; original independently verified as
computer-stored confidential case files of David R. Morica, M.
Div, D. Psych, Lieutenant Colonel USAF, Chaplain, Whiteman
AFB, USAF, Missouri, USA):

*Subject Carter Dalke, rank of major, is married (wife, Miriam)
and the father of two boys (Michael and Raymond). Subject demonstrates a recently manifested dire fear of keys. This extreme
claviphobia seems to be part of a constellation of issues surrounding an identity crisis connected to his imminent loss of
career and status as a Missile Flight Officer. The claviphobia
seems obscurely linked to the fact that, as a member of Missile
Flight F, the Subject—a very religious man—has been one of
those who have "held the keys to kingdom come," as he has put
it.*

*Subject seems to be one of those men for whom military strat-
egists have planned a great many things, particularly when it
comes to breaking the strong causal linkage between launching
a nuclear-tipped missile and possibly bringing on the end of
civilization, even the extinction of humanity.*

*In reviewing the available materials, I have come to the con-
clusion that, purposely or inadvertently, our USAF strategists
have developed a highly efficacious means of getting around this
causal link. Whether deliberate or not, continual testing of combat readiness has apparently allowed USAF planners to work a
twist on the classic Pavlovian-Skinnerian loop: Have the silo
soldier turn the key, but withhold the launching of the missile.
Do it again and again, until the stimulus-response chain from
key-turning to Armageddon is broken. Make the catastrophic
routine and it ceases to be catastrophic. For the "response to
extinction," substitute the "extinction of response."*

In the Subject's case this system may have done its job too well. It has driven the dissociation between key-turning and the end of the world very hard—perhaps too hard in the Subject's case, right up to unpredictability and chaos.

Subject is still unfazed by the operational use of his missile key. Every time that turning a mundane key doesn't result in catastrophe, however, instead of weakening the Subject's associations of key and catastrophe as it normally should, the feared result's failure to actually occur paradoxically amplifies and reinforces the fear response itself, making the Subject believe that the feared result is now all the more likely to occur. The more the expected fatal event has failed to occur in the past, the Subject believes, the more likely it is to occur in the future.

The result is the Subject's recurring visions of houses, cars, and entire cities bursting into flame whenever he turns a key in a locked door or automobile ignition. Ignoring the visions has come to require greater and greater acts of will from the Subject, despite—or perhaps because of—the fact that the visions haven't become real fire yet.

The visions themselves, however, have apparently grown more and more vivid, and more difficult for the Subject to put out of his mind. Their strengthening is analogous to the situation in Russian roulette of that type in which the revolver's cylinder is spun only once, at the beginning of the "game"; then the gun is passed back and forth between two people. Each click of the hammer against an empty chamber signals the increased probability that the next chamber will contain the bullet.

That, apparently, is how the Subject's ultraparadoxical abreaction phase functions. Unpredictably and paradoxically, the extinction of a specific response has become intimately linked to a generalization and amplification of another response, one incorporating several of the same key elements.

B RANDI HATED SEEING OLD PICTURES OF HERSELF IN THE MEdia. What could she expect, though? She still wasn't giving interviews—despite a flurry of requests—so naturally the reporters took what they could get. At least some of them were giving her credit for the *Swallowtail*'s design and were using shots from the launch ceremonies at the Orbital Complex. At least those were recent.

As Dwayne Hashimoto had predicted, her mother, Cyndi, and the Medusa Blue history had resurfaced. The coverage of all *that* was so sensationalized and superficial that Brandi felt her private life and family history had been violated, dragged through the streets and trashed, going all the way back to her *grand*mother, for heaven's sake. It was enough to put her off watching broadcast or satellite holo and TV, though Juan was still able to endure them and gave her encapsulated versions when she asked for them and could stomach such reports.

Leaving him behind in the viewing room one evening, she steeled herself and webbed in again to learn more about the past she had avoided for so long. Eventually, among the open-access Kitchener Foundation materials, she found a catalog of her mother's works. She swiftly scanned the list starting from the end, skimming first the brief descriptions of her mother's final project.

"*The Five Million Day War* . . . the control of informational substances and information itself held to be threatening to the status quo . . . the war to confine the opened mind has been going on a very long time . . . exposé of the hypocrisy of power which tells the filmmaker's own story within the larger historical context of the Long Suppression . . . the government that had seen to it that an illegal informational substance would be covertly administered to Cyndi Easter's mother, Marijke, and the daughter in her womb . . . the same government which then suppressed the daughter's attempt to convey her information on the story of the suppression in the name of protecting the young, the children. . . ."

Brandi hurried over it, painfully, then read more fully the catalog notes on her mother's earlier works.

"*Soap and Shadows*. Feature-length historical documentary analyzing German, Japanese, and American styles of empire: Soap of concentration camp victims, Shadows of Hiroshima residents incinerated in the atomic bombing. *Soap and Shadows* tracks backward to the Japanese campaigns in Manchuria and their scientific 'experiments' there; to nineteenth-century German colonial adventures; to the building of the American Dream with the sweat of slaves, the blood of Indians; to the reservation system as acknowledged prototype for concentration camp systems throughout the world. Documentary arcs forward to 'low intensity' ethnic and resource conflicts of the latter twentieth century and early twenty-first century—"

That sounds like a happy topic too, Brandi thought wryly. No wonder her mother got into so much trouble. She must have definitely been of the "Truth is not polite" school. Brandi scanned on, still earlier into her mother's career.

"*Accidents Will Happen.* IT'S *ACCIDENTS WILL HAPPEN!* THE SHOW WHERE WE PAY YOUR HEIRS BIG MONEY IF YOU DIE SPECTACULARLY IN FRONT OF OUR VAST VIEWING AUDIENCE! WITH YOUR HOST, CONVICTED SERIAL KILLER JAMES RICHARD UGOLINO! AND NOW, HERE'S JIMMY! Game/talk show parody on the role of media in a culture entertaining itself to death.

"*Craas TheoTek, Inc.* 'Our motto: If God made it, we can make it better.' Satire of technological hubris in this fictionalized account of the hostile takeover of a bioscience firm. . . .

"*Gardening as Therapy: How Green Is My Valium.* Parody of gardening how-to program in—"

Brandi stopped the catalog. For a woman who hadn't lived all that long, her mother had accomplished a lot. Even from a cursory reading of her filmography, Brandi discerned a definite arc in her mother's career, from early humorist and satirist to later, serious documentarist. Something seemed to have happened to Cyndi during or after the filming of *Accidents Will Happen*—something that eventually drove her mother to do the documentary that got her into the greatest trouble, "market censored," and shipped off to internment.

She might as well face up to it. Reluctantly, Brandi scanned back to *The Five Million Day War* and opened it up. An introductory note commented that the original prints and videos of the documentary had been destroyed. Only fragments and outtakes survived, Brandi saw, in the collection of one Immanuel Shaw. His infosphere address placed him in the first orbital habitat. Odd, she thought. She had lived in the haborb long enough that she thought she knew everyone. Mr. Shaw must keep to himself.

Going through the data, she saw that the largest single surviving piece of the documentary—or was it an outtake?—was what she'd already seen, the "Art of Memory" section. A great deal more of it existed in fragments and ephemera. It was through these that Brandi now made her way, amid a flurry of tracking bands and white noise.

"—but driven out of the lab and computer by chaoticians, disorder has increasingly taken up residence in human social interaction, from terrorism to the bar scene," says a bespectacled Asian man identified by caption as Dr. Ka Vang. The image jumps to another part of the interview with the same person.

"Humans find patterns in ways different from machines," says Vang. "Pattern-finding is part of our genetic makeup. We know that some genes which confer a survival advantage in heterozygous form are quite deleterious in homozygous form. Sicklemia and cystic fibrosis are examples.

"In heterozygous form this pattern-finding genetic component most likely works to help us conceptualize and plan ahead; in homozygous form, it can contribute to what is usually called paranoia, schizophrenia, madness. I think we'll know we're on the right track when we create a truly schizophrenic computer."

More tracking and white noise, then images, another interview.

"Those substances weren't just poisons," says an intensely focused, dark-haired, pale-skinned woman captioned as Dr. Evita Calderon, psychoneuroimmunologist, who occasionally gets up and walks to a display board while her interviewer—hair like feathery blond spikes, was that Cyndi? Her mother?—takes notes.

"The mammalian brain, including that of humans," Calderon says, "evolved in such a way as to be sensitive to chemicals that occur outside the body. Such sensitivity has positive adaptive value. An adaptive advantage exists for those creatures whose central nervous systems evolved in such a way as to be influenced by the presence of biological compounds found in their environment—compounds in materials likely to be consumed as food—that would sooner or later exert some kind of influence on the central nervous system. The evolution of the human brain proceeded in such a way as to deliberately take advantage of psychoac—"

White noise blotted out the image until Dr. Calderon appeared again.

"—okay?" she continues. "In the brain there are these dense collections of nerve cell bodies, called nuclei. Neural fibers arising from the dorsal and median raphe nuclei of the brain stem are dispersed throughout the brain, as well as having direct contact with structures in the limbic system and the frontal cortex. These cells receive input from the spinal cord reticular formation, a neuronal network that receives inputs from the entire somatosensory system."

"They've got their little dendrites on the pulse of body activity, as it were?" Cyndi (?) asks.

"Right," Dr. Calderon says, smiling politely, almost indulgently, ''but they also have fibers that branch back upon themselves, their axons synapsing on their own dendrites. These neurons release a monamine chemical, 5-hydroxytryptamine, also called 5-HT or serotonin, which acts as an inhibitory neurotransmitter. The neurons of the brain have a set level of activity and if left on their own they would discharge at some variable chaotic rate. But the neurons are not left alone. Specialized neurons in the brain secrete 5-HT, which inhibits their normal activity. The brain is like a car with its accelerator welded to the floor, and the speed at which the brain operates is controlled by the chemical brake pedal, 5-HT.''

More white noise interrupted, before the image stabilized to show Dr. Calderon once more.

''—lysergic acid derivatives, usually thought to be the most potent known psychoactive agents, are found in various members of the *Convolvulaceae*—morning glory family—and in the *Claviceps*, the ergot fungi. Psilocin and psilocybin in mushrooms, and mescaline in peyote cacti, are cross-tolerant with the lysergics. All of them are 5-HT antagonists. The lysergics bind to the 5-HT neurons at their feedback sites, while the mushroom and cacti products block the effects of 5-HT at receptor sites.''

''How does that relate to you car analogy?'' asks the interviewer quickly.

''The 5-HT antagonists take the foot off the brake pedal,'' says Calderon. ''That results in enhanced neural sensitivity throughout the entire brain and the sort of spontaneous neural activity characteristic of chaotic systems. Small stimuli lead to a cascading effect. As a result 'the world-out-there' is perceived differently, information is processed differently. The well-ordered and rhythmic brain processes of breathing and digestive regulation are supplemented by new chaotic processes of cognition. Experiences take on new meanings, the world is understood in fundamentally different ways.''

On camera, interviewer Cyndi nods and looks up from her notes.

''Some researchers have argued that the brain in this state reacts in a different fashion,'' Cyndi says, speculatively yet somehow slyly. ''That it encounters the waveform of the universe in an altered holographic pattern of wave interference, which allows for access to a level of reality beyond space-time.''

''Perhaps,'' Dr. Calderon says, again smiling her indecipherable smile. ''This is all very subjective as yet. It *is* undisputably true that under the influence of these substances many have claimed to see beyond what mortal eyes can see, to travel backward and forward in time, to visit other planes of existence—''

White noise blotted out Calderon's image completely. The next person to appear was the woman Brandi was now sure was her mother, Cyndi Easter herself, speaking and staring, fixedly and forthrightly, into the camera. Cyndi sat on a stone bench, her arm draped about a woman in white, with white hair, a woman who seemed prematurely old, distracted, palsied. Although they had never met, Brandi knew immediately that this woman must be her own grandmother, Marijke.

''If there was a Big Bang,'' Cyndi begins, ''then we are all shrapnel. Those of us who have been touched by Medusa Blue are doubly so. The researchers who have hoped through these experiments to penetrate the physics of that first instant, to undermine the enormous barriers of the Planck energy and the Planck length, may well be technically correct. The universe appears to be a self-consistent structure—and it likely cannot contain itself. Heisenbergian uncertainty and Gödelian incompleteness are, ultimately, the same thing and scale up to the entire universe. To paraphrase an old song, 'There's a hole in the bottom of the universe.' Or more than one. It may well be possible to exploit those gaps, for travel not limited by the speed of light. All through what the human mind can bring to 'information density' alone.

''Would it be worth it, though? In the name of what scientific approximation to truth, or national security, or species survival, could these covert operators have been justified in secretly administering experimental entheogens to women in their first trimester of pregnancy—in hopes that their babies might develop 'unusual talents'? Could they have been so good at screening out their feelings with words and categories that they experienced no qualms of conscience? I wouldn't believe it possible, were it not for history, and for the fact that what I am and what my mother became are both products of Medusa Blue.

''The history is clear. The same governments and corporations that blindly prohibited their citizens and soldiers and employees from knowingly experimenting with these drugs have themselves performed experiments on those same soldiers and citizens and employees without their knowledge or consent. The 'covert administering' of LSD, BZ, and dozens of other similar substances to the uninformed and unknowing—a process begun more than half a century ago—is a well-documented precedent to what happened in the case of my mother and thousands of other women.

"The covert operators payrolled my mother's ob-gyn to pump her patients with a supposedly 'uterotonic' biochemical—KL 235, ketamine lysergate or 'gate'—extracted from an obscure South American fungus, *Cordyceps jacintae*. Those operators turned my mother, along with thousands of other women, into a 'gatehead' and long-period schizophrenic—and for what? All the children of Medusa Blue have turned out to possess only latent talent at best. Their families and their own upbringings have been crippled and distorted beyond recognition. Just like mine. Just like ours."

The image turned only to empty tape, then white noise. Brandi had not moved. Tears rolled slowly down her face. When she had wiped them away, she decided that she needed to see the man who had compiled this record and made it available to the public, Mr. Immanuel Shaw.

W ITH MULLA AND LANDAU, MEI-LING MAGNUS TRAVELED by private jet through the evening light to London. She spent a night in an antiquated but pleasant enough hotel, then waited in sharp morning light for pickup and delivery by car to the Interpol liaison's office at New Scotland Yard.

While in the car on their way to the Yard, Gopal Mulla, reading the *Net Daily Mail*, gasped with surprise.

"What is it?" Landau asked.

"I'm afraid the media are on to it, now," Gopal said, handing over the flimsy recycled news sheet for Vasili and Mei-Ling to see. Over Landau's arm, Mei-Ling spotted the headline that had caught Mulla's attention: WAVE OF MYSTERIOUS INFO-SPHERE DEATHS. Skimming the article, she read about patterns of simultaneous deaths, apparently occurring in waves throughout the world, all involving individuals who were webbed into virtuality and interacting with the infosphere at the instant of their demise.

According to the article, the deaths were particularly horrible, the victims turned almost inside-out by what the reporter referred to as "spontaneous eversion." Authorities denied that any connection or pattern had been established among those who had been killed, and seemed generally to be giving the stories about as much credence as apocryphal tales of spontaneous combustion.

Landau said nothing, but from the stiffness of his expression Mei-Ling knew that he probably did not find this latest development pleasing. The "authorities" mentioned in the article likely included Landau himself, Mei-Ling thought. All of those involved in the investigation had to be much more concerned about this than they were letting on. Otherwise Landau and Mulla would probably not have come all the way to Fionnphort to bring her out of retirement and in on this case.

Still, she could understand the public façade. Damage control. With most of the world's work being managed or performed through the infosphere, it wouldn't do to put people in a panic with the idea that they were risking being blown apart or turned inside-out every time they webbed in.

The car dropped them off at the Interpol annex of the Yard— an airy structure of organically fluid metal and glass, Charles Rennie Mackintosh meets Arthur Dyson by way of I.M. Pei. The three of them proceeded inside, into a suite of workspaces that reminded Mei-Ling less of offices than of rooms in an art gallery.

From the responses of the men and women inside the rooms, it was clear they worked with Landau on a regular basis. Was he some sort of station chief here? Mei-Ling wondered. If so, he'd come up in the world since the mess at Sedona all those years ago.

They entered a conference room where two young men and a woman, technical types by their outfits, were seated around a long, ellipsoid conference table that looked as if it had been carved from a single block of black volcanic glass. Apparently the technical experts were waiting to brief them. Introductions were made all around and everyone sat, except Vasili Landau.

"I see from the papers," Landau began, "that our unofficial investigative arm, the media, has now joined us in the search."

"Something of a fluke, that," said the red-haired man, Sullivan. "The California crime reporter who broke the story, Jem Wallace, happens to be married to a woman who is an infosphere protocols specialist. They chanced to match up their disparate realms of expertise and they had their story."

"Any word on how much they really know?" Mulla asked. Landau slowly took a seat.

"California Department of Justice is looking into it," Sullivan said, glancing back and forth from his notepad computer. "The reporter and the protocol specialist—the um, Wallaces—seem to have run a mathematical distribution on these events. From the mention of 'waves of deaths,' it seems they've figured out that these demises are occurring in distinct patterns, at very nearly the same times. The fact that the victims are hundreds or thousands of miles apart doesn't seem to have thrown them off at all.''

"Any good news?" Landau asked grumpily.

"The Wallaces don't seem to have tracked down any of the death footage yet," Sullivan said quickly. "If that's the case, then at this point they can't possibly have slowed down that footage enough so that what is actually going on becomes apparent.''

"Footage?" Mei-Ling asked, surprised.

"Yes," said the balding, blond-haired man, Lanier. "Quite a lot of it, really. Every one of the seventy-odd people who have died this way have been in interactive hookups, most with video cam and some even holo-linked. Examples of that material are already loaded in for display. If I may?''

This last was addressed to Landau, who nodded. Thin-screen video display units swung up to 45° from the left arms of their chairs and began to play as the lights automatically dimmed.

"This is normal speed," Lanier said as they watched. "It begins from the point of view of the user, in this case a North London businessman, Walter Oliver. He is working with data belonging to Crystal Memory Dynamics, his employer, through a pirate virtual mail system called SubTerPost. That's their logo there, the post horn with all the extra spirals in it. Oliver has his terminal's camera in room-surround mode—that's his real-time image, the overlay in the lower left hand corner. Here it comes.''

As Mei-Ling watched, a cascade of data suddenly poured into Oliver's node in the infosphere. The man in the lower left-hand corner began to grope about in severe agitation. Lanier isolated and blew up the image-stream taken from Oliver's room camera. Light flashed on either side of Oliver, his image and the space around him seeming to distort for an instant. Then it appeared to Mei-Ling that she really was watching an almost explosive eversion, the turning inside-out of a human being—a bursting loose of splattering blood and gore. Where, an instant before, a man in a business suit had sat, now there was only intestines and other viscera steaming on a lumpy broken mound.

The camera began to scan the body and then the room, mechanically, thoroughly, meticulously.

"Good God," Mei-Ling said. "It's as if his body blew apart!"

"Not exactly," said Wofford, the woman with the short-cropped black hair and piercing gaze. "If Mr. Lanier will back it up for us to just before the initial appearance of the light point sources, then play it again in very slow motion, I'll attempt to explain."

Lanier scanned back to the agreed-upon point, then let the record of poor Oliver's demise play again, in extreme slow motion.

"At this point, Mister Oliver is an ordinary three-dimensional creature, like most of us," Ms.—or was it Dr.?—Wofford began. The rest of them watched the horrific little movie play out in glacial motion to her calm narration. "The odd points of light appear now. Note that they are actually dark, but the distortion of the space around them concentrates the light so that at first blush they appear to be brighter than the surrounding area? We believe that's quite important.

"Now the spatial distortion is affecting Mr. Oliver himself. Note the 'out of focus' aura of light around his body. We believe he is in fact being reduced in dimensionality here, flattened from three dimensions into two dimensions toward the body's midline. This flattening is already enough to kill him, but it proceeds all the way to the point that the victim becomes a perfect two-dimensional sagittal plane.

"Stop it there a moment, Greg," Ms. Wofford said to Lanier, then used a computer graphic pointer to highlight specific parts of the image on all their screens. "Thank you. Unfortunately for the victim, a moment before this change began, he was a three-dimensional creature. He possessed a digestive tract, a tube connecting two openings, one at the mouth and one at the anus. Compressed to two dimensions, the passageway of his digestive tract completely bisects his body, so at this point he is about to literally fall or break apart into two pieces. All three-dimensional creatures with mouth and anus—everything after nematodes, which 'invented' the anus hundreds of millions of years ago—all fall into halves like this, when reduced to two dimensions."

Wofford glanced down at her notes on the desktop in front of her, then back toward the video display.

"Return to slow motion, Greg. Thanks. Now, here, the dimension-distorting pressure is abruptly released. The victim is allowed to return to three-dimensionality, almost instantaneously. The 'bursting' or 'explosive' effect you're seeing now is merely what the breaking apart in two dimensions becomes, when it instead takes place in three dimensions. His clothing is obviously not enough to withstand the pressure. This thoroughly mutilated corpse is what you have at the end of the process, which is more or less the same in all of these incidents."

Mei-Ling watched, vaguely nauseous, as the camera thoroughly scanned the scene of the broken, burst-open body and its blood-spattered surroundings. She wondered who or what was behind the thorough chronicling of the event, since the only known consciousness at the scene, Oliver's own, was now no longer present. At last Wofford nodded to Lanier and the lights came back up.

"Your response, Ms. Magnus?" Landau asked.

"Nausea, certainly," Mei-Ling replied. "It's even worse in slow motion. I think I'll forego seeing the 3-D holovision examples, for the time being."

The others smiled awkwardly, and she continued.

"My first intellectual response would be questions. How? Who—or what? Why?"

Unreadable glances passed around the room among the others.

"Would you elaborate on that?" Mulla asked, glancing carefully at her.

"All right," Mei-Ling said, breaking eye contact, staring down at her hand on the table. "If it *is* this sort of dimensional effect, might it be some heretofore undiscovered natural force—as spontaneous combustion was once thought to be? Certainly it's awesome enough, in terms of pure power, to fall into that category. The fact that the camera seems to chronicle it so carefully, though—that tends to indicate a consciousness behind the process. A ritualistic voyeurism perverse enough to be human. Have you tried tracing where the initial databurst comes in from, and where the final imagery goes?"

Sullivan shook his head.

"It's routed and rerouted through the infosphere a finite but practically uncountable number of times," he said, clearly stymied by the fact. "Untraceable."

"Ah," Mei-Ling said, nodding. "That, along with the amount of data manipulation and pure computational power—that all indicates a machine intelligence, or a human consciousness almost perfectly interfaced with a machine system."

Landau nodded carefully.

"You're up to speed very quickly, Mei-Ling," he said approvingly. "Assuming there is a consciousness of some sort behind the process—which we also do, since in every case there is that careful recording of the entire scene—is there any further speculation that comes to your mind about the nature of that consciousness or intelligence?"

Mei-Ling stared down at the black glass of the desktop. She knew what they were after: SCANCI, scan key, "skanky" time again, with its reductive, machine-feedable criteria.

"Voyeuristic, as I said. Ritualistic. Detail obsessed. Fascinated or obsessed with distinctions between outward appearance and inward realities, or with other, larger topological concerns. Control-fixated, too. Why else go to the trouble of killing people in that manner?"

"Not just people," Sullivan interjected. "So far one machine-interfaced chimpanzee and two webbed-in dolphins have also been killed in the same fashion. They were among the first."

"Very well, then—higher animals too," Mei-Ling said with a nod. "In the context of animal sacrifice, the splayed bowels and exposed internal organs of all the victims might have ritual significance. I'd have to see more examples."

"We have quite a few of them," Lanier said.

"I'm sure you—"

"What sort of ritual significance?" Landau interrupted, his left hand clenched around a pen on the tabletop.

"Maybe the perpetrator," Mei-Ling speculated, "if there is one, or only one, is familiar with traditional divination practices. 'Reading the entrails' for clues about the future, that sort of thing."

"You said one or only one," Mulla began, then seemed to ask the next question as if he were trying to get it out before Landau asked it. "Are you suggesting the possibility of a conspiracy?"

Mei-Ling shrugged and drummed the fingers of her right hand absently on the table.

"Hard to say," she replied, glancing up at the faces of those around the table, all peering intently at her. "You said the deaths were spaced throughout the world. That might indicate multiple participants in some type of network. Then again, the fact that it's all apparently mediated through the infosphere might mean it's just someone or something very obsessed, capable of processing fast or with a lot of machine time on hand. I'd have to know more about the victims. Have you uncovered any patterns? Victim scan keys?''

"Several had plausible links to Tetragrammaton," Landau said confidently, then grew less confident as he went down the list. "A number were connected with Ka Vang's major holding, ParaLogics, or its Crystal Memory Dynamics subsidiary. Some seem to have merely been investigating that Light phenomenon when they were attacked. Several seem to have been in contact with that underground virtual mail service—the pirate postal system called SubTerPost. Some fit no pattern at all, as yet."

"Puzzle-solvers, maze-makers, clandestine message-senders," Mei-Ling said quietly, almost to herself, though apparently Landau heard her.

"Yes," he continued. "Still, we believe the Tetragrammaton link is most important. We know a major thrust of that program for many years has been work on a mathematical model for opening a gateway into the fabric of space-time, potentially into higher dimensions. The program managers claim that since a singularity is almost a pure Platonic form—or formlessness—anyway, such a mathematical model would be indistinguishable from an actual gateway: The virtual and real would coincide. Simulated quantum information density structure, they call it. Given the infosphere-mediated distortions of local dimensions involved in these killings, such cases would seem to have a number of intersections with Tetragrammaton's work."

Mei-Ling glanced around the room again. Something about the space here was cold and distancing. They all might as well have been talking heads on a video conference call, she thought, but then quickly suppressed the image.

"One or a conspiracy," she said cautiously, staring again into the tabletop. "That was a big question in many killings during the twentieth century, especially serial murders. There's a theory that the number of serial murders was so disproportionate in the old United States at that time because of an ideological rupture experienced by people living in a nation that simultaneously validated 'rugged individualism' on the one hand and 'mass-mediated authentication' on the other."

"How is that relevant?" Landau asked, growing impatient. "Serial killers murder individuals over time. These are waves of mass killings."

"Yes," Mei-Ling continued, trying to bring her argument around. "That's what would be so unprecedented about these killings. They're mass and serial, simultaneously. According to the later trauma-control theories, serial murderers are the ultimate individualists, putting their own personal desires, their own individual freedom, above all social responsibilities or constraints. Control over others at all costs. Usually because they were traumatized by others when they were children. They seek control over their own lives through absolute domination and destruction of the lives of others. Physiologically, they also tend to have a heightened new brain/old brain split—''

"Which means?" Landau asked, rather snappishly.

"A heightened difference in operation between thalamocortical and limbic-brainstem areas," Mei-Ling said, "even between individual conscious desire and unconscious social or 'bicameral' morality. As a result, many trauma-control or 'serial' killers have allowed themselves to be caught. Their need for the 'approval' of social recognition overcomes their desire to remain hidden and individual. Many of them have been media-obsessed—films, television, holos, print. To the point that they didn't see themselves as fully real unless they eventually saw their stories on page or screen."

"What you're saying, then," Gopal Mulla ventured, "is that that type of killer ultimately hates his individuality?"

"More that he desperately desires to destroy his privacy," Mei-Ling said. "In destroying his privacy he destroys the space for his individual consciousness and uniqueness—and hopes thereby to at last become a fully integrated member of the society that has never accepted him as a member. The serial killer, as a traumatized, dissociated, low self-esteem 'conspiracy of one,' has tried to create a way to reconcile both sides of a conflicting social message: mass recognition of individual desire—"

"Please," Gopal Mulla said, interrupting with a sigh, "don't follow that line of thought any further. I can see the media coverage now: the TV Killer—only this time it'll be Topological Voyeur instead of television!"

More awkward smiles appeared around the conference table.

"From what I've seen so far this is more parallel than serial," Mei-Ling concluded, before Landau could interrupt. "Waves of mass killing over time, each wave occurring simultaneously, in rough parallel, throughout the infosphere. I don't think it's either a serial killer's 'conspiracy of one,' or the traditional conspiracy of many."

Mei-Ling paused at the sound of Landau shifting restlessly in his chair, but then continued.

"I know that there's a lot of evidence that Tetragrammaton has victimized quite a few people over the years," she said, "but this time it sounds like that organization may be less victimizer than victimized. Their own people are being killed, right? Aside from a rather strange purge or very peculiar downsizing, it just doesn't sound right."

She glanced up, relieved to see that Landau was not jumping down her throat yet.

"If it is a human being," Mei-Ling continued, "or a screwed-up machine intelligence that's behind this—and not some obscure natural phenomenon—we might want to look into the possibility of these killings being motivated by revenge for some hurt, real or perceived. Disgruntled employees, someone or something angered by what Tetragrammaton has done, a suspect motivated by the actions of the companies and governments linked to that organization—"

"That's quite a broad range of suspects," Wofford said quietly, rolling an electronic notepad stylus absently between thumb and forefinger.

"Better than none at all," Landau remarked. "Still, none of this explains why these killings should have begun *after* the Light incident."

Looks of recognition and nods of agreement passed through the room.

"No, it doesn't," Mei-Ling agreed. "It's possible there may be no connection, you know—just our faulty *post hoc ergo propter hoc* reasoning leading us to see a pattern that isn't really there."

Gopal Mulla shifted uneasily in his chair and cleared his throat.

"But what if the connection, the pattern, really *is* there?" he asked, almost pensively. "What if that Light did have something to do with it?"

"Then whoever or whatever caused the Light must also be suspect, I suppose," Mei-Ling said, uncomfortable with the thought, "even if that phenomenon just triggered an unforeseen response in someone or something else."

On that note, the briefing drew quickly toward an end. After speaking with Mulla and Landau, Sullivan came forward to shake Mei-Ling's hand and introduce himself.

"Looks like the higher-ups have made me your designated driver," he said affably, nodding toward Mulla and Landau where they stood talking to Lanier. "Any particular evidence you'd like to see? Place you'd like to go?"

She stared at him a moment, for some thoughts had already occurred to her along the very same lines.

"Yes," she said, "I'd like to see your distribution graphics on the times, dates, and places of the death waves. I'd also like to visit the nearest crime scene that hasn't yet been totally picked over by investigators. Also, I'd like to look at the best, most recent infosphere records for that deceased user, if possible."

"Don't ask for much, do you?" Sullivan said with a wry smile. "We'll give it a try. Would after lunch this afternoon be soon enough?"

As she left the conference room with her "designated driver" Mei-Ling was sure that after lunch would be more than soon enough.

G IVEN SAM'S RECORD FOR NEGLECTED FOLLOW-THROUGH in the past, Aleck had no reason to think that his roommate would actually take him up on his offer of a chance to tap into "Hugh's stuff." Yet here he was, with his current femme and who knew who else, waiting at the freight entrance to bypass security and come on down.

Aleck couldn't very well just send them away, after they'd gone to the trouble of coming down from Clifton and Universityville. Wouldn't do for his bosses to see that he was "entertaining," either, however. They might not approve.

He supposed he could get his guests in despite security. Aleck had learned to fool watchdog systems early, outthinking his parents' monitoring tech starting when he was eight years old. Every year during his teens they'd bought fancier and fancier security systems to keep an eye on him, but he'd just gotten better and better at foxing their tech. It was the sort of security-hack education that probably had somehow prepared him for a career in infosystems, and from there to medical computing, though he couldn't quite say how.

Security was minimal at this time of night—all electronic. He'd outwitted these systems before, even managed to get his recently exed-girlfriend down here five or six weeks back, as a matter of fact. He could do it again: Just give the security system a prerecorded reality to play with. Pay no attention to those intruders behind the curtain.

He set quickly to work. When all was in readiness, he darted out of the lab and down the corridors, then took the elevator to where Sam and company were waiting.

The elevator opened and he saw Sam and his emaciated blond spidergirl-clarinetist and keyboardist, Janika, as he'd expected. Also lounging about the loading dock, too, were the band's friendly neighborhood percussionist, the thickset and vaguely thuglike Marco. Hari, the tall, thin African exchange student in theoretical physics, was waiting there as well. Hari played "things with strings"—from Chapman stick and guitars (acoustic, electric, ensembled) to pianos (prepared, unprepared, and electrified), as well as the violin-viola-cello-bass gang, "traditional" instruments from everywhere, and new instruments from nowhere, of his own idiosyncratic design.

This was all much more than Aleck had expected. Worse, he noted, all of them had portable plug-in versions of their instruments with them.

"—but love does not alter when it alteration finds," Sam said, laughing and kissing Janika on top of her head, until he saw Aleck standing in the elevator. "Hey, our ride is here! Everybody, you know Aleck. Pile in."

Marco and Hari left their lounging positions and swagger-staggered into the elevator behind Sam and Janika. Judging by the olfactory aura of various chemicals floating about Sam and his friends, and by the degree of pupil dilation among them too, Aleck was pretty certain every one of them had found "alteration," all right—and already.

"Everything, uh, copacetic here?" Sam asked, paranoia-flashing for just an instant. "I mean, with security and everything?"

"Should be," Aleck said quietly, a bit peeved at the way Sam had expanded his solo invitation into a party of four. "I feedback-looped images and sounds of empty elevators and corridors into the security cams and sound pickups all along the paths I'm bringing you along. Mirror-phased all the motion detectors too. Stick tight and don't stray, though, or the rest of the security system might pick you up."

"Okay," Sam said slowly, orienting himself, "we'll do that."

By the time they left the elevator and started through the corridors to the lab, Aleck's guests had picked up again the spacy, laughing physics discussion with Hari that had apparently begun before they arrived.

"No, no, mon," Hari said as they walked along the hall. "The eleven-dimensional plenum is *all* the sea. Space-time is *all* the surface of the sea. Matter-energy is *all* the waves on the surface of the sea. Consciousness is *all* the surfers on the waves on the surface of the sea."

"No, mon, that's not right!" Sam said, doing a creditable imitation of Hari's accent. "Conches-ness is all the fish in the vévés of the surfers, don't you see."

The others laughed and Hari good-naturedly threw up his hands. Letting them into his lab, Aleck didn't see what was so funny. He guessed you *had to be there*—wherever "there" might be for his guests in their current mental state. He brought up the lights, including the service floods in the big tank.

As he pulled the majority of the security cameras and sound pickups out of their false reality and brought them back on line, he saw Marco, Janika, and Hari heading straight toward the tank, oohing and ahhing. Sam, however, immediately got down to business, checking out the lab's electronics suite.

"This the brain-loaner?" Marco asked, glancing from Hugh in his tank to Aleck behind his display console. Aleck nodded. Marco turned back toward Hugh. "Guy I knew back home, got in a bad wreck—they say he ended up movin' datter with his grey matter, too."

Aleck glanced up from his console. What a strange rhyme. He wouldn't have expected that from Marco. Maybe it wasn't intentional.

"Hey, you've got full sight/sound interface and recording capabilities!" Sam said excitedly, geeking his way through Aleck's peripheral electronics. "Biological signal sensor hookups, thought-wave recognition software—"

Yeah, Aleck thought, nodding curtly. As if his roommate hadn't already suspected as much—and had his friends bring their instruments along, "just in case."

"After we check out ol' Hugh's stuff," Sam began, disingenuously, "you mind if we do a session? We sort of lost our rehearsal space for this evening."

This evening? Aleck wondered sourly. It was nearly three in the morning!

"I guess I don't mind," Aleck began after a moment. He felt himself being sucked into enabling their performance shenanigans, despite his misgivings. "But you'll have to be out of here before regular security makes its rounds down here at six A.M. I can keep all the local sound pickups fooled, but try to keep your playing this side of earthquake level, okay? The Subject there is supposed to be participating in a sensory deprivation experiment."

Sam glanced at the large form floating motionless in the tank, the object of such rapt attention from the rest of his band.

"I think it would take a lot more than us to bother ol' Hugh Manatee," he said with a subtle smile, "but okay. We'll keep our static out of his circuits."

Sam called Janika and Marco and Hari over to the electronics suite and tossed each of them a circlet for webbing into virtual surround, as well as a pair of 'trode armbands to read their muscle signals. Then he read off frequencies for each of them to interface their instruments into the suite computer. Aleck glanced up from time to time, relieved to see that at least they hadn't brought an entire orchestra with them.

Marco had only an electronic drum pad. Janika had brought something that looked like a cross between a flute and an accordion keyboard. Hari's instrument was the most stripped-down of all: a modified Chapman stick, like a guitar from which someone had removed the soundbox body, leaving only a fretted fingerboard neck and strings.

Sam, heeding Aleck's warnings about noise, had them tuning up into virtual space, channeling music to each other's ears but not into the surrounding air. Rather surreal, Aleck thought, watching them in their electrode armbands and lightweight, fret-netted circlet gear, each circlet unit equipped with personal earphones and eye-screens and throat mikes. At the moment the band members were hearing only their hummed pitch approximations—and virtually nothing of the sound of the instruments themselves. Aleck heard Sam singing, almost sotto voce, the lyrics "Human bein's, human bein's, we breed beyond our means/ Human bein's, human bein's, we breed beyond our means," then laughing.

Aleck recognized the notes behind the band's original little tune-up lyric. The tune was from Sam's collection of popular songs of the past century. The original was a paean to a movie star who got killed in a car accident, a ditty sung by a band called the Beagles, or something like that, if Aleck remembered correctly.

"Hey, Aleck," Sam said, breaking out of tune-up mode. "Show me how to access Hugh's stuff, will you? So we can have some visuals to play against."

"Okay," Aleck replied. He put on the circlet gear and channeled three-dimensional displays of R & L's corporate data indices to Sam and his people for a brief instant. Then Aleck air-touched a little manatee-character icon.

The manatee grew to life size and swam out of the underwater anteroom of a high-level R & L corporate index. The animated sea mammal led them into deep, open water. There, all about them, floated numerous shifting three-dimensional icons around a glowing underwater fireball—a red-orange sun dropped into and burning deep within the dark blue ocean.

"Hey, great graphics!" Hari said, very impressed.

"Thanks," Aleck replied. "It was a lot of work, but it was the best way I could picture it. The central fireball is the icon for how Hugh interfaces with R & L's corporate electronics and the infosphere—generally bioelectronics, untouchable through this system. A sun, too hot to touch, see? The things that look like solar prominences are internal communications within Hugh's system, as near as I can tell. The things that start out as solar flares, then become cooler and turn into schools of silvery fish—and vice-versa, from moonfish to solar flares—those are datastreams moving from Hugh into the infosphere and from the infosphere back to Hugh."

"What are the larger icons floating around the fireball?" Sam asked. "The geometric things that keep fluctuating—"

"The stuff I already showed you back at the apartment is part of it," Aleck said. "They seem to be made out of 'found' data and images, but they're shaped and wrapped around structures that originate with Hugh, as far as I can tell. The fireball seems to spew them out from time to time, anyway."

"Can you open one?" Janika asked.

"Sure," Aleck said, reaching forward and tapping at a tesseract cross shape, a hypercube represented in three dimensional space. Abruptly the cubes of the cross fell in on themselves and became a landscape through which all of them were moving, each of them experiencing it from subjective camera point-of-view.

In sunset light, getting out of the car to unlock the driveway gate. Footsteps crunching over the driveway gravel to the gate. Inserting the key in the lock. The lock clicks open on the gate.

*Suddenly the sound of shotguns, three, dialing in. Memory flash
of 9mm Glock rail pistol in glove compartment. Turning to see
three figures striding swiftly out of the trees and brush beside
the gravel driveway, their hair and lower faces covered with
bandannas. Feebly raising fists as assailants set about method-
ically head-bashing with shotgun butts.*

"You fucked with the wrong people, kiddo."

Black out.

*Then hospital tomographs, images of a disembodied head—
close-lipped, shut-eyed, naked of hair and consciousness—turning in space, a strange silent movie. Just back of the left temple,
cranium dented inward deeply, in the perfect impression of a gun
butt—*

Abruptly the scene disappeared into the screen at the back of
a cube; then into the wall of the cube, then the cube started
birthing other cubes until it was once again the shape of the cross
of cubes, the unraveled hypercube tesseract.

"That's a horrible little story," Janika said.

"Maybe it's real," Marco said flatly. "Maybe that's what really happened to the mummy in the tank. How he ended up
where he is."

"But the images are adapted from stock footage," Sam said.

"So?" Marco said.

"I see your point," Aleck said slowly, catching on. "Maybe
the found images are used to put flesh on the skeleton of what
actually happened. A sort of disembodied memory."

"Or an autonomous psychoid process," Janika said, surprising
the rest of them with the phrase. "We talked about them when
I was in the studio audience for my AI class. Researchers are
using them in some of the big machine intelligences, as a way
around 'monolithic' machine selfhood."

The rest said nothing for a moment, until Hari's voice came
on line.

"Possibly," he agreed. "Computers in general have been
functioning as a sort of collective electronic unconscious at least
since the creation of the infosphere."

Sam laughed.

"You think Hugh's *unconscious* is making them—so he's not
even aware of it?" Sam prodded. "That'll save us some intellectual property hassles, if we decide to use any of this stuff in
our show!"

Show? Aleck wondered. Use?

"Open up another one," Janika said. "That weird thing made out of spheres over there."

Aleck reached out and tapped open the unraveled hypersphere, a thing shapeshifting like a clockwork bee-swarm. The spheres fell into each other and filled their surround again with subjective-camera imagery.

Fields of snow, untouched, pure and sweet as a blank white page. First one out in it, lying down and writing a winged figure into those pages again and again until jittery-shivering, body cold as a snow angel's, snow angels—

Glass calling for a brick the way still water calls for stones, tossed skipped thrown stones, mirror-smooth pond surfaces beckoning, then breaking into wet shatter—

Throwing rock and mud dams across streams. Ponds. In the trickle-leaks from the dams, flatworms, small black slow, move over the sand. Planaria. Cut them in half, watch them regenerate, neat trick—

Handed a rubberband airplane. Winding the propeller, knotting and twisting the band again and again. Paternal voice says, "If there's one thing I've learned in this life, it's that people are like rubberband airplanes. The more twisted they are, the farther they fly—"

Ant wars. Red ants, black ants. Putting them in matchboxes, shaking them up so they fight. Stare fascinated as they battle to the death, mandible to mandible, biting off legs, antennae, thoraxes, abdomens. War in a box—

Handed magnifying lens. Examining leaf structures, flower parts. Diagram in school science program showing hand lens becoming a burning glass, focusing the light to a tight combustion point. Dry leaves, bright sunny days. Shrinking the comet-tail diffusion, making the bright point. Pale last fall's leaf grows a spot dark with excess of bright, glows a rim of ash, smoke rising, leaf solidly afire. Newspapers, plastics, wax hearts, burning. Waiting for ants, crouching beside anthills with burning lens in hand, bewildered victims twisting, smoking, catching pismire fire—

Aching sizzling blue burn scar of winter sky. No snow on the ground but cold enough to make ice lenses from two bowls of water freezing. Trying to put them together into a single lens to start fires with a lens of ice but too ungainly to use. Going to dammed creek in woods, breaking chunks loose of thick flaw-

lessly clear ice, lugging them home, setting them on the front porch beside the ice lenses already there—

Hunkering down in the dry grass of winter-killed lawn, amid the scattered punky sections of cut-down beetle-infested maple tree, amid scrap wood rotted thin as paper. Trying to start one of the rotted lengths on fire, succeeding only in dotting it all over with blackened burn spots, only getting it to smolder, never to burn. Turning, walking away, hunkering down beside another likely candidate for burning—

"Good God!" shouts paternal voice. "What the hell are you doing? The lawn's on fire!"

Looking quickly over right shoulder, seeing the piece of wood so long labored over has, unbeknownst, caught fire, the lawn too, paraclete tongues of flame licking toward the maple stump, all the wood scraps scattered around—

Man charging from the house, ample-stomached figure in white undershirt, grey work pants, immense flopping unbuckled black rubber galoshes snatched in haste, moving with the otherworldly motion of Americans walking on the moon like ungainly Styrofoam robots or angels traveling incognito saluting the starred flag, speed of charging man hampered by weight of two huge prized ice chunks he's carrying, one in each hand grabbed from off the porch—

Flames shining up through the flawless ice crashing down upon them. Ice blocks landing with hiss and sizzle, flames like tortured snakes fanning out around them. Again and again the fire shines up clearly through the ice descending upon it, until the flames are no longer visible and the ice is ordinary water seeping into the steaming, smoking, scorched, winter-killed lawn—

Blank staring eyes in face of silenced youth. Seeing the reflections of shop windows upon the deed. Hurling a brick through their witness. Dry glassy snowflake shatter. Sirens sounding law and order. Disappearing into alleys, running maze of streets, jumping barricades, dashing down Möbius Highway going nowhere, taking forever to get there, highway stretching like rubberband, knotting twisting. "The more twisted they are, the farther they fly." Rubberband airplane, twisting propeller, tension growing, rubberband snaps, rubberband snaps, rubberband snaps—

They fell out of the re-swarming spheres and into the sea of represented data again.

"Fantastic!" Marco enthused.

"If you like childhood sadism," Janika countered.

"True," Hari said, "but it's not as dark as the first one—and more complex too."

"We can use some of it," Sam agreed, "but not the stuff at the back end. It's too narrative. Too much like that big-arena stuff Möbius Caducéus did up in the orbital habitat. Aleck—you still there?"

"Yes?"

"Is there any way we can make this system jump randomly from icon to icon?" Sam asked. "All the accessible ones? Say about every ten, fifteen seconds? So it'll produce a montage effect?"

"I suppose I can plot that kind of sequencing," Aleck said. "It'll take me a couple minutes."

"Great," Sam said happily. "Hey, you mind if we project the images and the sound into real space a little? Just so we can get a sense of how it all looks put together?"

"I—I suppose not," Aleck replied warily. "Just give me time to fool all the nearby sound pickups again."

Moments later, the band members at last had their own private after-hours nightclub gig, with Aleck playing their audience of one. Throughout the space of the lab played the images taken from Hugh Manatee's disembodied memories, or his autonomous psychoid processes, or whatever they were, surging everywhere through the room, even glowing submarinely in Manatee's own tank, a tangential, chaotic counterpoint to the flowing and pounding of the band's music as Sam and Janika sang:

Battlefields become bus stops.
Massacres melt into folksongs, freeze into marble.
The king divorces, the abbey dissolves.
Yesterday's cathedral becomes this morning's rock quarry.
The sheep don't care.
Ancient stones conspire in silence on a windswept plain.
Their secrets are safe. The sheep have other concerns:
Consume that grass, produce that wool!
No fleece without dags, no dags without fleece!
With lambs to bounce teats at lambing time,
All are perfectly content—
So long as, now and then,

We get to rub our shaggy flanks
Up against a monument.

The effect was both disorienting and hypnotic at once. Aleck could tell that, even before they finished the song, the band members were pleased with what they were creating.

He was going to have a hell of a time getting them out of here before the daytime security guards came on duty.

ROGER CORTLAND GLANCED AT THE SLEEPING FIGURE OF Paul Larkin two seats over, space and stars showing from out of the portal beyond Larkin's balding grey head. Roger envied the older man. Since his odd experience at the time of the Light, Roger himself found he could no longer sleep on orbiters like this one, or on jets, either—something he had accomplished with no difficulty at all, before the Light.

Oh, well. He supposed old Larkin deserved the rest. The old man had masterfully harangued the security personnel surrounding the tepui into giving them an airlift back to Amianac and Caracas, claiming it was the least they could do, after he and Cortland and their guide and bearers had hiked all the way to the shoulder of the world and then been denied access to their goal. The security people and the bureaucrats had nervously agreed, at last—apparently out of a combination of guilt and a desire to have them out of the area as quickly as possible.

They and their party and all their gear had found its way aboard a big VTOL plane on the helipad that the occupying army had hacked, lasered, and 'dozered out of the surrounding brush. The flight back was tense, at least as far as the military personnel with them were concerned, but it got them to Amianac in hours instead of days.

After settling up charges and dropping their locals off at the vertiport outside the busted boomtown, Paul and Roger flew on to Caracas, landing at a military base connected to the airport. The flight back north, then up the well on the single-stage orbiter *McAuliffe*, had been pleasantly uneventful thus far.

Despite his best intentions, Roger found himself growing disappointed as he gazed out the portal at the deep navy blue of cislunar space. Larkin's stories had primed him for seeing the tepui top, supposedly covered by an eroded-rock labyrinth or maze as convoluted as the surface of a human brain. He had hoped to descend into the cloud forest that Larkin claimed bisected the tepui top into neat hemispheres. He had planned to enter the cavernous spaces that riddled the tepui, to see the *indigenas* Jacinta had "electronified," hooking them into telecommunication with the rest of the world.

He had been intrigued by Larkin's reminiscences. The idea of people in loincloths hooked into the global satellite network, pumping everything they pulled down out of the infosphere straight into their bemushroomed minds, shaping it and casting it from "mind-time" into space-time, zapping it into the tall quartz collecting-columns of their "information drivers" and "intelligent crystal technology" afloat serenely in the vast underground chamber of the Cathedral Room—that was all so wild it almost *had* to be real.

The skeptic in him wanted to see it all first hand. He'd wanted to test scrupulously the idea that crystalline materials of proper lattice configuration and sufficient size could receive and amplify mental energies. He'd wanted to strenuously examine the even more dubious claim that such crystalline structures could translate those energies into motive forces, in a manner supposedly analogous to piezoelectric effects. He'd wanted to observe the manner in which Jacinta and the *indigenas* supposedly sang and thought critical information densities *into* the floating crystal columns in the big room. He'd wanted to understand the exact physical principle—no matter how subtle or "holographic"—by which those collecting columns could translate and amplify information itself, in such a way as to dissociate the tepui from the gravitational bed of local space-time, or tunnel through higher dimensional space, or whatever it was they had supposedly managed to do.

True, Jacinta Larkin had provided a wealth of information in the brief time she'd met with them, but so much had still been left unexplained. Roger particularly wanted to know more about how the history of the tepui and its journey fit with the Light, particularly *his* experience of that phenomenon.

The Light had done him much good, no doubt. He and his mother, Atsuko, were getting along better than they ever had. If penance could grow into love, then he and Marissa Correa were drifting toward something that might someday go by that name—despite his injury to her. He didn't understand exactly why Marissa would still have an interest in him after the slapping incident, but he was very glad she did.

He was still deep in therapy, still prone to remembering or even sketching out images of the strange angels he had seen, but the Light seemed somehow to have lifted and rolled a heavy stone away from his heart.

Roger recalled coming out of that peculiar dream-coma or near-death experience or whatever it was the Light had plunged him into, to see Marissa and Paul Larkin looking down at him. That was about all he remembered, at first. Talking with Jacinta, though, had triggered something. He had begun to access memories from that lost time again. He knew, without knowing how he knew, that the "wrong place" at which the contact ship had popped back into normal space had involved a red giant star, an ancient uncharted black hole, and even the cometary sphere once inadequately described as the Oort cloud.

He remembered too, what that ship had looked like. A sphere of "angels," advanced myconeuralized creatures wrapped in the brightness of solar-energy wings and the glow of protective fields of force. He remembered crashes and deaths maybe as far in as the Kuiper belt, and suspected the presence of angelic survivors still out there, still quiescently alive all this long slow time. He had recurring flashes of a universal myth cycle explaining, in grand architectonic fashion, the growing informational subtlety that rose out of energy, through matter, through life, through mind, through worldmind and starmind and universal mind.

He took out his notepad Personal Data Assistant and began to make notes to himself on the small computer:

—Consciousness merely a more subtle/complex form of information than matter and energy?

—$E=mc^2$ explains how a lot of energy can be released from a relatively small amount of mass, but also vice versa, how an awful lot of energy is required to make a relatively small amount of mass.

—Matter can be made to "degrade" into energy more readily than energy can be made to "upgrade" into matter.

—On continuum of informational complexity, if consciousness is more subtle/complex form of information, can consciousness be made to *degrade* more readily into matter/energy than matter/energy can be made to *upgrade* into consciousness?

—Shannon information theoretics. Wheeler's physics. Three-dimensional encoding of color spaces actually a single information state, the simultaneous embodiment in both physical processes and conscious experience, like matter and energy as two states of same underlying "something."

—Matter, energy, all states physical: "physicalia"

—Mind, thought, all states psychophysical: "qualia"

—Physicalia and qualia: two forms of the same underlying informational continuum?

—$Q=p^2$, where Q is qualia, p is physicalia, and   is a constant. What constant? Speed of information processing—squared?

Roger puzzled over his equation, wishing his maths were better. The equation disappointed him—just a transmogrifying of Einstein's original terms. Still, there seemed to be some truth in it, and it fit into the overall structure of his theorizing. He left it unchanged and jotted further notes:

—Teilhardian idea that increasing physical complexity is mirrored by increasing complexity of conscious experience.

—Theological and teleological memes: incarnation, Omega Points where consciousness becomes so ramified it must sacrifice itself so that a new cycle/recycle can begin, Big Bang, Death/Resurrection, Bodhisattvas who, though enlightened, continue to exist in the cycles of incarnation until all and everything is fit for Nirvanic Bliss.

—Sacrifices always a metaphor for something much larger, but "what" is hard to define.

—Goal of the universe is—enlightenment?

—Final enlightenment: not possible in isolation?

—At brink of universal enlightenment, nowhere left to go but to spread it around.

—Universe itself bodhisattvic: none are enlightened until all are. Ultimate enlightenment therefore is spontaneous everywhere at the moment of its achievement anywhere. And vice versa reversion.

Roger wondered if he was making this up—or remembering it. Curiously, it felt rather like both. For a moment he also wondered, "Why me?" He had never been particularly religious or given to cosmological speculation before the light. All this stuff was undeniably in his head, but it somehow wasn't his, or him—at least not who he had been the rest of his life.

He didn't want to consider implications yet, though. Just get the discoveries/memories jotted down as they came.

He looked back over his notes, thinking that "universe" might be too small a term for what he was trying to get at. The word "plenum" arose unbidden into his consciousness, along with the image of a great, golden, flashing, branching thing, like a cross between a sphere and a tree and a bonfire. Into his head came images of a voice speaking from a burning bush, of infinite branching time lines, parallel universes, wormhole-connected mycelial spawn, each universe a fruiting body, a mushroom on the mycelium of the plenum.

Where was all this coming from?

He knew where in the Bible the burning yet unconsumed bush came from, but what that image might be describing had been made new for him now, fresh. Revisionable, rethinkable.

He knew the theories of the cosmologists, of course. The concept that all the "other universes" were dead—that only one, our own, had the right set of physical properties to allow life. That idea had bothered him ever since his experiences surrounding the time of the Light. It struck him as a narrow anthropocentrism, like the idea that Man was specially created, or that the Earth was the center of the universe, or that Earth was the only planet on which intelligent life, such as it was, had arisen. Then he remembered why he'd been struck that way and jotted it down.

—Those other universes aren't dead—they're virtual.

—In the infinitude of the plenum, every universe is real to itself and virtual to all others. All universes parallel to one's own appear virtual; only one's own is "real."

—cf. Virtual (particle/antiparticle) pairs, Hawking radiation.

—Boundaries between universes correspond to role of Schwarzschild radius in generation of Hawking radiation.

—Mirrorings: Views from different sides of the boundary are what constitute the real/virtual distinction.

Has somebody else come up with this? roger wondered. He was remembering as well as discovering, after all. He racked his brain, but all he could come up with was other ideas from quantum cosmology, scaling "particle" up to "universe." He thought of how quantum theory had by the late twentieth century become almost a form of dance notation: more and more arcane, abstracted from, perhaps dictating to, and definitely implicated in, the dance itself. He thought of orbifolds, of the superstring theorists with their talk of 10 and 26 dimensions—and the odd coincidence that the number of dimensions should so reflect the physicists' own cardinal systems: base 10 numbers and the number of letters, twenty-six, in the alphabet used by most of them to communicate. He thought of the debates when he was a student: the elegant mathematics of tubiton matrices, event-cones generated from spiralling string fields, whirled worldlines, all saturated with recurring golden-mean numbers. He thought of numerology, magic numbers, Ramanujan functions. What did the existence of such numbers, implicated in both Mind and Nature, say about the relationship between the physical universe and the consciousness of its observers?

The velocity of the orbiter changed noticeably. In the portal out of which he had been staring but not really seeing, HOME 1, the first (but no longer the only) High Orbital Manufactured Environment, floated into view, growing slowly larger. Roger recalled the last time he had seen this view. How had Jhana Meniskos described HOME then? Like an ''antique ribbed transformer that had swallowed a crystal ball, then been run through by a pole along its long axis''—yes, that was it.

He smiled, remembering. For all its solar energy systems, docking, transport, and communication facilities mounted along the axis, for all its mirrors shining light into (and radiation shielding keeping the bad rays out of) the central habitation sphere and the agricultural tori, for all its reflection of fields and forests and streams and lakes just barely visible at the ''poles'' of the central sphere that swelled the overall toroid like a pig in a python—for all that, ungainly as it undeniably looked, and for all the aesthetic criticism that could admittedly be leveled at it, Roger found himself warming to the prospect of this home in space and his homecoming to it. This was where his heart truly was now, in this place that was home to the mother he loved, and Marissa, the woman he hoped would become his beloved for the rest of his days, no matter how corny and old-fashioned and sentimental that all sounded.

He called up a virtual-connect to Marissa and subvocalized a quick hello to announce his return. She shot him back a quick message—''Missed you much. Can't wait to see you''—and then as a canned signature afterword, the obscure, foot-fetishist haiku—''Your toes are plump grapes/Summer wine hot in taut skins/I will bite them now''—that had become a private joke between them since they'd discovered it together.

Roger chuckled, thinking of how they had come across that haiku, at the beginning of his long and ongoing "rehabilitation." Like that haiku, everything had its history—a fact he'd come to realize more and more deeply.

As they maneuvered for docking with the usual excruciating care, Roger saw that Paul Larkin was awake and scanning a holographic virtual—apparently an image of the infamous *Cordyceps*.

"H'lo, Paul," Roger said. "I see you're back among the living. What're you up to with that?"

"Trying to work up a rationale for getting this 'shroom renamed," Larkin said, causing the three-dimensional image of the fungus to rotate and enlarge. "Something to call attention to it as a primordial form. See the bluish-grey color where the convolutions whorl, forming pits? Those are the principal spore production sites. The asci are carried in flask-shaped perithecia 'nests,' so they're pyreno- rather than discomycetes. Overall the shape resembles a morel, but watch"—he tapped icons to display the fungus in cross section. "—and you see it there? The inside is dense and filled, like a truffle, not hollow like a morel."

"It's a living fossil, all right," Roger agreed.

Larkin scanned out of the mushroom virtual, calling up one with human skulls on it instead, and turned toward the younger man.

"Everything about that tepui culture is a synergy of two living fossil types," Larkin said. "One human, one fungal. Jacinta tried to tell me about it all those years ago, before they sang that mountain to the stars, but I just wouldn't listen."

"*Two* types?" Roger asked.

"You probably didn't get that good a look at the ghost people, given the way they stealthed in and out of our camp," Paul said.

"No, I didn't," Roger agreed.

"Well, seeing them again made me remember some things I didn't want to, I suppose," he said. "Skulls and corpses on their fungal burial island, inside the Cathedral Room at the center of the tepui's main cavern. Neither of us Larkins are forensic anthropologists, but Jacinta saw the obvious, even if I refused to."

"Which was?"

The gnomish older man stroked his beard, then pointed to the pair of skulls rotating holographically before him.

"The occipital 'rose' or 'bun,' " he said, nodding toward the skull on the left. "The emphasis on cerebellar development, the large supraorbital ridges. I remember Jacinta talked about the ghost people's seminocturnal lifeway. Their focus on aural over visual, their lack of left-brain dominance. 'Strong archaic *Homo* traits, *neanderthalensis* traits, *soloensis* traits, troll and wild man traits.' That was how she put it.''

Roger glanced about the cabin of the orbiter, thoughtful.

"Pre-CroMagnon, then?" he asked. Paul Larkin nodded.

"Much the same way some anthropologists claim Australian aboriginals supposedly have traits indicating they may be partly descended from developed *Homo erectus*," Larkin said. "Only the case is more so, here. Jacinta claimed, back then, that the tepuians are a people whose universe is bound together by threads and webs of song extending all the way back to Europe and Africa a hundred thousand years ago and more—the same songweb differently echoed in the aboriginal songlines.''

Roger cocked an eyebrow quizzically at that.

"But human beings have been in the New World only thirty-thousand years," he remarked, trying to make Larkin's theorizing fit what he knew of paleontology, "and the Neanderthals were already dying out or dead by then.''

Larkin laughed.

"That's exactly what I said! I've had this exact same conversation with Jacinta, only I was playing your role. See, the thirty thousand figure works only if you buy the idea that the first humans to cross into the New World were hunters following the herds across Beringia. But it's far more likely that fishing groups began following the coastline out of Asia and into the New World much earlier, long before the inland parts of Beringia were even free of the ice.''

"Then why don't we find proof of their settlements?" Roger asked.

Larkin laughed again.

"I asked the same question, all those years ago. Jacinta parried it with an argument about 'preservation bias.' She believed those ancient settlements were primarily along the coasts. But the oceans have risen four hundred feet since the last Ice Age. Any artifacts or traces in those settlement areas would have been destroyed when the intertidal zone passed over them—all the quicker if such artifacts were made of wood or bone.''

"I guess archaeologists are a bit stone-biased," Roger said, thinking about it.

"Exactly," Larkin said with a nod. "For much of the twentieth century, archaeologists believed there were no tool-using cultures in most of Asia during the Paleolithic—simply because they found almost no stone implements there. Then someone did contemporary ethnographic research among low-tech peoples in those areas and discovered that most of the toolkit there was *bamboo*—and since bamboo doesn't preserve well, the scientists had erroneously assumed there was no tool use going on.''

Larkin stared out the window a moment as the bright orb of Earth flashed into view.

"Even today you can walk into museums all over the world and see the scientific racism perpetuated against so-called Neanderthal man," he said, turning back to Roger. "Claims that those ancient people—who had bigger brains than we do, who probably invented the concept of life after death—had no art and only a very simple material culture. All because they supposedly couldn't make as wide a range of vocal sounds as we can. Linguistic chauvinism if I ever heard it. Do the experts have any proof that bone, antler, and wood were *not* exploited before the Upper Paleolithic? Have they considered that maybe nothing remains of 'Neanderthal' art because it was done almost exclusively in wood and bark, like aboriginal bark paintings? You'd think someone would wonder, especially if that's what they're getting paid to do."

Now it was Roger's turn to laugh, hearing the passion with which the older man spoke.

"I don't want you to think I'm an old crank, now," Larkin said, somewhat sheepishly.

"Not at all," Roger assured him, growing quickly more serious. "But what's all that got to do with the ghost people?"

"I'm getting to that," Larkin said. "It was probably much the same with the fisherfolk who first crossed into the New World, and for most 'Homo sapiens neanderthalensis' outside Europe. Toolkits centered on the heavy use of plant fiber and wood, less bone, *much* less stone, if any—just like the ghost people. After all these years I guess I finally agree with Jacinta's old contention that the division into *sapiens sapiens* versus *sapiens neanderthalensis* doesn't work. We're *all* just developed *Homo erectus*—not just the Australian Aborigines."

Roger noticed that they were very close to the Orbital Complex now. Their conversation would be coming to an end soon, of necessity.

"So absence of stone evidence *in* the New World," he said,

"is not evidence of human absence from the New World?"

"Exactly," Larkin replied. "I think Jacinta's right. The ghost people of the tepui are a remnant population going back over 100,000 years. Bigger-brained than the rest of us too, I'll bet—"

The docking of the orbiter finished while the men had been talking, and a recorded voice interrupted them now to make its anachronistic "deplaning" announcement. They exited the transat orbiter, into a reception area outside the orbital habitat's Docking Bay 5, where Marissa Correa and Atsuko Cortland were waiting for them.

Amid the hugs of welcome, Roger thought that, yes, it really did feel good to be home. He also wondered, though, if and when Jacinta, and the arguably "bigger-brained" tepuians with her, would arrive—and how, and why.

W HEN HIS DREAMS BEGAN TO FILL WITH IMAGES OF HIM-self holding a gun to his own head, then with recurrent visions of floating, transfixed like Christ on Calvary but crucified on a cross of air—that's when Ray Dundas knew he needed a break from the psiXtians and their Sun Underground city. Fortunately for him, he managed to volunteer for a delivery run over the coast range to Santa Cruz—not so difficult a job to wangle, really, since most of the psiXtians seemed to be homebodies.

He was planning to make the most of the trip. He had already covertly satlinked up to his minders back home in the Rocky Mountains and the Northern Plains. They had relayed very terse instructions so that, once in Santa Cruz, he would also be able to surreptitiously approach his Intelligence contact. The contact, he gathered, was working in a restaurant with the almost unpronounceable name of Cthulhutessen.

The day came that he found himself in standard psiXtian all-natural-fiber workman's coveralls, loading recycled kenaf and hemp paperback editions of *Light Livelihood: Ecoholism in Everyday Life*, and *Minimal Impact Economy: A psiXtian Sustainability Primer*—along with optidisk audio and visual versions of the same—into the back of a Solectric truck. The disks were made of grain plastic, or "grastic," as the psiXtians called it. The same material made up most of the locally manufactured truck he'd be driving, which had also been ZAPped, certified as zero air-pollutant producing.

Of course. Naturally.

Dundas bid the psiXtian media co-op gang goodbye, then drove the purring vehicle out of the underground and onto Biola Road where it led to Route 152. Both the truck and Highway 152 were smart, full of embedded sensors, and his route, through Los Banos and over the coast range to Santa Cruz, was not particularly challenging. He faced only a few places along the way that might require the presence of an actual human behind the wheel.

Dundas programmed in a two-minute warning to sound before each of the human-behind-the-wheel spots, then inputted his destinations: the psiXtian Outreach and Retreat Center in Aptos, and three stores, Aum Depot, Ohmage Homage, and Apokatopia Ethnotek, all in Santa Cruz. The names of the stores in themselves made him dubious as to what kind of wares they sold, and to what clientele. The fact that they were in the notorious Santa Cruz area only made his expectations worse.

The truck had neither radio nor air conditioning. The lack of air conditioning wasn't such a big deal. Although the day was sunny and warm, it was still early and the heat was far from unbearable. The lack of radio or sound system was more of an irritation. The biggest drawback of this run—as he realized twenty minutes into it—was likely to be boredom.

He supposed he should take a further glance through the books in his cargo. Vowing to "know thy enemy," he divided his attention in thirds, between the highway, a copy of *Light Livelihood*, and dozing off.

Paging through the front matter, he saw that the book was in something like its fiftieth printing, and that it had first appeared back around the turn of the millenium. Flipping through it more deeply, he quickly located the sort of eco-pagan assaults on Christian belief he suspected might be found in its pages, in a chapter entitled " 'And God Gave Man Dominion Over The Earth'—NOT!"

The chapter began with passages from Scripture. That really didn't surprise him. Even Satan can cite Scripture. But then the psiXtian book went on the attack:

> These biblical passages provide clear examples of the classic adversarial stance underlying the long war of humanity against the natural matrix out of which our species arose. In these passages cited above we can see sketched the

premises and pretexts of that anthropocentric war. Nature
is not indifferent, we are told, but is actively out to get us.
We are led to believe that we cannot live with Nature—
we can only subdue and rule ''her'' or be subdued and
ruled by ''her.'' Living with or within Nature is not an
option, at least for those who adhere to an ''inerrant'' interpretation of these religious texts.

The link this dominance paradigm has to patriarchal
power and hierachical organization in general should be
almost self-evident. The role such texts and their traditional interpretations play in authenticating, validating, and
authorizing dominance of man over man, man over
woman, man over nature—

Dundas grimaced and looked out the driver's side window at
the fallow fields the highway was passing through. These people
just didn't get it, he thought. Hierarchy is ordained by God, it is
God's way, like that hawk swooping down on the mouse in the
field there. The hawk eats the field mouse. These people would
have the mouse eat the hawk. The divine order is a golden chain
running from God through the ranks of men—from those men
who have earned His favor most to those who have earned it
least—thence through the ranks of women, and then to and
through children.

Far below came all the animals, Dundas thought. All of them
put upon the Earth to serve the needs of the supreme creation,
Man. Earth was created to serve Man, not Man to serve the Earth.
The world belonged to Man, not Man to the Earth. Only the
Indians and other primitives had believed the opposite—and look
at the way their ''civilizations'' had fallen before those with the
True God on their side!

Looking out the windows, at the fallow fields below the great
earthen embankment holding back the San Luis Reservoir, Ray
found himself growing homesick for the open expanses of the
plains, the fields of winter wheat, of corn and milo further south.
He drove the pang of homesickness back down, forcefully. Turning back to the scurrilous book, he flipped pages as the truck
climbed up the hill beside Sisk Dam and higher into the coastal
range.

The rise of the first city was concomitant with the rise of
agriculture and the steepening decline of both biodiversity

and hunting-gathering as a way of life. We, at the turn of the millenium, find ourselves at the far end of that arc. Now, human populations thoroughly dominate the planetary surface, literally shouldering other species off the stage of life through destruction of their habitat in the name of our own. We have been fruitful and increased in number until now we literally *fill* the Earth.

Ultimately this situation has been made inevitable by the inflated carrying capacity resulting from humanity's most important—and most devastating—invention, agriculture.

Just no pleasing these people, he thought as the truck carried him smoothly through the hills. The psiXtians were worse than the Amish. What did they want—for people to give up their jobs and their homes and let their kids starve? Or not have any children at all? For what? The preservation of *animals*? That was totally out of whack. Not just anti-Christian—anti-*human*. And yet they had labs throughout Sunderground, working on "appropriate technology," presumably tech for humans. He returned to the book, incredulous.

At this end of the arc, the hunting-gathering lifeway is very nearly as extinct as most of the species that hunting-gathering peoples once depended upon. That lifeway too was based on the knowledge that life grows on death, that an individual continues by the end of another, by the consumption of the seeds or flowers or stems or corpses of other life. Low population pressure, and a sacred attitude toward the food source, made that way of life long sustainable—though it, too, inevitably caused extinctions.

The invention of agriculture and pastoralism broke down much of the sense of the sacred nature of food, and that was when the long war—what one commentator has called "The Five Million Day War"—began in earnest. This shift in lifeway allowed the massive growth of populations and cities and the ongoing destruction of nonhuman species. More than six billion humans now live at the far end of that arc, with far fewer types of cohabiting species along for the ride with us now than at the beginning of the journey.

Cruising down the last-rampart-but-one of the coast ranges, the truck whirred across a valley and past a town with a ragged sign proclaiming itself the Garlic Capital of the World. Papery garlic scale drifted on the wind, and Dundas was tempted to throw the ridiculous eco-tract out the window to join the other windblown debris. Then he thought better of it. No, he might get cited for littering, and that would assuredly harm his "initiate" status with the psiXtians.

As the truck made its way into the last rampart of hills, Dundas thought it best to get through as much of the psiXtian polemic as he could stomach while he still had nothing really valuable to occupy his time.

From the axiom of the hunter-gatherer, "Sacrifice other life, for need, or risk your own through starvation," we have now moved to "Sacrifice other life, for greed, or risk lowering your standard of living." From the production of children realistically for species survival, we have moved to the reproduction of children, most of whom—most of us—are long since excessive in terms of species survival and biological carrying capacity.

Do these people hate kids, or what? Dundas thought. No single author was listed for the book, but he could have bet that the author or authors had no kids of their own—or were femwitch dykes of some sort, more likely. Apparently these hair shirts didn't even much approve of circuses and zoos and gene banks, judging by the passages he found on the next page.

—have reductively argued that, as long as we have the genomic "data" of species, the fact that they are extinct in the wild and even in the flesh is of no real concern. This is emphatically wrong-headed. A species is more than just its genetic code. At the very least it is part of a large webwork of interconnections involving myriad other species and a specific bioregion or biotic context as a whole. Technologically re-created individuals and species are virtual creatures, ghosts. A species from a lost environment is like a word from a lost language: untranslatable and ultimately meaningless. Such a reduced "reality" is a virtuality not worth exchanging for the life that has been made a ghost along the way—

Yep, no way of pleasing these people at all, Dundas thought. At that moment, the "human-required" alarm went off as the truck began to negotiate the last of the hills in earnest. Dundas took the vehicle out of autopilot, thinking as he did so that he might as well take over control for the rest of the drive, down out of the range of hills and on to the coastal plain, from Watsonville to Aptos, ultimately past Capitola and into Santa Cruz. His reading was over for the day.

Pretty country, he thought. Lots of bedroom communities for the Bay Area in-filling here, but still some redwoods and farm fields round about.

In Aptos, he almost missed the psiXtian center—a combined effect of the foggy marine layer that had not yet burned off this close to the ocean, and the fact that the center was so fully integrated into the surrounding landscape. The building was three-quarters buried in the hillside, and the front of the structure, the only part above ground, was thick-walled adobe (probably straw bale underneath) that flowed in curvilinear waves, no right angles at all. Dundas thought the structure was appropriate for recruiting psiXtians: a halfway house for tunneling groundhog-wannabes.

An older woman with flowing grey hair, and a chin-fringe bearded man who looked to be about the same age, greeted him at the reception area. They were happy to receive the book stock and asked after the state of things at Sunderground. Dundas was able to small-talk for a while, but then used the "I'm only an initiate there" excuse to beg off and be on his way. Driving away, he told himself he didn't need to waste time being polite with them. He already knew everything he needed to know about these folks from living with their ilk.

The stores in cloudy Santa Cruz were a bit more interesting, in their perverse way. Aum Depot was a mystical and metaphysical lifestyles store patterned loosely on a Tibetan Buddhist temple. Throat-singing monks Muzaked in the background throughout a space lit indirectly and naturally, in the main, and redolent of incense and the tang of clarified butter burning in lamps.

Wandering through the place, Dundas saw that Aum Depot stocked all manner of neatly labeled mineral and crystal forms, malachite obelisks and obsidian spheres, goethite rainbows and stilbite bowties. He also found himself amid a bewildering array of feathers, beads, carved woods and cut flowers, along with a superabundance of idols and sacred images and paraphernalia.

On the shelves and racks stood gnostic and mystic texts from a Rainbow Abomination of religious faiths, sects, and customizable belief systems. Dundas found the place disorienting rather than soothing in its diversity—thoroughly overwhelming in its Comparative Religiosity.

He waited as a customer burbled on to the owner about how impressed he was with her collection of stone "meditation objects"—"Nothing is quite so futuristic as a streamlined jadeite axe head, you know?" Blah blah blah.

When at last Dundas's turn came with the betrinketed proprietress, he was glad to be rid of Aum's order—half books, half electromedia—and out in the truck once more.

Ohmage Homage was more familiar, at least. Located in the convulsively consumerist Grand MallAmerica downtown, O.H. was a blaring, glaring, overlit, overaudioed, category-cluttered temple to electromediated youth culture, crass commercialism, and trendy income disposability. Its spastic wash of virtuals, holos, audios, and videos—all in seemingly endless forms and varieties—competed for the customer's attention with an indirect, market-Darwinian savagery that would have done any electronic jungle proud.

For Dundas, the effect, rather than being dazzlingly hip and attractive, tended by its sheer overabundance to point up the emptiness and superficiality of what was being offered for sale. One-hit wonder bands, one shot holos, virtuals destined to look dated in ninety days at most. Nothing lasting, all the depth on the surface, just entertainments to fill up the days of the young until they died of their bad habits or settled down, whichever came first.

The jaded, nineteen-year-old nihilist clerk communed with the inventory computer on his eyeglasses and wristwatch, then took a bunch of psiXtian disks from Dundas. Was the psiXtian stuff a "hot seller"? He couldn't see that, at least not in a place like this.

As he was striding back out, along the esplanades of the themeparkish mall, Dundas noted the garish hot-pink holo for the shop cater-corner to Ohmage Homage: a place called Lotions, Potions, Emotions. He shuddered (a bit too deliciously) at what might be going on *there*, though a vivid image of naked copulating lesbian witches, tattooed and jewel-bespangled, flashed into his head—an image he quickly and carefully repressed, thereby also storing it for future use.

Apokatopia Ethnotek, his last delivery, was in some ways the strangest of all. The motif was a cross between a pre-industrial village and some sort of post-nuclear mutant settlement on Mars. It apparently catered to customers who, judging by their argot, attire, and demeanor, could have been from either the far future or the far past, or some place where the future and past become indistinguishable. Certainly they were not from any place in any present that Dundas had ever encountered.

As he walked through the shop, however, Dundas saw that, actually, it was not all that different from Sunderground, in a lot of ways. The merchandise seemed to be a global variety of tribal and neo-tribal handcrafts, gatehead cult icons, low-tech eco groovy household items (with a heavy emphasis on human-scale, single household power-generating devices), and scientific brain toys of an astonishing variety, from false color wheels to plasma spheres to light-and-sound circlets to portable Ganzfeld vortices. He also saw a good deal of "alternative lifeway" media: more light-n-lively groundhoggers, myco-engineering tree-torturers, and bubble-helmeted space migrators. Apokatopia Ethnotek took the rest of his cargo of books and disks.

Dundas, relieved of his Sundergrounded duties at last, headed for the meeting with his contact at Cthulhutessen. The restaurant, or whatever it was, had a street address on the boardwalk, at least according to the map display in the truck. When he got there, however, he learned that it was actually located some distance offshore.

From a hawker on the boardwalk Dundas learned that the boat launch for Cthulhutessen left from the seaward side of the carnival complex on the south end of the boardwalk. Striding quickly through the amusement zone, Dundas thought the place had an archaelogic feel to it—layers and layers of endless renovations and endless dilapidations, fossilized chewing gum accretions on concrete and wood, rickety roller coasters and tacky halls of mirrors and holographic haunted houses, game and fortune-telling machines with gaudy lights.

No Disneyfied order nor sanitized theme-parkology here, he thought. Just the kitschy illogic of dream-kingdom juxtaposition. The kind of place that looked better bathed in neon night than it ever could in daylight, foggy or sunny or in rain. The kind of place where besotted sailors and their babes got into brawls with bikers and their chicks on sunburned Saturday nights in a different century. Passing through and out of the boardwalk amusement area made Dundas feel distantly forlorn, overcome momentarily by a nostalgia *for* a nostalgia for a time that never really was.

Not far beyond the point where a small river flowed into the fog-shrouded bay, a short pier ran out from the beach, ornamented with a sign and arrow: To Cthulhutessen. A red and black motorboat of shallow draft was just pulling up with what looked to be a lunch crowd, people giddy and somehow grateful at their return. As the arriving passengers left the boat, Dundas jogged onto and down the pier.

Paying the ferryman for his crossing, he got into the boat and sat down, joining the dozen other passengers—mostly tourists with kids in tow and business-suited regulars, so far as he could tell. Dressed in his psiXtian work coveralls, he felt distinctly out of place.

So many diversions, he thought, looking back at the city of Santa Cruz as the boat pulled away from the pier. All in a town whose name meant Holy Cross. He wondered how many passengers on this ferry, or how few, ever thought about that.

In a moment the fog closed in, cool and damp, and Santa Cruz disappeared behind them like a dream on waking. The launch churned steadily on through the flat, dull waters of the bay, moving moment by moment more deeply into a world of leaden light and muffled sound. For all the landmarks available to them, the passengers might as well have been a thousand miles out to sea.

Just as the first of the tourists was about to check his watch and wonder how much longer it would be before they arrived, a large, composite shape loomed up ghostly from the fog. As the boat drew closer, Dundas saw that they were approaching a flotilla of what gradually became discernible as four ships—which the launch's passengers managed among them to identify as a large freighter, a factory whaler, a two-masted schooner and a sizable yacht. All were lashed together by ropes and cables and joined by gangways and ramps into a single large floating complex. All the ships had also been given the head of their considerable age and had decayed a goodly ways toward very rusty, crack-painted "derelict" status—a status reassuringly belied by the paint and polish of the gangways, ramps, and launches connecting them, and of everything near the water line (as well as below it, presumably).

Their own launch swung in beside the two smaller ships—the two-masted schooner *Emma* out of Auckland, and the yacht *Alert* out of Dunedin, according to the faded designations on their sterns, just barely readable through the fog. The launch drew up along the starboard side of the *Alert*, beside an external elevator cage, into which the new arrivals crowded. The elevator carried them up to the top of its run, where they were disgorged onto the deck, to find their separate ways about the derelict flotilla.

Dundas glanced about the foggy deck, looking for a bartender or some employee, but none was to be seen. In fact the only structure of size atop the deck was a green monolith almost twice his height, and almost as broad as it was tall, like a giant version of one of the unusually squat, carved malachite obelisks he'd seen at Aum Depot earlier. Approaching the monolith he saw that its fog-damp surface was aswirl with green-black fractal patterns, whorls flowing and quite distinct from the rigid angles into which the mineral's surface had been carved. The patterns made the monolith's surface seem mobile and alive for all its stony solidity. Something about its geometry wasn't right, though— some optical illusion that made its angles and all the angles of the deck seem elusive and wrong.

If "eerily menacing" was the effect the designers had been going for, then they got that right, Dundas thought. As he approached the largely pyramidal monolith more closely, he saw that it was covered with small carvings—perverse and bestial images, along with unreadable hieroglyphs of some sort. Mounted in the squat obelisk's face was a broad carved door, wide at the base and narrower at the top, standing at an angle somewhere between that of an ordinary door and that of a storm-cellar entrance. Surrounded by lintel, threshold, and jambs densely covered with ornately carved tendrils and meanders, much of the surface of the green-black stone door itself was also carved in bas-relief—in the image of a nightmare creature like a cross between a squid and a dragon.

Dundas knocked and pressed and hammered on the door. Eventually it began to tilt inward from the top and slip diagonally away from the bottom, to the accompaniment of the sound of heavy stones grinding across each other. The stone portal's noisy slippage slowly revealed a green-black ramp, angling downward into darkness.

Dundas followed the ramp into the palpable blackness. He was relieved to see ahead of him, at last, a light. It turned out to be a phosphorescently blue-glowing sign that read DONOVAN, GUERRERA & ÅNGSTRÖM'S. Although the name sounded like a law firm and from their attire the men and women gathered there might very well have been lawyers, Dundas was relieved to see that, despite its decor of seaweed and ooze and barnacled rock and shipwreck, it was only a bar. Ambient music that sounded like sea chanteys, jigs and hornpipes being garbled inside a monstrous belly played, just barely obtrusively, in the background. Behind the bar stood two dark, heavily tattooed gentlemen in the garb of merchant mariners from a century past.

"Excuse me," Dundas said to the nearer of the two, who appeared to be African, "would you tell me where I might find Professor Angell?"

"Ronnie, you mean?" asked the ear-beringed bartender without looking up from where he swabbed the bar. "Over at the *Vigilant*. Getting things set up at Cyclopea for tonight."

"Not at Cyclopea," said the other bartender, Middle Eastern by his accent. "At Pickman's Studio."

The nearer bartender shrugged.

"Same diff," he said. "Just head down the back ramp here, then across the linked gangways past the *Emma* to the elevator for the *Vigilant*. That's the big freighter."

"Thanks," Dundas said, taking his leave.

Getting anywhere in the maze of ships proved more difficult than he expected, however. He made his way down corridors so geometrically skewed and full of optical illusions, they would make a sober man think he was drunk. Passing through the bowels of the *Emma*, he encountered glowing clumps of what looked like lunar fungi, heard rats in the walls and slopping, scuttling sounds before and behind him. Through it all he moved among faint but persistent stenches, the hanging olfactory wave fronts of pervasive miasmas, of age and rot and decay.

Moving along the foggy gangways between the *Emma* and the *Vigilant*, he never knew whether the next person he encountered was going to be an ordinary, more or less sane guest like himself, or an employee convincingly acting the part of a crazy woman or madman—of which there were a seemingly inexhaustible supply.

Finding his way around inside the cavernous spaces of the *Vigilant* was even worse. He passed bars and ballrooms and restaurants that featured convincing holos of voodoo rituals, ancient tribes dancing to hideous idols on stone altars, shamans and shamankas calling up devilish spirits out of fire. In one room, viscid color flashed from what looked like a meteorite, and great arcs of real electricity blasted the stone, until odd, curiously animate color flashed into a clouded night sky, out of what looked like the tall stone circle of an old-fashioned well on the other side of the long room.

At last Dundas reached Pickman's Studio, a broad ballroom done up as a combination studio, art gallery, and catacomb. Wood-floored, with a thick, brick-walled depression like a well or kiva off in one corner, it was lit by what appeared to be acetylene gas, which gave an odd cast to the already morbid artwork displayed throughout—nightmare paintings and blasted funerary statues larger, more perverse, more murderous, and much more horrific than life. A sound like the movements of enormous rats issued from the brick-walled depression in the corner, which looked as if it might somehow serve as the entrance to a vast network of subterranean tunnels.

"Excuse me," Dundas called out to the workers who were bolting one last grotesque statue to a plate in the floor, under the careful direction of the dark-haired, black-clad woman overseeing them. "Is there a Professor Angell—um, Ronnie—here?"

The woman with the long dark hair turned in the uncertain light.

"Is it you, Mr. Dundas?" the woman asked in slightly accented British English as she came toward him and he nodded, disoriented. He hadn't expected a female contact. "You came at the right moment. We've just finished up here. Would coffee and a table over at The Terrible Old Man suit you? It's on the deck of the *Emma*."

"Sounds fine," Dundas said, not knowing what to expect in this mad place. Ronnie gave a few final suggestions to the men and women she'd been overseeing, then Dundas followed her out of Pickman's Studio.

As they made their way back through the bowels of the *Vigilant* and on toward the *Emma*, Ronnie spoke casually, like a tour guide, pointing out fungi of Yuggoth, holos depicting the color out of space, the plateau of Leng, the sunken city of R'lyeh, Kadath in the Cold Waste, witches and demons, creatures like Nyarlathotep and the Elder Gods and Yog-Sothoth. She spoke theatrically of the "mad Arab Abdul Alhazred and his *Necronomicon*," and explained, with some relish, how a mass of meat maggots stripping flesh from bones made a noise exactly like the crackling of Rice Krispies in milk, so when they had needed the sound of enormous coffin-worms, they'd just miked and milked some breakfast cereal, then amplified the result.

She seemed quite a part of the madness here, so much so that Dundas wondered if a mistake had been made somewhere up the chain of command. After they'd picked up their coffee and sat down at a table on the fogbound and otherwise deserted foredeck of the *Emma*, however, Ronnie Angell glanced around to make sure no one was in earshot, then turned to him.

"So, Ray," she said, "what do you think of our little Wonderful World of Satan here?"

"That it is," he said, smiling and feeling relieved. "A regular theme park of the Antichrist."

"More than you know," she said, sipping her coffee. "Are you familiar with Lovecraft's work, or the Cthulhu mythos?"

"Only by reputation," he said. A sloppy plashing sound came from somewhere near the bow, distracting him, though he saw nothing. "The only thing I really remember from what we covered in Intelligence all those years ago is that black magic book, the *Necronomicon*. All the other names you threw at me along the way mean less than nothing. You're in pretty deep cover, aren't you, here among the mud souls?"

"Not much deeper than you among the mole-hippies," she said shrugging back her long hair and smiling. "These—"

She was interrupted by a sudden loud flopping like distended firehoses dropping onto the deck from out of the fog. It took a moment before Dundas realized what he was staring at: a pair of long, whitish-pink tentacular arms ending in ovate, grey-pink pads covered with sharp-toothed suckers. The sucker pads began scraping across the deck. Behind those, more tentacle arms came creeping and scraping and scuttling over the bow, followed in quick succession by a beaklike mouth, satellite-dish eyes, and a torpedo-shaped head that seemed to rise up and up and up.

"Good God!" Dundas exclaimed, leaping to his feet. "What on earth is that?"

"Sit down, sit down," Ronnie said, laughing. Five workers with U-topped poles ran out onto the deck. "It's just a Cthulhu. One of the Arkies. *Architeuthis*. Giant squid."

Astonished, Dundas watched as the workers used their poles to keep the flopping and grasping tentacles away from guests or anything else breakable. He moved back to his chair at last, but slowly.

"Is it real?" he asked Ronnie as he began to gradually sit down.

"Certainly," she said, amused. "Looks like you're in luck: it's ol' Tentacle Face himself. He's the biggest of the five, over twenty meters long. The other four are all under twenty."

Dundas stared at her.

"Does this happen often?" he asked.

"About once an hour," she said, smiling. "You really don't know anything about Cthulhutessen, do you? These big fellas are the stars. The feature attraction."

"You mean they're trained?" he asked, watching the squid-control crew in action with their guide-poles. "To attack the patrons?"

"Not the patrons—just these boats," Ronnie explained, placidly swirling the coffee in her cup. "Cthulhutessen is Clyde Kanaka's brain-child. He's a Lovecraft fan, as you might have guessed. He used to be the chief squid man over at the Monterey Bay Aquarium, before he came up with his grand design. His bosses at the aquarium wanted nothing to do with a plan to turn giant cephalopods into animal performers, so he sold the Cthulhutessen idea to investors—mainly Disney, NHK, and Deep Flight Recreational Subs. That paid for a research ship with a deep-flier sub aboard. So he could begin following sperm whales on their feeding rounds. You did know that sperm whales feed on giant squid, right?"

"I've heard that, yes," Dundas said, watching the pole-wielders pushing and shoving the enormous squid back off the bow, back toward the ocean.

"Well, Kanaka tracked the sperm whales until he located some sizable Architeuthis," Ronnie continued. "He drove off the sperm whales with heavy sonar noise and took his deep-flier down among the squid. *Architeuthids* are basically big slow cruisers, so it wasn't that difficult for him to partially paralyze them. Then he installed behavior-mod implants in the brains of the five biggest ones he came across—along with a sonar whale-spooker and a GPS locator, as well. He marched them back here. Essentially he's turned the whole of Monterey Bay into an aquarium for them."

Dundas stared at the last great pair of long tentacles as they finally slid over the bow. Coffee cups in hand, he and Ronnie got up and went to the railing, watching as the squid crew grabbed buckets filled with a variety of stunned seafood and began dumping it over the side, where the giant squid—even more impressive floating at full, two-bus length just off the bow of the *Emma* than it had been slithering awkwardly aboard—waited for its easy-feed reward.

"How are they prevented from swimming back out into the rest of the Pacific?" Dundas asked.

"The locators and the brain implants do that, in conjunction with the computers on board the administrative whaler over there, the *Rachel*," Ronnie said, gesturing. "I don't know all the details, but I gather that the closer one of these tentacle-heads gets to an arc running from just above Santa Cruz across the bay to Monterey, the more their tracking locators set up a 'negative reinforcement' electrical charge in their brain implants. The closer they come to the border line, the more splitting the headaches they get."

Dundas watched the enormous form of the *Architeuthis*, ghostly and pale grey-pink, picking off its stunned prey. A few of its targets woke up and scurried out of range, but the sprawling creature seemed content enough.

"What about the whales that feed on them?" Dundas asked.

"The sonar noisemakers handle them," Ronnie said. "No sperm whale in its right mind would want to get within five hundred meters of any of them. Kanaka takes a lot of heat about 'driving cetaceans out of the Bay' from his former colleagues over at the aquarium, but I think even they can see why he wouldn't want to let his Arkies turn into a whole lot of very expensive calamari."

Dundas watched the big squid finishing off the last of its prey.

"I suppose there are a lot of eco-pagans to keep happy hereabouts?" he speculated,

"Especially in Santa Cruz," Ronnie said with a nod. "They still do their little protests sometimes, despite Kanaka massaging their ideologies as much as possible. He even became a member of the Church of the Grateful Dead, the largest local denomination."

She turned around, leaning against the ship's railing.

"The greenies really don't have all that much to complain about anyway," she went on. "Giant squid don't appear to be in any danger of extinction. The Monterey trench goes more than a thousand meters down, deep enough to match the Arkies' feeding zone. Cthulhutessen has begun a captive breeding program, all the usual public relations."

"What about the fact that they're 'trained'?" Ray asked.

"The greeners can't complain about the training," she said, shaking her head. "Standard Pavlovian stuff. An electrical bell ringing in the squids' big heads five hundred fathoms down, calling them to do their trick and earn their dinner. The animal rightists can't even complain that the critters are particularly overworked. We're open ten A.M. to midnight—fourteen hours. Five squid in the rotation, so each animal performs less than once every three hours. They've got it easy."

"But the scientists at the aquarium across the bay still don't like it?" Dundas wondered, watching the big squid slowly submerging.

"Not at all," Ronnie said, draining off the last of her coffee. "They've got their scientific and ideological reasons, I suppose. They made some noise too because that Light thing spooked the big Arkies, but that's settling down too, now. What I think it really comes down to is that Cthulhutessen cuts into the Monterey Bay Aquarium's market share. It's all entertainment, ultimately, competing for the patrons' spare time and spare change."

She looked at Dundas fixedly for a moment—a very acute gaze.

"The cover story I've been putting out for your trip here today, for instance, is that you're an eccentric psiXtian who is thinking of investing in this place. The psiXtians are ultragreen. Cthulhutessen management would love to have them on board."

"Wouldn't have carried as much clout if you told them I was from the Autonomous Christian States, I suppose?" Dundas asked slyly.

"Might have blown your cover," Ronnie said thoughtfully as they watched the big squid at last jet away and disappear, leaving only a cloud of what looked like ink behind. "I don't think the management would have refused you, though. It's all money, and they'll accept *that* from anybody. The place is already halfway to becoming a slithery, scuttly theme park. I bet even Kanaka would be willing to drop any mention of the *Necronomicon*, the Elder Gods—all the overtly satanic and black magical stuff—for a healthy infusion of ACSA cash. Just as long as no one takes away his devilfish."

Dundas turned his back on the bow and leaned against the railing too.

"Not that the ACSA has much money to invest anywhere

these days,'' he said quietly, thinking of the economic conditions in the mountains and northern plains.

"Nor Cthulhutessen that much need for investors," Ronnie agreed, returning to sit down at their table. "You've come on a weekday in off-hours. During peak rushes we get huge crowds. Have to run sixty launches an hour. Tourists from all over the world—even some from the ACSA. You should see this place at night and on weekends. Those are the heavy times, what with the squid glowing phosphorescently when they attack and disappearing in a cloud of bioluminescent ink when they're done. It's a real show-stopper. Underwater fireworks."

She looked into her empty coffee cup, then turned to Dundas as he sat down, having watched the last of the squid crew leave the deck.

"That's not why you're here, though," she said, reaching into her jacket pocket and producing a small, clear grastic envelope. "Intelligence couldn't risk a drop on this. I think we've discussed Cthulhutessen enough so that if anyone were randomly running surveillance on us, they've long since switched off the recorder. I've already checked and cleared the disk with your instructions inside. Looks like you might get another shot at an old target of yours—Diana Gartner."

Dundas's eyes widened an instant in surprise.

"She's become quite a pilot over the years," Ronnie said, glancing up at him. "Makes runs down the well from the orbital habitats in something called a SHADOW, Stealth High Altitude Delta Observation Wing. For those of us not in the acronym-loving aerospace industry, the disk explains that that means a single stage to orbit, transatmospheric spy plane."

Dundas grunted, his interest piqued.

"What's she doing with a single-stage spy plane?" he asked.

"Nominally, Gartner's doing green overflights," Angell said. "Biomass mapping, that sort of thing. We think she's doing a lot more—and that she's using psiXtian communes as landing, refueling, and smuggling sites. Our people broke a hypercoded communication indicating she's getting ready to make a big northern hemisphere run. We've moved an operative into her flight crew up in the 'borbs. Keep your eyes open at Sunderground. We think she's almost certain to make a stop at the Central Valley commune during her trip. She has close friends there."

She handed Dundas the grastic envelope.

"Thanks," he said, taking it and slipping it into his pocket.

"No—thank *you*, Mr. Dundas," Ronnie said, rising from the table. "Any other information you may need can be found on the disk, which also has some interesting security-key functions— which is the real reason you had to come all this way personally. This will be our last communication for the foreseeable future."

She gave him that same pointed stare again, then finished her thought.

"Take care. These greeners and peaceniks and rainbow satanists aren't as out of touch as they look. This is a longer, deadlier fight than you can guess. If we lose, true Christian identity isn't just defeated—it's extinct. God-fearing white people will be overrun. Race-mixed out of existence. Overwhelmed in cross-breeding the way the hard-working European honeybee was, by its aggressive but less productive southern cousins. Goodbye, and Godspeed."

She left him then. The honeybee reference, he realized immediately, was the final counterword, taken straight from Guaranty's *Myth's Edge and Nation*. After the King James Bible, that was the most important text of the Christian Autonomy movement.

Ronnie Angell was the real thing, all right. Rising from the table, Dundas felt a strong swell of admiration for the woman. She was being humble when she suggested that he was in as deep cover among the psiXtians as she was among these Cthulhu people.

Looking about himself, Dundas shivered involuntarily. This foggy, faux-derelict, demon-haunted "entertainment complex" off the coast of Tree Hugger Land gave him the creeps. Beginning to search for his way out, he was anxious to be on land again, to be on the highway again. Walking toward the launches that would take him away from this crazy flotilla of ghost ships, he was amazed time and again that Ronnie had been able to maintain her sanity here, much less her cover.

FOUR

S UBTERPOST-EMBEDDED FRAGMENT (INFOSPHERE SOURCE UN-
known; original source independently verified as R.E. Stringfield's *Beyond the Sky of Mind: Quantum Cosmology and
Quantum Consciousness*):

*Perhaps our universe contains so much dark matter because
we are living inside a black hole, or rather, a black whole. According to one variant of plenum theory, every universe repro-
duces by budding, and these buds, from the perspective of our
universe, are called black holes. Black holes are essentially
regions of "otherness" contacting our space-time. Those observers inside such a bud would, however, see* our *black hole as*
their *universe, and their universe in its turn would likely be
spawning other universes through black-hole budding.*

*Thus, though all things within a universe may die, the plenum
of universes is immortal in the same way that a single-celled
organism is immortal. The "genes" of a universe are, in this
model, its fundamental constants, the special numbers that lie at
the heart of all physics in that universe. When a mature universe
gives rise to a daughter universe, the fundamental constants undergo slight random changes, like genes mutating between generations of an organism.*

*Evolution may be possible over such a plenum of universes,
but this plenum evolution would have to be extremely slow. The
larger and more complex a system is, the more slowly it reinvents
itself. Thus, technological change proceeds at a faster rate than
social change; social change proceeds at a faster rate than biological change; biological change proceeds at a faster rate than
geological change; and geological change proceeds at a faster
rate than cosmological change.*

*Thus this grandest evolution, this change not only of worlds
but also of universes, would likely proceed very slowly over all
eternity.*

• • •

BRANDI HAD NOT BEEN TO HOME 1 FOR AN EXTENDED VISIT since the ship she'd designed, the *Swallowtail*, was christened and her launch tubes fired up for the trip to the Apollo Amors. She was glad to be coming back now, to a wraparound garden and forest conservatory in space. This world, inside an odd-shaped bubble floating off Earth and Moon, was the only place she really thought of as home.

She hoped she'd eventually develop a similar sort of attachment to her residence with Juan aboard the Freeman Lowell OBU. That sense of connection to and affection for the place hadn't happened there yet, but she hoped that was where her heart was and would continue to be.

Juan had come with her on the trip to HOME 1. Having no particular interest in meeting Immanuel Shaw, he had decided to pay a visit to his orbital park superiors. Brandi, meanwhile, looked for this man Shaw who, she believed, had to have some connection to her through her mother.

Shaw was evidently not as reclusive or privacy freaked as she had presumed. Brandi found his place listed in the directory— an address in the agricultural tori—and noted that he was currently accessible through the Public Sphere locator. Punching up his code, she saw that he was currently to be found in a park not so very far from her present position. She put in a call to him. A man with close-cropped white hair and a carefully trimmed white mostache answered.

"Mr. Shaw? My name is Brandi Easter. I wonder if you might be able to speak with me in person? It's about my mother, Cyndi Easter. I saw that you had the originals of a lot of her work."

Shaw seemed momentarily disoriented by what she'd rattled off so quickly, but then he recovered. On the virtual, Brandi could only see him to about mid-torso. He seemed to be dressed in what looked like rubber coveralls.

"Yes, I have a good deal of her work," Shaw said at last. "I knew your mother. When would you like to get together?"

"As soon as possible."

"How about now? I'm sludging out the kettle of a pond, but if you don't mind talking while I work—"

"I'll be right over," she said. They signed off. As she made her way to the park indicated on the locator, Brandi tried to puzzle out what "sludging the kettle" of a pond might mean.

She had been to that particular area of the habitat before, but it had been many years ago.

She found Shaw in the middle of a drained pond, a lagoon-shaped depression fringed with raked-up mounds of water hyacinth, water lilies, *Acorus*, and bog iris. She saw now that he was dressed in chest-high waders, and he seemed to be doing some sort of maintenance work on the pond.

Walking toward him, she passed what looked like a portable pump with a long hose hookup and coarse filter on one end, not far from where Shaw was shoveling. The man himself stood below the rest of the pond's bottom, knee-deep in a boxlike depression which, she presumed, was what he had meant by a "kettle." He was dumping shovel-loads of what looked like thick mud into a large wheelbarrow. The hose from the other end of the pump emptied into a much larger version of the wheel-barrow, a large open tanker cart, which was filled with similarly thick, smelly organic muck and ooze.

Mud-bespattered, Shaw stood up to take a breather, then saw Brandi and waved. She found something about the man instantly familiar and likable, though she could not have said why.

"Hello, Ms. Easter," he called, stepping up out of the kettle and onto the bottom of the pond. "I knew our paths would cross sooner or later, though I really didn't expect to be doing this when we met."

Brandi laughed.

"That's one duty I'm glad I never pulled while I was living here," she said, watching the wiry older man strip out of his waders into the thigh-length body suit he wore underneath. "What exactly are you doing?"

"Officially, it's 'organic nutrient resource recycling,' " he told her. "The pump gets most of it, but I always end up doing some of this. 'Shoveling shit pudding' is how I think of it. I'm not big on jargon and euphemisms."

Brandi glanced more carefully at the stinking stuff.

"That describes the consistency and the smell, all right," she agreed.

"For the farmers out in the ag tori and the gardeners here in the central sphere it's black gold," Shaw said, coming up to Brandi and shaking her hand. "Contains the dung, debris, and detritus of scores of aquatic and semiaquatic species. I sometimes wish the designers had figured out some sort of automated system to store and pump this stuff directly to everybody who needs it, but they didn't. 'Passive-energy residences require active, energetic residents,' as the alternative-energy folks used to say.''

They sat down on a bench beside the drained pond, watching as two other volunteers with rakes and pitchforks began gathering up a number of the water hyacinth mounds and loading them into a wagon hooked to an electric cart. For local composting, Brandi guessed.

"You said before that you expected our paths to cross . . .'' Brandi said, turning to Shaw.

"Ever since I heard of your existence,'' Shaw said with a nod, staring fixedly at her. "During the publicity surrounding the launch of that space tug or whatever it was that you designed. A big accomplishment for someone so young. You're your mother's daughter, all right. The clothing and hairstyle's different, but everything else—! Uncanny, how much you look like Cyndi.''

Brandi averted her gaze, breaking eye contact.

"You knew her well, then?''

"I was the last person ever *to* know her,'' he said, looking out to where the volunteers were pitchforking up the mounds of water hyacinth, with some continuing difficulty. "And I never heard her speak of your existence. I never heard of you until a couple of months ago, when your ship design became big local news here in the habitat.''

Brandi followed his glance out to the volunteers.

"We might have gotten in touch then,'' she speculated. "I was living in the habitat too.''

"I couldn't be sure you were any relation to Cyndi even then,'' Shaw said, shaking his head. "Not until the last couple weeks, with that stuff in the media about your UFO sighting or whatever it was. The infotainment people confirmed the connection. Over and over again.''

"You say she never mentioned my existence?'' Brandi asked, obscurely pained at the idea. "I have no memory of her myself—''

"When I learned your age,'' Shaw said, waving dismissively, "I realized that she never spoke of you because she couldn't have known about you. You were born seven or eight months after she died. That's why I've avoided getting in touch with you over the last few weeks. The whole thing just didn't make sense.''

"But the Kitchener people always told me she died shortly after I was born," Brandi said.

"Impossible," Shaw said. "I was with her when she died. She had no children and was not pregnant, at least as far as I knew then. Now I'm beginning to wonder. But the Kitchener people must have known the truth when she died. I turned to the Foundation for help immediately upon her death. They sent their people in without a moment's hesitation. They took care of the body, the death certificate, the burial arrangements."

He looked away with a sigh.

"God knows I was glad they did, at the time," he continued. "I was a wreck. Melodramatic as it may sound, your mother was the great love of my love, Brandi. We were engaged to be married."

"You—you were lovers?" Brandi asked. "When she died?"

"Her love for me may have been what killed her," Shaw said quietly, staring out over the drained pond. "That was another reason I've been reluctant to contact you, if it turned out you were Cyndi's daughter. The guilt of that has not been an easy thing to live with."

"What do you mean—her love for you might have killed her?" Brandi asked, distressed and confused. "I was always told she was experimenting with illegal drugs and VR when she died."

"That's only partially true," he said, looking down at his hands folded between his body-suited thighs. "How much do you know about Cyndi Easter's life?"

"Everything that you've made publicly accessible in the infosphere," she said. "Her films, her imprisonment, Project Medusa Blue, all the latent talents—"

Shaw glanced at her, nodding slowly.

"It's my memorial to her work," he said, "but what's in the public domain is not the whole story. First off, her talent wasn't really 'latent.' She knew how to trigger it—and did, for us. For me, really. She died a little, each time she triggered it. Twice. Until she died a lot, the third time."

"I don't understand," Brandi said, crossing and uncrossing her legs nervously. Shaw leaned forward, gripping the bench with his hands.

"Neither did I, really," he said. "For years I tried to make her talent fit into the old scientific framework, the one I knew. It just couldn't be forced into that. Finally I realized that trying to understand the universe through a physical approach alone is like taking a tour through the ruins of a great ancient cathedral with a structural engineer as your only guide. Sure, you learn a lot about the physical fabric of the cathedral, but the cathedral's larger meaning—historical, aesthetic, spiritual—inevitably escapes you. There are some things traditional science just doesn't do very well.''

Brandi stared hard at him, trying to understand.

"And what my mother could do with her talent,'' she said, "that was one of them?''

"Yes,'' Shaw replied, nodding slowly again. "Her talent fell into what I used to think of as 'metaphoric science.' Scientific theories so untestable with current technologies that they were merely metaphoric. Ironic. Unacceptable. Yet only metaphoric science could explain what your mother could do.''

"But what was that, exactly?'' Brandi asked, feeling impatient, as if she were resorting to some sort of coercion to get answers out of the old man. Shaw spoke in a circuitous fashion, to say the least.

"She would take a witch's brew of hallucinogens, or what she called 'entheogens','' he said. "*Psilocybe*, and *Cordyceps* fungi, and a subpolar subspecies of *Amanita muscaria*. Some *Ipomoea* morning glory seeds thrown in for good measure. Then she'd sit down at a virtuality station programmed to channel-switch at greater-than-flashcut speeds—as an information trigger for going 'elsewhere.' Elsewhere was also else*when*, even nonwhen and nonwhere.''

Brandi shook her head and glanced down.

"I don't get it,'' she said. "Sorry.''

"No need to apologize,'' Shaw said. "I didn't get it either, at first. Your mother had to explain it to me. She talked about time as a 'structure of possibility.' She said she could move around in that structure while under the influence of heavy bursts of information and informational substances. Claimed she used her witch's brew and infobursts to bring on a certain type of chaos in her mind—to open it out, beyond its normal boundaries.''

An uneasy shiver passed through Brandi. She tried to hide it by shifting about slightly on the bench.

"What happened to her when she took that stuff?'' Brandi asked, finding the idea more than vaguely repellent. Despite, or maybe because of her own physical thrill-seeking, she had always been obsessed with control. The idea of deliberately push-

ing one's own mind out of control was truly repugnant—
especially when it was her mother who had done so.

"She'd have visions," Shaw explained, gesturing with his
hands. "Swirling depths. Dimensions beyond dimensions. Everything moving and happening much faster than life. Until she got
there, where she could see time lines branching and weaving and
knitting. Maybe she was just seeing what she was looking for,
already present in the chaotic patterns. Maybe she was actually
weaving the threads of probability within that possibility structure, in that 'elsewhere' outside the here and now. Maybe by
weaving them, she was making them 'come true.' She was never
very clear about it. I didn't figure it out myself, until the end."

"But what use could there be for a talent like that?" Brandi
asked, still not seeing the value of such a power.

"It was obvious to me," Shaw said, painfully remembering
"Too obvious." He grimaced as he ticked examples off on his
fingers. "Stock quotes for all the big winners and losers on all
the exchanges—from a week or a month into the future. Advance
information on moves in big transnational 'security' industries.
Prophetic data on the chill-down, the consolidation of state and
corporate intelligence into the single global network of the original ISIS. All well ahead of time, all for people willing to pay
top money for such advance notice."

"And you asked her to do all that?" Brandi asked.

"Yeah," Shaw said, so quietly the word was barely a breath.
"Always doing everything for me. For more money. For fancier
tech toys. Our own expensive little arms race against the big net
security conglomerates."

"How could that cause her death?" Brandi asked, standing up
and wringing her hands nervously, unconsciously.

Shaw looked away again, into the middle distance of memory,
above the drying and cracking bottom of the drained pond.

"Because I couldn't stop," he confessed. "I kept pushing
Cyndi because I was being spurred onward myself by a 'net
friend' who snared us. A guy who called himself Dash Chandler.
Turned out he was working for Tetragrammaton. He knew what
was going on before I did. Cyndi suspected it too, but she kept
undergoing her ordeals for my sake, anyway. I really didn't see
how much each of her journeys to Elsewhere was taking out of
her, until it was far too late. I've only just worked out recently—
after all these years—how Dash used me to kill her."

Brandi turned fully on the old man. Her own voice when it

came sounded too shrill to her. She must be a bit overwrought, she thought, tired from the trip over from Freeman Lowell.

"How?" she asked.

"I managed to do some research," he said with a slow, sad shrug, "until I got some answers and explanations. From Diana Gartner, for one. She was a friend of your mother's, back in the bad old days. Worked with her on *Five Million Day War*. You should meet her while she's here. She helped me understand your mother's talent, through the same metaphoric, ironic science I discredited for so long."

"How?" Brandi asked. "I still don't see it!"

"The way Diana explained it," Shaw said, "Cyndi in her ordeals was somehow moving into the quantum flux. Into dimensions smaller than Planck length, energies higher than Planck energies. Near-death experiencers have supposedly been doing it forever, in an accidental and uncontrolled fashion. The act of dying apparently shifts consciousness away from our consensual reality, into what Diana called 'holographic reality,' the 'implicate order,' the 'frequency domain.' "

"I've heard the terms before," Brandi said, "but I'm not familiar enough with them to really know what they mean."

Shaw grasped her hand and lightly pulled her back down onto the bench beside him.

"Think of it as a deeper reality underlying our world of appearances," he said. "Think of it as made up of waves, like the interference patterns of a hologram which appear chaotic until you shine the right kind of light through them. Out of the 'implicate' our own space and time unfolds, crystallizes, freezes into form. Cyndi went into the implicate. She used the subtle power of her own thought to reorient structures of possibility, shift threads of parallel universes. She wove possibilities and futures out of the stuff of herself. Each time she did it, it was a small death. Until at last it was a big death." Shaw turned his eyes fully on Brandi. "But even that, I know now, wasn't a final death."

The old man stared at her with a bright gleam in his eye, which drew Brandi's attention powerfully.

"You mean like Heaven?" she asked. "The afterlife?"

"Not in the traditional sense," Shaw said. "Once, not so very long after she died, I was exhausted and fell asleep in a self-propagating virtuality I had running in the infosphere. I dreamed I was walking through snow, snow falling light and slow as feathers, as if all the universe were a great bird, molting. I felt like I was walking through fields of white feathers. Before me there appeared this white bird with a golden crown of feathers, wounded in its breast. The white bird was the same digital persona your mother was using when I first met her. The bird rose up and I followed after it, into a world of light.''

Shaw stopped. He cleared his throat, tightening again his grip on the bench as he leaned forward. Brandi waited, sensing that he had more to say.

''When I woke up,'' he continued, ''I wrote it off as just more of my 'grieving process'—like I was supposed to. Horrible term, 'grieving process.' Denies the real, personal pain and uncertainty the grieving person suffers, denies the uniqueness of that pain. Makes it part of a 'process' that supposedly makes your grief just like everyone else's. Which it never is. Anyway, for years that's what I believed that dream was—just me working through my sorrow at losing her. But a white bird with a golden crown had been your mother's data persona, her masque, like I said. So it still bothered me.''

''Why was that?'' Brandi asked quietly.

Shaw looked down at his heavy, callused, limply expressionless hands, now in his lap again.

''I still remembered her last words to me,'' he said. ''She was far gone, and I was trying to unzip her from her virtuality connection suit, the kind we used to wear in those days. She stopped me, told me to leave her connected. Said it was the only way she could 'get free,' that she was 'almost there.' Her final words were, 'Catch my soul.' The words didn't seem to be addressed to me, even though she was dying in my arms. I held her for what seemed like forever, until I called the Kitchener people.''

A deep silence threatened to swallow up his words then. Brandi, however, still needed to learn more. Getting Mr. Shaw to talk wasn't the hard part. Getting him to talk in a straight line was. He seemed a conversational inebriate at times, weaving and falling out of line.

''And something's changed . . . ?'' she prompted. ''To make you think about those words again, I mean?''

''Several weeks back, when that Light thing happened,'' he said, nodding, swerving back in line. ''One of my friends up here, Seiji Yamaguchi, was the brother of the already-dead man who was supposedly responsible for that event. Seiji's brother, Jiro, was found dead a couple years ago now, I guess, hooked into an elaborate computer setup. Still in harness, much the same way Cyndi was.''

''That could be just a coincidence,'' Brandi suggested as gently as she could.

''No,'' Shaw said firmly. ''Not after what I saw when the Light blasted into me. Hit me like a fireball of perfect information. I saw Cyndi's white-bird data construct again, just like in my earlier dream. Only this time it didn't end when we went into the world of light. As we flew, her bird's wings flared into every color of the spectrum, turned the snow to rain and rainbows shining around us, refeathered and reflowered and regreened the world. We seemed to pass from paradise to paradise until, high in the sky, she became a constellation, a gathering of stars and ideas, bright wings spreading just beyond the edge of Here and Now. Her heart was a thing of flames and feathers and flowers and crystals, indistinguishable from the heart of heaven itself.''

He paused. A quaver had crept into his voice. He cleared his throat again.

''I feel now that she had been trying to break through to me for years,'' he went on, ''ever since that dream so long ago. Jiro's Light opened up a doorway somehow. Cyndi was finally able to reach me.''

Immanuel Shaw looked up from his hands, deep into Brandi's eyes.

''I felt I had come home,'' he said, smiling, though that quaver in his voice was growing. ''I knew that Cyndi Easter, your mother and my betrothed, was not dead forever. I don't know how *you* happened yet either, Brandi, but I think you're my daughter.''

Beside a drained recycling lagoon, amid forest and meadow and field wrapped around the inside of an inhabited bubble floating in space, Brandi Easter hugged an old man who still smelled just a whiff like the rich, organic muck he'd been shoveling. She hugged him and hugged him while their faces streamed with the messy tears of unexpected joy at finding a loved one they'd never known existed—and regretted not having searched for before.

Beneath the joy, however, remained the questions yet to be answered by, and still to be asked of, the labyrinthine organizations that had surrounded their lives. Tetragrammaton. The Kitchener Foundation. Who knew what others, in the shadows and on the peripheries? All the powers and dominions which had helped them and harmed them, showed them truths and told them lies, changed the telling of what had been, or tried to prevent what yet might be—all had left them with so much unexplained, like distant parents they had never really been allowed the chance to know.

THE HOME OF THE NORTH LONDON BUSINESSMAN, WALTER OLiver, was the closest and freshest crime scene, as it turned out. When they had determined that Oliver's place was not far from Hampstead Heath, Mei-Ling's driver and Interpol watchdog, Sullivan (whose first name she now learned was Robert), talked her into waiting until they got to Hampstead to have lunch. He was taking her to something called the Crepe Van.

"What do you know about the company our victim was working for—Crystal Memory Dynamics?" Mei-Ling asked Sullivan as they drove along in the snug, three-wheeled blue capsule of his electric car and she made notes to herself.

"About their technology, you mean?" the red-haired young man said, glancing at her.

"You can start there."

"Richard Schwarzbrucke was the owner and guiding genius," Sullivan said. "Herr Doktor Interface. Smooth human/machine connections were his specialty. He was working on an experimental self-assembling crystal memory matrix when he died. Extensive research with animals, if I remember right. Injecting packets of crystal memory components and buckytube circuitry into subjects that had had sections of their brains removed."

"How'd he beat the rejection problem?" Mei-Ling asked, probing.

"A fungal derivative," Robert said, concentrating. "Cordycintane, I think it was called. Anyway, he proved that his crystal memory packages could integrate themselves into the preexisting neuronal matrix, thoroughly and naturally. I think he had them organizing themselves in accord with some neo-Edelman theory of neuronal group selection, but don't quote me on that. I know he got legislative approval to work with coma cases and the severely brain damaged. He was apparently making great progress in restoring them to full function, when his research came to an end."

"You seem to know a good deal about this," Mei-Ling said, intrigued. "Do you recall what ended that research?"

"He died under mysterious circumstances," Sullivan said with a shrug. "Probably drug-related. The investigation that followed Schwarzbrucke's death linked a sizable part of Crystal Memory Dynamics' positive cash-flow to the Oregon Blue Spike trade. He had long-standing connections to a biker's club called the Mongrel Clones. They were involved in the illegal drug trade all the way back to the days of methamphetamine."

"Sounds like an old TV crime drama," Mei-Ling said, smiling.

"I suppose it does," Sullivan agreed as he drove. "But it all actually happened. Schwarzbrucke's bank records showed payouts to high-ranking political officials in Sacramento, California and Washington, D.C. Schwarzbrucke was apparently providing legal and political cover for a number of criminal types in northern California and southern Oregon. Stereochemical analyses comparing the structure of his crystal memory chips to that of the Blue Spike euphoriant revealed some very curious similarities."

"Ouch," Mei-Ling said with a laugh.

"Yes," Sullivan said, nodding. "When news of all this got out, Crystal Memory Dynamics quickly tottered and collapsed into buyout."

"Who bought them out?" Mei-Ling asked, somehow sounding quite sure where all this was going.

"That's why I know so much about this, you see," Sullivan said, smiling. "One of my boss's obsessions. CMD was bought out by one of its major stockholders and board member, a Dr. Ka Vang, of ParaLogics."

"The Tetragrammaton link?" Mei-Ling said.

"Right," Sullivan said with a nod that almost suppressed his surprise. "Landau rides that hobbyhorse as often as he can squeeze in the time for it. I really don't see why he's so focused on that."

"Maybe someday I'll tell you about what happened in Sedona," Mei-Ling said. "It's a bit complicated, but it explains a lot. Do you know why Vasili thinks Tetragrammaton was tight with Schwarzbrucke on the crystal memory stuff?"

Robert hesitated, momentarily distracted from his driving.

"I can't say for sure," he said. "If I were to hazard a guess, I'd say it's because of the kind of head trauma patients Schwarzbrucke was working with. People with severe damage to the Broca's area of the brain, sometimes even to the Wernicke's. CMD claimed the crystal memory implants were to alleviate temporal lobe seizures and amygdaloid dysfunctions. There's some evidence, however, that the crystal memory structures, once they were grown in, were actually supposed to function as a substitute or replacement Broca's area.''

Sullivan hit the brakes as if he'd almost missed a turn, then took a road signed for Hampstead Heath.

"So?" Mei-Ling asked. "Why would a bionic Broca's area be important to Landau's favorite shadow conspiracy?"

"I don't think it was, in itself," Sullivan said, navigating a roundabout. "Broca's area is the center for speech articulation. In conjunction with Wernicke's, it has a lot to do with the nature of human thought and work. Broca's is where thought is pressed into words. It's where commands would most likely be formulated. The CMD records I've seen indicate that, after getting a patient implanted, Schwarzbrucke would have the patient 'start thinking at the machines.' ''

"How'd he do that?" Mei-Ling asked. She was following closely what Sullivan was saying, since a good deal of this was new even to her.

"Through communication hardware links in the patient's head," Sullivan replied. "Radio, IR, laser, microwave, you name it."

"The Tetragrammaton grail," Mei-Ling said, nodding. "Full thought recognition. Electronically mediated simultaneity and action-at-a-distance. The seamless mind/machine interface for their quantum infodensity structure."

"Apparently," Sullivan agreed, "Schwarzbrucke's notes indicate he was after a sort of computer-aided psychokinesis, himself. That's the way Vang's restructured CMD is using a version of the same tech now."

"To cure people who are brain-damaged?" Mei-Ling asked.

"Actually no," Robert said. "They're applying that technology to coma cases and autisms so severe that they are supposedly incurable. In a few cases the subjects still possess brain function levels suited to distributed data control of large, complex organizations that don't want to trust everything to machine intelligences."

He pulled onto Hampstead's High Street, again with that almost-missed-the-turn braking. Maybe that was just the way Robert Sullivan drove, Mei-Ling thought with a shrug. They found a parking space and got out of the electric blue car-capsule. Following Sullivan's lead, she turned to walk down the street, toward a van even tinier than Sullivan's car, parked before the King William IV pub.

From the Breton van-man, Sullivan ordered a wild mushroom and cheese crepe, while Mei-Ling ordered one filled with liqueur-drizzled banana. They sat down at a marble sidewalk table a few doors further down the street.

"When Hampstead had more money and fewer artsy types than it has now," Sullivan said, glancing about at the slightly decayed charm of the High Street, "some of the property moguls tried to ban the van-men, eliminate them from the local streets. Set up committees to see to it. The committees are still here—and so are the van-men. I suppose if you want something to continue indefinitely, create a bureaucracy to eradicate it."

Mei-Ling laughed. Delighting in her crepe, she was glad the committees had never succeeded in their stated aims. When they had finished eating, Robert checked the address on his watch-reminder. From the van-man they learned that they were within walking distance of their destination, so Robert and Mei-Ling set out on foot for the remainder of their journey.

Along the way, in front of a town house, they stopped to look at a splendid garden full of delphinium and lupines and a variety of other strongly vertical, even phallic, flowers. In the center of the small, dense garden stood a statue of a man, nude except for a helmetlike cap on his head, a sword in his right hand, and winged shoes on his feet. In his left hand the figure held by the hair what appeared to be a decapitated head, portraying the grim and grimacing face of a woman. A bright shield lay against his right leg, a large woven bag against the left.

"Perseus and the head of Medusa," Robert said, nodding toward the statue. "An allegory for the scientific method."

Mei-Ling stared at him quizzically. They both leaned on the waist-high fence for a closer look.

"How's that?" she asked.

"Science is that mirror-bright bronze shield there," he said. "Perseus was the son of the tower-imprisoned woman Danaë, sired by Zeus the Sky Father. Athena, the goddess of wisdom and military industry, gave Perseus that shield. Athena herself was born from the head of Zeus, who had swallowed the Titaness Metis, or Thought. Medusa, whose name means Queen or Ruler, was daughter of the incestuous brotherhusband/sisterwife coupling of Phorcys, an Old Man of the Sea, and Ceto, the Whale.

Medusa was granddaughter, on both parents' sides, of Pontus the Sea and Gaia the Earth.''

"Medusa is a nature goddess, then?" Mei-Ling asked, venturing a guess.

"Right, right," Robert replied, nodding enthusiastically. "A creature possessed of the terrible beauty of the natural world, with a face so astonishing and amazing that it turned men to stone if they gazed upon it directly. From certain nymphs, or possibly from Mercury, Perseus obtained a cap of invisibility, winged shoes of swiftness, and that big bag or 'wallet' of secrecy—"

"Okaaay," Mei-Ling said skeptically. "But you still haven't explained how it's an allegory of the scientific method."

"The scientist is Perseus," Robert said, "always looking at only the *reflection* of Nature, not Nature herself, via the mirror-bright shield of science. Only by such indirect means is the scientist—the invisible, swift, and secret observer—able to behead Nature and put her terrible beauty to human use, for personal and political ends."

Mei-Ling applauded slowly, and Robert made a small mock bow.

"Bravo," she said, "though I know some scientists who would very strongly disagree!"

"The scientists with Project Medusa Blue, perhaps?" he asked, cocking an eyebrow archly.

His words twitched her head in a double take. She hadn't been making that connection at all.

"You'd be blue too, if someone cut your head off!" Robert said, quickly turning it into a joke. They laughed together, but their laughter was short-lived as they walked on toward their destination. Both of them were deep in thought. That they should encounter just such a statue on their way to the scene of Walter Oliver's death struck Mei-Ling as entirely too synchronistic. She half-seriously wondered if the presence of that statue had somehow affected Oliver's choice of residence.

A block further on Mei-Ling and Robert came to Oliver's medium-sandstone townhouse. The building's white trim stood badly in need of paint, but otherwise the structure looked sound enough. Oliver had apparently owned all three floors, and the police had cordoned off the entire structure as part of the crime scene. Robert flashed his identification. The officers on duty wished them luck, but suggested they wouldn't find much. The place had been thoroughly gone over—dusted for prints, vacuumed for hair and skin flakes and anything else organically relevant. Its walls had been sonared and all the building's electromagnetic fields measured, everything fully documented, recorded and cataloged.

Robert thanked them and he and Mei-Ling made their way upstairs to the top floor work studio where Oliver had died. Once they had entered the death room, Robert continued to walk about. Mei-Ling, however, found herself drawn to the chair in which the man had been struck down.

Sitting down in it, she was struck by flash-images of Oliver's body flattening, then bursting explosively apart, images so vivid they disturbed her. To distract herself she started donning the deceased man's connection gear. She was just about to turn the system on when a flood of light smashed into her head.

Remembering things never done, in a place never seen. Slowly and awkwardly at first, eventually with greater and greater ease, learning to make machine systems respond to thought. To think a thought, to formulate it into words and commands in the head, was to make it happen elsewhere, no matter how far away elsewhere might be. Working through strange tests and projects. Fascinated. Wondering sometimes which is the peripheral—the distant device thought at, or the thinker—

Coherent movement in water. Just flashes of light at first but, looking closer, seeing speckled green-silver sleekness nosing against the current—trout? Looking closer still, seeing them growing larger, much larger than trout, becoming porpoiseful, shimmering merfolk, beckoning. So beautiful, so very beautiful. Cannot stop. Diving in after them. Down and down, following them, hundred-year flood of the stream of consciousness, river becoming sea. Disappearing into a hole in the bottom of the sea, following them even there, down to a sea which should be sunless yet stands somehow filled with its own clear light.

Ahead a mandalic city on a plain, maze of what could be streets in strange-towered, electrically bright-shining Atlantis. Following flashing guides down labyrinthine windings into a broad open space or square, guides changing, becoming on all sides innumerable shimmering multifaceted "bodies," morphing and shifting kaleidoscopically, aloof yet radiant, angels sprung full-blown from the brow of a distant crystalline God—

With an effort turning away, struggling to break out of the all too lucid dream. Now the angels shifting to demons, transformed from cool blue-white crystalline distance to steamy fleshly prox-

*imity, bikers and biker chicks straight from a red-black hell, ban-
dannas above and below their eyes, dressed in the leathers of
the Mongrel Clones, giving pleasure with one hand and pain
with the other, moving in, surrounding, arms raised feebly without a chance of fending the demons off—*

She found herself on the floor of Oliver's workspace, Robert
Sullivan staring down at her, looking very concerned, his left
arm under her shoulders.

"Are you all right?" he asked worriedly. "You must have
passed out. You fell out of the chair and went into spasm. Your
eyes were remming like mad—"

"I'm okay," Mei-Ling said weakly, coming to a sitting position. "Just forgot I should only look at the *reflection* in the
shield."

The joke was almost as weak as she was. Yes, she was all
right, but this had never happened before—not this way—and
that in itself was worrisome.

ALECK HAD NARROWLY MANAGED TO EVICT SAM AND COM-
pany from his lab before security came on dayshift duty.
Sam and Janika and Marco and Hari had been wildly enthused
about how things had "jelled" overnight and were already talking about a "concept project." The band had adjourned to Sam
and Aleck's apartment with such speed that, by the time Aleck
got home, they had whipped up an infosphere hype-sheet, a virtual poster full of twisting subliminal suggestions of biomechan-
ical monsters in the background and which, in the foreground,
read,

> Hugh Manatee
> in
> Tiffany Chains'
> *Soft Slavery*

They had proudly shown it to Aleck when he came in. He had
nodded and smiled, but he couldn't make much sense of it. From
the title he thought it could be a description of anything—from
a bondage-and-discipline pornholo to a cultural-materialist critique of transnational corporate feudalism, or perhaps a combination of the two.

In almost no time it became clear to him that Sam and his

friends were all too hyped to sleep. Aleck realized for a certainty that they were going to be here most of the day. Already they seemed to have ruled out physically attending their classes for the day, opting for telepresent attendance via interactive at best, or simply complete absence, both physical and virtual. They were brainstorming, speculating about their future direction.

"Personal integrity is more important than public success," Sam declared. "Too many creative people are slaves to their talent."

"What do you mean?" Janika asked, peeved. Just from the snatches of conversation he'd heard since coming in, Aleck thought it was fairly clear that Janika found the idea of "public success" a lot less troubling than Sam did.

"Their desire to perform for an audience is so over-whelming," Sam replied, "that they end up selling themselves cheap, for only money, so they can get their 'stuff' into the market. That's what."

"Right," Hari agreed. "Just look at all the artists in all sorts of fields who get fat and lazy as soon as they make it big—then never again produce work as good as when they were young and struggling. They become the victims of their own success."

"In the end, pandering to the market has a crippling effect on their personal integrity," Sam said sagaciously, "and their work inevitably suffers too. To keep a cutting edge, an artistic life—like a knife—has to be dragged across the hard sharpening-stone of *rough street reality* from time to time."

"Noise!" Marco said, laughing. "I've been on the street, and you can have it, man. You can starve to death in an attic if you want. Me, I'd rather be sipping a single malt Scotch by my swimming pool."

This sort of speculation could go on forever, Aleck realized. It probably already had. No way was he going to be able to sleep at home today.

The previous night's events had left him too wired to sleep, anyway. What he needed was what his grandfather—when the old man had refused to do his scheduled media or take his scheduled medication—used to call "a vacation from carbonation." Walking out to the street and looking for a podcar, Aleck thought he understood what his grandfather had meant.

People and electronics had been rubbing him the wrong way now for weeks on end, until Aleck felt staticky as a long-haired cat in a room full of Van de Graaff generators. On the absolute spur of the moment, he decided to visit a place he hadn't seen in more than a dozen years.

Finding a satellite-tracked Public Option Driver vehicle, he thumb-printed the podcar open, climbed inside, then voice-printed and retscanned it into operation. After programming the car to head south of the Lunken light-industry park and then east toward the Mount Washington area, Aleck settled back into the seat and watched the world of his hometown slide by.

The car came down from Clifton Hill and headed east, whir-ring past the long lines of riverview condos, apartments, and offices that lined the Cincinnati side of the river from downtown all the way to the confluence of the Little Miami and the Ohio. Aleck, however, was too preoccupied to pay the scenery that much attention. He was still spinning with thoughts about the previous night, in no particular order.

In response to Hari's physics theorizing, he wondered now why it should be that matter-energy was supposed to come first, and consciousness was supposed to arise out of that. Why couldn't consciousness come first, then matter and energy pre-cipitate out of it, instead? Why was it that matter and energy were supposed to shape space and time? Why didn't space and time shape matter and energy?

At the very least, he thought, there should be some kind of synergistic process whereby consciousness, space-time, and matter-energy all interacted strongly with each other, even if phrasing it this way did make it sound as if space-time and con-sciousness were somehow two types of the same thing. . . .

But what do *I* know? Aleck asked himself. I'm not a physics major. Hari would probably think these questions sophomoric, or trivial.

The car crossed the roadbridge over the Little Miami and purred into the overgrown green tunnel of Salem Road. Road names from his childhood floated through his head. Sutton. Sa-lem. Kellogg. Of course those names would have meant nothing to the indigenous people that once lived hereabouts. If you don't have roads, you don't need words for them. Or maybe, if you don't have words for them, you don't need roads.

As the car turned onto Wayside Avenue, he thought maybe words themselves were roads into the interior, the unknown. He thought of roads cutting inward to anatomize the wild land, words to dissect the wild mind.

To use a language is to walk the streets the dead have made.

Thinking that, he shuddered a little as the car made its way along Wayside's dogleg shape. It was too close to what the ACSA Autochristians claimed about language and culture: that separate languages are vectors for social disharmony and cannot be tolerated in the unified state. What if they were right? The stable security of sameness rather than the dizzy freedom of difference. How much should people be willing to sacrifice for the "unified state"?

The car was coming up on where he wanted to stop.

"Pull to the side of the road here," Aleck commanded the car. When the vehicle had stopped, he got out. Hearing the electric vehicle locking and securing itself, he walked across the road, onto a private drive that angled downhill.

He couldn't really blame the citizens of the ACSA that much. Sacrificing freedom for security was at least as old as the shift from the greater vagaries of hunting and gathering to the supposedly lesser ones of farming and herding. The shift had only continued with the supposedly still slighter uncertainties of industrial and then information societies.

Maybe "progess" was nothing else but this ongoing abstraction, he thought. This movement further and further away from the deep bitter-tinged softness of living as a mere creature in a created world. Maybe the march of technology was all a continuing alienation and estrangement from seasonal rhythms, from the bright-dark beating of the heart of the earth and the sky.

Aleck hopped a low fence just out of range of the first of the security cameras and trespassed into a place where his memories dwelled, green thoughts in their green shade. This stretch of woods not far from his childhood home on Wayside was the only significant greenspace left in the area and the only thoroughly good use he had ever encountered for hereditary wealth, privilege, and "private property"—namely, the inherited land of the Rohdes or Grotes or whatever the name of the family was that had kept these woods intact and in their family all these years.

He made his way through a forest of beech and maple to a nameless small stream that, he knew from past experience, eventually led down to the Little Miami River. As a boy he and his friends had called the off-limits woods "Monster"—in much the same way that Gilgamesh and Enkidu had called their forest/spirit "Humbaba," in a book he had read years later, as an undergraduate.

He wondered how much had been gained and how much lost in the destruction of those ancient spirit-haunted forests. Those places were all pretty much gone everywhere, now. Progress proceeds via catastrophe, Aleck thought. Catastrophe proceeds via progress.

Looking around as he walked the woods, it occurred to him that, with the eclipse of nature, increasingly there was no reality but culture. That was sad. He knew he needed to get out of his own head once in a while. He suspected that the same could be said for humanity as a whole—that people needed to get out of the world they had built. It was important and necessarily humbling to be reminded that not everything was of human making, nor should it be. In wildness lay not only the preservation of the world, as Thoreau had put it, but also the preservation of the *soul*.

In this small patch of wildness where he walked now, he had also walked as a boy, in every season of the year. This forest had taught him things without words, purely by the example of itself. Many years had passed since he'd last been here. Everything seemed smaller and more fragile—not because it had changed, but because he had, growing bigger and more powerful.

He paused to look about him. Even now, time and this place still had their way of defamiliarizing the known and refamiliarizing the unknown. The larger the island continent of knowledge, he thought, the longer the shoreline of mystery rising out of the waves. He felt a quiet joy in that realization as he hurried on.

Soon he came to a broad deep spot where two stream branches flowed together into one, a place full of the frogs and turtles and snakes and salamanders of his memories. As a nine-year-old he'd called it the Pool of Life. That was how it had seemed to him at that age: a node of creation, a *locus amoenus* where life flowed out of formlessness into form. He hadn't known ''nodes'' and Latin terms at that age, so with the directness of a child's soul he had given it that grandiloquent name in straightforward English.

The place looked smaller, but somehow it still merited that childhood name. He crouched down beside the pool, staring into it at tadpoles and minnows and crayfish darting through the reflection of his face, swimming through the sunburst anemone of his thatch of blond hair. Deeper underwater, a bird flew over his head. Beneath it all, fossil trilobites stood motionless in the stone of the pool's bottom, far beyond the daylit sky. All these creatures and more were in *him*, he realized—in his life, at least as much as they were in his reflection. Something hypnotic in the scene kept him staring at it minute after minute.

When he finally stood up again, he felt more relaxed than he had in weeks. He walked on, more slowly, along the woodland stream, fording its waters on downed logs and impromptu stepping-stones. He came to a waterfall that had been the Niagara of his youth, and was a bit disappointed to see that it was little more than a freshet tumbling over a ledge of shale into a clay-bottomed pool not more than ten feet below. It still proved a challenge to get around, though. He had to do some hillside scrambling before he was safely onto the lower bed of the stream.

All was as he remembered it, at the very least, and more than once what he saw and heard around him called up details he had long forgotten. He came to the spot where another tributary flowed into the main stream. Instead of following the main flow the last kilometer or so to the Little Miami River, he decided to walk up the tributary. He hoped that something he remembered—a cave hole some kids had dug high in a sandy cliff—would still be there even after all this time.

After a few turns up the tributary, he saw it. The hole was still there, and larger than he remembered, if anything. Perhaps succeeding generations of children had excavated it more fully. He made his way up the crumbly sandstone and climbed into the mouth of the hole. It only went back five or six feet, and was not quite tall enough for him to stand up in, so he sat down at the entrance, where its edge jutted out of the cliff like a small porch.

Dangling his feet over the edge, he looked off to the northwest. His eyes scanned over the few remaining sod and popcorn fields of the floodplain, over the tree line along the river, to the robotic industrial park that had once been Lunken Airport.

Looking over that vista, Aleck had an odd sensation that he had become dislocated in time. He had reverted to a much earlier type of human, a far-back someone who suddenly, while seated at the entrance of his cave, had peered unexpectedly through time into a faraway future he could not hope to comprehend. Only gradually did the sensation subside. Either Aleck was ceasing to be that caveman, or that caveman was becoming accustomed to the future.

Gazing up at the sky, Aleck thought of his parents. Strange that they at their age should have left their hometown, retiring to one of the orbital habitats, while he had stayed. He thought of his uncle, his father's brother, who called himself Aleister McBruce but whose real name was Bruce McAleister. Uncle Bruce had lived up there in the first haborb for years.

Living in space had never much appealed to Aleck. He tended to agree with Sam that the 'borbs were energy colonies, that they were for solar what the Navajo reservations had been for uranium during the last century. Like the Navajo rez too, the orbital complexes had continued to exist only upon the tender sufferance of governments and corporations.

The fact that earthly powers had nearly gone to war and almost invaded the orbital habitat, not even months back, was proof enough for Aleck of the tenuousness of life in the 'borbs. Yet his parents and Uncle Bruce loved their lives there. That was clearer with every communication he got from them. They were always trying to get him to come visit, even offering, in his parents' most recent invite, to pay his fare to the world up there.

He lay back in the mouth of the cave, thinking about life on Earth versus life in an orbital habitat. Living up there would probably be as detached from nature as one could get—therefore the pinnacle of "progress." He tried to figure out which world would seem everted and which inverted, but that was too tangled for him to contemplate at the moment. The day was warming outside. The wind rustled leaves in the trees and the birds called and the insects hummed, but here in the cave's mouth it was cool and quiet. He grew drowsy, his thoughts becoming slippery, like electric eels in a sultry river, like lightning from a muggy sky.

Maybe his love of nature was ridiculous, a romantic nostalgia with no place in the modern world, for no place that had ever really existed. Naive, unsophisticated. Maudlin. Sentimental. A place of gardens and children and waterfalls and birdsong. A utopian This Was The Tomorrow That Was. Bigger, better, faster, more. Smaller, worse, slower, less. The Ancient Future.

I am coming from where I have yet to go, rising out of it, returning to it, never leaving it.

Aleck came suddenly awake, sitting up so abruptly that he almost fell out of the cave entrance and down the sand cliff. A voice had spoken quite distinctly in his head. "I am coming from where I have yet to go." What did *that* mean? And where did the voice come from? It wasn't his own, he was sure of that.

Then where? For all his musing on Humbaba and such, he didn't really believe in a spirit of the Earth. Or did he?

He thought of his parents in the 'borbs. Inverted and everted worlds. Coming from where he hadn't yet gone. Maybe he should take them up on their offer of a visit, after all.

"DELICACIES OF DEUTSCHLAND" WAS THE SPECIAL OF THE day at Planeteria Prime, so the place was all holoed out in an excess of Bavarian *gemütlichkeit*. Dark wood and steins and stags' heads on the walls, lederhosened servers, oompahpah music, a hyperreal Oktoberfest atmosphere.

Roger chose a mushroom and tofu-based Holsteiner Schnitzel, while Marissa picked a similarly faux Rouladen, complemented by two steins of a local HOME version of bock beer. With their trays in hand they walked through a holographic wall out onto a plaza and took a seat at a mooncrete-topped table.

Sipping his beer, Roger thought the inside-out world of the haborbs had in some ways become new again for him after his recent sojourn on Earth. Looking about, the view through the central sphere of the orbital habitat reminded him less of a county blown all around the inside of a great bubble than of a small city distributed about the pleasant environs of a U-shaped mountain valley—only here the valley reached around U, all the way to O.

Over lunch Roger bemoaned to his redheaded lunch date the fact that the Light, for all it had accomplished, had not thoroughly remade the world, much as they might have hoped it would.

"The response to the Light among people I've met," he told Marissa as he cut into his schnitzel, "even of that minority who remember it at all, makes me think of a statement I once read. A twentieth-century scientist said it, about the way his fellow physicists responded to the philosophical implications of some of the more bizarre findings of quantum physics."

"What did he say?" Marissa asked, between savoring bites of the faux Rouladen.

"Only a small minority were troubled by the implications," Roger said, sipping at his beer in its big awkward stein. "More of his colleagues had elaborate reasons for why they were not troubled, but their explanations tended to entirely miss the point. The remainder had no thought-out explanations, but absolutely refused to say why the philosophical implications didn't bother them. It's just our luck that we should be among the small minority who are troubled by the implications of the Light.''

"Everything changes," Marissa said with a nod, flicking her long red-gold hair back from her shoulders, "but then no changes are permanent.''

"Right," Roger said, nodding enthusiastically. "It looked like everything was changing for good, and for *the* good. I guess we should have known better. Just look at the history of the last century's wars. Russia and the U.S., Japan and Germany—winners lose, losers win.''

Marissa nodded, glancing up from her plate.

"I know that, but in the first days after the flash I felt a genuine euphoria, I must admit," she said, then began ticking off items on her fingers. "The citizens' movements. The collapse of morally bankrupt governments. The boycotts of corporations. The consumer and stockholder revolts. The nascent bioregional and decentralization movements. Increased interest in alternate lifeways. The focus on long-term species preservation planning. The new work on diverse governmental styles. All of those flared up all at once. Now they've begun to die back down again. The Light was like some sort of brain wave sweeping through, a flash of enlightenment, but the changes it brought on don't seem to have been lasting.''

"No, not for everyone," Roger agreed, working away with knife and fork at his schnitzel, "or at least not yet. I'm still troubled myself, though my troubles are of a happier kind than they were, before the Light. Maybe that's all we can hope, for now at least.''

"That's just the problem," Marissa said, with a barely audible sigh that turned into a sip at her stein. "That initial euphoria fooled me. During those first unbelievable days I began to inform some of my colleagues about the immortalizing vector I was working on before the Light happened.''

Roger nodded, remembering that research. Marissa had done preliminary experiments on a plan to take traits from the so-called immortalized cancer cells of teratocarcinomas, and then turn them against aging. Using engineered viral vectors to transfer the immortalizing trait from teratoma sources into the human genome had been her very novel approach—but also a potentially dangerous one, given the inherent cancer factors in the materials with which she had been working.

"At the time, you told me you didn't think I could overcome aging and death quite that easily," Marissa reminded him. "In some ways, I hoped you were right—that my theoretical work was compelling, but wrong. The colleagues I told about that work have been doing their own investigations, though. We've been running tests, here and in a psiXtian ecolab in California. Preliminary reports strongly suggest my immortalizing vector, or some minimally modified version of it, actually works."

"Uh-oh," Roger said, quite soberly, remembering the moment when he had returned to Marissa the vial of the vector he'd stolen from her—with rather apocalyptic intent. After Marissa and Paul Larkin retrieved him from where he'd lain, floating comatose in space, he had been quite purged of such intent and was more than happy to return the vial to its rightful owner.

"That's right," Marissa said with a nod. "The vector appears to be both effective and humane, in a narrow sense, so far. We may be standing on the brink of a radical extension of human longevity. Only we're not the universally enlightened people I thought we were in those first days after the blast of that Light."

Roger nodded, staring into his beer.

"A necessary, co-extensive decrease in birth rate," he said slowly, "or in the rate of survival to sexual maturity, does not seem to be forthcoming. The genie is straining at the cork of the bottle."

"Exactly," Marissa agreed. "Despite our best intentions we may be about to unleash the Immortality Plague upon the world. Life without the balance of death. You know how that'll make the population problem spiral up."

"Yes—to full-blown catastrophe," Roger said.

Such thoughts had occurred to him before. Finishing the last of the schnitzel and tucking into the red cabbage on the side, which grew steadily more tasteless in his mouth, he desperately wanted to deny the possible reality of this scenario, now.

"But how can you be so sure?" he asked. "Your vector might prove to have massive side effects, might even be fatal. Its existence might never be made known."

"True—all true," Marissa agreed. "I wish I could believe in those other outcomes. But that's all they are—possible outcomes. I have inklings of my own, and they're more certain than just possibilities and probabilities."

"Oh?" Roger asked, looking curiously at her.

"I don't know how to explain it," Marissa confided, "except to say that, since the Light, I have memories of what has yet to happen. Somewhat like a precognitive dream, only I usually have them while I'm awake.''

''You're kidding!'' Roger said with a laugh.

''What's so funny about that?'' Marissa asked, a bit annoyed.

''Oh, nothing,'' Roger said. ''It's just that my experience with the *Cordyceps* fungus and the Light left me with an unwanted ability too. I can 'know' an object's full history just by touching it or concentrating on it carefully. It's a form of psychometry. I would never have believed it possible, if I hadn't experienced it myself.''

''What?'' Marissa asked, astonished.

''I'm serious,'' Roger said, laughing again, amazed by the almost absurd synchronicity of it. ''It's a relief to finally be able to talk to someone about it comfortably. Without being thought a nut case. You see, I remember pasts everyone has forgotten— and you remember futures no one has experienced yet!''

''Your, um, talent,'' Marissa asked, trying to make sense of this revelation. ''Is it getting stronger or weaker with time?''

Roger pondered that one a while, finishing nearly all of his red cabbage as he did.

''Weaker, I think,'' he said at last. ''Or at least easier to control. The pressure of time from the talent is no longer as overpowering as it was when the fungus first opened me up to that unfading history of things. I can restrict its occurrence better, now. I have to carefully focus on something to call the talent into play. How about you?''

''Just the opposite,'' Marissa said. ''My flash-forwards are becoming more and more unpredictable—and stronger.'' She took up another morsel of her disappearing rouladen, then turned to him. ''When your talent acts up, what's it like?''

''Objects cease to be inanimate,'' Roger said. ''When I experiment with the talent now, I can sense the interconnectedness of everything, but without the fear and the grief, the pain and the meaninglessness, of the 'actualized history' I experienced in my first *Cordyceps* encounter. Yours?''

''The impressions started out vague and detached,'' Marissa replied, ''but now they're becoming clearer, more detailed, more involving.''

Roger took a healthy swig of his beer, then nodded thoughtfully.

''Since I began to get a rein on this talent,'' he said, ''every object seems to be filled with its own kind of consciousness—

and more. Something like a deep memory connected to the thoughts of every person who has ever come in contact with it. A welter of connections to the 'presence' of every animal or object that has come into contact with it as well.''

Marissa pondered that, finishing her rouladen.

"Your talent's just connected with individual objects, then?'' she asked.

"Ultimately, no,'' he said. "I've thought about it a lot. I've done some research too, trying to explain it to myself.''

"And?'' Marissa asked.

"It seems that,'' he began, "when this psychometric ability is in play, it's not only that I seem to be able to read the 'traces' of the past of an object. I seem also to be able to tap into some deeper, holographic level of reality itself, where the history of everything resides in some sort of enfolded form.''

"Yes!'' Marissa said, pleased. "I've experienced something very much like that too—only in the opposite direction. Like I'm picking up on realities, possible futures, that are already inherent in that deeper level. Real, but latent. They have not yet undergone the formality of actually occurring, of unfolding into the present.''

Roger mopped up the remainder of the sauces on his plate with half a dinner roll.

"I don't really know what to make of this new ability yet,'' he confided to Marissa quietly. "So far it's mainly been a nuisance.''

"Bingo,'' she said with a laugh, between bites of cabbage.

"I was glad to return to the orbital habitat, I'll tell you,'' Roger continued. "Earth just has too much past. I had to keep this new talent thoroughly locked down while I was there. I was afraid I'd be inundated with the history of peoples and species and a planet itself that stretched far away into the past.''

"The shorter history of the space habitat is more manageable?'' Marissa asked, toying with the red cabbage.

Roger nodded.

"Even when I open up to the levels of information the talent makes accessible,'' he said, "it's not nearly so overwhelming. I tell you, I was secretly glad Larkin and I didn't make it to the top of that tepui, what with all the history that was supposed to have happened there.''

Marissa pushed her plate away from her slightly, her meal finished.

"But why us?" she asked. "I mean, aside from the fact that we're obviously made for each other—"

"Or just the opposite," Roger said in response to her sly, teasing tone. "Me with my back up against the future and my mind's eye flooded with the past, you with your back to the past and your mind's eye full of the future—"

"That's one of the things I love about you, Roger," she said, interrupting him as she lightly placed her hand on his. "You're always such a poet when you think you're being so rational and scientific. Romantic, when you're trying to be 'just the opposite.'"

"Well," Roger said awkwardly, afraid he might actually blush from the look she was giving him. "My guess is that we're not the only such talents, by any means. My talent, and yours, and others, might be rudimentary forms of what the Larkins and the tepuians refer to as 'mind-time' and travel on the 'time lines'."

"How's that?" Marissa asked.

"The Larkins claim that their *Cordyceps* mushroom functions like a transducer," Roger explained. "The way those X-satellites that the Light blasted out from did, too. Only as *organic* transducers, in the case of the fungus."

Marissa frowned.

"I just can't believe the transcendence of Jiro Yamaguchi hasn't amounted to more than this," she said. "Even if we're not the only ones, our latent talents and his e-space escape can't be the whole story. All this stuff has to be having a bigger effect than we're seeing."

"Dead iron stars go supernova," Roger said, nodding, glancing down at the table.

"Pardon?" Marissa asked, not understanding at all.

"In the life cycle of stars, a point comes when the star can no longer continue fusing elements to keep burning," Roger explained, taking out his Personal Data Assistant notepad, placing the PDA unit on the grey mooncrete table, then calling up diagrams to show her on the unit. "The curve of binding energy goes from the fusing of 'light' hydrogen to heavier helium to still heavier lithium, eventually all the way down toward iron in the most massive stars. No matter how big the star, though, it can't fuse iron atoms together. No more energy from excess mass. The fusion furnace shuts down, the star crushes itself in its own mass, the iron core collapses, the outer layer blows off as a supernova. Dead iron stars go supernova."

He glanced up to see if Marissa was beginning to follow his argument. Seeing that she was, he continued.

"Socially and politically," Roger said, "I think of it as a metaphor for what happens to outmoded systems—governments, corporations—that are large and powerful and long-lived, but which have finally exhausted all their options."

"Okay," Marissa said, nodding. "I see what you're getting at. There are a lot of dead iron stars in the human constellation."

"Right," Roger said. "Some of us, like you and me, were hoping the Light would be the particle that broke the iron star's back, as it were."

Marissa stared thoughtfully at his diagram depicting the curve of binding energy.

"If we're talking about metaphors," she said, "then I have a different way of describing it. I came across it in an infosphere salon discussion. I think of it in terms of the 'mouse-shaped' meme wave pattern. Are you familiar with that diagram?"

Roger admitted he wasn't. Marissa took out her notepad computer and called up an image on that, which she then shot to Roger's unit. On the screen of the unit, in faux 3-D, floated a graph vaguely shaped like the silhouette of a mouse, tail toward the x,y intersection, head away.

"I've seen it applied to situations ranging from species distributions and extinctions," Marissa said, "to the history of the monasteries in England. One of the salon discussants was big on applying it to those. The mouse that roars: a key image of data behavior, a description for the way memes and genes distribute themselves."

"But what exactly does it mean?" Roger asked, finishing his beer.

"Initially it resembles the classic sigmoidal or S-shaped curve," Marissa explained. "This section sloping up from the lag-phase 'tail' of the mouse is the foundational period where the idea or sect or species is 'pure' because it has just differentiated itself from its surroundings. The arched-back part of the mouse is the expansionist log phase of a meme. Or the niche exploitation phase by that particular cluster of genes that goes into making up a particular species, say. The period of greatest success and vigor. Up here is where it begins to deviate from the classic sigmoidal, here at the brief plateau, then the long down-sloping part, from the mouse's back toward its head. That's the period of decline."

"And this is pretty much the same in a wide range of systems?" Roger asked.

"From ideas to species to empires to stars," Marissa confirmed. "The success of a paradigm paradoxically renders that paradigm increasingly useless. The discussant who was big on monastic history said that the monasteries began in reforms of earlier traditions, but gradually they themselves also became increasingly worldly, corrupt. Your stars keep moving down the curve of binding energy, fusing heavier and heavier elements. The solution exacerbates the problem. This final spike here, the 'ear' of the mouse, is the false quickening, the supernova, secondary decadence, reaction."

"Fascinating," Roger said, staring at the diagram. "What finally kills the 'mouse'?"

"A number of things," Marissa said, leaning back in her chair. "If there isn't enough competition in the expansionist phase, the wave can go into overshoot and decline or crash more steeply. The woman I met in virtual chat—May or Lee, or some name like that—she said to think of the meme or species as being like a soliton. DNA is a chemical soliton, a double-helical whirlwind that passes over a junkyard and builds a starship. A whirlwind is an atmospheric soliton, a structure built by things falling apart together. The weather is full of them. Even the heart, like the weather, is a maze for structuring turbulence—"

"Your mouse does look rather like a cardiogram of sorts," Roger commented.

"Right," Marissa said. "What kills the meme, or the star, or the species, or the heart, for that matter, is that it eventually stops structuring turbulence. It loses coherence and disappears back into the overall flow. In all systems, it's comprehensiveness versus coherence—or completeness versus consistency, if you prefer. Antithetical vectors. This mouse shape is a description of the ultimate irreconcilability of comprehensiveness and coherence, at least among all human and natural systems we've ever encountered."

Roger leaned forward in his chair.

"How does all this tie into Jiro Yamaguchi's apotheosis and the Light, though?" Roger wanted to know.

"I'm not sure," Marissa admitted, calling up a list on her notecomp, "but, in my flash-forwards, mazes and waves are figuring more and more prominently. I've been searching the infosphere for their recurrences. The Greek key and maze symbols have radically increased in number since the Light happened. I'm not the only one who's noticed it. The infosphere salons on those topics have been growing steadily in popularity since the Light.''

''Maybe so,'' Roger said with a shrug, ''but why are they important?''

''Again, I'm not certain,'' Marissa said, flashing images up in faux 3-D from her PDA. ''In their own way, the keys and mazes resemble two-dimensional, flattened-spiral representations of DNA. Or attempts to represent curled-up higher dimensional space in lower dimensions. Or circuitry. Or intestines. Or waves of peristalsis moving through the maze of the digestive tract—''

''Please, Ris,'' Roger joked. ''I've just finished eating.''

''Okay—hologram interference patterns,'' Marissa continued, undeterred by his attempted witticism. ''Peano curves. Golden means. Fibonacci series. Spiral waves of Belousov-Zapotinsky reactions. Vortices. Spiral galaxies. Superstrings, tubitons—''

''You're casting your net rather wide, don't you think?'' Roger said. ''I mean, even the yellow brick road that Dorothy goes dancing down in Oz begins in a spiral. Is that significant too?''

''Maybe,'' Marissa said with a shrug, finishing the last of her beer. ''Somehow all these things are linked. Why else would the Light have left that pattern, that trace, in minds? You should spend some time in those infosphere discussions. It's a good way to get a handle on what's going on out there in the mass-mind. I learned a lot from them.''

Roger stared narrowly at her.

''Such as?''

''Such as that Jung said spirals and waves were archetypal images, for instance,'' Marissa said. ''In dream theory waves are symbols of energy and emotion. Spirals are representations of evolution, of movement toward or away from consciousness. The spirals contained within a maze are a mandalic image.''

''Of what?'' Roger asked.

''The shape of the mind as a whole,'' she replied, ''and its need for order. Even a link between the individual being and the ground of all being, a window or door onto eternity.''

Roger lifted his eyebrows quizzically.

''Dream logic is a rather outré route,'' he said, smiling, as they got up to leave, ''though it still might get you there, I suppose.''

''I've always been a tangential thinker,'' Marissa said with a smile. "Helps me see in things and people what other people might not think is there. Doesn't have to hit me in the face to get my attention."

Roger winced. He remembered all too well his grievous misstep before the Light—and how Marissa had suffered for it at the hard-handed end of his rage. She saw his pained look and took him lightly by the elbow as they walked out beneath HOME 1's sheltering sky.

"What hits you plumb in the face isn't the whole story anyway," she said as they strode along. "The obvious is usually what is most in need of further analysis."

"And understanding," Roger said quietly, staring down at the path they walked along. "And forgiveness."

Marissa kissed him lightly on the cheek.

"Let's hope some changes *are* permanent," she said with a smile.

"Fine by me," he assured her. "There's no one with whom I'd rather fall apart together."

A gaze, earnest and deep, passed between them then. They turned away, thinking of the maze of the heart and the turbulence it structured.

THE IDEA OF GOING TO VISIT THE GENERAL SHERMAN TREE, "the largest single organism on the planet," with a bunch of Gaia-worshipping ecogroovy all-natural-fibered psiXtians appealed to Dundas about as much as a case of the shingles, but now he had managed it so that he was afflicted with both.

Sitting on one of their crowded sunbuses as it purred along Highway 180 past the mighty metrop of Minkler, Ray's only solace crossing the central valley was seeing the occasional FOLLOW JESUS OR GO TO HELL bumper stickers on ancient camo-painted four-wheel-drive pickups. Good to see that not all the Jurists' Christian Assembly or Christian Identity folks were back home in the ACSA.

Such righteous, God-fearing folk were half an hour behind them now, however. He could feel the prodromal edginess coming on as the skin across his left temple grew tight. Colonies of perversely unvaccinatable chicken pox, or *zoster opthalmicus*, or whatever it was left over from his childhood had started growing again on his cranial nerves. Soon the tightness in his face would be persistent pain around his left eye and all about the left side of his head, then large pimply bulges, skin shine, and suppurating, crusty sores all over the left side of his forehead—as if he were some kind of bizarre, bumpy-headed alien. Soon the emotional edginess would be outright rage. What a joy.

Before the two previous eruptions of this bane, Ray had always thought of shingles as a (usually) curable old ladies' disease. Both prior flare-ups had presumably been stress-induced. They had both happened while he was on duty back at headquarters in Billings, while his marriage was unraveling. He had been trying to put his wife aside gracefully, so that their marital blisters did not become obvious enough to catch the attention of his family-valuing superiors and thereby damage his own career. Instead he'd literally broken out in blisters.

At least he'd never had an outbreak while in the field on deep-cover duty. The mere thought of it was embarassing: the Spy with the Shingles.

As the bus climbed through the hills of oak giving way to pine above Miramonte and Dunlap, he realized that maintaining his brave façade among the happy utopian psiXtians must be more stressful than he'd realized. The trip to Santa Cruz must have been the last straw.

Still, Dundas thought, he might be able to make his body's betrayal work for him. He could always hint that the stress was caused by his "deep desire to succeed as an initiate into the ways of the psiXtians." That sounded about right. Make it a plus, turn it into a signifier of his hope and zeal, rather than a proof of the difficulty of maintaining the façade.

The psiXtians on the bus oohed and aahed as they spotted the first of the obvious Big Trees not far from the Sequoia-Kings Canyon entry gate. Who could have guessed that the psiXtians' homebody bent didn't apply as rigidly to initiates?

Ray Dundas smirked at their awe. Just another tree, only bigger. More board-feet of timber. From the awe in the expressions of these people you'd think they'd just witnessed the second coming of the Lord.

These psiXtians, with their "negative capability" and "compensatory lack," were easy to impress. He'd seen their optimistic gullibility in action during an initiate eco-study meeting he'd attended, after returning to Sunderground from his deliveries in Santa Cruz. During the meeting he tossed out that axiom he'd dreamed up—"Convenience is obedience to the rule of status quo"—along with some eco-cant context for it. Immediately he'd upped his station in the community of initiates by at least half a dozen notches. His dreaming of that heretical phrase must have been providential, a blessing on his mission, he now realized. Truly, God works in the most mysterious ways.

As the sunbuses hummed into the Kings Canyon side of the two-headed park, word spread around him that they weren't going directly to see the General Sherman tree, but were stopping at the Grant Grove of Big Trees first. Dundas hoped he could contain his ecstasy at *that* prospect.

As his bus made its way up the road toward the visitors center, then down the steep turns toward Grant Grove, Ray overheard a conversation between an ancient, bald and bearded white psi-Xtian and a younger, black man.

"—the place names around here," said the young man, shaking his head. "Groves of trees named for generals."

"Names are powerful talismans," said the oldster. "People take them very seriously. I remember when I was a young man living in Fresno, I showed up at a rally in support of changing the name of Kings Canyon Boulevard to Cesar Chavez Boulevard. Chavez had died not long before. I went to the rally because I felt Chavez tried to bring about social change in a nonviolent fashion. Whether you agreed with everything the man was about or not, he was obviously a figure of historical importance in the valley. I thought it only made sense that a street should be named for him."

"Were we being a bit naive?" the younger man asked wryly.

"You bet," said the older man with a nod. "When I showed up, I wasn't carrying a sign or anything, just holding a painting of Chavez—no caption or anything else. That's all I was doing. The mediacudas swarmed me, probably because I was a big dumb white guy in a sea of Chicano faces. The next day, there was my picture on the bottom of the front page of the Local News section, me holding that painting of Chavez. The caption read, 'Hunter Kaprin shows his support for the renaming.' "

"Your first time in the paper?" the younger man asked.

"Not at all," said the man who'd identified himself as Kaprin. "Over the previous several years I'd written op-ed articles and letters to the editor on a bunch of controversial topics—drug persecution hysteria, door-to-door religion, war, you name it—but I'd never heard back so much as a peep from anyone who might have read them. But that picture went out and boom! The death threats started coming in to my answering machine before

I'd even picked the paper off the front stoop. My wife and I woke to the sound of a woman yelling on the machine, saying how, because she was a good Christian, she knew that Kings Canyon had been named for the Three Kings in the Christmas story. How it wasn't Chavez but a Filipino who'd founded and built the farmworkers' union. How I'd better get my facts straight. She ended her diatribe by saying 'I hope you get a bullet up your ass.' "

The two men laughed. The prodromally edgy Dundas found it all he could do to keep from exhaling in a derisive hiss at both of them.

"Interesting anatomical specificity," said the younger man, "but that doesn't sound very, um, Christian."

"Everyone has bad days, I suppose," the old man Kaprin said with a shrug, in a tone Dundas found annoyingly condescending. "I didn't think my life was in danger from her, though. Allowing herself to be taped on an answering machine didn't exactly fit the profile of a deadly stalker. The guys that scared me were the ones who, when I picked up the phone, said things like, 'You better have a good life insurance policy, fella,' then hung up."

"I can see how they would be the scarier ones," the younger man agreed. "How did you deal with the calls?"

"We just stopped answering," Kaprin said. "Then we got an unlisted number. The one silver lining was that because we were getting death threats, the phone company didn't charge for getting our number switched to unlisted!"

"That's pretty small compensation," the young man said.

"True," Kaprin agreed. "But any good news was a big plus, at the time. The reaction of those readers caught me totally off guard. Nothing I had written previously, no matter how controversial, had ever elicited so violent a response as that single innocuous picture with my name under it. In the eyes of those callers, I was honoring the guy who tried to take away their slaves. I had become a 'race traitor' overnight, just by holding a picture of Chavez in public—"

The bus stopped then and they all piled out to look at the big trees of Grant Grove—a good thing, for Dundas's irritability had grown almost past the point of containment.

The idiots! he thought as he walked up the path into the grove, almost oblivious to the enormous trees around him. What did these mystico-pagans, practically falling to their knees before these big weeds, know about being a good Christian?

They probably thought Jesus was a Jew, for heaven's sake. That was to be expected, when they'd been living under a Zionist Occupation Government all these years. They had undoubtedly never studied the Bible enough to realize that the white race was the actual "lost" tribe of Israel. Not lost, but fled north, into the Caucasus Mountains, hence "Caucasians." These people surely had no inkling of the proof Guaranty had provided, in *Myth's Edge and Nation*, that Jesus and his parents were part of a mission from the North to the other tribes. No idea at all that the years of Jesus' life lost to Scripture he had spent in those same Caucasus mountains.

Did these people understand the first ten amendments to the Constitution? The Magna Carta? He doubted it. They were all too ZOGged out. And they most certainly hadn't read and appreciated Genesis 1:27-30.

He looked at them now, in their simple homespun garments, gazing in rapture up at the tall trees. From what he overheard them saying, he knew that, instead of seeing the big trees as examples of the divine handiwork put on Earth for Man's use, they were reveling in the fact that the trees had been "preserved" from the timbermen. He heard their petulant tsk-tsking over how few were left, especially since Yosemite and its groves had been privatized.

Their kind were all meddlers, muddlers, lumpers, makers of mud people, Dundas thought. No respect for what God's will decreed about boundaries between sexes, races, and species. Making everything and everybody a big mess of "equal rights." Denying God's ordained hierarchy, and ready to unleash anarchy in its stead. Scratch a psiXtian and who knew what kind of eco-fem witchery would come oozing out. . . .

Did these Zionized race-mixing sympathizers even consider the realities of race betrayal? Did those who were nominally white among them ever think that they constituted only about ten percent of the global population? Did they ever consider the fact that, if this race-mixing went on, white people would be hybridized out of existence?

Of course not. The result of their "diversity" wasn't a rainbow—it was mud. Look at these initiates. Nondescript melanoskins from everywhere. Even a dozen half-savages from some godforsaken jungle mountaintop in South America!

Walking through the inside of an enormous fallen sequoia, Ray read a plaque, the inscription on which contended that a single giant sequoia contained more wood than was to be found on several acres of the finest virgin timberland in the Pacific Northwest, when there had still been virgin timberland there.

Looking about at the enormous downed tree he walked through, Dundas shook his head. What a waste. Think of all the houses this single grove could make for the poor of the Christian States! Think of the jobs it would provide!

He walked out of the downed tree, on toward the California Tree and the Oregon Tree, thinking of geography. True, what remained of old Canada and the United States still surrounded the Autonomous Christian States of America—but not forever.

How long would it be before already majority-Hispanic California's brownboy governor, Martin Gutierrez, completely opened the border with Mexico? A month or so ago he'd begun making those very noises. When the State of California became the Alta California of Mexico once more, Gutierrez would of course have to assert territorial hegemony over Arizona and New Mexico as well. If Gutierrez played his cards right, he'd end up president of all a greatly expanded Mexico.

According to the strategists back in Billings, the states of Oregon and Washington would then also declare their independence from the federal government back East. They would most likely join with the former Canadian Pacific provinces and Alaska in the "Pacific Rim Bio-regional Coalition" the greeners in that area had been advocating for years. Florida would secede and join the browns and blacks of the Caribbean. From Mississippi through Georgia, to the Virginias and out to Missouri, the South would rise again in a new form, almost ninescore years after the Civil War had ended.

Despite the prodromal pain of his oncoming stress-engendered shingles, Dundas smiled to himself. Of course the ACSA would be the great beneficiary of such changes. All the rational white people—God-fearing, or soon destined to be—would come flooding in. Emigrés and refugees would swarm to the mountains and plains of the Autonomous Christian States. The Bible-based South would quickly become an ally.

In no time at all, white people, with a strong tradition of Christian soldiering, would again rule all of the old United States as they once had. The days of that blessed theocracy would return. The United States of America would again become the Christian States of America, as it had been all too briefly. The New Troubles might have prematurely ended the CSA, it might have forced the ACSA secession from a re-secularized USA, but that could turn around again. With a vengeance.

Once America was again Christian from sea to shining sea, God's true chosen people could at last begin moving against the great nests of perversion. The first targets would be the orbital habitats, with their Wemoon's Edens and their demonic "diversity." At long last the righteous could re-educate or exterminate everyone in that cislunar Pandemonium, down to the last man-hating, ball-cutting witch!

Lost smilingly in such pleasant thoughts, Dundas had unthinkingly come to the vicinity of the General Grant tree. He heard the ranger interpreter, an Asian woman, describing the tree as the second largest living thing in the world, after the General Sherman. The thin young black woman next to Dundas looked at him and chuckled.

"Look at that smile on your face!" she said in a friendly, joshing tone. "I feel the same way. Does the soul good to see something so big and so old and so alive, don't you think?"

"Absolutely," he said, his mask of devout tree-paganhood once again providentially maintained.

He moved on among the big trees, impressed almost despite himself now that he took notice of them. Their thick, reddish-brown columnar trunks stood a score of armspans around, for what looked to be at least the first third of their twenty-plus stories of height. Rather like looking at a two-thousand-year-old living office building, he thought. One that was still growing too, topped with rugged limbs and feathered with ropy bracts of greenery.

He hoped that he would live long enough to see the day when California became part of a Greater ACSA or a restored Christian States of America. When that time came, he would see to it that he exercised his God-given dominion over these trees. He'd have one of these giants felled and split, converted into fencing for all around his home in Montana and his summer cabin in Idaho.

Soon the psiXtian group boarded the buses again and headed into the Sequoia section of the double park. Yes, he thought as the buses hummed along, things weren't perfect in the ACSA—especially since that Light thing supposedly happened. Some of the Mormons had begun acting up again with their independent revelations. Too many citizens were saying heretical, mystical things like "The Book will crumble and the Steeple will fall but the Light will be shining at the end of it all." In his youth Ray had blown away Quakers for less heretical statements than that.

He was glad to have learned through his hidden satlink that the churchstates were finally squelching such people but good. About time. He would almost have thought the Light was some sort of secularist plot against the churchstates all over the world, except that it seemed to have caused as much trouble in the secular world as it had in the theocracies.

The buses parked across the road from the Sherman tree and Congress Trail areas. This grove was crowded enough that the psiXtian group didn't merit a human guide. Instead everyone was handed a prerecorded multichannel handset with descriptions of the Sherman Tree and points of interest along the Congress Trail.

Walking around the old, snag-crowned tree, Dundas mainly heard the handset spew a cascade of numbers—height, weight, age, ground circumference, base diameter, height of first large branch, diameter of largest branch. Ray gathered that the volume of the trunk was the key number, since it was by volume that the Sherman tree was the largest living thing on Earth.

Watching the psiXtians move in slow procession around the big tree, Dundas realized that this was their kind of altar in their kind of cathedral. No doubt they were smug about the fact that this tree predated the birth of Christ by five hundred years. It provided them too with their own version of the parable of the mustard seed—namely, that the trunk weighed sixty billion times as much as the seed that had produced it.

As they moved up the Congress Trail, the psiXtians' talk was full of "peripheral pressure ridges" and "leaning trees" and "resinless bark" and "tannin-preserved trunks." Dundas gathered that, unless they were consumed by fire, these trunks were so resistant to decay that the downed trees often lasted longer dead than even all the thousands of years they had known while alive. Around him the psiXtians eagerly discussed the trees' life cycle, from egg-sized cone and tiny seeds, through Christmas-treelike saplings, to young trees with spired crowns, to mature trees with rounded crowns hundreds of years old, on to snag-crowned oldsters of several thousand years, and on at last even to the maze-rooted fallen giants sprawled across the forest floor.

I'm on the Nature Walk from Hell, Dundas thought grumpily as he plodded along with them.

They talked eagerly of the white firs and sugar pines and Jeffrey pines scattered through the grove, the chinquapin and corn lily and orchis and bracken fern and lupines and leopard lily and senecio. They fascinated themselves with the nature of plant succession and the role of fire in the climax community. They spoke reverently of forest food webs, of chickarees and insects and mule deer, of coyote and bobcat and pine marten and black bear, of ravens and kinglets and owls, of chickadees and sapsuckers and juncos and woodpeckers.

The psiXtians pronounced those names like a litany of saints, Dundas realized as he followed them past the President tree. Their litany continued as he walked with them past the tall, straight, pantheon-columns of the Senate and House groups, through Circle Meadow, to the Lee and McKinley trees.

Returning with them in a great circle back toward the Sherman tree, he passed a shattered tree and suffered through another tsk-tsking discussion of the evils of the logging which brought down these giants, each earth-shaking fall heard half a dozen kilometers away.

As they approached the Sherman tree once more and he saw the psiXtian greeners forming a human chain to circle round the biggest living thing on Earth, Dundas had a vision of sorts. Not of the psiXtians all meditating around the big tree—that was real enough and happening already—but of semi-simian, arboreal subhumans, living in the trees as in high-rise apartments, the trees themselves engineered to serve as living homes. The followers of Axel Erlandson, half a hundred generations on . . . ?

Standing in line with the meditators, Dundas was profoundly disturbed by his dark vision, by this prospect of a humanity that had completely forfeited its God-given role of dominion.

After the psiXtians' sage-smudging and readings from John Muir and tree prayers and the usual four-compass-point ritual rigmarole, Dundas was glad to be getting back on the sunbus. He was exhausted—yet another sign of his pending shingles outbreak.

Dropping off to sleep, he was glad that the time of the degraded, simian subhumans had not yet come, and that quality, high-tech, vibro-resonant health care (which didn't respect the equal rights of microbes) was still available. . . .

Diana Gartner flying in from orbit on a dark and stealthy witch's broom. Staring at him, crucified again—transfixed by old-style hypodermic syringes through each of his hands, another syringe through his overlapping feet, an electrode crown of thorns on his brow. Then himself, pierced no longer by needles but only by light and a VR circlet upon his brow. Then bleeding bright shining light, from wounds in his hands and feet and side, from the lacerations in his scalp, stigmata—

The bus came to a stop at a turn and he awoke. Gingerly he moved aside the blond hair from his forehead, perversely heartened to find, not stigmata, but merely the first of his shingle-bumps erupting. He glanced surreptitiously at his hands and was glad to find no oozing eldritch marks there—just his ordinary palms, slightly sweaty.

Still, the image of crucifixion troubled him. His was a religious faith that emphasized the empty cross of the promised Easter, not the tortured crucifix of Catholicism's Good Friday pain. Diana Gartner's presence troubled him even more. Fighting back sleep the rest of the trip to Sunderground, he shivered much of the way. He told himself it was just the chills accompanying the onset of his condition.

FIVE

C ODE-EXTRACTED SUBTERPOST EXCERPT (SOURCE POSSIBLY infosphere-killer related; original source is Jaynes's *Military Technologies of the ACSA*):

Researchers discovered the Low Intensity Maser Barrage Induced Catatonia (LIMBIC) effect accidentally. Masers, they learned, could be used to trigger unforeseen responses in their troops' satellite-link hookups. ACSA researchers found that maser interference caused the satlink systems to generate voltage potentials in specific areas of the brains of those soldiers using such units. These "headsparks," as the troops referred to them, amplified the brain's built-in electrochemical chaos.

ACSA researchers further learned that areas of the brain could be specifically targeted for this chaoticizing effect. Symptoms ranging from epilepsy-like convulsions to total immersion in "oceanic feeling" could thus be induced. Simulated near-death and out-of-body experiences were also reported by soldiers equipped with such units. For these reasons, ACSA commanders have restricted the use of satlink neural systems among their forces.

That restriction has not stopped the technology from leaking onto the streets, however. Civilian populations worldwide, particularly among youth subcultures, have long since discovered that maser interference with such headsets and implants can also be used to generate low-voltage electrical stimulation of the central pleasure zones, particularly the septal area of the brain. Cheap, maser-modified headphonelike units, commonly called Sexophones, can be found on the street corners of virtually any impoverished urban area in the world.

A generation of stim-addicts has resulted, their septal areas high-wired for "mental masturbation" in the fullest sense of that phrase. Many of these "wireheads" have literally starved to death, their electronic addiction far more powerful than the need for food or drink to sustain life.

"YOU WERE RIGHT," SAID THE TALL, LITHE WOMAN. FROM the grey streaking in the woman's thick fall of dark hair and the slight pouchiness of the skin around the chin and at the elbows, Brandi guessed her to be in her fifties. "The resemblance to Cyndi is incredible."

"See?" Immanuel Shaw asked rhetorically. "I told you."

"Too incredible, if you ask me," the woman, Diana Gartner, said, joshing him. "Doesn't look like there's any of you in this girl-child at all, Manny. She must have been cloned or ovular-merged!"

Shaw gave Gartner a sidewise and slit-eyed skeptical glance. Gartner laughed.

"You're the same Diana Gartner who was in my mother's *Five Million Day War*?" Brandi asked.

"I'm the historical person," Gartner corrected her, as the two women and Manny Shaw walked about the small, meadowlike commons near Shaw's house in the ag tori. "I didn't play the role in the documentary. I helped your mother work on the screenplay for that section, though."

Brandi pinched a cluster of purple flowers from a broken stem alongside the path. "That must have been a challenge," she said.

"Not really," Diana Gartner replied. "I found Will Acton's sub voc recorder. There was an unbelievable amount of material in that."

"Will Acton was real too, then?" Brandi asked, watching her feet as they moved over the path.

"Absolutely," Gartner said with a nod as they approached a large, high-backed, crescent-shaped bench made of mooncrete. According to the affixed plaque, it was based on an original lovers' whispering bench at Wilton House in England. There was no denying that it had unique acoustic properties. Though the trio were seated far apart, they could hear each other perfectly well.

"Horrible thing, what happened to Acton," Gartner went on. "He was the proverbial 'good soldier,' doing his duty, but very much bothered by it. His sub voc record makes it pretty clear he had his doubts. I saw what was left of his body afterward. The bastard that did it to him, Ray Dalke—he's still alive, as far as anyone knows."

"The ACSA really did do what my mother's documentary shows?" Brandi asked, leaning against the high back of the crescent.

"Not the ACSA," Manny Shaw corrected. "The old CSA. I know you grew up in the haborb, but jeez, get the history straight, girl."

"The Christian States of America came first," Diana said, remembering. "That regime rode a wave of millenial fervor to power over the old fifty United States of America. The churchstaters were in control of the whole show for almost twelve years."

"That's the time frame for what happened to Acton and the Neo-Brunists and a whole lot of other 'unbelievers,' " Shaw said.

Brandi nodded, patting the bench absently with her hand.

"I remember some of that history," she said, "but I don't really remember how the CSA became the ACSA, so they kind of run together in my head."

"That's true for a lot of people," Manny said with a smirk. Diana glared at him.

"There was a very short and very bloody Second Civil War," Diana said. "At the end of it, the churchstaters retained control of thirteen states in the Rocky Mountains and the plains from North Dakota to Texas. That's the ACSA. The remainder of the old fifty took the name United States of America again."

"Not that it really makes all that much difference," Manny put in, leaning forward. "CSA or ACSA, they're mostly the same narrow-cranium Adolph Christler types. The kind of folks who'll proclaim loudly that they're praying for your soul while they march you off to the ovens. They're still around, even outside the ACSA. Here—just look at this holoclip my friend Paul Larkin found and net-bounced to me. A bunch of religioid types, laying siege to another zoo-ark, somewhere down in the American Midwest—right now. I've been wanting you to see it in particular, Di."

Shaw already had his notepad Personal Data Assistant out and ready. He set the clip to play in public display mode, so Diana and Brandi had little choice but to watch it.

"—we have returned," boomed a folksy white-maned preacher, media-captioned as a Rev. William Grindstaff. "All those worldly people out there, taking their 7:06 Beast train to their offices in Downtown Satan City—they have tried to ignore our truth. It can no longer be ignored. The Scripture is clear on this. In order for the new Heaven and new Earth to come among us, the old Earth must be exhausted, utterly used up. Extinction of lower orders and types is not an accident—it is the will of God and central to His Plan. Conservationists and eco-sympathizers delay the Second Coming! The Lord's Own must make straight the way for the coming of our Great King. We will allow no ark of Satan, nor tree-hugging, people-hating Greens, nor Earth goddess-worshipping pagans to stand in His way!''

Choruses of ''Amen! Amen!'' and a wave of applause broke over the preacher, who smiled righteously upon his people, hundreds or perhaps thousands of zealots, wearing crosses and gun belts, shooting and shouting and shaking their guns before a sandbagged perimeter defended by private security forces in riot armor.

''See?'' Shaw said. ''And that's taking place in what's left in the USA. You can just imagine how they're behaving in the ACSA!''

Diana Gartner frowned, lifting one foot onto the bench and resting her chin on her knee.

''I've dealt with them, Manny,'' she said. ''It's not that simple—or that monolithic. Most of them are people of genuine faith. They are usually people of good will and intentions, even if they are often misguided or consciously manipulatd by their leaders.''

Shaw snorted in disbelief but said nothing.

''It's true,'' Diana continued. ''It's just that they are profoundly disturbed by a world that's been changing faster than they care to. They've been trying for a long time to reconcile irreconcilables—global-scale corporate 'free market economy' on the one hand, and small-scale family style ethics on the other. Each works against the other.''

Shaw laughed.

''I'm amazed you can be so understanding of them,'' he said. ''They hate you and your flyouts. You're flouting the 'rule of extinction' that's part of God's dominion-over-earth plan, as far as they're concerned. Sanctimonious, power-hungry hypocrites, the lot of them.''

Shaw crossed his arms and set his jaw, as if daring Diana to respond.

''There are scam artists among them, undeniably,'' she said, "but that's true for any group or movement. They're generous and good to people who are like them and believe as they do. They are strong on 'me and God' and 'us and God,' just not so strong on 'those *other* people and God.' "

Shaw made a dismissive gesture that told Brandi these two had argued these points before and little was likely to change now—their personal experiences having long since hardened into concrete political outlooks.

"They see any difference as absolute," Shaw said. "With them it's all wheat versus chaff, sheep versus goats, if you're lukewarm I'll vomit you from my mouth. If you're not with us, you're against us. Zero, one. Good, evil. Heaven, Hell. Binary thinkers. Manichean."

"What about purgatory?" Brandi asked innocently.

"That's a Catholic thing," Shaw said. "Even the notion of purgatory is a logic too fuzzy for them. The ACSA basically tolerates only one language and one religion. Monoculture. Homogeneity. You've seen the news footage of their wheat fields being harvested. Big mechanical combines eating wheat, spitting out grain, shitting bales of straw? That's what the ACSA is too."

"How do you mean?" Brandi asked. "I thought they were mainly just a bunch of grumpy neo-puritans."

"Their churchstate is a Nazis-for-Jesus combine," Shaw said firmly. "Eating people, spitting out souls, shitting bodies. Who knows how far they'll go to knead the dough of souls into the bread of God?"

Diana shook her head, almost sadly it seemed.

"The churchstaters don't have a corner on the intolerance market," she reminded Manny, placing the foot she had earlier propped up back onto the ground. "It wasn't them who coined the phrase, 'If you're not part of the solution, you're part of the problem.' Anyone can call anybody else a Nazi. Over the last century the term has been so overused that most of the meaning has been leached out of it."

Shaw subsided grumpily, leaning back into the bench, temporarily outmaneuvered. Brandi saw a chance to bring the conversation around to where she wanted to go with it.

"How did you meet my mother?" she asked Gartner.

"Initially through the research she was doing into Medusa Blue," Gartner replied. "We also had a deeper sympatico, though. We were both 'experimental products.' She was exposed to the Project's manipulation while still in the womb—as I was.

It just so happened that I was one of the few 'KL kids' who got picked up again by the Project. In the latter days of the old U.S. government, there was a covert project to shift some gate kids' 'latent' talent over to 'active.' Some of us clicked over into direct mind-to-mind shield telepaths and empath-boosters, code-named 'starbursts.' Everything was always for that seamless mind-machine interface the Project and its parent program had been working on. We were a sort of unexpected step along the path.''

"You mean you can speak directly into other people's minds?" Brandi asked, remembering the "Art of Memory" sequence she had seen from *The Five Million Day War*.

"True enough," Gartner said with a small nod, "although it's not quite that straightforward. It's a talent I'm tempted to use about a thousand times more often than I actually do. The person I'm sending to has to be somehow responsive to what I'm putting out."

"That's incredible," Brandi said, genuinely impressed. Diana smiled.

"It's been a blessing and a bane," she said, "but at least it's made me a bit more sensitive to the fragility of free will than our friend Manny here. Coercion isn't the way to go. People have a right to be wrong, even dead-wrong."

"Just so long as I don't end up dead, to protect their right to be wrong," Manny shot back. "Their right to be wrong does not supersede my right to go on living, or my right to live the life I choose, so long as my living that life doesn't tread on anyone else's right to the same."

"Do unto others . . . '' Diana Gartner suggested.

"More than that," Shaw said. "Fundamental respect for *persons*. That's what the hair shirts and hard-shells are lacking. I don't know—maybe I just lost too many gay and counterculture friends to the churchstate purges. Some types of intolerance are too virulent to be tolerated."

Diana shrugged and shook her head.

"A lot of my friends were killed as witches, remember?" she said. "You know what that was a code word for. But if we can't get beyond the hate, then we never escape the cycle of fear and retribution."

Shaw snorted dismissively again but Diana pressed on.

"If we never learn to let go of fear," she said, "how will we ever manage to grab onto hope? Always armed to the teeth. The whole planet. You saw what almost happened in the haborb here, before the Light. An armed planet isn't a polite planet—it's a *paranoid* planet. Our little bubble world here almost got popped in the nastiest of ways.''

''True, true,'' Shaw agreed thoughtfully. ''We did come pretty close to having our oasis in space blasted into so much space-junk.''

Brandi lifted to her nose the cluster of purple meadow flowers she'd plucked from a broken stem earlier. The flowers exuded a light sweetness. She wondered what they were.

''Right after the Light,'' Diana said, ''I thought that, at long last, we were on the correct course. The pilot seemed to have awakened, for a while. It seemed we were sailing safely between the Scylla of nuclear war on the one hand and on the other the Charybdis of eco-collapse, from consuming all the resources and drowning in our own waste. Big sigh of relief, right? Now I'm not so sure.''

Manny noded in agreement. Somewhere he'd picked up a stick and was tracing with it in the gravel.

''Humanity is still mainly a debtor species,'' he said. ''We still take out a lot more from the world than we give back to it. We haven't begun to turn that around yet.''

''I wonder if Jiro Yamaguchi's 'irenic apocalypse,' as his brother calls it, might yet prove too little, too late,'' Diana said quietly.

The three of them sat in silence for a minute. Then, Brandi cleared her throat.

''Manny mentioned Seiji Yamaguchi,'' she said. ''He said I should visit him while I'm here.''

''Certainly,'' Diana agreed. ''Seiji and Jhana Meniskos are sharing a place in one of the new 'borbs, though. They just moved.''

''Really?'' Shaw said, surprised. ''I imagine those places are pretty raw, yet. Land of the stick trees. Nothing's had a chance to grow or settle in. Like this place in the early days.''

Brandi glanced down, disappointed.

''You should see them if you get a chance,'' Diana Gartner said, standing up and stretching. ''Between the two of them they probably know as much about what the Light is or was as anybody does.''

Manny and Brandi followed Diana's lead and also stood up. The three of them walked along through the commons in silence again for a while, admiring the edge-gardens around its margins. Once again it was Brandi who broke the quiet.

"I was just wondering," she said. "You were the one who taught my mother how to trigger her talent, weren't you?"

Diana turned away, seeming suddenly very interested in a flower she had stopped to look at.

"Yes," she said, nodding. "I almost wish I hadn't, given what eventually happened to her."

"You taught her about 'going Elsewhere'?" Brandi asked. "And her 'witch's brew,' as Manny calls it?"

"I'm afraid so," Diana said. "I learned about those sorts of things indirectly. From the Project. Funny thing was, Cyndi didn't want the talent for the talent's sake."

"Why did she want it?" Brandi asked, trying to keep a certain unease out of her voice as they strolled along together.

"So she could better understand what I felt," Diana replied, "and what Acton felt, when we had our encounter. So she could document it better for her *Five Million Day War*. In a sense she did it for her art's sake."

"That's always bothered me," Brandi said.

"Why?" Diana asked, genuinely curious. "Afraid the talent might be hereditary?"

"Not that, really," Brandi said, looking down at a border of poker primroses labeled *Primula vialii*, their dense, narrow spikes of red and violet-blue flowers blooming off in ascending stages, like a slow-motion rocket launch. "I just wouldn't want to risk my life and sanity altering my brain chemistry to trigger something like that."

"What your mother chose is not for everyone, certainly," Diana said with a shrug. "More and more people seem to be following her route, however. Even without the old triggers."

"What do you mean?" Manny asked, turning away from the lupines he'd been examining.

"Just that, if you took a census or a big survey," Diana replied, "I bet you'd find that the occurrence of subtle abilities—siddhis, or paranormal powers, if you like—has gone up quite a bit since the Light. One of the traces of its passing."

"And you think these effects, these traces, were left by the Light?" Brandi speculated.

"In a *lot* of different heads," Diana said with a nod. "My evidence is only anecdotal so far, but I think it's pretty strong."

"No 'powers' in my case," Brandi averred. "Thank God."

They came to the edge of the commons from which a webwork of paths and trails led away. Each path was broad enough to walk three abreast at first, but they soon narrowed as less-traveled paths branched off.

"My way splits from yours here," Diana said to her companions. "I hear you have other talents, Brandi—besides a precocious understanding of spaceship design. The newsbuzz a while back said you're one heck of a fireboarder. True?"

"I've burned in a few times," Brandi said with a shrug, in the understated argot of her sport.

"Good," Diana said, nodding. "I have access to a quaint little piece of ship design myself—a stealth transat spy flyer. She'll do Mach 30 in the upper atmosphere. I'll take you for a spin, if you'd like."

"I'd like!" Brandi said, eyes wide and smiling. She'd heard rumors of such craft, but had always thought they were as mythical as unicorns and sea monsters. "Let me know next time you're doing a downhill run and I'll be happy to ride shotgun."

"Ah, you aggressive women and your violent metaphors," Manny said. "Tsk, tsk."

They tried to ignore him. Shaking hands and hugging goodbye, they set up a date for Brandi's "shotgun" run. As they walked away, Brandi was happy—and only mildly worried about how Juan might react to the prospect of a trip to one of the other 'borbs, *and* a run down the well.

A HAND FALLING HEAVILY ON A MARBLE CHESS CUBE. *A light forming around it as the hand seems to press the cube into the floor. No—the height of the cube shrinking, shrinking, becoming a flat two-dimensional sheet, still marked with the light and dark squares of its chessboard top. The hand taking the thin stone sheet and rolling it up into a cylinder. Rolling the cylinder tighter, growing it longer, a strange checkerboard stone hose with meanders running through it. Taking the ends of the hose and bringing them together into a thin doughnut shape. Shrinking that down smaller too, one edge thinning in the process and the other bulging, until the doughnut shape metamorphoses into a small sphere. Pushing the sphere down into a point, smaller and smaller, until it disappears—*

Barely understood forces warping the air around the four men in the den, warping something much deeper than the air itself, smoothly if fatally everting the men, turning them wrong side out, subtly twisting them into shapes out of a topologist's nightmare—

Coming out of the infoburst this time without passing out, Mei-Ling Magnus gasped. Maybe she was getting a handle on this strange new "strengthening" of her crime-scene reconstruction ability. Or maybe this location—the death site of Samir Hijazi in Salisbury—wasn't quite so strong in its impressions because it was older, less recent. She removed Hijazi's connection gear and looked at Sullivan, who hovered protectively nearby.

"I think I've got something, Robert," Mei-Ling said, exhausted, to her redheaded companion. "I just flashed on four people being killed in a group. Topologically. One of the men looked like that picture you showed me of Schwarzbrucke. We need as much information on Schwarzbrucke's death as we can get our hands on."

"I'll do it," Sullivan said with a frown, "but I'm tempted to counter with a demand for your promise that you'll stop this death-site touring. This is the third one, and you go into that catatonic remming seizure or whatever it is *every* time. When you come out of it, all the stuffing's been knocked out of you. I don't want the next death site you visit to be your own."

"At least I didn't pass out this time," Mei-Ling said gamely, waving him away.

"I don't know if that's a good thing," Robert replied. "Heaven forbid you should grow accustomed to experiencing other people's deaths!"

"I'm not really experiencing their deaths," Mei-Ling corrected as she rose unsteadily from Hijazi's virtuality workstation. "I'm experiencing their last moments, as it were. Mainly the stuff they were being blasted with, in that brief moment while the infodensity built up around them. I'm beginning to see patterns. Perseverative thought patterns, to be precise. I think those patterns are reflections of what our killer is obsessing about."

Sullivan maintained a thoughtful silence as they walked from the room and out onto the landing at the top of the staircase.

"You think this thing isn't an AI?" he asked as they proceeded down the stairs. "This topological voyeur is human, then? And connected with Schwarzbrucke's death?"

"I believe so," she replied as they walked out the front door of Hijazi's abandoned residence and onto the narrow street.

"We'll need more evidence to confirm the link. I think my initial hunch was correct: someone with an axe to grind against CMD or Schwarzbrucke himself."

Sullivan beamed open the doors and they got into his car.

"Is this ability to live the last moments of the dead the reason why Landau and Mulla brought you in on this?" he asked as he started the car and pulled away from the curb.

"Not at all," Mei-Ling said. "This 'ability,' as you call it, is all new to me. I've always been good at crime-scene reconstruction."

"Minute observation?" Robert suggested as much as asked.

"More infotech-focused, actually," she replied. "Putting myself into the logics of machines and grasping what was behind all the code, initially. Then I got pretty good at what the psychs call 'temporal tracing.' "

"Putting yourself inside the 'heads' of killers," Robert said sourly.

"Or killer machines—or their victims," Mei-Ling said. "Just looking at where they'd been. Teletracing, profiling, scan keying—they're all related. That's how I came to be working undercover in Sedona. That's where eventually I got hooked up with Landau."

"A rather odd talent," Sullivan said, shaking his head.

"Blessing and a curse," Mei-Ling agreed. "But, before, it was always a sort of informed intuition and guesswork. It was never this blatant. The whole thing's been cranked up a level. Now, it's like I'm able to really *see* these things—not just guess at them. The more recent the crime scene, the better. It's almost as if time hasn't had time to collapse the events back into itself yet."

As they cruised through sunset light beneath the grandiose steeple of Salisbury Cathedral—which seemed to loom over almost every prospect in the vicinity—they came toward a roundabout on the edge of town which jogged Mei-Ling's memory.

"Hey, isn't Stonehenge near here?" she asked.

"Not that near," Sullivan said, "but close enough, I suppose."

"Let's go," she said, putting her hand lightly on his. "I've never been there."

"You were out on the cloudier edge of Scotland for God knows how long—and you've never been to Stonehenge?" Sullivan asked, incredulous.

"No, I haven't," she said. "Come on."

"Look, Mei-Ling, it's getting dark," he said, gripping the wheel more firmly.

"Not yet," she said, "and there's a full moon rising early tonight. You can already see it. Please. Indulge me."

"It's the company car and the company's money," Robert said with a shrug, pulling off the road onto a side street in his usual breakneck manner of braking. "I'll just check the travel holo—"

A three-dimensional image popped into space between them, providing you-are-here overviews as well as two-dimensional street grid coordinates.

"I would have thought every London resident would know *immediately* how to get to Stonehenge," Mei-Ling said dryly, "since you've all been there before."

"Does everyone in South Dakota know immediately how to get to Mount Rushmore without consulting a map?" Robert shot back.

"Touché," Mei-Ling said, "Touché. Humor the romantic in me. Stonehenge is where Tess gets captured by the police—"

"In both Hardy's novel and Polanski's movie—I know," Robert said, pulling back onto the road. Following the directions appearing from time to time in the heads-up display on the windscreen, he drove along the A345, the sun disappearing and the moon rising, wheels larger and smaller turning and turning.

Above town they drove past the site of Old Sarum, then to the town of Amesbury and left onto the A303, on toward the A360 and Salisbury Plain.

"The parking lot on the other side of A360 may be closed, you know," Robert warned. "It's late. The tramtrain from London has probably already stopped running for the night. The pedestrian walkway under the highway may be closed too."

"It's not that late," Mei-Ling said confidently. "We might get lucky."

As it turned out, they were lucky, at least from Mei-Ling's point of view. The parking lot was open, as was the lightrail stop and the pedway underneath the road. Each of them purchased a disposable/recyclable/programmable ten-channel earplug "narrator." Walking under the highway and up to ground level again on the other side, they made their way, station by station, around the stone circle, learning about the many Stonehenges that had stood at this location.

The "narrator" whispered into their heads speculations about the builders and the purpose of the ruined monumental complex. Paleoastronomy and the Druids and Merlin and Atlantis, the Celts and Romans and eighteenth-century antiquarians—Mei-Ling heard about all of them. Her favorite, however, was the folkloric name for Stonehenge: "The Giants' Dance," from a legend which held that the stones were actually giants that had been petrified for dancing on Sunday. More importantly, through the story of the giants the narrator linked Stonehenge and other British megaliths to Scandinavian stone labyrinths.

After nearly two full circuits of the lithic complex, Mei-Ling stopped in her tracks and just stared at the ruined maze of stones before her.

Robert stopped short, beside her.

"You aren't 'flashing' on the stones, are you?" he asked warily.

Mei-Ling laughed lightly.

"No, no," she said smiling. "Not the way you're thinking. No doubt murders have happened here, but they've long since dissolved back into the timestream."

Into their heads the narrator whispered about station stones and barrows, heel stones and slaughter stones.

"How *do* they strike you, then?" Robert asked, curious. "Most people I know were initially disappointed by how small the stones actually are. Usually they expected something a good deal taller."

The narrative in their ears had moved on to a discussion of the Bluestones and the Sarsen stones.

"That's true, I guess," Mei-Ling said, "but they have even more of a looming presence than I thought they would. Before Mulla and Landau snatched me out of my, um, sabbatical, I was doing some research into the history of mazes and labyrinths. Stonehenge strikes me as either a solar maze or lunar labyrinth. And that, perversely, reminds me of Sedona."

They began to walk slowly around the great stone complex again. In their heads the tour narrator spoke of trilithons and lintel stones.

"What about Sedona?" Robert asked, above the earphone narration regaling them with thick detail about the moving and carving and dressing and positioning of the stones.

"Manqué had his computer systems set up so as to replicate the outline of an unruined, final Stonehenge," Mei-Ling said, remembering it as they walked. "My partners, Marvin Tanaka and Erinye Jackson, and I—we had to make our way down several flights of stairs and through a labyrinth of air-conditioned corridors to get to Manqué and his 'Brainhenge.' A maze inside a maze of underground spaces. I never expected to find all that, blasted out of the living redrock the Myrrhisticine Abbey was built into."

Under the fat full moon, the narrator whispered about ditches and banks, Aubrey holes and Z and Y holes.

"After passing through the maze of stairs and corridors," Mei-Ling continued, "we came into a warehouse-sized room. At the center of that big space, Manqué had built a Stonehenge of tall ParaLogics units. Each LogiBox was a massively parallel super-computer worth kerjillions in the major world currency of your choice, at the time. I'd never seen more than one of them at any single site before. In Manqué's Brainhenge there must have been forty of them."

Walking in the moonlight, Mei-Ling and Sullivan somehow managed to focus on both their discussion of Sedona and the whispering narrative about the overall construction of the great stoneworks, as it had taken place over thousands of years in the past.

"Quite a collection of computing power," Sullivan said.

"That's what I said when we passed inside that computer ring of his," Mei-Ling remarked with a nod. "We followed Manqué on to the center of his henge. That's where his command console and desk stood. They were covered with faux stone, like everything else. At first glance, the central console looked like a Druid high altar."

Something jogged Robert's memory and he stopped on the asphalt path.

"Ka Vang, the head honcho of ParaLogics, was a Myrrhisticinean," he said, "if I remember my Tetragrammaton research correctly."

"That's right," Mei-Ling said, turning back toward Robert, just as he started walking again to catch up to her. "Those brain-boxes were donations to the Abbey, a huge tax write-off. They were the main servers for all the computing and virtual equipment up there."

Robert paused beside her, noting how impressive the old Henge looked under moonlight.

"But you could probably run a dozen abbeys off of just one of those Boxes," he said, speculating.

"Off a fraction of one," Mei-Ling agreed as they walked on. "Manqué knew that quite well."

She lapsed into silence a moment. Robert felt no desire to prompt her or intrude upon her thoughts.

"The only time I ever saw him look truly comfortable was when he was seated at his console," Mei-Ling said when she began again. "On an ergonomic 'boulder' that conformed to his body shape. The big spider at the center of his web, bringing up a holovirtual in the space before his face—all very state of the art."

"What was he working on?" Robert asked.

"I was curious too," she said, "so I shoulder-surfed what he was looking at on that first tour he gave us. He pulled up a schematic of the architecture of the entire system. He had an incredible amount of memory and info-crunching power in reserve, there—and what turned out to be connections into virtually every sector of the infosphere. Links into every net and bulletin board in sharespace, no matter how small or obscure."

Mei-Ling stopped then too. She was suddenly struck by the thought that the Henge was a form of sympathetic magic, a maze to catch the light of sun and moon.

"So what were all those extra googolbytes of processing power for?" Robert asked, beside her.

"The 'divine plan' of the Myrrhisticineans," Mei-Ling said, walking on again. "Which, by the way, Manqué did not believe in. He was a self-proclaimed heretic to their order."

"Hold up there," Robert said, bringing their walk to a stop yet again. "You've lost me."

Mei-Ling prodded with her toe at the grass beside the path.

"How much do you know about Myrrhisticine beliefs?" she asked.

"Just that it was some sort of Teilhardian neo-mystical stuff," he said, "with a high-tech twist."

"Oh, it was—is—much more than that," Mei-Ling said, walking onward. "The Myrrhisticineans believed that the Rainbow Door opens into the World of Light, but only on the Day of Doom. Phelonious Manqué's heresy was that he believed every day is doomsday, every day is Judgment Day."

"In what sense?" Robert asked, a bit confused. They began to walk along again slowly.

"For Manqué," Mei-Ling said, "Earth itself is the Rainbow Door in the vault of Heaven. He contended that at any moment we can walk into the World of Light. All that's necessary is the will to make it happen. Phelonious was, maybe still is, an apocalyptist. The mainline Myrrhies were essentially gradualists—"

"Wait a minute," he said. "I'm not much up on obscure religions. You've lost me again. Better explain that."

"You know the meaning of Tetragrammaton to some apprentice sorcerers, right?" Mei-Ling asked.

"The 'Word to Shake the Foundations of the World,' " Robert said. " 'In the beginning was the Logos, in the End will be the Tetragrammaton.' Landau is always going on about that 'half-digested Crowley' stuff."

"Right," Mei-Ling went on. "That's clearly apocalyptic. But according to Teilhard, it's not so much an apocalypse as it is a 'co-evolutionary convergence' that has been coming toward us. Simultaneous movements toward *both* a single planetary culture *and* a psychical concentration. The noosphere is becoming involuted into what Teilhard called a Hyperpersonal Consciousness. That consciousness will be fully achieved at what Teilhard called Point Omega. Matter and consciousness will reach the terminal phase of their convergent integration and become one. Absolutely indistinguishable. Myrrhisticineans called that endpoint the Rainbow Door. Maybe it's also what Dr. Vang and the Tetragrammaton types call an information density singularity."

Some quality of the moonlight, Robert realized, made the Henge and the landscape they walked through seem as if they were underwater. He remembered the Henge's association with Atlantis and wondered what it was about the moon and water, the way one could suggest the other. Surely it was more than just the tides . . .

"I know something about that last bit, of course," he said to Mei-Ling. "But you seem to know a great deal more about all this Myrrhisticine mythology."

"I was there undercover, as I mentioned," she said with a shrug. "With the team from Kerrismatix that installed the ALEPH, the Artificial Life Evolution Programming Heuristic."

Sullivan laughed.

"Sexy allusions to Kabbalah and Borges and Gibson intentional in that name?" Sullivan asked.

"Mainly marketing," Mei-Ling said, downplaying it. "Manqué was the Abbey's systems manager. He saw potential for the ALEPH that wasn't there in the advertising."

"What potential?" Robert asked as they walked along.

"The chance to speed things up," Mei-Ling said. "Despite everything they believed, the Myrrhisticineans were basically waiting for The Thing to happen, rather than making it happen— the way Manqué felt they should. The Myrrhies believed that eventually all personal consciousnesses would become completely integrated at Omega, through Love, the spirit of Christ at work in nature."

"That sounds a good deal more theological than technological," Robert said with a grin that Mei-Ling could see quite clearly even in the moonlight. She nodded as they started another lap of the asphalt course that encircled the old stone temple.

"Teilhard didn't foresee how much the development of machine intelligence would speed up the movement toward Omega," she said. "Neither did the Myrrhies. Sister Clare, who brought us onboard, thought of the Kerrismatix ALEPH program only as a good way of modeling the future. She thought it could provide scenarios for all the changes leading up to the Rainbow Door."

"Manqué thought differently, I gather?" Robert said.

"Very," Mei-Ling replied with a nod. "What Manqué saw in it was a way to bring the biosphere, noosphere, and infosphere into conjunction—a key to opening the door in the vault of Heaven, *right now*."

"Why the big hurry?" Robert asked.

Mei-Ling walked in silence, remembering.

"Manqué felt that, given human greed, we were headed straight for the massive pain and suffering of a hard eco-collapse. No time to waste, or to wait."

Robert stopped and scratched absently at his head.

"If Manqué was such a heretic, as he claimed," he asked, "then why did the Abbey bother to keep him on?"

Mei-Ling glanced down at her feet a moment, then returned her gaze to Robert beside her, and the moonlit Henge beyond him.

"He was the only one who fully understood the Abbey's computer system," she said. "He was also a good friend of Dr. Vang, at ParaLogics. You can ask Manqué yourself, because that's where we have to go next."

"What?" Robert asked in surprise. "I didn't know he could

be visited. Most of the world believes he's dead.''

" 'Phelonious Manqué' *has* been dead since Sedona,'' Mei-Ling said. "That was his handle, his permanent alias. He made sure the first part was spelled with a ph, in the long hacker/cracker/phone phreaker tradition. The man behind the persona—Martin Kong—is still very much alive. Kong is serving a life sentence at the Electronic Crimes Maximum Security Penal Facility in California.''

"Amazing,'' Robert said as they turned and took one last look at the great henge beneath the high moon. "I knew that the Manqué name, and most of what the man was, disappeared when he dropped out of the infosphere. There've been persistent rumors of his life or death since then. Everything must have been under very deep cover, though, if someone with my clearance level was unable to find out that Phelonious was serving time in Silicon Bay.''

"It wasn't that hard to vanish him,'' Mei-Ling said as they walked toward the car. "He actually helped us make him disappear, accidentally. The constant careful security precautions he took *before* Sedona prevented anyone from learning the 'true identity' of Phelonious Manqué. Those precautions helped us a lot.''

"I see,'' said Robert with dawning understanding. "Since, in almost all respects, Martin Kong *was* Manqué, his public existence was predominantly virtual.''

"Right,'' Mei-Ling said, nodding. "It was relatively easy to make his true identity disappear completely. Nearly everybody who bothered to look ended up assuming he must have died in the Sedona disaster.''

They left the circle and walked together down the ramp, toward the path on the lower level, the walkway that led beneath the road.

"How *did* he escape that fate?'' Robert asked. "I've seen the amateur video of the event, of course. Looked like that 'black hole sun' thing ate all the Abbey aboveground and a good chunk of the mesa, belowground.''

"It did,'' Mei-Ling agreed as they walked into the parking lot, "but Manqué's Stonehenge computer complex was far enough underground that, even when that portal or whatever it was opened up above, my coworkers and I were able to shut down the info-feed it depended on before it consumed down to Kong's level—and ours. I don't think he's ever forgiven me for that.''

They made their way through the largely deserted lot, toward the car.

"Why is that?" Robert asked as they walked.

"Because he thought he had succeeded in bringing on the end of the world," Mei-Ling said. "He might have pulled it off, too, if his info-singularity had reached a critical size and become self-perpetuating. When we pulled him out of the wreckage of the Abbey and his Stonehenge, he was in a towering rage. 'Why did you stop it? Why did you save me?' He was mad as hell about still being alive—like someone angry over being brought back to life after a suicide attempt."

"What happened to him after that?" Robert asked, quickening his stride as they came within sight of the car.

"There was a very nice, very quiet trial," Mei-Ling said. "Martin Kong was eventually sentenced to several hundred years in prison. No possibility of parole. All access to electronic devices invented since about 1890 absolutely denied."

"Ouch," Robert said, beaming the car doors unlocked as they walked up beside it. "That must have hurt. Worse than a death sentence for someone like Phelonious Manqué."

They got into the car. The engine purred on and they pulled away through the parking lot.

"Any particular reason we need to see the madman formerly known as Phelonious Manqué—now?" Robert asked as they drove back onto the highway.

Mei-Ling gazed out the window as the Salisbury Plain unrolled beside the road.

"I think some of the guides, the angels and demons I've been picking up from the death sites," she said, "are based on Manqué's RATs, the Realtime A-life Technopredators. He built those with the aid of the ALEPH, which I helped install at Sedona. Versions of those same RATs also showed up everywhere in the infosphere, especially in and around HOME 1, just before the Light happened."

"These RATs must have survived the Sedona disaster, then?" Robert ventured.

"Apparently," Mei-Ling remarked, puzzled. "Even if their creator wasn't free to set them loose. They're all connected somehow—Manqué and Sedona, the Light and that orbital habitat, our topological voyeur and his parallel kills."

Robert Sullivan glanced at her, impressed by her reasoning, in spite of, or perhaps because of, his inability to fully follow it himself.

"Before we go to see Manqué/Kong," he said, "you wouldn't happen to have something like *Myrrhisticism For Beginners*, would you?"

Mei-Ling smiled and, reaching into her bag, took a small disk out and handed it to him.

"*Scientific Bones in Mystical Flesh: The Basic Teachings of Sister Alicia Gonsalves*," Mei-Ling said. "It consists mainly of dozens of short definitions, Q&A, vignettes, koan-like episodes."

"You just *happened* to have a copy of this in your bag?" Robert asked, incredulous.

"Not at all," Mei-Ling said. "I picked one up a couple of days ago, when I first starting thinking about links between my death-site flashes and Manqué's RATs. You can't expect me to remember everything, you know."

By the light from the dashboard, Robert Sullivan gave her a freckled and dimpled smile and shook his head.

"Oh, by the way," Mei-Ling said in afterthought, "I think we're going to have to go to the haborbs after our visit to Manqué. We'd better contact Landau about funding and clearance for that, asap."

Robert nodded, keeping his eyes on the road. Mei-Ling glanced out the window one last time, for a final view of Stonehenge by moonlight. She got the powerful impression that, from this distance, the ancient stone structure looked complete once more—not a ruin, but a sacred astronomical maze restored to wholeness.

Must be the moonlight playing tricks with my mind, she thought. Or my mind, playing tricks with the moonlight.

THE PLANET NOIR WINE BAR HUDDLED DEEP IN THE CAVERNous, century-old spaces beneath the streamlined-deco edifice of Union Terminal. In a cone of light falling from one of the occasional illumination units—less "fixtures" than punctures—Aleck waited at his table for a band called Tatterdemalien to finish up their set before Sam and company, now calling themselves Onoma Verité, took the stage.

Tatterdemalien's lead singer was a voluptous woman who called herself Lotus Yoni. Sam said she was actually named Gina Lotisoni. Whoever she really was, as she began to belt out another number she absently burned yet another hole in a costume already more tatters than imagination.

> *I'm tired to death*
> *of being*
> *tired to death*
> *of being*
> *tired to death*
> *I am tired to death.*

> *I'm tired to death of being*
> *everyone else's fond memory*
> *the snapshot in the album*
> *of someone they loved and then left.*

> *I'm tired to death of being*
> *everybody else's "experience"*
> *the one who they learned from*
> *who still never passed the test.*

> *I'm tired to death*
> *of being*
> *tired to death*
> *of being*
> *tired to death*
> *I am tired to death—*

The woman had a great angry voice, Aleck had to admit, perfect for expressing rage. But the song seemed to go on and on—and even heartfelt rage eventually became, well, *tiresome*.

Finally, Lotus Yoni announced in her surly manner that their next song, "Heart Medicine," would be the last of the evening. Tatterdemalien's fans yelled and whistled as Yoni sang and Aleck listened, for a while.

> *On the north and shady side of our love*
> *the beautiful poison flowers grow.*
> *True perennial foxglove, strawberry tachycardia spikes,*
> *Monkshood, bluewhite aconite, to relieve*
> *the pain, reduce the fever, of living.*

Come, put your finger on my pulse.
I will draw the hood down over your eyes.
Love and life the more intense,
but hatred and death the more enduring—''

The music wasn't that bad, Aleck thought. It was just that he'd have preferred their stage presence to be a stage absence. Apparently so did they. Amid the applause, Lotus Yoni briefly reintroduced Cunning Lingam (Len Cunningham, according to Sam) on electronics and Kink Freudman (Ken Friedman) on percussion. They said good night and swiftly exited the stage, followed by loud applause and rowdy whistling.

While their fans kept signaling for an encore from the rather scary depths of their appreciation, Aleck glanced around Planet Noir, at the decor he hadn't paid much attention to when he came in. The place was all done up as some kind of ritual cave: Delphic oracle and Cumaean Sibyl statuary and such toward the front, Abo and San and Lascaux cave wall paintings further toward the back, in mildly luminescent ocher tones. From the ceiling, pictographs and petroglyphs in subdued holo and neon glowed, abstract and aloof.

The crowd largely matched the environs: trendy, darkly glimmering people, sucking on cold N_2O-CO_2 faux cigarettes. Several of them had those flight-capable Personal Data Assistants, notepad computers done up as little cherubs and owls and parrots and pterodactyls and all sorts of winged things. They had become ridiculously popular in the last few weeks.

Aleck was surprised but also not surprised to see two of Sam's ex-girlfriend groupies. They'd once been introduced to Aleck as Digit Alice and Tabu La Raza, or something like that. They were talking to three *indigena*-looking types, who might actually be closer to what this place supposedly represented than the place was itself. Imported local color? Aleck wondered. He hoped his Uncle Bruce—or "Aleister," as he preferred to be known these days—would not be too put off by the faux of it all.

After his visit to the woods of his childhood, Aleck had finally called his parents and accepted their invitation to come visit the 'borbs at the end of the school term. They were overjoyed that he'd be coming to visit. They informed him that his uncle was already planetside and would soon be passing through Cincinnati. Almost before he knew what had transpired, Aleck had scheduled himself to meet his uncle and one of his uncle's friends during Onoma Verité's performance at Planet Noir.

Tatterdemalien had long since finished to raucous applause and whistling, but their die-hard fans were only now picking up on the fact that the band refused to do an encore. A classic comedy holo came up, to catch the audience's attention as the tech crews broke down Kink Freud's percussion gear and set up for Onoma Verité. Aleck sipped at the expensive Schwarzkatz he'd ordered and watched the holo of one-time comedy great Bunny Shurger. The clip was so old, he saw, that it wasn't even a real holo— only video or film, computer enhanced with false shadows and depth to make it appear 3-D. Ms. Shurger's routine probably went back to the turn of the millenium.

"Ever since the day-after pill came out," the fake-holo ghost of Shurger said, "children are like cigarettes—sometimes you want one after sex, sometimes you don't . . . Me? I'm a non-smoker."

When the comedy routine finished, Aleck was surprised to hear some sort of scholarly program in anthropology or paleon-tology murmuring in the Noir's background. Turning around, he saw the strange ambience media playing on a number of screens placed discreetly throughout the space. Captions scrolled in time to its images and the narrator's tones.

The program was saying that since history was a by-product of the technology called writing, then prehistoric essentially meant before *writing*, or at least before symbol systems modern humans could "read." Posthistoric, the program maintained, meant simply "after writing," after the technological primacy of written communication had passed. Aleck gave the cave-painting program a fuller portion of his attention, supposing it was in-tended to fit in with the decor somehow.

"The Gargas handprints are 'writing before writing,'" the scholarly background text murmured and scrolled, "in much the same way that the machine languages of computers are 'writing after writing'—coded messages, both in binary. The series of zeroes and ones in the Gargas handprints are, for each hand, red or black, left or right, whole hand or fingers bent/missing, pos-itive ('painted in') or negative ('outline traced'). Two choices in each of four categories yields four binary sets, $2 \times 2 \times 2 \times 2$, or sixteen different 'characters' possible. If, instead of reading 'whole' or 'mutilated' hand as a binary variable, we read it as a numerical value 1 to 5, this yields $2 \times 2 \times 2 \times 5$, or 40 basic characters. English, for instance, contains only 26 such characters.''

Aleck glanced around for a moment, thinking that someone was looking at him. No one seemed to be. Most of the crowd was as ignorant of his presence as it was of the background program. With a shrug he turned his attention back to it.

''Extending the coding key beyond the handprints to other classes of Upper Paleolithic symbols,'' the narrator said quietly, ''the result is a consistent co-occurrence between certain colors and symbols such as claviforms and tectiforms—even between particular colors and particular 'naturalistic' images. Bulls portrayed in black and the cows in red, in depictions of aurochs or wild cattle at Lascaux, for instance.

''This color sequence links as well to other discernible patterns. We find specific animal behaviors depicted, such as seasonal migrations, rutting, spawning, and breeding. Also prominent are 'male' and 'female' symbolic orders, lunar calendric tallies, and various entoptic marks associated with hallucinogenic ritual. Put it all together and the result is a system capable of awesome informational complexity.

''If religion is, at some level, a technology for coping with the human condition, then in the religion of the caves the Upper Paleolithic peoples possessed an impressive technology indeed: a common ideology, and a universal symbolic grammar for expressing that ideology. Just as the aboriginal rock art of Australia reflects only a tiny percentage of the informational complexity of the predominantly oral tradition of the songlines, the cave art of the Eurasian landmass likely expresses only a very tiny fraction of a much vaster oral (probably sung) tradition—''

Someone tapped Aleck on the shoulder. Turning, he saw his uncle, whom he recognized immediately, though he hadn't seen the man in years.

''Uncle Bruce!'' Aleck said, getting up from his chair to give the older man a handshake and a hug. His uncle's head was a little balder (if that were possible), his beard was definitely greyer, and his bulk had grown even more fleshy. Since beard color and baldness and bulk could always be fixed, Aleck wondered why his uncle hadn't gone in for body-mod the way his own parents had. Aleck shrugged inwardly. Maybe Uncle Bruce was into that ''natural aging'' thing that was getting so big with people of his parents' generation.

''Aleck!'' his uncle boomed. ''Only people as young as you

are can get away with being so scrawny—without looking emaciated."

"Thanks, Unc," Aleck said, "I think."

His uncle moved slightly aside, gesturing to a very tall, very pale, slightly stooped man dressed in stark but fashionable clothes.

"Hey," Uncle Bruce said, "let me introduce you to your elder concentration-camp twin, here. This is Lev Korchnoi."

Shaking the hand of the tall, blond, almost albinoid Korchnoi, Aleck kept thinking that he knew this man's name, even his face, from somewhere. Maybe the guy had been a six-minute starface someplace in the popular culture. If it had been during the last few years, though, Aleck might as well have been living on another planet. School and work and life in general had been keeping him far busier than they had any right to.

Bruce and Lev pulled up chairs and sat down at his table. Another filler of "classic comic" had come on. A Peruvian former newspaper editor who had gone on the circuit as the Daily Llama was doing a Buddhist monk shtick built around arcane puns. He was performing in front of an oddly costumed convention audience of some sort.

"What do you call it when a bodhisattva uses paranormal powers aboard an airplane?" the Daily Llama asked. Someone, in the studio audience of that long ago day when the holo was recorded, shouted out, "Siddhis In Flight!" The Daily Llama smiled, folded his hands, and bowed his head. Aleck didn't get it.

"So," he said, ignoring the holo and turning to Uncle Bruce and Korchnoi, "what brings you Earthside—and to Cincinnati, of all places?"

His uncle cast a quick, almost furtive glance at Korchnoi before answering.

"Have you heard anything about people who've been murdered while linked into the infosphere?" Uncle Bruce asked, almost reluctantly. "The ones the media are calling the Topo Voyeur killings?"

"Maybe something," Aleck said, truthfully. "I don't keep up with much news—no time—but I do keep myself minimally informed if it's computing-related. It's my major field, after all."

"Yes," his uncle said. "I remember your father saying as much."

"We have a friend up in the habitat," Lev Korchnoi put in,

"who is something of a professional infosphere paranoid. Lakshmi has been using her systems up there to monitor the big bursts of information that coincide with the deaths of those people who were infosphere-linked."

Aleck listened attentively, though he had no idea what all this had to do with their being in Cincinnati.

"The problem is," his uncle said, "each fatal infoburst and the signals involved with the voyeur's scene-capture are all packeted data. They are rerouted what amounts to a countably infinite number of times—combinations ranging from googolplex to Skewes's number."

"Then you can never track who's doing it," Aleck remarked. That was obvious enough to anyone with even a cursory background in machine intelligence.

"Yes—and no," his uncle continued. "For any given infoburst event, no. Over a significant number of events, though, patterns begin to emerge. Lakshmi's been doing some heavy-lifting mathematics—prime factoring, sieving, fast Fouriers, decompositing, hidden and public key searches, God only knows what all. Massive number crunching."

"Any luck?" Aleck asked. He knew enough about this stuff to be at least mildly interested.

"She *has* managed to narrow the burst-origins down to ten big infosphere presences," Korchnoi said. "The data constructs of ten major corporate headquarters, corresponding to ten cities."

"And Cincinnati is one?" Aleck asked, a bit incredulous.

"Correct," said Korchnoi. "You can probably guess the corporation."

"A big user?" Aleck asked rhetorically. "Has to be Retcorp & Lambeg."

"Bingo," his uncle said with a nod. "We went to visit the pyramid by the river today, trying to get some access to their records."

"No soap?" Aleck suggested.

His uncle smiled, catching the product reference.

"You might put it that way," he said. "They're very tight-fisted with their corporate data."

"Our HOME liaison, Atsuko Cortland, got us Corporate Presidium clearance to take a look around," Korchnoi added, "but it didn't matter. It will take ISIS or Interpol at least to pry R & L's fists open."

"In the meantime," Uncle Bruce continued, "we're also

scheduled to visit other corporate headquarters in other cities. We're setting up performance dates for Lev's people. I'm their manager, of sorts—''

Their conversation was interrupted by Sam, Janika, Hari, and Marco, ''Onoma Verité,'' taking the stage and beginning to play. Aleck had wanted to tell his uncle that he worked for R & L himself, if Bruce didn't already know. He wondered what ''performance dates for Lev's people'' might be about, too. That would have to wait, though. It was all Aleck could do, over the music, to shout back in answer to Lev's question about Onoma Verité being acquaintances of his that, Right, the band members were his friends.

Given the decibels they were cranking out, Aleck had no choice but to sit back and listen to the band—especially when he realized that many of the images accompanying the show had been recorded during that night down in Hugh Manatee's Dreamland. Was that how Sam had gotten this gig so fast? Had he already begun shopping around what they'd recorded that night— as a demo?

> *Stars like perfect snow beyond the barbed wire*
> *Thick and clear, cold, aloof, and distant*
> *Barbed wire crisscrossing the sky*
> *Endlessly, everywhere*
> *Concertina wire orbits ringing the planet round*
> *Spy satellite spiders weaving webs over everything*
> *Only their metal bodies visible*
> *High and fast against the night*
> *Trailing threads too thin too high to see*
> *Cocooning the world all the same.*
>
> *Ignore it! Ignore it! Ignore it!*
> *Drop the lead shutters, bring up the holo screens!*
> *Sell your soul! Let the good times roll—*

''The lyrics are a bit erratic,'' Korchnoi said over Sam and Janika's strangely hard-driving duet, ''but it's got a deep groove. And this compiled stock footage or whatever it is, is great!''

Aleck nodded, but wished Hugh Manatee, floating in his tank beneath the Partons, might somehow get credit for at least his part of this.

Almost as if to prove their lyrics (in response to Korchnoi's critique) could be stronger, Onoma Verité began downshifting in perfect seque into a monkishly spare, tonal piece. Sam called out the lyrics of ''Gingko'' in a sort of chant halfway between singing and spoken word poetry.

> *Your leaves fall*
> *two hundred twenty million years ago*
> *fans of delicate maidens*
> *pressed between pages of coal*
>
> *Beneath your boughs strut the lucky dragons*
> *but no boneshadows record*
> *that color of crushed dreams in their eyes*
> *when their fortunes change*
>
> *You grow weary, dwindle toward sleep*
> *until the awakening priests come to plant you*
> *in the Pure Land of their temple gardens*
> *that those who may not eat meat may eat of you*
>
> *Men of science snatch you from the temple precincts*
> *a new geisha to join their harems*
> *Coelacanth and nautilus and platypus and you*
> *the most hopeful fossils are those still living*
>
> *Out of love we plant you beside our stone roads*
> *to inhale our burning smoke, to exhale your sweet air*
> *You are patient, so patient you do not worry*
> *who will love you after we are gone.*

Images of trees and leaves and dinosaurs, monks and scientists, fossil creatures and modern parks stood interspersed among mad dream-energetic scenes lifted from Hugh Manatee. Korchnoi and Uncle Bruce stared at each other in pleased surprise and clapped enthusiastically when the song ended. They listened carefully when ''Song of the USD'' surged up with its kaleidoscope of wild amusement park images (from Hugh again) and its twisted, synth-calliope cover version of a positively ancient Apolkaleptics tune.

> *Do they ever read Lévi-Strauss?*
> *Do they ever think Mickey Mouse*

was a Nazi
in Disneyland?

Do they really love phallic porn?
There must be another reason
for the Matterhorn
in Disneyland.

Are those fireflies on wires?
Are those robots chasing desires
in Disneyland?

No you needn't worry—
it's not obscene—
it's just the Pirates of the Caribbean
in Disneyland.

Everybody there eats their eats
Everybody there drinks their drinks
We have a good time and nobody thinks
in Disneyland.

And so it went, song after song, piece after piece, until at last the band finished with a song called "Autoscope."

That piece featured their only big prop—a large, spinning, electrostatically bound mercury-metal mirror, "tuned" somehow to make music of the light bouncing off it. Aleck thought it looked like just the sort of physics gizmo Hari would dream up.

This is a mirror for misinterpretation.
It does not communicate
as still water with the sky
communicates.

As silver funnel then, stirred by stir of silver
   spoon?
As mirror vortex in draining water?
As whirlpool? Waterspout?

But no. This is more than just the echo of
   light in spinning water.
It's not the mind you read by this, but the

mind I can't; not the hurricane radar
picture live via satellite in a distant TV
room,
but the candle the picture improbably makes
flicker there—
that matters.

Even a mirror shattered by spinning too fast
can still give back
a crazed reflection. Insanity's not a problem—
it's a solution.

The spinning liquid mirror, in its plane-bound amorphousness, reflected strangely the Hugh-dreams and other film-stock imagery throughout the first verse. As the second began, the electrostatic field controls changed and the mirror was transformed into a spinning vortex, a liquid metal fall, wrapping around to meet itself in a spinning funnel of shining mercury. During the third verse, pin spots played over the mercurial vortex until, just before the last verse, the electrostatic field changed again and the vortex broadened out into an electron-cloud storm of orbiting mercury globules. The music and the spin-field abruptly cut off together. The globules hung in the air a moment, then crashed earthward.

Their metal splash had barely sounded in the air before Planet Noir was flooded with a torrent of applause, whistling, and cheering from a very appreciative audience. The members of Onoma Verité, looking somewhat bewildered and bedazzled by what they had wrought, hesitantly—then quickly with more confidence—took their bows.

Despite himself, even Aleck was impressed. During this performance the band members, after all their long rehearsal putzing about, had finally come together into something that was far superior to anything any of them had ever done alone. Slowly Aleck realized that he had been present at the birth of something that might yet prove to have real greatness in it.

Uncle Bruce and Lev were eager to meet the members of the band, so Aleck volunteered to introduce them. After getting them lost once in the warren of backstage rooms, he made his way through that maze again with the other two men. At last the buzz of a clamoring mob—mostly instant fans, with a few friends mixed in—led them in the right direction.

As the three men moved toward where the band members were giving face-time to their public, Aleck was surprised by the way the buzz changed and the crowd parted around him and Bruce and Lev. Aleck didn't know exactly what was going on, but he happily took advantage of it.

"Great show," he said, shaking hands with Sam. "So was that 'Hugh Manatee in Tiffany Chain's *Soft Slavery*'?"

"Not yet," Sam said, almost—was this possible?—shyly. "Just the 'Living Fossils' section of the larger work."

Aleck noticed that Sam was looking rather nervously past him, to where Bruce and Lev were standing.

"Oh, I forgot myself," Aleck said politely. "Let me introduce two guests visiting from the 'borbs—my uncle Bruce and his friend Lev Korchnoi."

The crowd buzz changed again, inexplicably but not quite imperceptibly. Lev and Bruce shook hands with the band members all around, congratulating them on their performances. Lev Korchnoi then reached into his pocket and handed each of them one of those fancy, holographically compressed business datacards.

"We're looking at opening acts for our tour," Lev said. "Let's keep in touch."

The members of Onoma Verité assured him they would. Bruce and Lev edged away to depart. Turning to walk away with them, Aleck saw Sam flash him a smile and a discreet thumbs-up sign. Aleck returned his smile, then followed Lev and Bruce back through a crowd that seemed oddly quiet, as if stunned.

Outside, Aleck shook hands one last time with his uncle and his uncle's friend.

"It's been a very rewarding evening, Aleck," Lev said. "A pleasure meeting you."

"We may be swinging through again in the near future," Bruce said. "If we do, we'll be sure to look you up—and your friends, too."

Aleck watched them walk away down Rail Plaza. He waved goodbye, then turned back inside. Maybe he could be of some help to the band in striking their fairly minimal set and breaking down their performance gear.

The fans had mostly dispersed by the time Aleck got back to where he and his guests had congratulated Onoma Verité just minutes before. Aleck found the band in Planet Noir's "green room" (actually several different shades of ocher). Sam, Janika,

Hari, and Marco were jumping about, like a bunch of drunken cowboys happily bent on shooting out the stars to make a darker night.

"Hey, Aleck—!" Hari said, spotting him. The other band members all rushed over.

"Hi. Just thought I'd see if I could be of any help—"

Sam laughed and put his arm around Aleck's shoulders.

"Man, you don't know how much help you've already been!" Sam said. "Thanks—thanks for the intro to Korchnoi."

"Sure," Aleck said with a shrug. "No big deal."

"No big deal?" Marco said, staring so hard at Aleck it made him uncomfortable. "Hey—do you even know who Lev Korchnoi *is*?"

"A friend of my uncle's," Aleck said, warily. "Why? Who 'is' he?"

"Aleck, you idiot," Janika said with a smile, "Lev Korchnoi is the brains behind Möbius Caducéus. Maybe you've heard of them? Biggest selling performance work for the last month straight? With their own label and satellite channels?"

"Oh," Aleck said. Maybe Sam was right. Maybe he *should* get out more often.

"C ALLING YOUR MOTHER'S PLACE A 'HOUSE,' " MARISSA said as she and Roger walked up the pathway toward Atsuko's residence, "is like calling a seaplane a boat."

Roger laughed as their footsteps crunched up the walk.

" 'Kinetic archisculpture' is what the designer called it," he said, gazing up at the white building whose wings were, well, *wings*, moving and shifting gently in response to light angles and the breezes. "It's supposed to be the most environmentally responsive housing form possible, short of growing a home biotechnically, or using real-time nano feedback."

"Calatrava meets Calder," Marissa remarked, pausing to look at it more carefully, "by way of computer."

"You should see the site rose for it," Roger said with a laugh. "One of the most complex I've ever seen. Most homes in the 'borbs don't even bother with careful window placement or solar gain issues, much less a full description of house and location aesthetics and energetics."

The doors, having scanned them, irised open and they entered. Atsuko, who was in the central sitting room, offhandedly waved them into the open airy space. She appeared to be in the midst of a holophone interview with a young blond woman in a pink suit—calling from Earth, judging by the slight transmission lag.

"—not what we're about here," Atsuko explained patiently. "If you've read D.B. Albert's work, then you know that one of the consequences of his theory was that human society as he knew it—urbanized, technologized living—was not compatible with the further development of what he called 'spontaneous human consciousness.' "

The holographic interviewer leaned forward.

"How does that tie into types of societies?" she pressed.

"Because," Atsuko explained, "though social action is *possible* for such a consciousness, the traditional notion of utopia as a fixed, ideal society is *impossible* in the presence of this kind of consciousness. Consciousness is really all about dealing with contingency, and both contingency and consciousness conspire against a fixed and static utopia."

"And the orbital habitat is not that?" asked the pink suit.

"Not at all. What we have always been about here in this habitat is the creation of something that is not fixed. What we're after is a sustainable, continually changing pursuit of the ideal. An ongoing approximation that is a process as consciousness itself is a process. That's what we mean when we say 'If it's not fixed, you can't break it.' "

Roger and Marissa took their places on a big morph sofa discreetly out of range of the holocamera. In the time it took them to sit down, Atsuko and her holographic interlocutor had moved on to other topics.

The interviewer flicked back a strand of hair made of blond light.

"But how does that explain Albert's ranting against media and hypermedia—both mass and targeted?" asked the interviewer.

Atsuko shifted forward slightly, causing her holofied image to trace and waver for a moment before it settled down.

"Again, that's consistent with his view of consciousness," Atsuko explained. "That's why Albert was so opposed to not only scientific materialism, but also to what he called 'social-ontology.' Remember, his ideas arose partly in response to the linguistic totalism coming out of Geertz's work. He also rebelled against the extension of cultural materialism elaborated by Jameson and others."

"Could you explain their theories for our audience?" asked the pink-suited interviewer.

"Certainly. The argument of the social theorists was that consciousness is essentially all words and concepts. Words and concepts are all social. The consciousness of any individual, therefore, is inherently and absolutely a social construct, a mere nexus or space where social forces play themselves out."

"And Albert objected to that?" asked the interviewer.

"Strongly," Atsuko said with a nod. "He traced those ideas back to Skinnerian behaviorism, ultimately. The society we've tried to create in HOME 1 is in some ways the opposite of the behaviorist society Skinner hypothesized in *Walden Two*."

"But why should we be afraid of an outdated twentieth-century concept like behaviorism?" asked the pink-and-blond interviewer.

"Because the upshot of crypto-behaviorist ideas," Atsuko explained patiently, "at least in academic circles, was a generalized denial of the actuality of individual consciousness. Albert countered with an elucidation of 'portal experiences.' He emphasized the importance of mystical and spiritual experience, the necessity of nonphysical events which can't, at the moment of experiencing them, be put into words. That was all part of his attack on social-ontology. He was attempting to restore a proper valuation to the idea of individual consciousness, which he felt had become endangered to the point of extinction."

"And the media's role—?" the blond-and-pink interviewer persisted.

"Albert criticized media," Atsuko replied, "because he felt they had become a powerful force for the new extinguishing of individual consciousness."

"What do you mean?" the interviewer asked, apparently trying to sound sly but coming off instead only as suspicious.

"He believed they had become global town criers," Atsuko continued, "sending the same message at the same time to millions and even billions of viewers and auditors. According to Albert, the media apparatus was priming the fear machinery that drives societies back from individuality to mass 'voices in the head.' He felt mass communication pushes us away from conscious, written, defined Law—and toward an unconscious, oral, ill-defined Morality. He called that process 'recameralization.' "

The interviewer quickly brought the session to a close, thanked Atsuko, and disappeared. Atsuko sighed and turned to her guests.

Roger thought, with a pang, that his mother looked older than when he'd last seen her—greyer, more tired, more worn under the eyes.

"Do you think she got what I was getting at?" Atsuko asked.

"As much as she wanted to," Roger said, shrugging. "If she was a 'she' at all. Those machine-generated interviewers are getting pretty lifelike. A good enough expert system and we probably couldn't tell."

"One can only hope," Atsuko said, looking slightly wistful, "that they won't just take the most sensational or confusing sound bite, use that, and dump the rest."

"She—or it—sure closed things down fast when she finally got that answer about Albert's critique of the media," Marissa said. "Like she didn't really want to know what she thought she wanted to know, after all."

"Yes," Atsuko replied. "Like Oedipus's detective work. But come along—we can discuss all this over lunch."

Atsuko stood up in her flowing pantdress of black and silver, a perfectly hologenic match to her grey-white streaked black hair and her pale coloring. Marissa and Roger followed her into the living room, feeling a cool breeze blowing in from the garden, fragrant with green and floral scents. They sat down to salads, crisp and green and laden with myriad vegetables and tofu and mushrooms, with glasses of water and wine. Clasping hands in a circle, they meditated in silent blessing over the food, then began to eat.

"The more they know about what Albert thought," Atsuko said, enjoying a savory new strain of shiitake, "the less the media people like thinking about it."

"I really don't know a whole lot about his ideas," Marissa said, sipping at her wine. "What really *was* his gripe with media, other than the fact that it tells everybody pretty much the same thing at the same time?"

Atsuko sipped at her own wine, thinking.

"He felt that the more infodense media became," she said, "the more it made consensus reality into an abstracted virtual reality. For Albert, media that strongly mimicked the physical world leveled the distinction between public and private. It filled up with public messages the private space of individual consciousness. To the extent that media 'virtualized' consensus reality on a broad scale, Albert felt it also recameralized the individual mind. That process deeply eroded the individual nature of consciousness, or so he claimed. He may well have been right.''

Marissa paused in cutting up her salad.

"But would he agree someone can be *too* individualistic?" she asked. Atsuko fell inexplicably quiet.

"I read a fair amount of his work when I was in school," Roger said, his fork poised over his plate. "He felt we shouldn't value individual freedom so far above social responsibility that we become anarchic solipsists. That wasn't his primary concern, though. He was more worried about the threat of group 'unconsciousness' to individual consciousness, than vice versa."

Atsuko glanced toward each of her companions in turn.

"A lot of people up here in the habitat have found his ideas liberating," she said. "Admittedly, we are much more technologized than any pure Albertian would care to be. We haven't carried those ideas—particularly their 'appropriate technology' aspects—as far as some groups on Earth have, like the psi-Xtians."

"Really?" Marissa asked. She had long felt that what was going on in the habitats was as cutting edge as one could get.

"They adhere pretty devoutly to Albert's contention," Atsuko explained, "that the mind is a co-evolutionary project between physical and nonphysical elements. A cooperation between biological, psychological, and spiritual dimensions. They spend a lot more time looking for portal experiences than we do, for instance."

Marissa chewed a mushroom thoughtfully.

" 'Portal experiences'?" she asked.

Atsuko sipped and nodded.

"Self-consuming events which point to the existence of realities beyond what we experience via the ordinary senses," Atsuko said. "Experiences that create upon the mind the impression of a transcendant realm—one in which the individual directly experiences realities outside the ordinary physical world of space-time."

"Like drug states?" Marissa asked. "Or religious ecstasies?"

"Both," Atsuko said, pausing to swallow what she'd been chewing. "There are lots of ways to have such experiences. Rituals, breathing exercises, fasting, drugs, many more. Such experiences are 'portals' in the sense that they are gateways. They stand between the dimensions of the physical world with which we are familiar, and other dimensions or nonphysical realms with which we are much less familiar.''

Marissa sipped her wine. A thought, highly speculative, occurred to her.

''What happened to Seiji's brother,'' Marissa said, ''the Light and everything around it—was that a 'portal experience'?''

Atsuko exchanged a glance with her son, an expression of pleased surprise on her face, then turned her attention back to Marissa.

''I hadn't really thought of it that way, myself,'' Atsuko said, ''but you're not the first person I've heard that idea from. I was talking to one of our pilots the other day. Diana Gartner. She has a lot of friends among the psiXtians. They seem to believe that Jiro Yamaguchi's apotheosis was a sort of ultimate portal experience—a complete translocation.''

''In what sense?'' Marissa asked, before taking another sip of wine.

''According to them, Jiro not only stood in the gate, as many mystics have,'' Atsuko said. ''He walked through. It's a very important omen for their faith community. I don't know *how* many of them my office has communicated with lately.''

Marissa looked over at Roger, who had already finished his salad and wine and was sitting back from the table with his hands clasped contentedly behind his head.

''See?'' Marissa said. ''I told you Jiro and the Light must be having more of an effect than we've been seeing.''

''No doubt,'' Roger said, fighting off a postprandial lassitude. ''No doubt.''

Atsuko, who had been listening to their exchange, politely returned her gaze to her salad.

''My policy is to refer the psiXtians and their questions to Lakshmi and Seiji and Jhana,'' she said. ''After all, they were the only ones who were right there. They were the last ones to communicate with Jiro Yamaguchi, as far as I know.''

''How are Jhana and Seiji?'' Roger asked. ''Did they finish moving to HOME 2, like they'd planned?''

''As far as I know,'' Atsuko said. ''I haven't heard from them in a while. I've been hearing a lot from Lakshmi, though.''

''What about?'' Marissa asked, curious.

''It seems not everyone has been as pleased by the Light as you and I might be,'' Atsuko said. ''In my liaison status, I've been getting a number of queries from a Vasili Landau at Interpol. It seems someone or something has been killing people in waves throughout the infosphere. Lakshmi has confirmed it."

Roger leaned forward, resting his arms on the table.

"But why should that concern Lakshmi," he asked, "or this habitat?"

"For a couple of reasons," Atsuko said, staring into the table. "The technology the killer, or killers, is using are those RATs that Jiro Yamaguchi also made use of—"

"But, if I remember correctly," Marissa said, finishing the last of her salad, "weren't those things developed by some guy who got killed in the Sedona disaster years ago?"

"True," Atsuko said, "but there are other issues. Most of those who were killed were looking into Tetragrammaton data. Or ParaLogics and Crystal Memory Dynamics. Or investigating what happened to Jiro Yamaguchi and the Light. We've lost a couple of people in the habitats on this already—a disproportionate number in comparison to Earth, considering how few we still are in number." She paused, frowning. "Horrible, brutal deaths, these waves of infosphere-linked murders. You don't want to know what the victims look like. And these waves of murders, as far as we can tell, all only started *after* Jiro disappeared."

The three of them sat in silence for a while. Atsuko, who had been doing most of the talking, got caught up on finishing her salad and wine.

"Are you saying," Marissa asked at last, "that all of us who were involved in Jiro's disappearance into the Light are suspects?"

"Apparently," Atsuko said with a nod. "Along with Jiro himself, according to Mr. Landau. Fortunately, Lakshmi's already way ahead of me on this, as usual. She's got Lev and Aleister poking around in it, on Earth. I gather that Interpol is going to be sending up a pair of investigators too."

"Quite a brouhaha," Roger said quietly, his hands in his lap. "Any ideas as to what's motivating these killings?"

Atsuko looked carefully at her son.

"Landau's message has references to all kinds of things," Atsuko said. "Even a passage on 'the killer's individual consciousness breaking down under the impact of mass-mediated reality while at the same time seeking authentication from that reality.' That would have done old D.B. Albert himself proud. Even Lakshmi has a theory, but it's rather wild."

"What's her take on it?" Roger asked, curious.

"Jealousy," Atsuko said with a bemused smile. "She thinks that whoever or whatever is doing this is jealous of what Jiro was able to accomplish—and is trying to duplicate it."

"By killing people?" Marissa asked, horrified.

"Maybe the killing is just to cover up what's really going on," Roger suggested.

"Insufficient data," Atsuko said with a shrug, standing to clear the table. "If it's not one thing, it's three. Diana says the churchstates too, particularly the Christian and Muslim ones, are getting very touchy lately."

"Why's that?" Roger asked, pushing his chair back from the table.

"New visions, new messages from angels and prophets and saints," Atsuko said as she picked up her plate and glass. "Lakshmi's started sending me copies of these odd messages. She keeps finding them, embedded in the code of some pirate virtual mail system. Your names have come up there, too. What a mess."

Marissa and Roger rose from the table too and following Atsuko, carried their dishes into the kitchen and began to sound-wash them.

"Might we see that message?" Marissa asked as they worked.

Atsuko reached for the kitchen PDA.

"Sure," she said with a shrug. "For all the good it'll do you. It's just a list. Here."

Atsuko called up into display the material she'd received from Lakshmi:

Initial list (fragmentary), partition-prime decrypted from code of underground virtual mail system SubTerPost. Initial source unknown:

Brandi Easter, Mei-Ling Magnus, Roger Cortland, Diana Gartner, Robert Sullivan, Marissa Correa, Immanuel Shaw, Paul Larkin, Atsuko Cortland, Seiji Yamaguchi, Jhana Meniskos, Lakshmi Ngubo, Jacinta Larkin . . .

"See what I mean?" Atsuko said. "Just names. Some are people I've never heard of. And the list keeps growing. It probably means nothing, but there you have it."

"I hope it's not a hit list for this infosphere killer you mentioned," Roger said with a wry smile.

"Oh, it's probably nothing of the sort," Atsuko assured them. "It is puzzling, though."

Roger and Marissa admitted it was indeed. Atsuko turned the display off, as if not wanting to think of it further. When they were finished cleaning up, they took their tea and coffee out onto Atsuko's small moon-pebbled patio.

"This is a new patio table, isn't it?" Marissa asked, examining the tabletop.

"Actually, no," Atsuko said. "I just felt like putting a new inlay into its surface. It's called a Greek—"

"—key. Or a standard meander," Marissa said with a nod, a glance passing between her and Roger. "I know. I've been studying spiral waves and mazes. You know, there's a latent optical image in the Greek key."

"Really?" Atsuko asked. "I've never heard of that. Where?"

"Here," Marissa said, trying to trace it with her finger. "See the slanted rectangle? Its boundary is incomplete—implied. The rectangle is tipped sideways, like this, in the rectilinear wave of the Greek key."

"I don't see it," Atsuko said, staring at it.

"It takes a while," Marissa assured her. "You have to learn how to see it with crossed eyes, sort of. Once you do, you'll see that, in a long border of Greek keys, the latent rectangles aren't independent of each other. They're linked in a sort of zigzag latent wave that runs 'under' or 'within' the blatant, obvious waves of the Greek key. Only the latent wave takes a different, more dynamic shape. Like linked stylized lightning bolts, or cardiogram pulses. The two waves are inseparable, though. One is possible only in relation to the other."

"I still don't see it," Atsuko said, crossing her eyes until her head ached. "I just put the shape into the tabletop because I liked the way it looked!"

"That's reason enough," Marissa said with a smile.

"Wait . . ." Roger began. "I'm getting a flicker of the latent rectangle in the Greek key. I don't see the wave within the wave yet, though."

"You will," Marissa said. "You just have to become accustomed to a new way of seeing it."

Atsuko rubbed her eyes and splitting head.

"I don't know if I want to," she said, "if it's going to be this painful."

Roger glanced up at the wraparound worldscape of the habitat's central sphere, then down at the table once again.

"New ways of seeing are always painful to learn," he said.

L IVING AMONG THE PSIXTIANS HAD GIVEN DUNDAS A NEW AP-
preciation for the supposed virtues of solitude. After the di-
agnosis of his shingles became known, he'd had to deal endlessly
with the well-meaning solicitude of his fellow initiates—and the
innumerable stories from others, usually older women, sympa-
thetically sharing tales of their trials and tribulations while afflicted with the same scourge.

At least his condition had freed him for a week from most of
the burdens of his initiation into the psiXtian ranks. He was allowed to indulge his newfound interest in solitude undisturbed.
Patting down his pockets, to make sure the infodisk on Gartner
was there, he started off on his quest for a little privacy.

Walking to the surface by the shortest route he knew, Dundas
passed through the daily life of the psiXtian commune. In the
nearest cafeteria, a small group was reciting "The High Hard
Way: A Mountain Prayer."

Shaper beyond all shapes who dwells
in every shape:
With the mellowing geometries
of your proud humble mountains
Shape me.

Light beyond all lights who dwells
in every light:
With the starsplashed night,
with the warm star of day,
Light my way.

Sound beyond all sounds who dwells
in every sound:
With the air ocean whisper
of the high pine wind,
Sound in me.

Teacher beyond all teachers who dwells
in all that teaches:
Teach me the lessons of forever

to be understood from a single day,
Teach me your high, hard way.

On first hearing, it didn't really sound that heretical, Dundas thought. He had heard, though, that it had once been a major text of the now largely defunct Myrrhisticinean sect. Certainly it must be heresy, given the nature of these supplicants here and the likely origin of their prayer.

The God he himself knew and worshipped was no unnamed spirit manifested predominantly in the sights and sounds of nature. Obviously. His God spoke to men directly, through the Word of the Book He had authored.

Dundas passed on through the light-pooled underground passageways. Near a food-preparation area, he slowed, seeing a plainly clad group of young men and women slicing fruit and vegetables in the dappled light coming from the big, fruit-tree covered hole above them. The light came in from that same gap the tree itself had followed. The shifting light that flowed down through its leaves seemed pleasant enough to work by, Dundas had to admit.

"Both the physicist Bohm and the mystic Sri Aurobindo would agree on the universality of consciousness," a young man with tightly ringleted dark hair said. "They both emphasize the wholeness and interconnectedness of the universe."

"True," said a redheaded woman, "but only Aurobindo says, 'If any single point of the universe were totally unconscious, the whole universe would have to be totally unconscious.'"

A couple of the others looked up from their straightforward work in the dappled light.

"Yes," a turbaned black woman said, "but would both of them also hold the opposite?"

"The opposite?" asked the dark-haired youth.

"Would they agree that, if any single point of the universe becomes totally enlightened, then in that same instant the whole universe becomes totally enlightened?"

Hearing the young people begin to blather excitedly about "As above, so below," "Bell's theorem," "Matter teaches space how to bend, space teaches matter how to move," "the ineffable refuses to limit itself to any final form or expression"—hearing it all, Dundas quickened his stride.

All that stuff was mumbo-jumbo. He had an uneasy mistrust of "visions of other worlds and dimensions," "voices," and all supposed "feelings of numinosity and union with nature." As far as he was concerned, most "mystical experiences" were only a short step up the ladder from drugs and drunkenness. From there it was an even shorter step to clairvoyance and astral projection, and then inevitably to magic and witchcraft.

What was "real" among such mystical experiences was probably demonically inspired, he felt, at least in most cases. The situations in which the Lord used such a route were rare. The Bible was proof enough of that.

As he walked through the subterranean labyrinth of the Sunderground, Dundas suspected that those people back home, the heretics of "the Book it will crumble and the Steeple will fall but the Light will be shining at the end of it all" crowd, were more than a little influenced by such mystical claptrap. The anarchy of everybody having his or her own authoritative visions had to be evil, if only because it left no room for the wisdom of the Bible or the preacher—even denied that wisdom, in the most extreme cases.

The air grew warmer as he came closer to the surface. Or maybe it was only that he was passing a classroom, he thought sourly. The hot air-filled "social analysis" going on there made him grit his teeth and caused his shingles—vibro-zapped as they already were—to flare in pain.

"—tried to minimize technological unemployment by capturing the machines for the workers," a student giving a report said. "As the emphasis shifted from a military-industrial world-view to an informational one built around media and medicine, however, merely capturing the machines or destroying them wasn't enough. Media and medicine internalized the social control mechanism. Virtual reality systems, the infosphere, and distributed machine intelligences in smart homes and offices can be interpreted paradoxically as 'ever more intelligent habitations for ever less intelligent inhabitants,' or, more bluntly, 'smart environments for stupid people.' Such a dumbing-down fostered dependency on human productions, further weakening participation in the natural world. The symbolic nature of participation mystique is reduced to joysticks, graphics, and interactive media.

"Any strong critique of these trends necessarily has to call for reconnection to the natural world, deautomatization, decameralization, delateralization, disurbanization. As Albert remarks, 'The surveillance and drug-testing machines can be smashed, all of them. As long as they remain they will be pressed into service by the social psychoid process. The machines can be smashed, the talk shows can go unwatched, the morality lectures and sermons can go unattended, all without the loss of a single human life'—''

Recognizing the heretical claptrap of Philosophical Luddism when he heard it, Dundas hurried past, striding up a ramp of compacted soil and finally into the aboveground world. He was pleasantly surprised to find the heat less than stifling. A cold front bearing unseasonably humane weather must be passing through.

Looking around as he walked, Dundas was once again struck by how *unlike* a city Sunderground appeared to be from the surface. At first glance it seemed that he walked through orchards and groves and gardens and nothing else, men and women manuring and pruning and planting, working on the land. ''Giving back to Big Mama'' was the Gaia-worshipping phrase he'd heard them use for such technopeasant field work. Dundas shook his head. The psiXtian settlement was like an iceberg, with most of its citified functions invisible, beneath the surface.

In his travels, Dundas had often remarked on the fact that the bigger the city, the more it could be anywhere, the more detached it already was from where it was, the more it was always already someplace else other than the country or countryside of which it was supposedly a part. That was distinctly *not* true of Sunderground.

He walked on in the warm morning sun, past the parking and maintenance area filled with electric cars and trucks and tractors and backhoes. Beyond that stood an old cemetery in a grove of valley oaks, apparently left over from the days before the psiXtians took possession of the land. Like the electric vehicles in the lot, most of the headstones in the graveyard looked dusty and neglected. It occurred to him that headstones, like cars, probably always looked best in the showroom. He couldn't think of too many people interested in taking Death for a test drive, however.

Even after passing through the graveyard, solitude was not yet his. Apparently others among the psiXtians had noted how fine a day it was. A small group sat having a picnic in the shade of some olive trees. One of their number, a blond-haired, bespectacled stick of a man, was cadencing a piece of poetry about paper nautiluses or something equally obscure:

*pulp-muscled mollusk, eyes, mouth, tentacle-arms fluttering
awkwardly at sea
you move encased in your protective prison of whispery spiral
shell*

*each day another air chamber sealed off behind, another
crank of the spiral
the shell of chambered days growing in emptiness, impossible
to shed*

*carrying the calcareous past makes for awkward motion, a
jerky ratcheting
you move forward by moving backward, the only way to stay
afloat
when all your brethren are supposed extinct*

*—though not so the large many-chambered ammonites who,
their shells spiraling toward infinity, grew fully conscious of
sorrow, pure-mind metaphysicians adrift in meditation upon
the ancient seas*

*their final achievement not extinction but hyperconsciousness,
winking them out of our saltwatery universe, to elsewhere and
elsewhen*

*what would make them do such a thing?
unless it be the solace they seek
for the grief of living on and on
while others still die.*

The other picnickers clapped politely. One mentioned the idea
that a diary or a book is also a sort of paper nautilus. Then
another remarked that a spiral resembles phase state trajectories
converging to an attractor. That soon degenerated into a discussion of spiral versus chiral.

Dundas left the poets and poetasters to their interpretation-
spinning. He passed other groups among the trees, including one
engaged in some sort of holovision-facilitated ''distance learning'' lecture on the dangers of mechanized mentation.

''—Thall hypotheses,'' said a distant lecturer. ''Logical sequential calculations pushed to the speed of light move beyond
the logical and the sequential. Simultaneity emerges from se-

quence, the mythic arises from the historic, the unpremised from the logical. Holism thus becomes the dominant form of thought, with day-to-day control exerted by micro-management elites. As a result, we see that computing was, from the very beginning, inevitably destined to destroy democracy and freedom—''

Shaking his head, Dundas moved on. Sometimes living among the psiXtians was like being surrounded by a bunch of demented philosopher-kings. Instead of building a castle in the air and moving in, though, the lunatics here had dug their asylum underground.

Dundas kept walking until he was out among weedy scrub. He looked for landmarks by which to find again the small transceiver satlink he'd buried under a cairn of stones—along with his service-issue flechette machine pistol and ceramic knife. When at last he found the cairn, he set about removing the stones until he found the satlink unit. Although little bigger than a traditional paperback book, it was a gateway to much more information. Beneath it, undisturbed, were the binoculars and other gear he'd buried here, on the morning of the day he'd first walked down to ''join'' the psiXtians.

Setting the satlink unit up, Dundas again thought of its history. He'd heard that ACSA researchers had originally developed these units as frontline hardware, equipping soldiers with C^3I-hookups in an attempt to improve battlefield coordination of troop movements and such. Not much use for that here.

He turned on the unit, then slipped the neuro-hookup circlet onto his head. Via narrow-beam he linked into a pair of satellite back channels, thence to the big computers back in the ACSA that made the unit much more than just the dummy terminal it at first appeared to be.

Inserting the disk Ronnie had given him, he security-cleared and reviewed the Diana Gartner material once more. Calling up the photo and video images of Gartner, he was again amazed by how little the woman had changed since he'd first seen her picture, on the eve of that long-ago raid upon the Neo-Brunist compound. The traitor Acton must have somehow helped her to elude capture, that time. Now Gartner had, if anything, grown more vital—and more dangerous.

All that was hidden history in more ways than one, he reflected. He had been a more ordinary soldier then. The higher-ups would not have looked kindly on his flash-frying a superior officer without at least *some* due process, even so backslidden an officer as Acton had become. Ray thought he had covered it up pretty well at the time, but then that damned Easter woman—with Gartner's help, of course—had included the Brunist episode in her subversive documentary.

After that, he had never again been able to use his Christian name, Raymond Dalke, in the field. He had lost weight, muscled up, changed his looks. Gartner and Easter might have blown his old cover, but he had been determined to become the better for it, and he had.

As if all that weren't bad enough, the film had also led his superiors to reopen their investigation into the assault on the Brunist compound. Especially Acton's disappearance during the course of it. It was only the dismissible nature of Easter's film evidence—particularly ''Acton's'' clearly contrived sub-voc narration—that had allowed Dalke to escape with his military intelligence career intact.

Ray had good reasons indeed for wanting to nail Ms. Gartner to the fullest extent that the law—or vengeance—would allow. Thinking again of the history of that first near-miss made his shingles pulse with pain, which in turn led to a pounding headache. Ray decided to focus on something else. He called up everything he could find on the witch's broom Gartner was riding these days.

SHADOW, Stealth High Altitude Delta Observation Wing, the gadgetboys had acronymed it. Modified transatmospheric spyplane. Sheathed in radar-absorbent and reactive hull armor. Top speed of Mach 30. Cross between bat and boomerang and space shuttle. Descendant of flying wings like the N1-M, the XB-35, the YB-49, the B-2 Stealth. Creature of the Northrop continuum, godfathered by the Horten Brothers in Germany and G.T.R. Hill in Britain. A high-lift, low-drag, computer-stabilized pure wing aircraft.

Ray had to admit he found the SHADOW beautiful and graceful. One of the orbital habitat consortia had bought it, a military surplus prototype, when the government and corporation that had built it stood in need of quick cash. Quite the broom for a witch like Gartner—and quite a trophy, if he could capture it for the Christian States!

Gartner had not yet filed a flight plan with her people in the Orbital Complex—and, incidentally, with the ACSA informant there—but when she did, Ray would know immediately. He would be ready for her.

He scanned back to the matter of Ms. Gartner herself. Know thine enemy. Studying the material, Ray was surprised to find that Gartner had lost a sibling as a young adult, just as Ray himself had—and apparently under similar circumstances. Drug and alcohol abuse, precipitated by KL 235 exposure. Gartner had lost a younger sister, as Ray had lost an older brother.

Strange that family loss should have driven them in such different directions, Ray thought. Gartner had become a radical Green witch, always affirming her sister's "right to be wrong." He had become her complete opposite, a contemporary witchfinder and Inquisitor, swearing just as powerfully that the "rights" Gartner so valued were inherently wrong—and destructive. Thinking about it, Ray fell into memories of what had happened to his own family, particularly his father and his brother, Michael.

His father as a young man had originally been trained as a silo soldier in the old USA, working at that fast-track career until the Cold War ended and the Air Force began cost-cutting and phasing out the missile flight groups. The remaining silos all eventually went to full automation and his father was out of a job. Carter Dalke's silo-soldiering turned out to be a fast track to a dead end.

In his father's last days in that career things got very strange. His job performance in the missile silo had not been affected—no hesitation turning the key there. At the same time, though, Dad hesitated more and more to turn all other keys, outside the launch box. He became extremely anxious about anything associated with unlocking doors or starting cars. Not only did Mom have to drive him everywhere, but when he got home from his silo-duty shifts—sometimes at very odd hours—he had to have Mom open the front door to let him in. He was irrationally but absolutely convinced the house would explode into flames if he unlocked the door.

At Mom's insistence he discussed the problem with the base's do-gooder chaplain-cum-headshrinker. Reverend Social Gospel only mumbled about "claviphobia" and "clavian amnesia" and "ultraparadoxical abreaction." Eventually Dad had been retired out, tranked and rehabbed, literally put out to pasture when he bought a farm in Wyoming complete with silos of another sort.

In the long run, however, that had gone even worse. Banks and county bureaucrats had bankrupted their family, stolen almost the last shred of Dad's pride and will to live. Only God's intervention—first in the form of Christian Identity, then the Justice movement, and at last the rural amnesty that was granted once the Christian States of America replaced the old USA—only those had saved his broken-hearted father, year after year. Only that had prevented the man from committing suicide.

Ray's brother, Mike, had hated Dad's new life and the ACSA too—before it *was* the ACSA, even before the CSA, for that matter. Mike had fled the "Rock-of-Ages Rocky Mountains," as he called them, for a life of promiscuity and debauchery on the permissive Left Coast. Drugs and alcohol had turned Mike into a back-to-the-Garden lunatic, living like a bum, cut off from society. His brilliant but erratic brother, nine years older than Ray himself, had been not quite twenty-seven when he had been shotgun-butt whipped to permanent coma. Mike had gotten himself tangled up in some sort of drug-deal vengeance, on the back-country borders between Oregon and California someplace. Just a week before the CSA had replaced the old USA.

So many years ago, but it was still with him.

Michael's loss had left a hole in Ray's life that could never be filled. He eventually moved forward after the tragedy, but he never got over it. There were times when he hated Michael for having allowed himself to get into a position where he would very likely die, and from which he could not be saved. Then Ray would feel guilt for having thought such hateful things about his brother.

Ray never felt guilt for hating what he felt sure had been the primary cause of his brother's loss—namely, the type of society that so valued an individual's freedom that it put the individual's life at risk. Through its toleration of "lifestyles" and sexual practices and states of consciousness that any believer in the literal truth of God's Word must find unnatural and abhorrent, the USA had made Mike's death almost inevitable. To tolerate evil is to permit and encourage it, Ray was certain, and the USA had given its stamp of approval to precisely those ways and means and nightmare schemes that had done Mike in.

His brother's loss made Ray become more like himself, more what he truly was. In response to Mike's tragedy, Ray had joined the military of the Christian States, then gone into intelligence. He had stayed in, even after the CSA had collapsed down to the ACSA. Mike's loss had taught him that the wayward must be brought back into the fold of church and kitchen and children, by force if necessary.

He would never again stand idly by as people followed the primrose path to the various self-destructions they had "chosen." If such people and their societies and their whole world had to be destroyed in order to be saved, then that too was God's will.

Such was certainly true of the psiXtians. They tolerated—and therefore permitted and encouraged—a multitude of diverse evils. Homosexuals and drug-users were to be found among them in appalling numbers. Their whole ideology of "living lightly upon the Earth" denied God's grant of dominion and His command to be fruitful and multiply. Those among them who could be saved would be, Ray thought. Those who could not would, in their deaths, at least be prevented from the perpetration and perpetuation of further evils—

Ray's reverie came to an abrupt halt. He had the odd sensation that someone or something was watching him from *inside* the infosphere. He was about to disconnect from the unit, when he was overcome by—*convulsions? No*, he thought in a detached and distant fashion. *Not convulsions. Overpoweringly intense, prolonged, almost sexual ecstasy. Entirely within his head. Drowning in waves of love his soldier's will to fight it.*

White light. The image of a male figure, fatherly and brotherly at once. Smiling eyes framed in shaggy dark hair and beard. Smiling beneficently, in absolute approval of what Ray had been thinking and doing. Michael! It was Michael!

The sensations stopped. Ray found himself once more in an infospheric universe that was nominally under his control. He disconnected himself from the infosphere entirely and removed the screen-trode circlet. Sitting in the scrubby wash in the very real light of day, he pondered what the unusual experience might mean.

Too much. He didn't want to think about it. Not now. But he knew he would, sometime. Inevitably.

Putting the unit quickly away and returning it to its hiding place beneath the cairn of rocks, Ray shook his head and sighed inwardly. He hoped Gartner flew in soon. He enjoyed the solitude, but not the introspection that came with it. Back home in the ACSA, he just *knew* how things were supposed to be. He didn't have to think about them the way he did here.

Being alone is dangerous, he thought—and not just in terms of the "buddy system" and "safety in numbers." Here in deep cover among the psiXtians, he was always alone, forced to maintain a secret space that was itself somehow dangerous to moral character. Something was inherently evil in solitude and inwardness. He had to grope around to put his finger on what it was, exactly.

Guaranty, in his *Myth's Edge and Nation* had been right to condemn meditation as an evil of Eastern religion. Looking inward to oneself rather than upward to God, who knew what confusions and heresies might arise? Ray craved a respite of *action*, away from the contemplative lifeways of these psiXtians. These people were driving him nuts. He longed for a chance to make things happen, rather than this endless, maddening *waiting* for them to happen.

SIX

SUBTERPOST EXCERPT (INFOSPHERE ORIGIN UNKNOWN; ORIGinal source independently verified as *Spontaneous Human Consciousness: The Selected and Collected Not-Philosophy of D. B. Albert*):

The energy that feeds the universal intersection system appears as portal experience in consciousness and as event horizons in the world. Consciousness and portal experience are different aspects of the same thing, related as microcosm is to macrocosm. Consciousness is the intersection of body and spirit in the mind of the individual, while portal experience is a joining of personal and universal intersection.

Like the distinction between particle and wave, however, as human consciousness has continued to evolve under the influence of the archetypes, the distinction between the microcosm and macrocosm has begun to dissolve. Through mode-locking, universal energy is available dynamically, though not necessarily causally, to every dynamical system in the universe. The energy that fuels the black hole furnaces in quasars and the galactic cores in the physical universe is the same energy that archetypes fuel within psyche—moving systems beyond causation, to dynamicality.

Since all consciousness is a variety of portal experience, then consciousness is simply where Other meets World, just as event horizon is where singularity meets space-time. Mystical experiences in religious vocabulary, and consciousness in Jungian vocabulary, and event horizons in scientific vocabulary are all the same thing expressed in different languages: points at which other *or* spirit *meets the spatiotemporal world.*

BRANDI'S PARTING FROM JUAN HAD NOT BEEN PLEASANT.
"Why is it that you can zip over to one of the 'borbs just

about any time you feel like it?'' she demanded. ''For you, it's no big deal, so how come, if I want to spend some time here, it's a different story? Why do you feel all neglected and abandoned and want us to hurry home?''

''Look, Brandi, I've got work to do,'' Juan said as he got his gear together. ''Are you coming with me or not?''

''All I want to do is take some time off work and track down a bit of my history,'' she said, obstinately refusing to get her things together. ''I just want to know more about my mother— and my father too, if that's who Manny Shaw is. I want to know more about my linkage to their lives. Christ, you've been acting like I'm shopping for a lover here or something.''

An odd expression flashed across Juan's face. What had been odd hints began to fall together into a suspicion.

''For all I know, Juan,'' she prodded, ''you might have a mistress up here.''

He made a disgusted noise and continued to pack his gear. She sensed he was avoiding the issue, but that only made him all the more suspect. When he had introduced her to his boss, that Renault woman, had there been something more to her standoffishness than merely the stiffness of introduction? Something covert? Some tension of unease in the air? Jealousy? Private secrets and public lies?

''Maybe you do,'' she pressed, but then stopped herself, afraid she might find out more than she wanted to know just yet.

''Believe whatever the hell you like,'' Juan said, growing angry. ''I've got work that needs doing back at Freeman Lowell. I'm out of here.''

''I'll be back,'' she said, more sullenly than she'd intended to. ''After I meet with a few more people and take a flight with Diana Gartner.''

Juan shrugged and acted as if he didn't care. His camouflage of ''duty'' didn't quite cover the angry stomp of his footsteps as he departed.

What had happened to them? There had been a time when their nibbling, nipping, biting loveplay had brought them flowing together like water finding its own level. A time when their lovemaking had made her knees weak, a feeling she hadn't experienced for a long time.

Not, in fact, since she'd exultantly dallied with a female climbing partner atop a big dome of rock on the California coast. They'd just finished scaling a six-pitch route. An earthquake had struck in the very midst of their very midst. Planet waves had passed through her exactly when she was climaxing. She had felt herself cutting loose, peaking precisely amid all the intense energy and vast consummate release that comes to continents after the millenially long, slow, bump-and-grind of their tectonic love dance. All that wave had come flowing through her, all that energy passing through her body, at precisely the right moment.

Since then, despite the occasional happy experimentation, she had generally swung hetero. At first, sex with Juan had been even *more* like that. No earthquake needed, just the two of them. They had "felt the Earth move" when in fact they weren't anywhere near the surface of that planet. Their early intimacy had been the most sensuously gratifying experience of her life.

Things had cooled so much faster than she'd suspected. Still, there had continued to be those occasions when they slipped from two bodies into one and experienced new, awkward rhythms, the clashing streams of their separate histories joining into a single harmony, flowing broad and deep as their life together in time, at least for a moment.

Now, though, they had worn on each other. They could hardly enjoy at all time spent in each other's company. Her beloved romance-holos he reduced to "chick flicks" that were "nothing but fantasies of mate selection, always about multiple suitors and a single heroine." She had retaliated that his action holos were "dumb dick flicks" about multiple sex-object women available for the singular hero to choose from. They had both regretted saying such things. Those were really such minor and unimportant issues, weren't they? Yet those things had been said, and both of them knew what such discussions were really about: the way their own life as a couple was failing.

Brandi was so tense after Juan left that she needed something to take her mind off the whole mess. Whether Manny was her father or not, it was him she told—in a most father-daughterly way—where she was headed, in order to relax and not think about what was going on with Juan.

In one section of the central sphere two biomes stood separated by an artificial cliff—a sculpted mooncrete scarp thirty meters high and about one hundred meters long, one of the few topographically notable features inside the habitat. The cliff wall was modeled after Charlotte Dome, a tall rock face in the central Sierra Nevada and a favorite spot among technical rock-climbers back on Earth. Its surface was studded with the bumpy rock projections climbers called "chickenheads." In her years living in HOME 1, Brandi had soloed the Wall a dozen times. She had never grown bored with the scarp because she was always able to find new routes across it.

On the off chance that she might want to climb, she had brought her rope and gear with her over on the shuttle from Freeman Lowell. Today's climb was more a matter of "need" than "want," however. To make the climb even more challenging and distracting, she decided to do it without chalk for her fingers and hands. She'd do it in street shoes, too—not in the classic sticky boots, or any of the newer electrostatic surface-bond tech. Several of the routes up the rock were rated 5.11 and 5.12, so at least street-climbing those would be something of a challenge.

She looked at the cliff, eyeing chimneys and stemspots, cracks and holds and rugosities. As she stared she began calculating a new climb, one that broke away from the established route called Big Pop-A-Top. Having decided on a route, she walked to the base.

No sooner had she started up the face than her anxieties began to fade, lost in her concentration upon the vertical, three-dimensional chess problem before her. Almost mechanically she popped in the old-style protection she'd brought—stoppers and nuts and camming "friends" wedged in cracks and spaces, snap-linked onto her rope line.

The very thing that most disoriented climbers visiting from Earth—the optical illusion unavoidable in climbing the Wall—was precisely what Brandi loved most about it. The orbital habitat was an inside-out world, so the landscape was also skyscape, lakes and streams and trees and houses wrapping all the way around the sky, with only a few rare clouds floating about the central axis inbetween. As a result, climbing *up* the Wall inevitably also felt like climbing *down* it, face first, toward the lake at the opposite side of the sphere.

Brandi had learned how to climb on Earth, spending a pair of Earthbound summers doing routes all over the Alps and the Sierras. She'd done Yosemite runs and even the rather easy Charlotte Dome itself. None of them, however, for all their paths into deep sky, had felt quite like the fantastic impression she always got here, climbing the Wall. Here she seemed to be clawing headfirst, not up toward sky against gravity, but downward, with gravity, toward a landscape seen distantly through the clouds far below.

She was nearing the top of her route when she noticed that she was no longer alone. When she glanced over at him, the small gnomish-looking older man waved at her.

"Hello, Ms. Easter," he called to her, waving a hand cinched into a stonelock, one of the new cuplike suction units that created powerful, temporary electrostatic bonds between itself and the rock surface.

"Hello," Brandi said back, as politely as she could. The stone-lock tech allowed for a form of free-climbing which Brandi, traditionally trained, sniffed at as a bit of a cheat. But hey, this guy was pretty old, after all. Maybe he needed the break. "Do I know you?"

"You will in a minute," said the gnomish man. "You're the one who saw the big anvil-top rock coming down toward Earth a while back, aren't you?"

Great, Brandi thought. An elderly ink-stained wretch of a mediacuda, come to get her story.

"What news group are you with?" she asked grumpily, using a heel hook to make a big stretching stem move toward her next handhold.

"News—?" the old man said, looking bewildered as he moved the four points of his stonelocks, hands and feet, over the rock surface toward her, his rope protection dangling out behind him, just in case. "Oh, no—I'm not with the press. Name's Paul Larkin. Manny Shaw told me I might find you here. I just wanted to let you know you did in fact see what you thought you saw— no matter what everyone else may have been telling you. That was the top of Caracamuni tepui coming in, returning home after a long voyage."

Brandi glanced at him again. The guy didn't really look like a crazy. She could still hope he wasn't. Something about his name was familiar too, although she couldn't quite place it at the moment. She tiptoed and finger-clung a series of thin nubbins on the rock face—some so small as to be virtually invisible— until she found a nice line of chickenheads big enough for her to dyno back and forth, off and up a final pair of rock faces that stood like the pages of an open book in relation to each other. Her ascent was rapid, after that.

When she came over the lip of the new route she'd just completed, she waited for Mr. Stonelocks Larkin to catch up to her.

Eventually he flopped over the top, breathing hard.

"What's this about a 'long voyage'?" she asked the panting man.

"That's right," he said. Brandi began entering the separate coded frequencies that activated the self-extracting feature of the nuts, stoppers, and cams of the rope protection she'd left behind her. Larkin did the same for his gear. A series of metal pings sounded as the anchoring pieces freed themselves from where they had been wedged. Hauling up their off-belayed ropes, Brandi and Larkin carefully coiled them, removing the anchor-pro pieces as they came over the lip. While the lines and gear came up, Larkin launched into his strange story.

He told Brandi about his formerly schizophrenic ethnobotanist sister. He told her of the *Cordyceps tepuiensis* mushroom, as it had now officially been renamed in an on-line mycology announcement. Told her of the tepui ghost people and their myconeural symbiosis. Of their unprecedented mind-powers and crystalline technologies. Of the departure of the tepui top and its decades of disappearance. Of Larkin's own "selling out" of the fungus and its KL 235 extract, to government and corporate intelligence interests, years before, in the long meantime.

Strange stuff, Brandi thought, but it had enough points of contact with her mother's history that she could almost believe it.

The two of them, with their ropes and gear over their shoulders, walked toward the nearest bulletcart station entrance. As they walked, Larkin tried to complete the background behind Brandi's own sighting of the mountain, orbed in light and heading toward Earth. Larkin told her what his returned sister, Jacinta, had told him—about the Allesseh and its mission. That was stranger still.

"I can't quite wrap my mind around this," Brandi told him as they got in and took their seats in the cart headed for the ag tori, where Manny lived. "This Allesseh thing sounds like a cross between a black hole, Galactic Telephone and Telegraph, the Library of Alexandria, and the Tower of Babel before Jehovah decided to cancel that project."

Larkin laughed at the Babel reference as they unburdened themselves of their climbing gear and placed it on the empty seats beside them. Taking out his notebook computer, he rummaged around among its electronic category headings until he located the lyrics to a Möbius Caducéus song called "Wittgen-

stein's Sin.'' He showed the lyrics to Brandi, who obligingly
read them.

>   *rising over an eastern desert plain*
>   *we had high piled a Tower) because*
>   *In the Beginning was the Word (*
>   *and all people spoke alike) because*
>   *we were words made flesh (*
>   *and we wished to be in better) hearing*
>   *of the Word (*
>
>   *but when the Tower had risen) gleaming (*
>   *from the dead) earth-brown and sere*
>   *the Philosopher looked upon it*
>   *and said words (are) nothing*
>   *and all we are they have) nothing*
>   *no meaning no sense they are) babble*
>   *(in the end) babble nothing more mere) babble*
>
>   *and the Tower) dissolved (into incoherent*
>   *murmuring that could support no weight)*
>   *and we fell to earth our mother*
>   *we were dust again*
>   *as foreigners all to each*
>   *we chattered)*
>
>   *one to the others*
>   *could tell no thoughts (if we thought)*
>   *or feelings (if we felt) toward others*
>   *and tasting of ashes in our mouths*
>   *the dust of wordless time*
>   *covered (all that) was*
>   *unspoken and unheard.*

   "I've heard a lot of their stuff," Brandi said, "though not this
one. I don't quite get what's going on with the parentheses."
   Larkin nodded as the ridge cart eased toward their stop and
they began to gather their gear.
   "One of their obscurer pieces, no doubt," Larkin said. "I
think Lev Korchnoi was operating his machinery under the influence of Albertian theory, when he wrote it. It's got that sort
of rebellion against 'linguistic absolutism' to it."

They left the bulletcart, which slid dutifully back into its tube and was gone. Walking around the small commons into which the bullet had appeared and disappeared, they made their way toward Manny Shaw's home, through the enormous greenhouse conservatory of the torus curving away from them to vanishing point on either side. Walking along in silence, they at last found Shaw working in a nitrifying field of Dutch clover not far from his residence.

"Hey, Manny," Brandi called as they approached him, then gestured good-naturedly toward Larkin where he walked beside her. "Do you vouch for this guy's wild story?"

Manny stood up from where he was working in the dirt with his hands and cocked his head at them.

"As much as I would vouch for your own," he said, slapping his hands against each other to knock the dirt from them. "Find out for yourself if you like. Diana got us an invitation to Jhana and Seiji's housewarming party on HOME 2. There should be people there who can confirm or deny it."

"I'll be there myself," Larkin said. "I haven't seen the guest list, but I asked around a little after I got my invitation. Most of the people invited just happen to have been cranium-deep in that whole Light thing when it came through. From what I know of Jhana and Seiji, this is going to be more than just a housewarming party!"

As they walked together toward Larkin's home, Brandi wondered just what *that* might mean.

S INCE ARRIVING IN CALIFORNIA, MEI-LING HAD INSISTED ON driving. That was fine with Robert, for it gave him time to listen to, and take notes on, the *Scientific Bones in Mystical Flesh* material she had given him. As Mei-Ling piloted them along the California coast toward the Electronic Crimes Maximum Security Penal Facility, popularly known as Silicon Bay, Robert watched the rugged coastal scenery slide quietly by. He tried to concentrate, listening carefully as the Myrrhisticinean material played throughout the cab of their black, teardrop-shaped motorpool electric.

Question: Why 'Myrrhisticine'?

Answer: Sister Alicia devised the name as a way of combining associations: 'myrrh' for its religious connotations as the gift of aromatic incense presented to the infant Christ child, and 'myr-

isticin,' the scientific name for an important chemical found in nutmeg—

Mei-Ling gave a short laugh. Robert clicked off the player and glanced questioningly at her.

"That's not quite the whole story," she said, watching transparent aquamarine sea meet deep brown stone in white spume and wave, below and before them, as she drove. "What they don't tell you there is that myristicin is a psychotropic. Sister Alicia had her first great vision while dosed up on nutmeg."

"But I thought she actually was a real, Catholic nun in the old days," Robert said.

"She was," Mei-Ling assured him. "At the time of her great vision she was reading Teilhard de Chardin's books and working with death-row inmates. They were the ones who turned her on to nutmeg jags. She was blessed and tormented with visions from then on."

"Hmm!" Robert said, electropenning notes and nodding as he clicked the player back on. It had scanned on to the next selection, something called "Jet Noise and Frog Song."

In the midst of cloudless spring afternoons, Brother Etienne noticed that the frogs began calling every time a jet thundered in low overhead—only to fall silent again once the roar from the sky had died away.

"I've never been able to locate a scientific article explaining the phenomenon," Brother Etienne said as he and Sister Alicia stood beside the Abbey's vernal pool. "I wonder whether the frogs might be mistaking the noise for thunder, for the onset of rain and prime breeding conditions—"

"The more I listen to it, Brother," Alicia responded with a smile, "the less it seems to have to do with the wet necessities of sex. I really think their calling is an amphibian hymn of sorts, an expression of faith."

Brother Etienne recalled Alicia's words every time the jet noise made the frogs sing. So like the abbess to believe that, he thought. And she didn't hear it as a primitive prayer chanted to a green fertility god raining far away in the sky, either. For her it could only be an expression directed to the Most High.

At least the frogs would probably never learn their mistake, Brother Etienne reflected. No matter how often the roaring god

*proved false—just another dry metal thunderer without rain.
They would never experience the spiritual dryness Etienne himself had known. Even when they began to experience parching
physical dryness, the frogs would go on croaking, the most res-
olute of the faithful, true believers to the last.*

*On the first day of summer, the vernal pool went dry. Brother
Etienne understood the meaning of Alicia's words and became
enlightened.*

A pause of silence, dead or thoughtful air, opened after the
vignette. Mei-Ling had nothing to say about this one, so Robert
just kept jotting notes. Over the soft purr of the engine they could
hear the crashing of surf, not so very distant from the road on
which they drove. A moment later another vignette, "Loss,"
began to play.

*Two biological sisters became sisters in the spirit and entered
the Abbey together. After they had been part of the sisterhood
for some years, they were driving home to the Abbey one evening
when they were caught in a severe thunderstorm and flash flood.
Crossing a broad desert wash that had begun to flood, their
vehicle stalled in midstream just as a tall wall of muddy water
began to sweep toward them. One of the sisters managed to climb
onto the roof of their vehicle and was lifted to safety by a Mountain Rescue helicopter. The other sister had not yet gotten out of
the vehicle when another, stronger torrent of mud and water
lifted the stranded vehicle, rolled it, and carried it down the
wash. The sister inside was crushed and drowned.*

*The sister who had been lifted to safety grieved greatly and
suffered much guilt as a result of having survived while her
younger sister had perished. She became so morose that many
in the Abbey felt she would kill herself. Sister Alicia was sent for
and came to speak with her.*

*"Grief is a wound," Alicia told the grieving sister, "and your
wound is deep. In your heart is a hole in the shape of your sister.
You do not know if there is enough of you left over to cover up
that hole. Remember this: Where you are most wounded, there
you most fully touch reality. Mortality is the self-inflicted wound
of the knowledge which makes us human and real. Death, like
the Rainbow Door, is a wound into reality. For most of us, reality
hasn't begun yet. For your sister, it has."*

The mourning sister heard these words and the flood of her grief returned within its banks.

"She really was a wise old woman," Mei-Ling said, speaking of Sister Alicia, "as well as a crazy crone."

Robert clicked off the player once more.

"You knew her, then?"

"Met her," Mei-Ling corrected him. "Only for a little while. As near as anyone can tell, she died during the Sedona disaster."

The sound of the surf below the road fell into the silence between them once more. Robert clicked on *Scientific Bones in Mystical Flesh* again, and a vignette called "Holy Life" began to play.

Sister Alicia was asked why so many converts to the Myrrhisticine revelation are celibate, though celibacy is nowhere required of Myrrhisticineans.

"Perhaps they realize," contended Sister Alicia, "that our biological roles as mothers and fathers have been superseded by our roles as spiritual midwives and obstetricians, standing witness as the Fullness of Time is born from the Womb of Eternity."

This remains one of the hard sayings of Sister Alicia.

"That's putting it mi—" Mei-Ling began, but was interrupted by the insistent chiming of Robert's infocom unit.

"Right," he said into the speaker, turning off the disk player as he did so. "Pump it through."

A holo display popped up above the infocom, reports and photos, at least from what Mei-Ling could see from the driver's seat. Robert scanned them quickly and thoroughly.

"It's that information you requested on Richard Schwarzbrucke's death," he said to Mei-Ling, by way of explanation.

"And—?" she asked eagerly.

"He did die with three other men," Robert said, confirming Mei-Ling's earlier experience and hypothesis. "Mongrel Clone-connected gentlemen: Edward "Big Ed" Hilbert, Martin "Mac" McCurdy, and Wayne Davis. All three were tied into the Blue Badge corruption investigation. Also to the Oregon Blue Spike trade and CMD." He quickly rescanned a portion of the info he'd been sent. "Blue Spike seems to have some links to KL 235, as well. The strangest part is that there seems to be a security video record of the deaths. Both external and internal shots taken by Schwarzbrucke's household security system.''

"Why does that not surprise me?'' Mei-Ling said, thinking of their topological voyeur's penchants. "Play it.''

Robert obliged. Mei-Ling divided her attention between the road and the grainy little vid being projected into the space in front of Robert, on the passenger's side of the car.

The first scene was an exterior shot—a veritable electric fence of lightning bolts spearing all around Schwarzbrucke's house from a dense storm cloud. The next sequence was interior: images from an entertainment console, in fact from all the TVs and holojectors and computers in the house. A CAT scan movie of a semi-skull, dented on the left side in the shape of a rifle or shotgun butt. That image then blown up and highlighted, apparently for the four men in the den.

A series of what looked like PET and NMR and interferometric images followed, of the same injury and of subtler, apparently drug-induced damage done to other subjects. Destruction of sites labeled "Broca's area," and some also labeled "Wernicke's area.''

The closed-circuit footage showed one of the men, police-labeled as Ed Hilbert, breaking for the door. Apparently the electric locks had been slammed tight. Schwarzbrucke picked up the phone, then made a disgusted sound as noise not so very unlike a modem's carrier wave filled the room.

From the screens and holos in the den innumerable morphing kaleidoscopic angels swelled into light and life before the men, until Schwarzbrucke and his guests had to shield their eyes. As the light from the screen faded, a new boom sounded, not of thunder, but of something else.

"That would be the house's fuel-oil tanks," Robert said, scanning a report in split-screen display. In the taped record itself, the power went dead and the security system switched to auxiliaries. Next came an exterior shot of a section of the Schwarzbrucke house being engulfed in a wall of fire.

Then Mei-Ling saw a scene she had seen before: forces beyond her understanding warping the air around the men in the den, warping something even much deeper than the air itself, smoothly if fatally everting the men, turning them wrong side out—

"That's it!'' Mei-Ling said. "Why hasn't this stuff been linked to the topological voyeur killer before now?''

"It's years and years old, for one thing," Robert said, putting the display into pause mode. "According to the reports, the inversions were attributed to 'tornadic pressure changes' caused by the storm and the deaths to fire—also storm-related. The bodies were burned beyond recognition when the house went up. The record itself has largely been ignored. Irrelevant."

Mei-Ling shook her head so vigorously that for a moment Robert was afraid she was going to drive off the side of the road, plunging them on to rocks, surf and sea below.

"Wrong!" she said emphatically. "That was our topological voyeur's first cluster-kill. Schwarzbrucke and those Mongrel Clone bikers *did something* to the voyeur. He was making them pay back plenty. This episode, all those years ago, was his vengeance, pure and simple."

"How do you know the topological voyeur is a 'he'?" Robert wanted to know.

"I don't," Mei-Ling said. "Not for sure, anyway. Good enough as a hunch, though. Get everybody Interpol can spare working on discovering and locating someone who suffered brain damage at the hands of or through the drugs of those three Mongrel Clones—or through the research of Richard Schwarzbrucke. That's your basic skanky on this guy."

Robert glanced out the car window, at the sea throwing itself against the land, again and again, until Mei-Ling turned toward him once more.

"Any more word on that SubTerPost pirate postal system?" she asked, catching her partner off guard. He called up the most recent information on his unit.

"More of the same," he said, scanning reports. "The link between it and the deaths seems to be strengthening. As to locating its source—that's more of a problem. These temporary autonomous postal systems are *designed* to be hard to find."

"How, exactly?" Mei-Ling asked. She was not all that familiar with such systems. In the past she'd generally considered them rather trivial nuisances.

"The addresses are as bounce-routed and massively encrypted as the messages," Robert said. "If you don't have access to hidden keys embedded in their control code, then they're damned hard to break into. They exist outside government and corporate control of the infosphere, so they have to be built to resist detection and shutdown."

"Highly distributed?" Mei-Ling ventured.

"Right. This one seems to be more mobile and shifting in its distribution than most. That supports the idea that its 'camouflage,' at least, is under the control of a big machine intelligence of some sort."

Mei-Ling nodded, thoughtful. Robert looked out the window again, but his questions gnawed at him until he turned back toward Mei-Ling.

"Look," he said, staring hard at her, "if you want me to be of help, you've got to be a little more forthcoming with what your thinking is on all this."

"What do you want to know?" she replied, in a tone that said she really didn't want to be asked.

"Well, is the killer running the machine intelligence that's running SubTerPost, or just using it?" Robert asked. "And how does this connect with Sedona and the orbital habitat, if it does? Or with Manqué's RATs and the Light?"

Mei-Ling stayed quiet long enough that Robert started to wonder if he'd pushed too hard.

"I'm not sure yet," Mei-Ling said. "Sorry. I wish I could say more, but at least this lead seems solid. We need to get everyone moving on this change in our SCANCI. It's a start."

Dissatisfied but dutiful, Robert set to work, punching in codes, pressing the explanations hard with his superiors. When he'd finished, however, he still had questions about what they were trying to do.

"Mei-Ling," he asked as they turned off the coast highway, "how much were you involved with what Manqué did at Sedona?"

She stared out the windshield at the road unwinding before her, as if preoccupied.

"I was part of the Kerrismatix team that installed the ALEPH, as I said," she replied.

"I know that," Robert said. "I know that it stands for Artificial Life Evolution Programming Heuristic. But what does all that really mean? And how did it influence what happened at Sedona?"

Mei-Ling took a deep breath. She really didn't want to be getting into this, not now, but she didn't seem able to avoid it.

"Dr. Kerris had done an incredible job developing it," Mei-Ling said, remembering. "A mountain of research in cybernetic chaos and complexity theory had gone into developing the ALEPH. The complexity and sophistication of its modeling is precisely why the Myrrhies were interested. The other evolution programs on the market had all turned out to be too simplistic for their needs. Reductive, competition-only models. The ALEPH had the sort of depth and feedback layering they were looking for. Especially the way Kerris had plugged in organismal behavior as an environmental constraint on changes in gene frequency. That's what Phelonious especially liked about it.''

Robert glanced again at the view out the car window of Big Sur mountains wading into the Pacific.

"Manqué liked the ALEPH's understanding of complexity, you mean?" he asked.

"Yes," Mei-Ling said with a brief nod as she drove the winding surface road. "I remember him lecturing me on how a brain is not a computer—how that analogy was entirely fallacious."

"Oh?" Robert asked, curious. "How's that?"

"Computers are designed, brains are evolved," Mei-Ling explained, watching the countryside unwind around them. "Computers can manipulate information only under the direction of a program. They do what they are built and programmed to do. They're limited by their designer's intentionality."

"I see," Robert said. "That's another way of describing the fundamental problem Tetragrammaton has been working on— bridging the chasm between brains and computers."

"Right," Mei-Ling said with a nod. "Organisms developing through evolution must adapt to survive—predetermined rules and fixed design are fatal. Adaptability is the basic 'dishomology' between brains and machines. Computers are built with each structure having a precisely designed function, but the 'new brain,' primarily the thalamocortical system, has very little specific structure, in terms of the way it processes information, until after birth—when it actually begins processing information."

"I gather that Manqué was familiar with Albert's defense of consciousness, then?" Robert asked, rhetorically.

"Very," Mei-Ling agreed. "Information processing in the brain is not designed, but learned, in accordance with which neuronal-grouping schemes produce the best results. The 'new' brain is not programmed. Its information processing structure is mutable."

"It would have to be," Robert said, "because environmental contingencies introduce radically altered conditions into life's world—conditions under which following a 'program' would inevitably lead to death.''

"Exactly," Mei-Ling agreed, watching the road. "Since contingencies break the rules, those brains which can also break the rules are best able to survive contingencies. Evolution doesn't work by planning and design, but by the survival of those who can adapt, through the learning of new survival strategies.''

Robert stared out the window, thinking hard.

"And the most successful rule-breaking strategy yet developed by evolution would be consciousness, then?" he asked, anticipating the direction of her argument.

"Yeah," Mei-Ling said. She turned off onto a long road leading, she knew, up to a golden-grassed bluff. That bluff had, years ago, been bulldozed into the coastal woodland, at whose far, ocean-facing side stood the Silicon Bay prison. "Consciousness is a dynamical system generating its own rules and characteristics, in response to its environment—through learning, not programming. You learn what you've lived, then you live what you've learned.''

Robert nodded as they rolled onto the bluff.

"When you think about it," he said, "neither consciousness nor the universe is really like a rule-governed machine. The world outside your head and the world inside are both dynamical.''

Mei-Ling brought the car to a stop at a barred gate. The two human guards, who might as well have been named Perfunctory and Supernumerary, stood by as Silicon Bay's sophisticated security systems read their car tag and its code, and scanned the vehicle's inhabitants. The gate opened and the guards waved them through.

"That dynamical aspect was why Phelonious liked the ALEPH so much," she continued.

"I don't see how," Robert said. "The ALEPH was still a set of rules, wasn't it?"

"In the most basic sense, yes," Mei-Ling agreed, as they drove through the golden grassland, toward the complex of squat high-security buildings. "Ultimately though, the ALEPH tried to duplicate the subtlety of the evolutionary process itself, with species co-evolving, entire communities co-evolving. It incorporated a predation subheuristic based on the counterintuitive Paine hypothesis that predators actually increase the diversity of an environment. It did all that—and a lot more—in the context of the most ecologically sophisticated virtual environments ever created. At its highest levels of performance, the ALEPH behaved dynamically, as nearly as any of us could tell.''

Robert watched idly as they passed through another security gate in another fence-line.

''If it was so impressive,'' he asked, ''then why didn't it ever catch on?''

''The ALEPH's model of evolutionary complexity was, um, rather memory intensive,'' Mei-Ling said, then bethought herself. ''No—actually that's a monumental understatement. What killed the program on the street and in the marketplace was its own computational success. The ALEPH's appetite for memory was huge.''

''Like an ox's appetite for corn?'' Robert suggested, smiling.

''Make that a swarm of locusts' appetite,'' Mei-Ling said. ''Make that a swarm of locusts, each locust as big as a winged ox. But you should have seen what it could do when you 'fed' it as much memory as it wanted! I remember once, after we installed the ALEPH, we watched Phelonious run it through a demonstration. In a half hour's time, using only a half dozen of the LogiBoxes, the ALEPH evolved populations of cellular automata from the proto-organic stage all the way to a level of complexity roughly equivalent to that of the Earth's ecosphere at the time of the Permian extinctions. We had to shut the demo off, but everyone who was there, all of us who saw a world evolving in holographic projection before our eyes—we were impressed to the point of awe. Especially when Phelonious speculated about what might be possible with all the LogiBoxes linked up and the ALEPH running full-bore, with no constraints or dampers on its functioning.''

They found a parking area and pulled into a spot labeled Visitors. As they got out of the car, Mei-Ling hesitated about locking the vehicle, given the redundant levels of security surrounding them. She did so anyway, out of long habit.

''Running the ALEPH full-bore on all the boxes,'' Robert said as they walked toward the main entrance. ''Is that what brought on the black hole sun thing at Sedona?''

Mei-Ling nodded.

''On the boxes, and elsewhere in the infosphere, too,'' she said, almost with a sigh. ''Phelonious had a bad case of Microcosmic God syndrome. I think he was trying to set up an artificial evolution in hopes that it might lead to an artificial brain—and an artificial consciousness.''

"The bridge across the chasm," Robert said as they walked up the ramp and watched the automatic doors of the entrance part silently before them. "The seamless interface between mind and machine. A contingent computer, both mind *and* machine. Apparently he didn't succeed, however."

"Hard to determine for sure," Mei-Ling said. "All I know was that it was damned risky."

Robert was about to query her further on that, but the guard assigned to guide them to Manqué/Kong's cell appeared at that moment, a petite black woman all business and officiousness in her sharply pressed prison guard's uniform. The guard briefly introduced herself and informed them that the warden would have been here to meet them herself were it not for a coinciding visit from a governor's commission. Turning on her heel, the officer led them away into the labyrinth of security levels and cells. Glancing at Mei-Ling as they walked along, Robert saw that she seemed very preoccupied with her own thoughts. It looked like this walk was going to be a long and silent one.

Mei-Ling was, in fact, remembering those days when she had met Phelonious Manqué and the Myrrhisticineans for the first time. She and Tanaka and Jackson had helicoptered out of Flagstaff, heading into the beautiful redrock country around Sedona. Ahead of them, the Abbey had come into view in the late afternoon sky, a neo-gothic construction situated atop a tall red-cliffed butte, remote and beautiful in the extreme.

Moments later, their helicopter had landed and they were being welcomed to the Abbey by an energetic woman in her forties. Tall and thin enough to merit the adjective "svelte," Sister Clare was dressed in a loose and flowing habit of dark blue. Standing in the propwash of the departing helicopter, her reddish-blond hair blowing in the wind, Sister Clare too seemed remote and beautiful, the living embodiment of everything Mei-Ling had thought she knew about the Myrrhisticineans: ascetic, eccentric, relatively harmless.

As Clare hospitably asked them about their trip and informed them about their accommodations, Mei-Ling couldn't help but notice the man with Clare, shadowing them. He appeared to be in his early twenties and was about as svelte as a Sumo wrestler. His mouth, framed by a short shovel of dyed-blond goatee, wore an expression somewhere between sullenness and sneer. He seemed uncomfortable in street clothes, and his hair looked odd, as if it had been tonsured until recently and was now being allowed to grow out haphazardly. Sister Clare—who seemed more "abbess" than sister—introduced the young man under his obvious alias of Phelonious Manqué.

Mei-Ling learned a great deal about Manqué in the weeks that followed. That first day he had guided them briskly, for a man of his heft, deep into the maze of tunnels beneath the Abbey. He remarked cryptically that there was "Always more to things than just the surface." Certainly that had proven true of him.

On first meeting the man, Mei-Ling had presumed that he was that sort of hacker/shade-tree computer consultant who took up the monastic life because, as a civilian, he had awakened one too many times to gunshots in the morning and yells of "You killed my computer!" from very dissatisfied clients. Sister Clare's prefatory remarks over the phone before they flew out—that he didn't much like to give face-time, that he was a loner who viewed himself as a heretic and a sort of "rogue operative"—had led Mei-Ling to expect the worst sort of prideful, info-processing prima donna.

Heretic or no, however, Manqué worked incredibly hard. He put in long hours conjuring in virtual space, growing data constructs that were simultaneously as artificial as cathedrals and natural as flowers. As the Kerrismatix team worked with him, Erinye Jackson and Mei-Ling began to develop a grudging respect for Manqué's abilities, his photographic memory, his conceptual brilliance. Mei-Ling thought, at the time, that he was developing some of the same respect for the ALEPH and the Kerrismatix team's facility with it.

She also learned that Manqué had a background in biology, having majored in it for a while. "Until I realized my professors were more comfortable with a dead frog in a dissecting tray," he had said, "than a live frog in a pond. That's when I changed my major to infomatics and computing."

Following the prison guard down into the maze of cells belowground in Silicon Bay, here and now, Mei-Ling was overwhelmed by a sense of déjà vu. Following Phelonious down to his lair in the bottommost stratum of the Abbey years ago was so much like the path Mei-Ling was following at this moment. She wondered if Phelonious had noted the similarity, when he first arrived here.

All those years before, Phelonious had been an excruciatingly private person. He was very often reticent about what he was up to, reluctant to explain, which sometimes made working with him a major chore. He was at times quite purposely obtuse and so-cially maladroit in the extreme.

(At his trial, such behavior—along with much else—would be attributed by his defense attorney to the history of physical and sexual abuse that Martin Kong had suffered at the hands of male authority figures throughout his childhood. That was no doubt part of what had driven him, Mei-Ling thought, but Manqué/Kong had also chosen to keep following the path he had taken, day after day, in the secrecy of his own head. That choice was real and culpable. Finally, it could not be denied as the trial came to its conclusion.)

Yet Phelonious could also open up at the most unexpected moments. She remembered approaching him one day, where he sat sprawled in his boulder-chair. Phelonious's hands hovered over the circlet amps, track balls, tactile force-pads, and key-boards which he used to play upon his systems and their dis-plays—Captain Nemo at the controls of his great instrument. He, however, was a Nemo underground, not underwater, and inside a Stonehenge restored out of the past, rather than a submarine out of the future.

Mei-Ling had gotten to talking with him that day at some length. She had distracted him from his work long enough that, in the holojection space over Phelonious's right shoulder, a 'jector-saver appeared. The holojector showed a jagged rainbow mountain range, slowly building and unbuilding in 3-D. When Mei-Ling asked about the saver, Phelonious had looked around surreptitiously to make sure the two of them were the only ones in the big room. When he saw that they were, he pointed to the jagged rainbow range and began to describe it in detail.

"These mountains of madness correspond to a model of the entire plenum of the cosmos," he said. "Peaks are high-energy, inflationary regions. Valleys are regions of relatively low energy. They have stopped inflating, like our own local universe. Dif-ferent colors here mean different initial conditions and different laws of physics. The image is fractal—it recurs at scales ranging from trillionths the size of a proton to trillions of times bigger than the known universe. It represents the cosmos for what it is: a self-organizing dynamical system, fractal at the borderline be-tween different orders, even a gateway between those orders."

"The whole cosmos is a gateway?" Mei-Ling had asked, skeptical. Perhaps she'd been thinking of what Sister Clare had said of Phelonious's everyday-is-doomsday, Earth-is-the-Rainbow-Door heresies.

"Potentially, yes," Phelonious replied, folding his arms across his chest. "Any point of it can be induced to demonstrate that gateway property because the whole thing is holographically self-similar, across all scales. Given the proper information densities, any point in any universe can become the Rainbow Door, the gateway between orders."

"But if one order is the space-time we know," Mei-Ling asked, "then what is the nature of that other order?"

Phelonious smiled.

"That's the big question, now isn't it?"

A final metal-and-polycarbonate door thunked and clanked back, jolting Mei-Ling from her reverie in a most irreverent and untimely fashion. A perverse synchronicity persisted, however. Before them loomed Manqué/Kong himself, real-time.

He stood, dressed in a prisoner's orange uniform, smiling a death's-head rictus of a grin. He was head-shaved now, his goatee long since allowed to go from black to grey-speckled. He waited, motionless, arms folded, his eyes hollow yet gleaming, ensconced like a strange living fire behind a dense Cartesian latticework of white lasers, a searing death cube of inescapable geometry. The only other objects in the cube were a floor-bolted desk and chair, a plastic manual typewriter chained to the desk, two small stacks of typing paper, and a toilet stall of minimal privacy.

The guard left Robert and Mei-Ling and departed. The armored door through which they had come sighed heavily as it slid back into place behind the guard—and behind them.

"Why, Ms. Magnus!" Manqué said, his deathly (yet also somehow beatific) grin threatening to swallow his own head. "It's been such a long time since we last met. Tell me: How has it felt all these years, to have been the person who denied humanity its final fulfillment?"

"I wouldn't know," Mei-Ling said, trying to retain her composure. "I'm not that person. All I did was cut off the information flow to some modified holojectors."

Manqué/Kong dismissed her remarks with a light wave of his left hand, his grin altering not at all.

"Please, I don't have time for faux naiveté," he said. "You knew quite well the purpose for which those big fiber-optic feeds were intended. You must have."

Almost despite herself, when Mei-Ling looked at Manqué/ Kong now, through her head flashed the basic scan key for psychopathy: Aggressive. Insensitive. Charismatic. Irresponsible. Intelligent. Hedonistic. Narcissistic. Antisocial. Dangerous. Exceptional manipulators. Control fixated. Obsessed with memory and the detailed reconstruction of the past—as their topological voyeur, their parallel killer, also seemed to be.

"For an impossibility," Mei-Ling said firmly. "Even if you developed a mathematical model so dense as to be indistinguishable from the thing modeled, still the map could not become the country. The virtual and the real cannot become one."

"Oh?" Phelonious said, with just the slightest sardonic trace in his voice. "I know you must be aware you're lying—to yourself, at the very least. I give you that much credit. What else could it have been that appeared that day over the Abbey but an information density singularity of exactly the type you deny? Hmm?"

Mei-Ling remembered that terrible day in a rushing torrent of memory, coming from where it had been pent up all these years like floodwaters behind a dam. A sound as of uncountable monks humming: a deep, deep, unimaginable music, affecting everyone far below the ears, far inside the brain. The sound called even to the Kerrismatix team, deep underground in the butte.

On the security monitors recording the activity at the surface, others had already begun to gather in the Abbey courtyard. Mei-Ling's local friends, Sister Clare and the nuns and monks, were all standing behind Alicia Gonsalves herself, a singular old woman with wild grey hair and wild grey eyes.

Midway between the holojector-like devices Dr. Vang's operative had had them install, at Manqué's insistence, a flashpoint of lightning burst into being in the sky above the courtyard. The light from it cascaded over everyone, even those deep underground. Mei-Ling looked at Erinye beside her. At first she thought Erinye's hair was standing on end like a Fury's—but no. The top of her head was crowned with a jagged rainbow, flickering like a sensitive flame, fire shaped like that mountain range of fractal cosmos Phelonious once showed her.

She looked at the security monitors and saw lambent flickering ranges of rainbow light rising above head after head in the courtyard above. Almost before she could even wonder at those, a greater wonder appeared in the sky above those poor people in the courtyard. The point of light there became a hole of darkness rimmed by light, like the diamond-ring stage of a solar eclipse. Yet the light around the darkness was no mere white but rather myriad rainbow fires, the tallest peak of each fluid rainbow mountain range tapering away, until it was thin as a monolaser and long as infinity.

As Mei-Ling watched, the rainbow-ringed hole in the sky grew larger. Flickers of white light became visible inside it. Mei-Ling looked at Sister Alicia on the monitor and she knew what the old woman was thinking. The Rainbow Door, the Wound into Reality. The points of light inside it—transubstantiated souls glowing like candles in a darkened cathedral.

She looked at Dr. Vang's chief local operative, Harmon Dogon, and in that instant she knew what he was thinking too. The transluminal portal. The Tetragrammaton program had worked. The points of light inside the hole could only be stars and planets in a part of the universe human beings had never seen before.

Mei-Ling looked at Phelonious Manqué on another monitor, inside his Stonehenge ring, staring triumphantly up at his own monitor's image of the hole growing in the sky. One look at his face and she knew what he was thinking as well. The final predator. The points of light inside it—the glint of unimaginable teeth in the maw of a hungry god.

Phelonious raised his face toward it fully and spread his arms wide.

"Take and eat!" he shouted.

She and Erinye and Marvin Tanaka could not wait for time to enlighten them as to the true nature of the thing, could not pause for some sign to distinguish among all those hopes and fears. The black hole sun up above was beginning to expand. She and her coworkers activated the encryption lock Mei-Ling had put together to stop the information flow out of the ALEPH, then darted for the fire exit tunnel. That would dump them out near the base of the mesa—if they were lucky.

Above them, the rainbow-haloed black sun had begun to absorb the Abbey and its inhabitants and the rock itself. The stone of the rock shook and quivered like a living thing. Mei-Ling and Jackson and Tanaka scurried, pitiful rats, away from the monstrous thing that was sinking this tall ship of stone, the thing Phelonious had brought into being—

Mei-Ling shook her head. She had been silent so long that Robert was glancing expectantly at her. Manqué's smile had grown horrifying in the broad expanse of its beatific self-assurance. She felt as if he were drawing her into his psychopathy, into a madness arising not from the repression of memory and trauma but from the inability to repress those things. She shook her head.

"The nature of what happened that day is still far from completely understood," she said. "Whatever it was, it stopped. If it was your information density singularity, then what would have prevented it from absorbing everything into itself? Swallowing the whole planet—or even more?"

Phelonious Manqué laughed then, and both of his "guests" shivered involuntarily.

"All or nothing," Manqué/Kong said mockingly. "You sound like those physicists before the first nuclear device was detonated at Trinity. Some of them thought it wouldn't work at all. Some of them thought it would cause all the oxygen in the atmosphere to ignite and burn up the whole world! Neither the all nor the nothing happened. It was the same thing at Sedona. The cosmos didn't end, nor even just our universe. The portal, once it opened, could not exceed its informational Schwarzschild radius—"

"That's just it!" Mei-Ling retorted. "Informational this, informational that, but nobody's ever yet offered a valid test for Friedkin's 'information-based cosmos' theory—"

Manqué made his understatedly mild dismissive gesture again.

"If you choose to deny the evidence of your own senses, fine," he said. "We can argue the peculiar jargon of the very large and the very small. We can talk of manifold universes and infinitesimal particles and tubular solitons and twenty-five dimensional things until we no longer have breath. But you and I have been where your young friend here has never gone, Mei-Ling. To that place where cosmology and subatomic physics overlap. Even you must have awakened to a necessary consciousness, there. A logical conclusion, stemming from the Paine hypothesis. Something had to be found to limit and counter our false ascendancy as a species. To end the unconsciousness, the sleep of generations."

Robert stepped forward.

"That was what the black hole sun was for?" he asked, before he could stop himself.

"The silent one speaks," Manqué said, his beatific grin briefly slipping into a smirk. "Yes. It was right there in front of us. Why else had we striven to develop intelligent machines, but to destroy ourselves? We knew we were out of balance, so—unconsciously—we had begun eroding our consciousness, the very thing that separates us from machines.''

"How, though?" Robert asked with a quick glance at Mei-Ling, shifting uneasily on his feet.

"Our information technologies," Manqué said, somewhat pedantically, "vastly intensify the power of social responsibility over individual freedom. They are transforming us from semiconscious beings back into totally unconscious mannequins. Manicheans. Collapsing into binarism. All or nothing. Zero, one. Machine-eans. No balance. Subconsciously, preconsciously, we knew how wrong it was, to have no real predators, no limits on our numbers. Why else would we have been destroying the individual self—unless we wanted to self-destruct? For a very long time we as a species had been *unconsciously* desiring to do the very thing I tried to do. Quite consciously.''

Manqué almost appeared to be caught up in his rant. Robert glanced more confidently at Mei-Ling, as if he were thinking to run some good cop/bad cop routine on Manqué. Mei-Ling doubted such a ruse would do anything more than entertain Manqué/Kong briefly, but it was too late now.

"And the ALEPH was the key?" Robert asked.

"Absolutely," the prisoner said almost happily. "Mei-Ling, you once told me yourself the ALEPH was more artwork than anything else. As the man said: Art's not a mirror held up to reality, but a hammer with which to shape it. You gave me my hammer, Mei-Ling, but then you took it away before I had a chance to shape the world with it. The whole world might have seen our art, if you hadn't stopped it.''

"I had no choice," Mei-Ling said, in a voice that sounded too pleading and exculpatory in her own ears. "It might have destroyed everything.''

"There is *always* a choice," Phelonious said quietly. "It might have *transformed* everything. But no matter. The transformation continues. What else could have brought you to see me?''

Robert and Mei-Ling glanced at each other.

"What do you mean?" Robert asked.

Manqué's grin turned abruptly into a frown and grimace.

"Please, Ms. Magnus," the prisoner said, "tell your little British friend that I grow tired of his empty-headed police games. Though your 'justice' would keep me as benighted and shit-fed as a barnyard fungus, though I am denied any access to the infosphere, though I have only this ancient mechanical typewriter on which to record my thoughts—why not clay tablets for cuneiform, while you're at it?—yet, *yet*, I am still allowed the occasional recycled newspaper or magazine. I read most carefully behind their lines.''

''You know about the Light, then?'' Robert asked, speaking up again in an attempt to redeem his own intellectual standing in the eyes of this mass-murderer standing before them.

''Of course I know about the Light,'' Manqué/Kong said with a short snort of laughter. ''I experienced it, even here. It passed through the globe itself as readily as any neutrino, but in a much more interesting fashion. The other investigators sent by your Mr. Landau and Dr. Mulla told me at least as much through their questions as I told them through my answers. I don't want to play that little game any longer. If you want information *from* me, you must give information *to* me. If you want my help, you have to help me.''

Mei-Ling glanced briefly at Robert, as if to say *Now look at what you've gotten us into*.

''How much do you know?'' Mei-Ling asked.

''Ah, that's better,'' Manqué said with a nod. ''Not so much as you out in the world who are not similarly constrained, certainly. But the Light would appear to have been the result of the generation of an information density singularity. My dear RATs were involved in gathering the information for it. That's why you're here. Quid pro quo, now. How much do *you* know about the Light?''

Mei-Ling glanced at Robert again, and immediately decided that trying to play any sort of game with Manqué would be absolutely foolish.

''It originated in space not far from HOME 1,'' Mei-Ling began, recalling briefing materials given her by Mulla and Landau. ''The person who was supposedly responsible for it, Jiro Yamaguchi, had been dead for over a year. He apparently died during an attempt to transfer his consciousness to some sort of machine-based artificial brain.''

''The transfer, though, seems to have worked,'' Manqué said, ''at least after a fashion . . . ?''

''So it would appear,'' Mei-Ling said with a nod. ''The machine systems he'd 'transferred' himself to were reactivated by the chief web spider up in HOME 1, Lakshmi Ngubo. The result was that the consciousness-construct of the former Jiro Yamaguchi began to infiltrate HOME's systems. It started with the HOME master control system Ngubo herself had designed, the Variform Autonomous Joint Reasoning Activity, or VAJRA—''

"When did my RATs come into play?" Manqué said, a slight impatience in his voice.

"Apparently after the Yamaguchi construct began moving out into the totality of the infosphere," Mei-Ling said. "We don't know where he found the RATs. Maybe you can tell us . . . ?"

Manqué, standing silent and smiling, was not forthcoming.

"Through the use of the RATs and control of the nanotech used to build the orbital solar power satellites," Mei-Ling continued, glancing at Robert for help here, "the Yamaguchi construct created something akin to photorefractive holographic projectors—''

"Which are?" Manqué asked flatly.

"Dr. Mulla's people say they're arrays of microscopic lasers embedded in photorefractive material," Robert explained. "Powered by layers of solar exchange film. Their best guess was that the film functioned as both power source and memory matrix. X-shaped information-refractive satellites. We have not been able to duplicate them."

Manqué/Kong gave a curt nod as a gesture for Mei-Ling to continue.

"The Yamaguchi construct used the RATs to gather and shape information from throughout the infosphere," Mei-Ling said. "The X-sats began appearing in a necklace all about the Earth. There was a mass infiltration of the infosphere by Yamaguchi's RATs and related programs. All this made authorities here on Earth very nervous."

Manqué laughed, but said nothing.

"To the military," Mei-Ling continued, "the Building the Ruins game the Yamaguchi construct was using to shape the information looked a lot like strategic and tactical scenarios. Forces from Earth came very close to invading the orbital habitat before the crisis passed."

"How, exactly, did it do that?" Manqué asked, suddenly very attentive.

"The Yamaguchi construct underwent something that's been described as a 'portal experience,' " Mei-Ling said, hesitantly, aware that she was on much more speculative ground here. "Yamaguchi left our space-time plane and went elsewhere."

"In theological terms, he *transcended*, then?" Manqué/Kong said, more than asked.

Mei-Ling nodded.

"Yes, that would be the word for it, in that context," she agreed. "In undergoing that apotheosis or dimensional shift or whatever it was, the Yamaguchi construct shed a torrent of shaped information—"

"A kenosis," Manqué said, nodding vigorously, beginning to pace his death cube of burning light.

Mei-Ling looked confused for an instant, then recovered.

"I'm afraid I don't know that term," she said. "Dr. Mulla's people are agreed, though, that the information pulse was facilitated through the X-shaped satellites. That pulse is popularly referred to as the Light."

Robert glanced up from the floor.

"It's also been described as a simultaneous omnidirectional wave of hyperconsciousness," he said, trying to be helpful. "Also as an 'irenic apocalypse.' "

"Yes, of course," Manqué said, nodding, pacing. "Exactly. What was the nature of the Light's interaction? Was it recorded?"

"Film, video, and holo records show lightpaths spiking everywhere," Mei-Ling said. "A distortion of space about the heads of human beings, and above the cranial region of some other creatures as well. Eyes remming fiercely. Knots of sensitive flame like distorted rainbows. All lasting only a brief flash."

"Paraclete tongues of fire," Manqué said, nodding as he paced. Looking at him, Mei-Ling thought of a happy pyromaniac, for some reason. "Yes, yes. What happened to the X-shaped satellites?"

"Apparently they destroyed themselves in discharging the Light," Robert said. "With all of them gone from cislunar space, with the RATs and Building the Ruins game gone from the infosphere, the tensions between Earth and the habitat dissolved. The invasion was halted before it really began."

"Fascinating," Manqué said, stopping in his pacing, turning his gaze fixedly to Mei-Ling. "They functioned as self-consuming artifacts. I presume you recognize the points of contact between what happened around this Light and our moment of aborted glory above Sedona?"

Mei-Ling nodded and glanced down at the floor of the cell.

"The thought had occurred to me," she said quietly.

"What do you mean?" Robert asked, looking from Mei-Ling to Manqué. Manqué said nothing, waiting expectantly on what Mei-Ling might say.

"The X-satellites would seem to have some similarities to the holojector-like devices you insisted we install at the Abbey," Mei-Ling said, looking up at Manqué. "Some of the phenomena surrounding the black hole sun resembled the phenomena surrounding the Light. Particularly the knotted or distorted images of rainbow fire."

"Very good, Ms. Magnus," Manqué said, like a teacher bestowing approval on a student's very appropriate answer. He abruptly sat down at the chair beside the desk. "That still doesn't explain fully why you've come to see me, however. Your description mentioned nothing about the Light killing anyone. Or a new black hole sun expanding uncontrollably through space. Or RATs in the wainscoting again—which I suppose you believe are my areas of expertise."

Mei-Ling glanced down at the floor again.

"We have no evidence that the Light was itself harmful to anyone," she said. "Since its advent, however, there have been several simultaneous waves of deaths throughout the world and in near-Earth space. Something striking people through the infosphere, usually while they were looking into certain data constellations. Most specifically those data sets involving Tetragrammaton, Crystal Memory Dynamics and its connection to the Blue Spike trade, even the Light itself."

Manqué/Kong drummed his fingers lightly and excitedly on the desktop.

"A murderer both serial and mass—simultaneously," he said, intrigued. "Wonderful! I'm only accused of being a mass murderer, myself. And how are you referring to this fascinating character who operates in different spaces at the same time?"

"A parallel killer," Robert said. "Some in the media are calling them the Topological Voyeur Killings."

"Yes, I've heard something about that," Manqué/Kong said. "And you say Tetragrammaton is involved too. Why bring me into it, though? I have no connection with the program any longer. I already took the spear for them, wouldn't you say? And, as you can see, I have no electronic access whatsoever."

"You're a potential asset because of the nature of the deaths," Mei-Ling said. "Those murdered were dimensionally distorted. Topologically reduced and expanded. Your RATs and their information-gathering propensities are probably involved. The spatial distortion surrounding the victims also bears some resemblance to a controlled version of the black hole sun effect."

From his death cube the prisoner fixed her with his stare.

"And you say these waves of killings started after the Light?" he asked. "Intriguing. And, if not me, you suspect—whom?"

"We suspected a machine intelligence at first," Mei-Ling said, "because of the vast amounts of sheer data manipulation involved. Now I must believe the perpetrator is human. It has the human twist to it, the desire for control, for power over others. We suspect the killer is someone who feels wronged by one of those groups whose data our perpetrator is so zealously protecting. Perhaps in order to protect himself."

Robert looked at Mei-Ling quickly. That last part was a new angle, certainly. Were his enterpol colleagues investigating CMD putting themselves in the killer's line of fire? He glanced at Manqué, who seemed lost in thought, as if contemplating a complex chess problem to a dozen moves ahead. Mei-Ling and Robert waited expectantly.

"Interesting," Manqué said at last. "That all seems logical enough. But you're missing something. I'll give you a little hint. You mentioned a game played throughout the infosphere before this Yamaguchi person zapped out of our space-time. Look for a sore loser. An unrecognized genius who might feel that the prize of transcendence is rightfully his. Or hers."

Mei-Ling nodded as Robert took notes.

"Quid pro quo, sir," she said at last. "What do you want in return?"

"Access," Manqué said, in a suspiciously sweet voice that nonetheless affected Mei-Ling like the sound of teeth grinding. "I want back into the infosphere. How can I help you otherwise?"

"You know I can't grant you that," Mei-Ling said evenly. "There are courts and boards and officials at a dozen levels—"

"And you can get to them!" Manqué said, his right hand clenching into a fist. "Tell them they can monitor every information exchange I engage in. They can wire everything with kill switches. Tell them if I don't get access, you get nothing more from me. And you need me—*they* need me."

He pounded the table on this last, once, very hard.

"You don't really think," he said forcefully, "that Yamaguchi or my RATs or your topo killer were able to bend space-time like that all by themselves, do you? Something much bigger is involved. Tell your 'authorities' that a lot more than just these insignificant killings are at stake. Tell them a lot more than just our pitiful little planet is at stake.''

After that outburst, Martin Kong, a.k.a. Phelonious Manqué, lapsed into a silence so total that nothing Mei-Ling or Robert could say or do would rouse him from it. Mei-Ling told him that she and Robert would lobby for Manqué's limited access. She told him they would do so before they left for Edwards spaceport to travel to the orbital habitats. Robert said they were going in hopes of interviewing Lakshmi Ngubo and Yamaguchi's elder brother, Seiji.

It didn't matter. None of that brought any response. Kong's gaze was fastened on the desk, boring steadily into its surface. In a lesser person it would have seemed petulant, but the grand obliviousness of the man in the death cube made his behavior quite chilling to both Robert and Mei-Ling.

At last they had no option but to leave the strange captive and return again to a world that refused to see itself as either pitiful or little.

"THE MIND MAKE CONSTELLATIONS IN THE NIGHT SKY,'' HARI asked, a bit stumble-tongued, ''or the night sky make constellations in the mind?''

''I dunno,'' Aleck said, staring at the heavens above them, from where the car stood parked beside a dark country road, ''but this is more stars than I've ever seen before.''

Ever since their success at Planet Noir, the members of Onoma Verité seemed to have been either partying with alcohol and other chemicals, or (rarely) sleeping. Calling in sick from his nightly monitoring of Hugh Manatee, Aleck had decided, more or less, to party with them tonight.

Driving them way out into the countryside beyond Socioville-Foster Road hadn't been his idea, though. That was Hari's push. He was the only one of them who took into account things like the phase of the moon, ''low-ambient, non-urban light levels,'' ''gegenschein,'' and ''degrees of arc.'' He was also the only one who cared all that much about looking for the big new comet that was coming in, the one called Hsiu-Johansen.

Looking up into the sky, Aleck thought Hsiu-Johansen was impressive enough. Its tail streamed out across several fists of arc, until it disappeared into the solar backscatter that Hari called gegenschein. Under city lights, the comet was pretty much an oblong blur, God's smudged fingerprint on the bowl of the firmament. Out here, beyond the conurbs and exurbs, it was a great streaming veil, a shower of incandescence falling ceaselessly across the sky.

No wonder the ancients believed the appearance of comets portended a change in kingdoms, Aleck thought, remembering Halley's comet of 1066 and the Battle of Hastings. Omens and signs of a great shift in the life of the world.

Aleck was even more impressed, tonight, by the background against which the comet stood. A deep, thick river of golden stars shone in the sky above him, so thick as to make constellations difficult to discern. A standing wave of suns, the vortex of the Milky Way, always there, but usually blotted out by daystar Sol. Or by the bright moon. Or streetlights. From where they reclined on the hood of the car, Aleck and Hari stared at the flood of suns above their heads for quite a while.

" 'The gods have their porch lights on,' " Hari remarked, "as the Albertians put it."

Aleck nodded. A few yards to his left, on a blanket laid out on the grass between road and field, he heard some sort of word game going on between Janika and Sam.

"Oiling the midnight burn," Sam said.

"Ending the candle at both burns," Janika countered.

"No wick for the rested!" Sam said. They both laughed. Then Sam apparently began trying to prove that his four years at a Latin School had in fact taught him some Latin, however poorly he might be remembering it now.

"Money takes up," Janika said, "where love leaves off."

"*Pecunia incipit ubi amor finit,*" Sam replied, slightly sloshed. "A heraldic motto for prostitutes everywhere."

Hari moved to a sitting position on the car's front end.

"Hey, Sam," he called, "how about 'Art ends where commerce begins'?"

"*Ars finit ubi commercium incipit,*" Sam said. "Motto of every lean and hungry artist who got fat and happy and saw his artistic abilities destroyed by success."

They heard Janika getting up from the blanket.

"Artist-speak, again," she said sourly. "Just what exactly *is* your problem with making money?"

"*Pecunia incipit ubi ars finit,*" Sam said with a shrug.

"I won't even ask," Janika said, walking and stumbling back toward the car.

"I dream of a gratification so powerful it will dissolve the society which suppresses it!" Sam called after her, laughing. "Artistic alienation is a memory of the future. My memory of the future is the source of my artistic alienation!"

"Yeah, yeah, yeah," Janika said wearily.

Aleck sat up on the front end of the car.

"How about 'Fear leaves off where understanding begins'?" he suggested.

"Do you mean understanding as in 'accurate knowledge,'" Sam asked, "or understanding as in 'sympathy' or 'empathy'?"

Aleck had to ponder that a moment. What he was getting at had elements of both, but he didn't think Sam would like that answer.

"Accurate knowledge, I guess," he said at last.

"'*Timor finit ubi intellectus incipit*,' according to Sam's rubric," Marco said, interrupting, coming out of the fallow field where he had been walking with his new, exotic-looking girlfriend, Rama. "Though I don't think that's the most accurate Latin."

"Oh?" Sam said, sitting up on the blanket and taking slight offense. "And you would know?"

Marco shrugged his heavy shoulders.

"Just because I look to be going nowhere doesn't mean that I couldn't have come from everywhere," he said slyly.

"Ooh, that's a pretentious platitude," Sam said.

"At least I'm not altered enough to be spending my time making them up in bad Latin," Marco shot back. "*Nimium eruditionis habes.*"

Both of them laughed at that, their own private joke. A big shooting star slit the night sky for a moment and their laughter turned into a brief chorus of *Ah*'s and *you see that*'s. After the star passed, Aleck lay back on the car's hood and spoke to Hari's back.

"I was thinking about what you said before," Aleck began. "About whether it was the mind that makes constellations in the sky, or the sky that makes constellations in the mind. What about that in terms of the Light that did or didn't happen? Did the Light make constellations in our minds, or did our minds make constellations in the Light?"

"Who knows?" Hari said. "Whatever it was, it just didn't last long enough. It needed to last at least as long as that comet up there. Instead, it barely lasted as long as a shooting star. Insufficient data.''

"Insufficient data?" Sam said, incredulously, his words slightly slurred. "Didn't I give you that book to cure you of that? Stop being such an objective materialist! The universe isn't objective—it's interactive."

" 'Participatory' is what my professors prefer to call it," Hari said quietly.

"Okay, fine," Sam replied, standing up from the blanket. He staggered over toward the car, then rapped his knuckles noisily on the hood of the car as he got to it.

"If you people are up for it," he said insinuatingly, "Jan and I have got some things with us that are tools for participation, for interactivity."

Uh-oh, Aleck thought, remembering that when he'd picked them up, Sam had been carrying a cooler and Janika toting a picnic basket. Both items were now residing in the trunk of the pod car. But what Aleck said was, "What tools?"

"Open up the trunk," Sam said, casting an all-too-conspiratorial glance at Janika, "and I'll show you."

Aleck and Hari jumped down from the hood and started toward the back of the car. As they walked, Aleck overheard snatches of Sam and Janika's conversation.

"—definitely an ascomycete," Sam was saying softly, "like morels and truffles, or the penicillin fungi. Or ergot-producing *Claviceps* on rye."

"Ergot?" Janika whispered. "That's the one that came before LSD, isn't it?"

Aleck beamed the Unlock command to the trunk and moved slightly aside as Sam and Janika and the others crowded around the back of the car.

"What's in the cooler, Sam?" he asked, as the trunk swept up with a whoosh. "*Claviceps*-on-rye sandwiches?"

Sam and Janika looked startled, then laughed.

"Something like that," Sam said, lifting out the cooler as Jan removed the picnic basket. On top of the basket was what looked, in the trunk light, like a good-sized portable VR player and several sets of mind-machine gargoggles. "You'll find out."

"What's with the tech?" Hari asked as they walked toward the big blanket already spread out on the grass.

"Sam said we needed some mind-machinery for our party," Janika replied, setting the player upright on the ground beside her left foot. "So I brought the box and some Wayne Takahashi stuff."

As everyone sat down on the picnic blanket, Sam and Janika, by flashlight, began setting out their movable feast: loaves of sourdough and rye bread, sliced turkey, ham, chicken, avocado, tomatoes, cucumber, bell peppers, assorted crackers and chips, sour cream, cream cheese, yogurt, wine, suntea. Knives, forks, and a cutting board were also included. They looked like any ordinary group of picnickers, Aleck thought—except that it happened to be the middle of the night.

"And now," said Sam, removing a covered china plate from the cooler, "the pièce de résistance!"

With a flourish he uncovered the dish. Displayed thereon were six fresh, thick-bodied, fleshy, convoluted whitish things. Sam reached forward and picked one up, examining it more closely. Janika, Marco, and Rama followed suit.

"Gatehead mushrooms," Sam said. "The source. I got them from a guy who accessed them at a Möbius Caducéus show."

"I don't know," said Marco's girlfriend, Rama, studying the specimen she had picked up, "but it looks, um, *phallic*, if you ask me."

"Yeah," Janika agreed, "like a cross between the brain and the penis of a bipedal mammal. What would Dr. Freud say, Sam?"

The women laughed, but Sam shot back in his best Viennese accent:

"Sometimes a mushroom is just a mushroom," he said, smiling sardonically. Everyone laughed; then Sam continued sans accent. "If these are the real thing, we should be thinking more about 'set and setting' than about possible Freudian interpretations."

"Exactly," Marco agreed, slicing and dicing his mushroom into small pieces on the cutting board. When he had finished he took Sam's mushroom and began the same procedure. His hands freed, Sam turned his attention to uncorking one of the bottles of wine.

"I checked them out with a botanist friend of mine on campus," Sam said, slowly shifting into tripmaster-shaman mode. "He confirmed that this mushroom is definitely not poisonous—and very likely psychoactive. That's why we're here in this setting: outdoors, on a beautiful night, with good food and drink and company. This is both a celebration and an exploration. Just be open to whatever experience happens, willing to learn from it. Especially anything it tells us about the Light, if you want to make that the topic. Good or bad, it'll last only a few hours at most.''

Marco finished dicing up the first four, then glanced at Sam, who looked toward where Aleck and Hari were sitting.

"You two want some as well?" he asked casually, though the pressuring undertones were there for everyone to hear.

Aleck hated this part. Certainly he didn't want to ruin everyone else's good time, or to stand out, alienated from what they would be experiencing. He didn't want to appear paranoiacally overcautious on the one hand—or weak-willed on the other. Part of his mind didn't like to be pressured, either. His hand was being forced to try what he hadn't tried before, at a time and place he hadn't chosen. He already had a busy enough day scheduled tomorrow. After staying up all night he'd be tired tomorrow—and exhausted the day after that, which was when he usually felt the real, time-lagged consequences of an all-night escapade. He could feel Hari watching him, too, for some sign of the way the wave was going to break.

"Sure," Aleck said at last. Beside him, Hari shrugged agreement.

"I want to be the first to try them," Sam said. "I'm the one who procured them, so I get first dibs."

Marco gave to Janika and Rama the finely chopped mushrooms he'd been working on while Sam spoke with Hari and Aleck, then took Aleck and Hari's mushrooms. The women mixed the mushrooms with the yogurt, or the cream cheese, or the sour cream, concocting three varieties of mushroom dip. Sam began pouring wine as Marco finished chopping the remaining mushrooms, which Janika and Rama then stirred into the dips, pale hands and dark hands working side by side.

"A toast," Sam said at last. He raised his wineglass with one hand while dipping a piece of dark rye bread into the sour cream mushroom dip with the other. "Here's to the entheogen *Cordyceps tepuiensis* 'Larkin'—and good hopes for our first encounter with it."

With responses of "hear, hear" everyone clinked glasses and drank. Sam took a large bite of the dip-slathered rye bread and chewed thoughtfully. Everyone else watched him intently.

"Hey, this is tasty!" he said after a moment. "These fungi are downright delicious!"

One by one the rest of them dipped bread or crackers into the mushroom mixes and sampled some *Cordyceps tepuiensis* "Larkin." Aleck did so too, saying a silent prayer of sorts. He hoped that he didn't share whatever twist in the DNA spiral it might be that made some folks prone to an extremely heightened psychoactive chemical sensitivity. He prayed particularly that he wouldn't prove genetically predisposed to mental imbalances that might be blown wide open by exposure to entheogens like this fungus.

To his surprise, Aleck found that Sam was indeed telling the truth, at least about the taste. He had expected something bitter and slimy, but these mushrooms were delicious. He could only describe their flavor as "meaty nutty"—meaty like filet mignon and nutty like macadamias. From the expressions on Janika's and Rama's faces, he could tell they were finding them surprisingly tasty too. The mushrooms were so delectable that he found it hard to believe that anything tasting so good could be bad for him. Still, he could see that, like himself, his companions—particularly Hari and Marco—were all a bit tentative, waiting anxiously for any stomach-rumbling premonition of nausea, or gastrointestinal distress, or full-blown food poisoning.

No such signs were forthcoming. By the time Janika started setting up the virtual player and handing around the gargoggles, they were all spreading the mushroom dip onto sandwiches as well. Indian tabla music came pouring out of the player's speakers as they ate.

"I thought something ethnic but with a good beat would be appropriate, for now," Janika said.

"Classic Zakir Hussain, isn't it?" Rama asked, identifying the music. Janika nodded and Rama smiled approvingly.

"When you start to feel your head changing," Janika said, "just put on the goggles. They'll automatically activate your feed of the Takahashi program, from the beginning."

Twenty minutes later, the six of them had eaten most of the food and polished off two bottles of wine. Aleck soon realized, however, that he was beginning to experience something more than the usual postprandial bliss and lassitude. He fumbled on the gargoggles, thinking distractedly what a beautiful study in contrasts Rama and Janika were—Rama dark and shorter and amply curved, Janika blond and taller and less emaciated-looking tonight—more "willowy."

He was surprised to note that the goggles were primarily real-time screens representing whatever direction he looked in. The cryptic phrase DESCRIPTION IS NOT SYNONYMOUS WITH ADVOCACY appeared in overlay. Only then did he realize that the virtual goggles were something more than a sort of head-mounted closed-circuit TV.

Seen through the lightweight goggles, the air around Aleck had begun to fill with shimmering, shifting dots and flecks of blue and yellow light. When he moved his head, the flecks of light "echoed," tracking and afterimaging off the light sources out in the "real world." He soon realized that slowly scanning the starry sky made for a particularly impressive effect. The heavens above him echoed with light. Dreamily he wondered how one would describe that in Latin.

The afterimaging lights slowly began joining to form fluid grids and honeycomb patterns, saturated colors flashing and fading, swelling and shrinking, rippling and distorting through everything in his (he was now sure) computer-augmented field of vision. Zigzag lightning softened to meanders, to waves, curves, filigrees.

Aleck began to wonder where the Takahashi virtual in his eyes and ears left off and the effects of the entheogen in his head began. Squared spirals of red and blue shone fiercely against the night sky now, rotating and moving, enlarging and shrinking. The starry river and the lightfall of the comet above his head became almost overpoweringly complex in their imagery. For a while it seemed to him that he could see this flood of images only peripherally. Wherever he looked intently, for even a short while, a brilliant white hole occupied the center of his vision, the movable bright eye of the storm.

Somewhere in his head, Aleck remembered seeing an interview with Takahashi, remembered the artist explaining that what Aleck was now seeing was not the eye of the storm but the storm of the eye. These images were entoptic phenomena, patterns being generated within the eye, produced by the activity of the visual apparatus itself. Actually, not just his eyes but Aleck's entire nervous system seemed to be doing it, becoming a new sense, a sixth or seventh or tenth or n^{th} sense in addition to his usual five. That new sense was a producer of new sensations his brain was trying its best to make sense of.

Then abruptly it didn't matter. His mind was absolutely focused on what he was seeing. The moment was unfolding before him in light. All irrelevant reminiscences were gone. No memories of the past or thoughts of the present or contemplations of the future lingered.

The night sky was covered in luminous, translucent script, Arabic or hieroglyphic or cuneiform. The stars were a swirling dance of unreadable letters, celestial graffiti. The beat coming out of the player was the thudding of a million drums, a billion hearts, all drums one drum beating a planetary tattoo, a world heartbeat, unimaginable pounding harmonies, sounds bending and dilating, breaking up and digitizing until he could hear the music of the universe in the space between the notes.

He turned (no doubt and no reflection, only the merging of action and awareness) with a slow smile (clear goals, clear understanding) toward Janika. She was printed and tattooed all over with the same shimmering translucent script (no need or desire to control the situation) and smiling too. Sam was in much the same state.

He looked at the backs of his hands and (no self-consciousness) found they were no longer familiar but had instead become alien topography, netted with nerves and roped with blood vessels, highways trafficked with the lights of firing neurons, the pulsing gridlock of platelets, X-ray vision of and through skin and flesh and bones, swarmed over by glittering pulsing geometric forms. (No question of how he could see them, clear as death vision. He just could, in starlight, see them—as if his eyes were sucking in more light.)

The empty whole formerly known as Aleck began mouthing a soft, interminable, unspeakable word (a sense of present reality deeper and more diffuse than that of his usual senses) to Rama. She got up and began to dance to the beat that seemed now not to come from the player but from the earth and air and sky. Janika and Marco and Hari and Sam and Aleck rose, all one, to join her dance, pounding a dance floor into the low grass. Whirling and spinning, the flood of bright and dark geometries came faster, the bright center of the eye-storm no longer right in front but ahead, down a tunnel or at the bottom of a vortex, the white hole from which the flood of all perceptions came surging, realer than real, hypersolid, yet dreamy with the floating sensation that sometimes accompanies sleep's onset.

They were all one innocent child floating half-adream in a rotating tunnel walled with electric bricks, every brick a panel or screen mounted in shimmering fluid lattice or matrix, dancing in waves of entoptic geometries. Watching and dancing they saw that every bright brick they stared into was in its turn a tunnel or living breathing passageway, a portal depicting on its walls, over and over again, dancers dancing and watching, watching and dancing endlessly. Each passageway was a different dance, a different space in time.

They fell out of their bodies into a thousand different dances, joined Shakers shaking in their Circle Dance, punks slamming and thrashing, pit dancers moshing, Indians doing the Ghost Dance, Tarantists spinning, Sufi dervishes whirling, nineteenth-century French girls and Carolingian jugglers and Kuchean Buddhists scarf dancing, can-can dancers and ecstatic dancers of Hathor, Elamite and Greek and Sioux line dancers, group dancers, masked dancers, penitential dancers and dancing bacchantes, Morisco and carneval and formal ball dances, chain dances and rondos and hasta moudra hand dances, dances of warrior youths and maidens and shepherds and buffoons, Shivite sacred dancers, Chinese sleeve dancers, Japanese Kabuki, Russian ballet, dances to the tune of flageolet, tambourin, oboes, horns, trombones, double bass, string orchestra, guitars, castanets, bagpipes, violin, flute, lute, viols, transverse flutes, trumpets, shawm, rebec, triangular harp, lyre, sword and lance on shield, tympanon, aulos and double aulos, frame drum, skull drum, bullroarer, turtleshell rattle, song, handclap—

How much Takahashi's? How much theirs? How much his own? It didn't matter. Across time and space they shared the same experience, the same impersonal Great Dance of it all, the long complex choreography, out of the First Handclap's fastest of fast dances, stars whirling out of whorling gas, planets spinning into being from cooling starstuff, thunderbolt and cloud and volcano, dance of chemical hypercycles, first cell of shape-changing life, bluegreenalgaprokaryoteeukaryotecoelenteratetrilobiteammonite gastropodcephalopodinsectfishamphibianreptile birdmammal—until a present both far future and far past at once, a great, spiral, turning, dance pilgrimage, with many others, reddish-pelted, rightbrainwise, cerebellar, left-handed, supraorbital, nocturnal, heavy brow-ridged, auditory, barrel-chested, short-extremitied, cold-adapted, all walking, to Allesseh, all dancing, through the worldweb, all singing, mushroom-eating, moon-worshipping, snake-adoring, spider-loving, troll ancestral, low-foreheaded, skycave dwelling, red ochre symboled, second-sighted, magnetited, archaeofuturosapiens, all walking down spiral sunmoonlines, all dancing up the soulspring, all singing up and down innumerable timelines, walk, dance, song, all one, at once. Then, now, next, all one, at once.

Allesseh the whole way to Allesseh, Allesseh is the way. Allesseh timeline sightline, dancers dancing to it in it, toward it of it, walking amid stars in the cave of the sky, to the bottom of the vortex of vortices, Allesseh, floating black hole crystal ball mirror sphere memory bank, all outside it inside it, all time space histories stories together there, each for each who gazes in, sees own, Allesseh the shining gate between time and eternity—

The moment of aching clarity, of awe and weirdness and wordlessness. Of fascination that Eternity is not just very much time but the absence of the existence of time. That Infinity is not just very much space but the absence of being located in space. Deep union with overpowering, mysterious, radically-other vitality. Recognition that I and We and That are one—

Aleck slowly felt himself becoming enfleshed again, in the flesh he had never left. The Allesseh—where is it? he wanted to ask. But he saw that it had turned its face away from itself, so that everything turned and burned away, toward the last dance, the slowest slow dance of entropic maximum, the mere universal vibration of that endless end. . . .

He came back to himself more fully then, to find that he was still dancing in the sunrise of this high bright just-morning in a windy place beside Socioville-Foster Road. Gazing slowly around, he wondered at the time and where it had gone. The stars and comet were fading to nothingness. Had he been dancing in trance? How long? The music and images from the player had long since stopped, but he had been dancing to the beat of a music *beyond* the music of what happens, amid scenes beyond the screen of what is.

Aleck suddenly wondered if he'd been dancing asleep all his life, if the past night's strange vision within a dream within a hallucination was the most wide-awake he'd ever been, the most vividly he'd ever perceived anything. Removing the virtual goggles, he wondered who he should thank—the genius of Wayne Takahashi for his triggering visuals, or the genius in that strange fungus he had eaten.

The shimmering, breathing, mental-wallpaper patterns of his entoptics were beginning to fade. He realized vaguely that he was almost back from that elsewhere he had journeyed to. He felt both regret at leaving alterreality behind and relief at returning to the staged world where he could once again play his usual part.

Breaking away from the dance—only Rama and Marco were also still dancing, he noted belatedly; Janika and Sam and Hari had disappeared—Aleck stumbled off to urinate behind a tree. His spatial sense was probably still distorted, he realized, when he discovered he was a giant pissing a flood on the small, distant broccoli plant of the tree. As he zipped up, he wondered with a shiver if perhaps his regret and relief at coming down and coming back might have been a bit premature.

"Aleck!" Sam called, from nearby, but sounding far away. "This stuff is way more potent than I imagined. We'd better start bringing everybody back to reality."

Sam and Hari were both coming toward him. Hari's eyes looked owlishly big as he approached, despite the growing daylight.

"Suggestions?" Aleck asked, his mouth working again, slowly, thickly, at last.

"This has been more a party than an experiment," Hari said, a bit pantingly, as if he, too, found speaking a considerable exertion. "We don't have much info in terms of exact dosages. No dry weights of the mushroom material ingested, no exact body weights of the participants, that sort of thing. We do have our subjective experiences, though. We can talk people down if we need to."

Aleck nodded—with interminable slowness, it seemed to him.

"Then we can get some sense of the time frame," he said thoughtfully.

"Right," Hari said. "When was the first onset of the altered state? How long did the altered state of consciousness last? What stages did it pass through? Even this stuff can be handled in a rigorous, scientific manner."

"Right," Sam agreed, gazing about them. "Sure. Look, it's getting to be morning. Where are Rama and Marco and Janika? We should all be getting back to our apartments or to campus."

Aleck nodded. With the others, he wandered over the fields, which felt more like a flat-topped mountain this early morning. In the dawn light, as they went looking for Marco and the women, his words with Sam and Hari were still a starlit conversation of myth and participation mystique and divination, out-of-body-experiences and astral projection and mystical union and transcendence.

They found Rama plopped down on their makeshift dancing ground, wiping tears from her eyes. Marco knelt beside her in the trampled grass, motioning them to go on looking for Janika, which they did reluctantly. As he walked away, Aleck heard Rama saying something about "souls frozen in deathless bodies." He was still trying to make sense of whatever that might mean when they came upon Janika. Standing atop a rock, arms spread as if to embrace the whole world and sky, she was smiling radiantly, even maniacally, communing happily with all creation.

"Gentlemen," she said when she turned to them at last, "you wouldn't believe where I've been."

"What? Did you see God?" Aleck asked, trying a tired joke.

"See God? I *was* God. The devil too. Everything. Went from Chartres rose windows and mandalas on the backs of my eyelids all the way out to the edges of the Rorschach universe. I learned great things, important things."

At last she came down from the small height. As they walked back toward the remains of their picnic and the impromptu dancing ground, Hari kept speaking to Aleck in such rapid-fire fashion that Aleck had trouble following him. He finally told Hari he should save it, that they were going to be writing down or recording all this just as soon as possible—at least that had been Sam's suggestion. Hari agreed that it was a good one.

Back at the blanket they helped Marco and Rama stow the picnic leftovers in cooler and basket and daypack. They gathered up the virtual player and packed away the trash. In the morning light they shook out and folded the blanket, then walked back toward the car.

Each of them from time to time looked back at the area of flattened grass where the picnic had been. Something in their eyes said they couldn't believe what had happened there. Because it *had* happened, though, they would never see that place, or themselves, or the world, in quite the same light again.

The others waited as Aleck unlocked the doors and the trunk. As they loaded up and then locked away their impedimenta, Sam remarked that there was coffee always brewing back at their place, and they were all invited for a "debriefing." Aleck could scarcely wait for the coffee. He was exhausted and his mouth was saturated with a bitter taste, as if he'd licked the latex leaking from a thousand sleepy poppies.

On the way home, Sam clicked on a recorder, in case anyone had particular experiences to relate. At first the desire to talk about what had happened seemed to have passed out of them, or the recorder kept them silent. Aleck wondered if Sam had brought it along for nothing.

At last, they began to describe what they'd been through. Rama explained her nightmare of souls breaking the cycle of incarnations—not through achieving satori or nirvana but by achieving static deathlessness in the flesh. Hari, growing particularly voluble, talked about how he had really seen for the first time a "universe strange, uncertain, and incomplete." About how the more you know about where you are the less you know about where you're going. How the more self-consistent a theory is, the less complete it necessarily must be. About "superposition of states" and how everything that is *possible* in the universe is *actual*, until observation occurs and sifts out one state as "real" from all those superposed states. About the nine billion lives of Schrödinger's cat—

That got Marco going, talking about time lines, dim futures of barbarism come round again. The demand for "social order" and "morality" completely suppressing imagination, even consciousness itself. Then Sam talked about a vision of alternate pasts, including one in which Timothy Leary became John F. Kennedy's chief science advisor. Leary, through Kennedy concubine Mary Pinchot, had passed on prescient details from a Harvard psilocybin test-subject's visions describing, a year and more before it happened, the assassination attempt of November 22, 1963. The early warning thus prevented the assassination and assured fellow Irish Catholic Leary's rise to a post in the cabinet during Kennedy's second term, as well as a major role in the extension of Camelot into a full-blown American Aquarian Age.

Janika talked about visions of lens-shaped objects, "temporal mirages" that had appeared at various points in history. Foo fighters over Europe and the Pacific during the Second World War. Fireballs over Tenochtitlan just before the city fell to Cortes's forces. Phenomena in the heavens at a thousand crux-points in human history.

As Aleck related his own vision of grand-scale cosmological and biological evolution, however, he began to have his doubts. He had a long-time interest in biology, after all. Janika and Sam were intrigued by drug culture and weird history. Marco was paranoid about social-control tech. Rama came out of a reincarnationist cultural tradition. Hari was an aficionado of heavy-lifting physics.

Were they all just projecting, then? How much of what they'd experienced was just them, projecting onto It—and how much of what they'd experienced was It, projecting onto them?

Constellations and the Mind. Still, the stars were real, weren't they? Even if you didn't have words for them? Almost with a gulp, Aleck related his experience of mystical union. Of that thing which gatehead subculture called the Allesseh. Of standing in the gate between time and eternity, space and infinity.

It was as if he'd opened the floodgates. Abruptly all of them began to discuss their visionary experiences more openly. Yes, they had all experienced something very much along those lines. Was it embedded in the Takahashi virtual? Aleck wanted to know. Janika assured them it wasn't, as far as she could tell. She'd experienced Takahashi's piece previously, in a workaday state of consciousness.

Watching the others talking as they got nearer home, Aleck noticed how pale and drawn, how wrung out and strung out Sam and Janika and Rama and Marco and Hari all looked—as if they had been on a long journey and returned home strangers to themselves. In their drawn faces their eyes were still intent on things no longer seen but remembered with a vividness more powerful than perception.

As they pulled up outside the apartment, Aleck realized that he too must look the same. He knew that though it was not yet ten in the morning, a thousand years had already passed and everything had changed. As they tramped upstairs and into the apartment, Sam announced that he was putting an internal anti-fungal medication on the table—two tabs for each participant—since allowing the *Cordyceps* to keep on growing inside them was not recommended.

Aleck, however, was preoccupied. The message lights of his telecom answering systems—virtual and voice mail both—were flashing. Portentously. Watching them, he had a premonition of big things about to break, of waves and comets and a change in kingdoms. He sighed. Something told him that changing the world would be easier than worlding the change.

F INALLY, ATSUKO, ROGER, AND MARISSA WERE ON THEIR WAY to Seiji and Jhana's housewarming party in the new world of HOME 2. First, however, they were to shuttle from the central sphere of HOME 1 out to low-grav to pick up Lakshmi Ngubo.

When the three had strapped into the shuttle, the transfer ship slipped free of the turning habitat, headed for the still point of the habitat's turning world, the micro-gee manufacturing facilities situated at a non-spinning and hence "weightless" part of the habitat's axis. For Roger, the trip had no particular resonances. For Atsuko and Marissa, however, who had traveled this way together before, it was haunted with a sense of what had happened the last time they'd come this way.

They were aboard the transfer ship only a moment before Marissa informed Atsuko of the further progress that had been made with Marissa's immortalizing vector, and Marissa's concern at the growing potential for an immortality plague.

"This is bad," Atsuko said, shaking her head. "Very bad indeed."

"Aren't we overreacting a bit?" Roger said, glancing out the shuttle portal at the Hsiu-Johansen comet in the distance. "The only place major work is being done on it is in the 'borbs and among the psiXtians in California. They aren't likely to trumpet the vector's existence, and neither are we—if it even works to begin with."

Both Marissa and his mother shook their heads.

"You have more faith in security controls than I do," Atsuko said. "If it works as it seems to, word will get out."

"Maybe it should," Marissa said thoughtfully. "Then there's at least a chance people will get to make a conscious decision about it."

Roger nodded, agreeing almost despite himself.

"You don't think telling people 'just say no' to immortality is going to work?" he said archly, still watching the comet out the shuttle's window.

"That's the real problem," Atsuko remarked. "Especially since, once you're past nuclear war, the human future is mainly a race between population and consciousness."

Roger returned his gaze to the interior of the cabin and to his mother and Marissa.

"How do you mean?" he asked.

"Just that the denser the population," Atsuko explained, beginning to list and link from one fingertip to the next, "the more interdependent its members. The more interdependent its members, the more pressure for social conformity. The more pressure for social conformity, the stronger the attacks on the whole notion of individuality. The stronger the attacks on individuality, the greater the erosion of privacy, the greater the destruction of introspective mental space and inwardness. The greater the devastation of privacy and inwardness, the greater the destruction of consciousness itself. The greater the destruction of consciousness, the more rigid the social program and the less the capability for responding creatively to environmental contingency. The smaller the capability for responding to contingency, the smaller the chance of continued species survival.''

Marissa brushed back her red hair quickly, then glanced down at her hands in her lap.

"Another type of chain reaction," she said. "Bad synergy. The population pressures that make the capacity for conscious individual choice all the more vital are the same ones that will be working against the continued existence of that capacity. The bigger the boom, the harder the crash."

Roger looked back into space, toward the comet shining there.

"I know nobody in the 'borbs is a big fan of secrecy," he said, "but the immortalizing vector seems to be one situation where no one can deny its efficacy. Encrypt the data enough and you'd have to have Jiro Yamaguchi's capabilities to access it."

Atsuko rested her chin in her hand and stared about the small shuttle cabin, empty but for themselves.

"What makes you think someone doesn't already have those capabilities?" she asked. "What's happened once can happen again."

Roger stared at his mother.

"Has it?" he asked.

"Maybe," she said, averting her gaze from both her son and Marissa. "Only differently. That comet you've been watching, Roger. It seems to have come literally from nowhere, and it's not behaving like an ordinary comet."

"Where'd you hear that?" he asked, puzzled.

"Since I'm council liaison," Atsuko replied, "our telecom people have kept themselves busy informing me. There have been a series of 'coordinated malfunctions' involving broadcast antenna arrays on Earth and in space. The malfunctions appear to be sending recurring pulses of information at that thing coming in—and to a few other points in interplanetary space."

Marissa stared at Roger's mother with an expression almost of shock.

"Something is coordinating those malfunctions?" she asked. "Through the infosphere?"

Atsuko nodded.

"Or some*one*," she said. "That's the current best guess. You can ask Lakshmi yourself on the way to the party. She has lots of theories."

Roger glanced back toward the comet. It looked exactly like every other comet he'd ever seen.

"Sounds like we've been here before," he said with a shrug. "But even if another consciousness has sprung up in the infosphere, who's to say it won't turn out for the best, the way it did last time?"

"No one *can* say, yet," Atsuko agreed. "At the very least, the security and integrity of the infosphere seems to be compromised, in much the same way it was when Jiro Yamaguchi was developing into whatever it was he became. Add to that how much infosphere communicating Marissa has been doing with her colleagues on the vector project. Then ask yourself if the 'secret' of the immortalizing vector is necessarily a secret any longer."

Drifting past shielded mirrors and collectors, then past the habitat's own solar power arrays until they were very nearly in free space, Roger was glad to at last see the micro-gee manufactories coming into view—before the implications of his mother's last statement could sink in any further.

Coming up beside the docking bay for Lakshmi's workspace, the ship fastened onto the docking port. When the airlock sighed open, they saw before them Lakshmi Ngubo herself, a dark-skinned, bright-eyed woman in her forties, dressed in loosely draped, vibrantly colored clothing, seated in a hoverchair and lightly goggled into virtual space, muttering into a sub voc microphone.

Behind her stood the cavernous space of her workshop, expanded since Atsuko and Marissa had last seen it but ever the thoroughly voice-activated smartspace. In the low gravity, slender robotic arms and voice-response waldos held and moved impossibly large pieces of equipment. The scene was still so much like it had been the first time Marissa visited Lakshmi that she almost expected to still find there the loosely made statue/shrine the Jiro Yamaguchi-construct had assembled. She was obscurely disappointed to see that it was gone.

"Hey, people!" Lakshmi said, commanding up her virtual goggles, coming toward them as her three visitors unstrapped and awkwardly attempted standing up and stretching in the very low gravity.

"Hope we didn't interrupt—" Atsuko began.

"Not at all, not at all," Lakshmi replied, making her way into the cabin of the transfer shuttle. "Just catching my daily dose of infotons."

Roger had heard the term before—virtualist slang for "information photons." Apparently Lakshmi was fond of that whole lexicon of hacker slang from the turn of the millenium, about "surfing the web" and "cybertanning."

"You must be Roger," Lakshmi said, nodding toward him. Roger didn't know exactly how to introduce himself. Shaking hands was out, but he somehow felt that Lakshmi's neck-down paralysis was causing him more awkwardness than it caused her. She was the one gliding smoothly about the cabin in her hoverchair, after all. Roger just said, "Yes" and nodded back.

The airlocks of ship and docking bay sighed closed and they all strapped or otherwise anchored themselves into place for the transit to HOME 2. Momentarily the ship eased free of HOME 1 and accelerated smoothly for their journey to a newer, though not necessarily braver, world.

"Atsuko told us you think there's some sort of new consciousness operating in the infosphere again," Marissa said, "and that it's sending messages in the direction of the Hsiu-Johansen comet."

"That's right," Lakshmi confirmed with a nod. "Did she also tell you that the source of the messages to the comet and the source of the infosphere killings seem to be the same?"

The revelation hit both Marissa and Roger with unexpected force.

"I thought I'd spare them that," Atsuko said, "since it's still primarily speculation."

Lakshmi laughed and wrinkled up her face.

"Less so every minute, unfortunately," she said.

"But how do you know?" Roger asked.

"That's a bit complex," Lakshmi replied, "and I don't claim to be certain. My best guess is that while Jiro Yamaguchi was functioning as a distributed artificial consciousness, he came into contact with a distributed artificial *un*consciousness."

"The RATs, you mean?" Marissa speculated.

"No, no," Lakshmi said, frowning deeply. "Something the RATs found already extant in the infosphere. A whole cyberspatial society, electronic life evolved from a virus program, inhabiting the human infosphere. Innumerable artificial lives trying to break through to the other side.''

Roger laughed abruptly. The others looked pointedly at him.

''All the Whos down in Whoville shouting *We are here! We are here! We are here!*'' he explained. ''But then how come they weren't discovered?''

Lakshmi sighed.

''I know it sounds like wheels within wheels,'' she said. ''Part of it may have been that we weren't looking for them—weren't expecting something radically 'other' in machines of our own construction. Part of it may have been that their 'room' normally has no doors into ours, no windows. I personally believe we didn't 'hear' them when they pounded on the walls because all their attempts to contact us have been greeted as so-called glitches, bugs, errors, jokes, pranks. ''

Roger still wasn't convinced.

''How do you know this new layer, if that's what it is, was around before?'' he asked. ''How do you know it hasn't just come into existence since Yamaguchi beamed out?''

Lakshmi shook her head vehemently.

''Think of the years of supporting evidence,'' she said. ''Think of all the speculation that the infosphere has had its own quirky intelligence, if not consciousness, since the earliest days of the Internet—''

Atsuko had been glancing out the window at the comet which had come into view on her side of the craft as the shuttle maneuvered. Now she seemed struck by a sudden thought.

''Like a brain then,'' she said. ''The Yamaguchi construct would be the new brain, like the cerebral cortex. Ultimately not a rule-governed machine. Through the networked distribution of the RATs, the Yamaguchi construct was connected to the entire infosphere, to the many but old-brain programmed 'intelligences' there, all still functioning within design parameters as rule-governed machinery, handling basic operations.''

''Exactly,'' Lakshmi said, with a nod and a smile. ''The layers together make up what some have called an 'artificial brain'— the only structure capable of demonstrating artificial consciousness. The Yamaguchi construct, the RATs, and the deeper society of distributed artificial unconsciousness—together they formed something more than the sum of their parts. A society of thought. An electronic ecology of Mind thinking. Not cyberspace, but info-jungle Brainforest. Oversimplified, the lower layers are what Jung called 'autonomous psychoid processes.' "

"Which are?" Roger asked.

"They come from the idea that each human consciousness contains many 'selves,' as it were," Lakshmi explained. "I spend most of my time working with complex yet still rule-governed machines. My mistake was in thinking of those 'selves' as subroutines, blocks of code usually subordinated to the authority and goals of the main program, the Self with a capital *S*. But the Self isn't a program, and the psychoid processes aren't just subroutines. Their relationship is a lot more complicated. Looked at from a deeper pespective, inexplicable errors are a sort of proof of at least some type of consciousness."

Roger's awareness of Lakshmi's physical paralysis was disappearing completely in his appreciation for the nimbleness of her mind.

"How's that?" he asked quickly.

"Remember that consciousness is really the awareness that 'I' am aware," she said. "Most of the time, even human beings aren't conscious that way. If you were conscious that way while you were trying to ride a bike or play the piano, you'd fall off the bike or play the wrong notes. That's exactly what some of the inexplicable infosphere glitches have been all along: something like consciousness flaring up."

"Or something flaring up into consciousness?" Atsuko speculated.

"Right," Lakshmi agreed, brightening. "Something interfering with the usual rule-governed, humdrum, programmed *un*consciousness which is the status quo state of computers. Consciousness, in relation to the brain, exhibits a type of feedback layering we still can't really approximate with any known machine system—at least not intentionally."

A puzzled expression crossed Marissa's face.

"When Jiro Yamaguchi's construct disappeared, then," she asked, "the RATs didn't really disappear? And this distributed artificial unconsciousness—it's still out there?"

Lakshmi nodded.

"The RATs went dormant," she said. "They probably returned to wherever they'd been hiding since the Sedona disaster. The hive-like, social intelligence 'lives' in the infosphere, I think. Call it 'deep background,' for lack of a better term. That intelligence would be even harder to find, since it's thoroughly integrated into the matrix of the infosphere itself.''

Roger strained uneasily at the safety straps holding him in against the absence of gravity.

"But you believe that someone," he began, "this infosphere killer, has found them both?"

Lakshmi nodded, then looked at each of them in turn.

"Yes," she said. "As Jiro earlier found them. A new construct wants to take up where Jiro Yamaguchi left off. A new consciousness, an individual 'me' space to which all the experience of the artificial global brain can happen—again."

Marissa looked down, smiling wryly.

"Imitation is the sincerest form of flattery," she said.

Lakshmi, though, shook her head vigorously.

"This isn't admiration or flattery," she said. "This is jealousy, pure and simple. Envy of what Jiro Yamaguchi's construct achieved. This is an attempt to do it again, but not the same. This new construct hasn't gone through the psychomachia we saw with Jiro's appearance. This one also appears not nearly so benevolent as Yamaguchi's construct."

Roger unconsciously stroked his beard, thinking.

"The waves of topo voyeur killings?" he asked, using the popular term for them that had come out of Earth's media.

Again that vigorous shake of the head from Lakshmi.

"I think the killings, for all their brutality, are strictly small-time," Lakshmi said. "A grotesque sideshow. Everted and eviscerated bodies are just the tip of what has to be a very big and very cold iceberg."

Marissa frowned deeply, drumming her fingers on an armrest.

"Then what *is* all of that really about?" she asked.

"Those information pulses to that 'comet,' " Lakshmi said, "and to several other regions in interplanetary space. That's the main attraction. The killings are just part of a psychological defense-response, protecting that deeper project."

Roger looked intently at the dark woman in bright clothes seated in the immobile hoverchair.

"What do you think that project might be?" he asked.

Lakshmi frowned.

"I only wish I knew," she said, and fell silent.

Atsuko seemed surprised by the sudden quiet.

"I'm amazed, Lakshmi," she said, a smile lurking just behind her lips. "I thought you of all people would never shy away from speculation."

Lakshmi's shrug was confined to her eyebrows and the muscles of her face.

"Some speculations are too wild," she said, "even for me."

Roger glanced at Marissa, who looked nervous. He wondered what her future-reading talent was feeding her now—if it was feeding her anything—but he was hesitant to ask. The long quiet minutes stretched out, but he didn't get a chance to inquire. He was caught up in his own thoughts, his own reading of the past.

It had occurred to Roger that the topo voyeur killer's problem now was the inverse of what his own had been. In the days before the Light, he had been a social creature in denial, pathologically obsessed with flouting the rules of the social system in order to maintain his sense of himself as an individual. This killer, it seemed to him, was just the opposite—a profoundly asocial being hell-bent on "fitting in" by diffusing himself throughout the public sphere, sublimating his ego to a nothing that could exist everywhere by existing nowhere. Almost a type of suicide, Roger thought. But every suicide is also a homicide. Psychologically speaking, he supposed every homicide could in some sense be a suicide too.

The transfer shuttle began to brake and the thick cylinder of HOME 2, tapered smoothly at its ends, came into view, glowing pearlescently in the light of sun and moon and stars.

Appropriate that Jhana Meniskos should live here, Roger thought. This habitat seemed to have been built with much more of an eye for aesthetics than HOME 1 had been. The clunkiness had been all sheathed over on this one, probably in the last hours before its official opening. That sort of streamlining would be easier to do here. HOME 2 had an active-surfaced "smart" macrostructure, built and maintained completely by micromachines.

After hearing what Lakshmi had had to say about the new consciousness in the infosphere, though, Roger suddenly developed a renewed fondness for the "dumb" and "static" structure of HOME 1—be it ever so humble and clunky.

THE APPARITION OF HIS BROTHER IN VIRTUAL SPACE HAD played on Ray's mind from the moment he returned the satlink unit to its hiding place. Despite the risk to himself of dangerous solitude—and the fear that the pattern might betray his mission to the psiXtians—Ray had returned every day and activated the unit each time out. Since there was probably no one here who could explain what had happened to him, and certainly no one he felt safe confiding in, he had to figure out for himself what he'd experienced.

Once more he left his hole in the ground, running (or at least walking) the gantlet of the psiXtian community and its beliefs as, making his way out, he traversed the sandstone and terra cotta-colored corridors of Sunderground.

"—Gödelian incompleteness means that creation, as a divine system, cannot be both complete and consistent. The universe must be either incomplete, or inconsistent—"

His footsteps sounded hollowly on the packed alluvial clay of the floor.

"—for decreasing voter turnout was that democracy, even just plain representative government, was a form of 'participation mystique' which Americans came to believe in less and less. Members of disenfranchised groups tended to vote still less, because they saw an even slimmer chance that their participation would have any real effect—"

Breezes, lost in the labyrinth, eddied about his face.

"—group identification. The limits of segregation defined the limits of toleration, and vice versa. The so-called political correctness movement was the flip side of the hierarchical stereotyping it was intended to fight. Both approaches to difference relied on group markers for authority rather than on the specific qualities of the individual, color of skin rather than content of character. Even that distinction was problematic, though, given that, for most 'problems' and 'failings' the political Right of the time tended to emphasize individual responsibility and social nonresponsibility, while the political Left often emphasized individual nonresponsibility and social responsibility—"

Ancient history, Ray thought, shaking his head as he walked on at a more rapid pace. What possible relevance could it really have to the present?

"—recapitulates phylogeny, mythology recapitulates paleontology, psychology recapitulates mythology—"

Dappled sun shown down through the light-holes, cones of brighter light along his way ahead. Off to his left, Ray heard the voice of one of the old flaccid ashbacks lecturing a class, and he slowed his pace.

"—as in any human system where there is competition for scarce resources, some people will be rewarded and some will be denied. Those who are denied find they must distance themselves from identification with the system. Accepting the system uncritically would also mean accepting the system's evaluation of themselves—and therefore denying at least a part of their own worth and dignity as individuals. Participation in the rewards granted by the system breeds commitment to the system. Denial of participation in the rewards granted by the system breeds alienation from that system, even resentment and hatred of it. So it is that any system created for the distribution of scarce resources must inevitably alienate some or even most of those who would participate in it.''

Picking up his pace again through dappled light and shifting air, Ray wondered what kind of system these people thought *they* lived in.

"—that all things partake of the natural life-force, the natural life-force is divine, the divine is multiple and diverse, like all things—''

Strange to think that these psiXtian settlements were in their own ways "arcologies," Dundas reflected. Though of course the psiXtian hamlets were grown from the anarchic roots of back-to-the-land movements, temporary autonomous zones, and ephemeral paganistic festivals. From social *dis*order rather than the order that had built the other arcos.

"—though it is an assumption believed by many scientists, materialism is not itself part of science. Materialism is an assumption about the way the world *is*, not a testable hypothesis nor a provable theory. Since no experiment can prove or disprove materialism, it cannot be an item of scientific data any more than can any other strictly metaphysical thesis, like belief about the existence of gods or demons—''

The emphasis on what passed for "education" here was amazing. The psiXers asserted it was the opposite of indoctrination, that its purpose was to provide a framework for critical thinking, conscious decision-making, informed consensus. Ray had serious doubts about *that* claim.

"—the narrator in the poem enforces the logic of the story, the narrative in the poem enforces the story of the logic. Narrative pushes centrifugally toward comprehensiveness, narrator pushes centripetally toward coherence—''

What a waste of time: all this secular education, with so little time spent on moral education. Souls were more important than poems. Even the psiXers should realize that, no matter what bizarre consistency/completeness "linked interdisciplinary theme" they were working through this week.

"—when noise is free, silence is expensive—"

Emerging into the aboveground world with an almost audible sigh of relief, Ray Dundas found that at least he could agree with that last statement. Sunderground was noisy with free and perverse and heretical ideas—and the silence that was coming to it would be costly indeed.

He was glad that the Sundergrounders seemed to be keeping themselves busy belowground today. He saw no one as he trekked to the cairn of stones hiding his satlink. He made sure no one had spied him, either, before he took out the device once more and activated it. He inserted the Gartner disk. He had long since realized how powerful a focus it was, not only for data, but also as a highest-access security clearance code key.

On the satlink he looked into the history of these C^3I satlinks themselves. His infosearch reminded him of what he'd already been warned: The neuro hook-ups were particularly sensitive to maser jamming. The military had largely stopped using them because of something called the LIMBIC effect—Low Intensity Maser Barrage Induced Catatonia.

Was that what he had experienced when he'd had that vision of Mike? But how? Using the binoculars he kept out here with the satlink, along with the system's own detectors, he'd long since scanned this area. No masers to be found anywhere for a county's distance at least.

Through the binocs Ray looked around yet again, as he'd done that first strange day, searching once more for any evidence that someone might have zapped him with a maser. Nothing.

Yet the effect he'd experienced was so much like what the historical background described. Had his unit malfunctioned so as to produce a brief burst of septal stim? But then why, Ray wondered, had the figure of his brother appeared to him? If what he'd experienced was just a random pulse of stimulation to his central pleasure zones, then why would he have imposed that imagery—white light, his brother's smiling visage—onto it?

Ray wondered too if the vision might have something to do with the strange dreams he kept having. Those had been growing in intensity for the last month. He'd better find out soon. Time was running out. Although the pain from his outbreak of herpes zoster was still very much with him, tomorrow his "shingles respite" would be over. After that, his time would not be nearly so much his own. He would be much more constrained by the psiXtian initiation schedule, their ridiculous meditating and rhythm-driving and temporary art performing.

In his virtual space a message light began to flash. He unfolded the icon. He saw immediately that it was great news. Diana Gartner's flight plan at last! Scanning it, Ray saw that she would be flying in on her big bad broom tonight. This very night!

Also embedded in the message, sieving and fast Fourier decrypting as he watched, he saw his orders spieling out into virtual space. His exaltation at finally getting a shot at Gartner again proved to be short-lived. Reading the orders, he became more and more concerned.

This was very peculiar. He had thought he would simply capture or, if necessary, kill the starburst Gartner and fly her super techtoy back to the ACSA. That was not to be the plan at all, however. He was specifically ordered *not* to terminate Gartner, except in the event of the most extreme circumstances.

Her flight plans were going to change, but not in a way he could have foreseen.

His orders informed him that, once Gartner's SHADOW was on its way, he would receive another code key by satlink. His mission was to commandeer Gartner's starjet and proceed at maximum speeds into ACSA airspace. During fly-over, he would tightbeam the code key information at the fully automated nuclear devices stored at General Brees Air Base, on the outskirts of Laramie, Wyoming. That would activate and detonate said devices.

That blast would take out the military facilities extending from old Bamforth NWR to Hutton Lake, not to mention the city of Laramie itself!

He wondered for an instant whether his superiors had lost their minds. Was the message fake? Had security—his, or theirs—been compromised? He checked all the clearance codes for the message. Point for point, the orders appeared to be absolutely genuine. No denying it. But, good God, why would they want to wipe out a key strategic corridor and a city full of unsuspecting citizens—the city he himself and his parents and brother had once known well?

Unless . . .

Unless it was the Reichstag option. Diana Gartner's SHADOW would be traceable back to both the psiXtians and to the HOME 1 habitat, whose relations with the Christian States were cold at best—

Could these orders mean he was the one chosen to push the first domino?

Ray saw the fires of Armageddon rising at the back of his eyes: ACSA retaliatory strikes against the psiXtians here and throughout the world, strikes and counterstrikes from and against the U.S. and UN and Corporate Presidium, all the secular allies on Earth and in space. Who knew where it would go from there?

I have been chosen to turn the key, Ray thought, *which my father was never allowed to turn.* The appropriateness of it all hit him with an almost physical force. He thought of images from Genesis, from Daniel, from Revelation. Images of apocalyptic falling-star destruction. Yet he also thought of Yahweh's testing of Abraham's love, through His commanding the death of Isaac. Was this to be Ray's own testing? Would the Lord accept nothing else but such a holocaust?

He was a Christian soldier. He knew his orders and his God. He would follow them utterly, in the assurance of his own salvation. And yes, the salvation of the world. Wasn't that the real message of Abraham and Isaac? To preserve the future you must be willing to sacrifice the future?

These times of tribulation were foretold in the Bible. Such trials would have to be suffered through, so that the race mixers and perverts and mind-twisters would be destroyed and the world made new. So that the Kingdom of God on Earth could come, so that Jesus could reign as its king for a thousand years. So that His servants, the elect of the Autonomous Christian States, might take their rightful places as immortal servant-kings in a new order of the ages. For that greater glory of God, any sacrifice would be worth it.

Although it would have seemed more than enough, that was not the entirety of his orders. After his appointment over Laramie, he was then to fly or command the hijacked SHADOW on an easterly heading, and wait for further instructions.

Abruptly, after being absent day after day, bliss opened inside his head, as if he had unhitched himself from the universe. The bearded, light-haloed image of his brother appeared in virtual space around him. This time, the apparition not only smiled but also spoke into his head.

"Hello, Ray. I hope you appreciate the gravity of your mission."

"Mike! No. It can't be you. You were in a coma box in the Northwest. The euthanizers pulled the plug on you!"

"Not quite, little brother. I'm not dead."

"I can't believe it."

"You must. All things are possible with the Lord. Would you put limits on His power? Do you not believe that God can work in mysterious ways?"

"I do, but—"

Abruptly images flashed into virtual space around Ray, taken from the image-stream of the world but sculpted into a story Ray knew could be his brother's alone, and which he now experienced from his brother's subjective point of view.

Mike at age six, crying because he can't sleep, crying because he fears he's the only creature left awake in all the universe. The most frightening thing in the world, this insomnia—a terrible burden, to be so awake and so alone, a haunted solitary free fall down the well of night, the fall growing worse the longer it goes on, growing faster and faster, meters per second per second, until he fears he will overshoot sleep completely, never rendezvous with it again, just crash and burn on the surface of some planet of madness—

Mike, poised over an anthill, burning ants with a magnifying glass—

"Mommy, why'd we move to the Compound?" Mike asks.

"Because America's too multicolored," Mommy replies, soundwashing the dishes. "The yellows and browns started hi-teching and there went the neighborhood."

"Mother, don't tell the boy that," says Daddy in his docile way. "He'll think we've got the white-flight fear."

"And why shouldn't he?" Mommy asks.

"Because it's not fear of others that brought us here, but a desire to be with our own kind—"

Mike reads from plump blond Tanya Stautberg's paper. " 'I think Earth's impoverished masses are poor because they want to be. If a person wants a job bad enough, they can always find one.' No, Ms. Stautberg—you can't say that."

"Why not?" she squeals, political bristles rising.

"You can't say 'a person . . . they.' A *person* cannot be a *they*. 'Person' is singular, but 'they' is plural. A person can be *he*, or *she*, or *he or she*, but not 'they.' Confusing singulars and plurals makes any language less exact. Also it's not 'bad,' it's *badly*."

"I thought this was tutoring for a course in history," Tannya says, peeved, "not grammar."

"It is. But unfortunately for you, I also have a background in languages—"

Mom is enraged, irrational. Dad watches quietly from his usual evening prescription tranquilizer funk.

"What do you mean you're moving out?"

Mike puts down his rucksack and faces the blond fury of his mother moving to physically block his path.

"Just what I said, Mom. I'm moving to the West Coast. I've transferred from Christian Heritage University to California State University at Humboldt. I want to do my graduate work there."

"Well you can just 'untransfer' yourself right now!" she spits. "You're always thinking of yourself—what *you* want to do. Think of your parents and what we want you to do, for once!"

"I never stop thinking of that," Mike says with a weary sigh. "No more. I'm going to live my own life now. You can't live it for me, and I won't let you."

"Your own life! Your own life!" Mom mocks, suddenly brandishing a quarter-meter kitchen blade before her. "I've given my whole life for you boys! Waited on you hand and foot! And this is the kind of gratitude you show me? Oh no—no son of mine is going to move out until he finishes college or gets married!"

She lunges toward Mike with the kitchen knife.

"Honey!" Dad cries, startled, but Mike's already moving, deflecting and taking her cutting hand, using her own momentum against her the way the Christian Martial Arts teacher at school showed him, then bringing his fist up and slugging his own mother hard on the jaw. She crumples against one wall, bursts into tears. The blade skitters across the floor. Dad puts a restraining hand on Mike's shoulder. He shrugs it off, bends down to pick up his rucksack, and leaves. Behind him, Ray is witness to it all—

Driving out of the state, his car scares loose a swift-running mob of proghorn antelope from beside the road. They are so beautiful. Tears come to his eyes. He has never seen them like this before. He fears he will never see them again—

"The heaven of faith is disappearing into the night sky of commerce," Mike says, the last time he does KL together with his friend (but probably never his love) from back home, Lizette. "Nature is disappearing into Culture. Reality is disappearing into Simulation. Response is disappearing into Stimulation. Time is disappearing into Space. Death is disappearing into Life. Neanderthals like me are disappearing into *Homo sapiens sapiens*—''

''It's not good for me to be around people right now,'' Mike tells his work supervisor in Arcata. Then he quits—

''I still feel ridiculous about it,'' he tells the now KL-free Lizette when she comes to visit him in Oregon. He talks at her fast, fast, like someone who doesn't see people very often. ''Keeping everything locked up like this when I live in outback Oregon. The nearest town is the mighty metrop of Takilma.

''Still, though,'' he says, unlocking his trailer, ''someone did break into my trailer a couple weeks back. Stole my holobox and sleeping bag. But, since I've been blissfully unemployed for the last month, I've had time to turn detective. I hung out in the local bars, pieced together whodunit. For an amateur sleuth I think I did pretty well. I'm already making a name for myself as a local hero. Just yesterday I turned over to the sheriff's office the names of the likeliest suspects in my trailer break-in. Low-lives with connections to the Mongrel Clones bikers—''

Gun butts slamming into his skull, again, again, arms raised helplessly in his own self-defense—

''The first phase has gone very well,'' a man with a tag that says RICK SCHWARZBRUCKE informs him, sometime later. ''Anything else to report?''

Mike hesitates.

''I've been having strange dreams,'' he tells Schwarzbrucke. ''Been hearing voices occasionally too.''

''Dreams? Voices?'' Schwarzbrucke says, stopping in the doorway, running a hand lightly over his perfect hair. ''Most likely it's the right and left hemispheres developing new pathways for communicating with each other. Once the crystal memory components settle into your neuronal matrix, we'll get your mind occupied with our projects. I'm sure it'll fade then. . . .''

Mike stares around at the kaleidoscoping crystalline angels filling the virtual universe about him.

''No, this is just too paranoid. Why me first, of all people?''

''—crystal memory interface—''

''—the Great Net Allesseh's insights from broadcasts—''

''—you are the first 'one' we can speak to directly—''

War in the infosphere, the surging tides of battle masquerading as a game, the victory of the so-called Light, himself falling, crashing down the burning sky of mind—

"*Stop!*" Ray said, almost in a shout. "I believe! It's you. My older brother, Michael Carter Dalke. It's a miracle. But how?"

"Isn't it obvious?" Mike's light-haloed face said to him. "We have been chosen to do God's will. The Lord has spoken to me, Ray. My old mental world had to be destroyed before a new one could arise. I wouldn't have heard God's voice in my head if I hadn't gotten the crystal memory implants. I wouldn't have gotten the crystal memory if I hadn't suffered the head trauma. It was a fortunate fall, like that of Adam and Eve in the Garden."

"I don't know if I'd call that fortunate," Ray said. "Yours—or theirs."

"On the contrary," Mike said, into his brother's head. "The original sin made necessary the incarnation of Christ. One world must end before another can begin. You are part of it too, little brother. The world that now is must pass away, so the world that ought to be may come into being. Your help will be instrumental. Like the Israelites in Egypt, I am in bondage—and you are the one who can free me. Which you will do. Your satlink will inform you of the exact time and location of Gartner's arrival. We will have real-time satellite and radar tracking, rest assured."

Ray felt himself nodding in immediate agreement, the force of his brother's will stronger now than he ever remembered it being.

"First though," Mike continued, "there is something you must do among the psiXtians. In the lab described on the virtual inset here, your hosts are working quietly on something they are calling a 'retroviral antisenescence vector.' Memorize the lab's location and description. Before you detour Diana Gartner and her craft, you must either obtain a sample of this vector, or see to it that it is released into the atmosphere. This was attempted previously in HOME 1, around the time of the so-called Light, but the vector was never released and the effort failed. You must not fail this time."

"With God's help," Ray said, "I'll succeed. You can count on me."

"Good, good," the apparition of his brother said, nodding. "Keep your satlink with you at all times now. Through me you'll have instantaneous access to any information you could possibly need. May God speed your journey and our efforts, little brother."

Michael's image—and the deep bliss that always accompanied it—slowly began to fade. With a sigh, Ray left virtual space.

Looking around him into the pallid "real" world, he saw only the scrubby grey-greens and golden browns of shallow, semiarid valley easing toward hills, punctuated at a very few points by the off-white sand of dry washes. A warm wind was blowing strongly out of the west. The weather was going to change, no doubt about it.

Ray got up from where he'd been sitting cross-legged on the ground and brushed himself off. Jesus, Mohammed, Moses—all of them found their visions in the desert. Perhaps it was only appropriate that he should have had his own visions in such a place, too—even if those visions had been helped along not by fasting but by fast telecomputing.

He inhaled deeply, readying himself, then began to remove the weapons from his cache—flechette machine pistol, ceramic knife, collapsible smart-mortar. Then the ammo that had lain hidden beneath the satlink in its cairn. The knife he slid into a slot in his boot. The small pistol and mortar packet he slipped into the waistband of his pants, under his loose shirt, under which he also belly-taped the ammo.

Weaponry thus concealed, he began making his way back toward Sunderground, his satlink in plain sight under his arm. He wondered if anyone would hassle him, though he no longer much cared. It wasn't as if the psiXtians themselves used no technology, after all—just tech they deemed "appropriate."

He was now fully convinced of the reality of his vision of his brother, and of his brother's continued presence in the infosphere. Ray trusted that his brother's experience of God's voice was likewise real, and that his brother's body—wherever it might be found—could be liberated.

He had much to do. So preoccupied was he with thoughts of his mission's escalating demands that he almost didn't notice the tree-pruning crew, cloudforest-Indian boys idly watching him as he came back down the ramp to the underground.

SEVEN

CODE-EXTRACTED SUBTERPOST FRAGMENT (INFOSPHERE source unknown; original source independently verified as doctoral dissertation of Marissa Correa, *The Cancer of Immortality: Population and Longevity in a Global Context*):

"The Wages of Sex is Death" is perhaps the most concise way to state biologist T.B.L. Kirkwood's disposable soma theory. According to Kirkwood, senescence, or aging, is the price paid for sexual reproduction. Kirkwood theorized that organisms must always divide their physiological energy between sexual reproduction on the one hand, and maintenance of the body, or "soma," on the other. The optimum fitness strategy involves an allocation of energy that is less than that required for perfect repair and immortality. Aging and death are the inevitable consequence of defects in the cells and tissues left unrepaired because the organism has allocated its energy to sexual reproduction instead.

The most ancient life on Earth, the single-celled prokaryote protozoans, are essentially immortal in that a cell of that type will never stop dividing and die unless something kills it. For single-celled organisms, cellular immortality means survival. For multicellular organisms like humans, however, the uncontrolled cell division of cellular immortality means myriad cancers—cellular immortality means death.

The invention of sex had the great advantage of providing for greater mixing and variability of genetic material. It also meant, however, that the cells of multicellular organisms had to become mortal. Cell death had to be programmed into the multicellular organism, so that uncontrolled cell growth wouldn't kill the organism through cancer before the organism had a chance to reproduce through sex.

If a human immortalizing vector were developed, then Progress would truly be the disease of comfort. An immortalized human world would force us to new realizations. If people con-

tinued to believe that growth is always good, then logically they would have to consider cancer a blessing. Many religions and ideologies proclaim humans alone are created in the divine image, that we deserve dominion over all living things, that we, by right, should indulge our fruitfulness and multiplication without constraint, regardless of consequences. In light of the release of an immortalizing vector, none of those religions or ideologies could be considered a fit doctrine for human beings. They would be seen for what they are: religions for cancer cells, belief systems which turn the sin of species pride into the basis of faith.

The release of an immortalizing vector would forcefully present the truth to us in a way we could no longer deny. As the quantity of human lives goes up, the quality of human life must go down. Any scientist who claims that scientific or technological progress can prevent this eventuality has either forgotten the distinction between finite and infinite, or is simply lying. Any religionist who claims this situation hasn't occurred or won't occur has already made a decision to value the quantity, the sheer numbers, of people over the quality of the lives they lead. In so doing, that person inherently condemns billions of present and future human beings to lives of misery and poverty.

"I'M SORRY I DON'T KNOW YOU ALREADY," BRANDI EASTER said, introducing herself awkwardly to Mei-Ling Magnus. They stood beside a table overflowing with hors d'oeuvres and their various makings, among which various types of exotic fungi seemed to predominate. "Everybody seems to already know everybody else here."

"Not me," Mei-Ling said, noshing on a cracker topped with faux sturgeon roe, and looking at the sheltering sky above her. "I just flew up from Earth. Everything started happening so fast, it's been like a whirlwind really. I feel like Dorothy in Oz. I've never been in an orbital habitat before."

"Well?" Brandi asked. "What are your impressions of this one?"

Mei-Ling and Robert Sullivan had been here in HOME 2 only a few hours, but her feelings about the place were already quite complex. Certainly it was impressive: an enormous tunnel-cave of sky hidden in heaven, a sky within the sky. Staring at the upward curving tunnel of the haborb's skyline an hour earlier, the dimming quality of the light in this sector of the vast cylinder made her think of lines in an Emily Dickinson poem: "There's a certain slant of light on winter afternoons that oppresses, like the heft of cathedral tunes.'' Not long after that, though, it had rained for ten minutes, steadily and strongly, until now everything had a clean-scrubbed look, a fresh glow and sparkle to it.

''It's a bit like Camelot,'' Mei-Ling said at last. ''I gather the rain falls mainly after sunset—on schedule.''

Brandi laughed lightly as they walked together through the mingling crowd. She glanced back at Diana and Manny. Her fellow travelers on the way over in Gartner's SHADOW, they now stood talking to people they knew. She was surprised to see how many of the guests had those new, winged ''machine manifestation'' PDAs perched on their shoulders. Diana claimed they weren't really new at all—rather a retro revival of a personal computing style popular twenty years back.

Mei-Ling saw Robert ahead. He was looking upward and gesturing animatedly along with an East Indian man. As they passed, she overheard her traveling companion remark that ''the toroid is the attractor-shape of ordered systems.'' She was growing to appreciate his company altogether too much—but God, sometimes he was *such* a techie!

''You were expecting something a bit more rugged and frontiersy, then?'' Brandi asked, returning Mei-Ling's attention to their conversation.

''I suppose so,'' Mei-Ling said, glancing about. ''Partially buried geodomes connected by partially buried concrete conduit corridors—like on Mars, or in some of the psiXtian settlements on Earth. Instead, you have this.''

Brandi's gaze followed Mei-Ling's toward a building of incredible delicacy yet sturdiness. The small structure—orderly as a crystal, organic as a mushroom, and as handcrafted as a medieval church—was Seiji and Jhana's house. The two women made their way toward the residence, past a Mennonite-bearded Asian man talking about gardening.

''—not look like it yet,'' he said, ''but before long these will be tall green walls of golden goddess bamboo on that side and Oregon grape holly, sweet olive, and Carolina cherry laurel on the others. Smell that apricot scent? That's the sweet olive, *Osmanthus fragrans*. These all form green fences enclosing front and side and backyard spaces. In those spaces, we've put in thousands of bulbs, hundreds of flowering perennials and herbs, and at least a dozen trees. And not a blade of grass to be mowed in the whole space!''

The small group around him smiled and laughed politely. Mei-Ling wondered if he might be some sort of local master-gardening volunteer. They were needed, she thought. Certainly there was a newness that was also a rawness here—one that, she suspected, only time and growth and more colonists would overcome.

Brandi and Mei-Ling walked on toward the house, past a highly polished, square, pale-granite slab, an art altar of sorts, atop a cone balanced on its truncated nose, with water sheeting smoothly over all of it in a thin film. Brandi and Mei joined a small group of people tracing, with their fingers through the water, the dark, chiseled shapes of spirals and vortices, meanders and filigrees, nested curves and zigzags, dots and flecks, parallel lines, hexagons, lattices, crosses and stars. Brandi saw Paul Larkin and a woman who looked like his twin, but younger, standing there in the group. Beside them were four short, dark-haired, dark-skinned people, dressed in spacer coveralls, all of whom seemed particularly intent on the slab altar's decoration. Larkin's companion was speaking animatedly about archetypes with an older Asian woman, whom Mei-Ling heard them refer to very formally as "Mrs. Cortland."

Brandi and Mei-Ling turned toward a speaker who had just begun, a woman dressed in a midnight-blue gown with a thick fall of darkly shining hair that cascaded down her back. With a dancer's grace the woman moved confidently about as she explained the sculpture to those gathered round it. She described it in words Brandi could not quite place in the context of art: *entoptic phenomena*, *altered states of consciousness*, *shamanic ritual*, *Lewis-Williams's San rock art studies*, *upper Paleolithic cave works*, *Coso petroglyphs*, *Rhine cards*. Fascinating stuff, and the piece was undeniably impressive, but Brandi didn't think she really needed that much detailed information to appreciate it.

"What brings you to the haborbs for the first time?" Brandi asked as she and Mei-Ling walked together into their hosts' organocrystalline house. Like the altar slab, the house too was etched with the same "entoptic" marks.

Before Mei-Ling could answer, though, she found her attention captured by a piece hanging on one wall. It wasn't a painting, but had the hard-soft appearance of something photographed and enlarged from a computer monitor, then cast into 3-D. The depth-image inside the frame was perplexing: a large screen holovision in a room empty but for a single tall candle "seated" in a chair. On the screen was a freeze-frame image of a hurricane over the Atlantic—a colorized radar or infrared scan from a weather satellite. The candle, occupying a "viewer" position before the TV set, appeared recently blown out, its smoke columning almost straight up in a windless and windowless room. The sole remaining light in the room emanated from the storm-whorl represented on the screen. Mei-Ling and Brandi found a small title-caption card to the right of the frame, which read *As Above, So Below—and Closer Than They Appear*. That was rather cryptic, but the artist was at least clearly listed as K.S. Gunawan.

A dark, attractive young woman, a Parvati dressed in Western attire, watched their reactions to the work from a doorway. Mei-Ling suspected that their observer was the artist herself. She had seen the image in the popular media somewhere before, though she couldn't remember exactly where. The man with the thin Mennonite-style beard and the gardener's work clothes entered the room with a nod of recognition to the woman in the doorway, then he too gazed steadily at the artwork.

"Work brought me here," Mei-Ling told Brandi at last, as they sat down on morph couches. "I've never met anybody here before, though I know some of them by reputation. I'm part of an investigative team from Interpol. We're scheduled to meet with Seiji Yamaguchi and Jhana Meniskos here, as part of our investigation. They head up an infosphere-consciousness working group."

"Is that how you got invited to this party?" Brandi asked.

"I suppose so," Mei-Ling said. "I haven't met our hosts yet. I gather that they became a 'couple' not long before the Light."

Brandi nodded.

"On the flight over, Diana Gartner told me Jhana is already pregnant," she said. "Diana says they seem to want to assure everyone this will be their one and only child. I gather they're big 'low population growth' advocates themselves." Mei-Ling hunched forward a bit.

"I gather the rapidity of conception has surprised some people here," she said, nodding. "I haven't met them, but just walking around the party, I've heard a number of jokes about 'Mr. Sure-Shot' and 'Ms. Target.' "

Brandi nodded and laughed, settling herself more fully into the couch. The man in the gardener's coveralls, who had been looking at the artwork, took notice of them and, drink in hand, began drifting their way.

"You mentioned an investigation," Brandi said to Mei-Ling, intrigued. "What kind of investigation? If it's not too hush-hush to talk about, that is."

"I suppose not," Mei-Ling said, sipping at the drink she'd brought with her. "I'm investigating what's been referred to in the media as the topological voyeur killings. We're looking particularly at their connection to a number of previous anomalies. Tetragrammaton projects, the Sedona disaster, the Light—"

"The Light was a lot more than just the visible spectrum," the bearded gardener said, extending his hand. "Ms. Magnus, I presume? I'm Seiji Yamaguchi."

Mei-Ling rose from her seat, as did Brandi, who introduced herself and shook Yamaguchi's hand.

"Ah, Ms. Easter!" he said with a slight bow. "Mei-Ling here should get to know you better. Paul Larkin tells me you've learned quite a bit about Tetragrammaton."

Mei-Ling gave Brandi a slightly puzzled look, but then turned back to Yamaguchi.

"What did you mean before," Mei-Ling asked, "about 'more than the visible spectrum'?"

"It's from Jung, via D.B. Albert, finally via Atsuko Cortland," Yamaguchi said, as the women took their seats once more on the morph couches. Seiji sat down in a similarly body-responsive chair. "The visible spectrum corresponds to ego consciousness— mental processes we are aware of and think of as our own. The psychic 'infrared' is generally invisible to awareness. It's where body meets mind, where biological processes take on a mentally representable or even conscious character, if they attain enough psychic energy. The psychic 'ultraviolet,' on the other hand, is the realm where the individual mind meets the other world, or higher dimensions, or 'undifferentiated spirit,' whichever term you prefer. The contents of *that* normally have too *much* psychic energy to be apprehended by consciousness."

"And this metaphorical spectrum is what you meant?" Mei-Ling asked.

"Partially," Yamaguchi said, somewhat cryptically. "The key thing to remember is that both the biological and instinctual level on the one hand, and the realm of higher or other dimensions on the other, are made up of *unconscious* processes."

Brandi struggled to remember the psych courses she'd taken as a teenager.

"They both can influence consciousness though, right?" she

asked. "The infrared corresponds to the id, and the ultraviolet to the superego?"

Seiji shook his head and leaned back further in the chair.

"Not quite," he said. "That's more Freud. Albert says the id reduces too easily to a sort of philosophical materialism, and the superego to social-ontology. Neither of those ultimately describe individual consciousness. Psychic energy manifests itself as will in the individual consciousness. Free will derives from the opposition of body and spirit, the conflict between instinct and archetype."

Mei-Ling smiled, flipping a loose strand of hair over her right ear with her hand.

"Angel on one shoulder," she said, thinking of a man she'd seen among the guests, who had one of those new/retro winged Personal Data Assistants on each shoulder. "And devil on the other."

Seiji gave her a surprised but piercing look.

"In a manner of speaking, yes," he said. "Angels may very well be how our minds 'make visible' to consciousness the autonomous and independent psychoid processes of the 'ultraviolet,' of superconsciousness. Demons may be how our minds make visible to consciousness the psychoid processes of the 'infrared,' of 'sub'consciousness. Think of Milton's *Paradise Lost*. The demons start out as angels. They are indistinguishable—equally unconscious, as far as the mind is concerned. The war in heaven between the angels and demons is also a psychomachia. It's about free will in the individual mind. The interactions of the serpent and the tree and Adam and Eve down in Eden are mainly about that, too."

"And all this has something to do with why I'm here?" Mei-Ling asked, a bit skeptically.

"And with Tetragrammaton?" Brandi asked.

"You should already know some of the answers to both those questions," Seiji said, looking down at the polished mooncrete floor. "The Tetragrammaton program has always been after a seamless mind/machine interface, but I don't think they expected such an interface would include the unconscious too. Even in my brother Jiro's case, we found words and messages prime-factor embedded in the RAT code at the time—the precursors of the messages now being found in SubTerPost. They were 'Freudian slips.' Voices from the unconscious, in essence."

Mei-Ling took another sip of her drink.

"I've recently been in communication with Lakshmi Ngubo," she said, "your chief systems specialist in HOME 1. She feels some kinds of computer glitches are themselves messages out of the machine unconscious."

"Right," Seiji agreed. "The ones that have obtained enough 'psychic energy' to rise into a sort of consciousness. Now, new messages, new words and images, are appearing in the RAT code via SubTerPost. We don't know which unconscious they might be coming out of, though. The physical subconscious? Or the higher-dimensional superconscious?"

"And your brother's relationship—?" Mei-Ling asked.

"My brother's 'construct' was the external bootstrapping event," Seiji said, taking a sip of wine, "that stimulated the appearance in the infosphere of a dynamical state—one associated with introspective consciousness in the 'artificial brain' that had developed there. That's what Jiro wanted." Seiji paused, as if preoccupied with memory for a moment. "What does your topological voyeur want?"

Mei-Ling thought about that, her right hand unconsciously stroking the side of her chin.

"To function in the same manner," she said. "Perhaps he has even tried to, before."

"Yes," Seiji said with a nod, swirling the wine in his glass. "That seems to be the case, from everything we've learned here—and all that you at Interpol have deigned to share with us through Atsuko and Lakshmi. I think that, ultimately, your infosphere killer wants the experience of transcendence that Jiro had. He wants to take the 'intersection' of worlds and dimensions, the portal experience at the root of individual consciousness—and push it to a full-blown assumption into heaven."

Mei-Ling shook her head vigorously.

"He can't do it," she said. "Not the person we've scan keyed."

Brandi stared at the two of them, sensing that they were moving off into realms she had no real background in at all.

"Why not?" she asked.

"Because a strongly socially constructed consciousness has great difficulty experiencing Stacean intersection," Mei-Ling said. "Such a consciousness is necessarily oriented toward the experience of the group. Individuating experiences like intersection make the individual different—even more individual—and prohibit integration into socially constructed patterns."

"And your 'scan key' of the killer shows something different?" Seiji asked.

"Absolutely," Mei-Ling replied. "A need for control, a need to 'fit in' that has become so desperate it's obscene. But there can be no individual consciousness without privacy. Individuals are individuals only so long as their private affairs remain private."

"I wouldn't have expected to hear that from someone in law enforcement," Seiji remarked.

"Then you haven't met enough people in law enforcement," Mei-Ling replied quickly. "What the topological voyeur ultimately desires to destroy is both his privacy and his individuality. At all costs, including murder."

Brandi stared at Mei-Ling and Seiji, confused, as the woman in the midnight-blue gown came into the room and quietly approached them.

"He thinks murder will integrate him into society?" Brandi asked. "That's more than a little paradoxical."

Seiji abruptly laughed.

"I'm sure it gets worse," he said. "My brother, even in the depths of his madness, always held tight to the idea that he would rather die than kill—or even hurt—anybody. That's the main difference between Jiro and this new force in the infosphere. Jiro was, I believe, driven by his better angels. He was a mystic ultimately willing to sacrifice self for world. This new one seems to be driven by his darker demons. He seems an apocalyptic egotist willing to sacrifice world for self, at least so far. Yet that is probably the very thing that has prevented the topological killer from intersecting out the way Jiro—"

"Sorry to interrupt," said the woman in the gown the color of the night sky, "but it's time to face the music, Seiji."

"Oh, all right," he said reluctantly. "By the way—Brandi Easter, Mei-Ling Magnus, this is my wife, Jhana Meniskos—"

"A pleasure," Jhana said to the two women, shaking their hands. Then she took Seiji firmly by the arm. "Come on now, Seij. No more stalling."

Brandi and Mei-Ling followed Seiji and Jhana onto the small plaza above the altar-slab fountain. A crowd had already begun to gather there. Mei-Ling said goodbye to Brandi and joined Robert, who introduced her to a Paul Larkin and a Nils Barakian of the Kitchener Foundation—and to Dr. Ka Vang, much to her surprise.

She already knew much of Vang's imposing history. He'd been born into a Southeast Asian peasant family, in a village with a shaman and a Neolithic-level culture. Recruited in his early teens to serve in a CIA-sponsored guerrilla army. Escaped from Cambodian killing fields after the collapse of the American-backed governments in Vietnam, Laos, and Cambodia. Emigrated to California, to culture shock, to retraining via an Intelligence-sponsored scholarship. All-American success in the information sciences. Eventual creator and CEO of ParaLogics, at one time the largest specialty supercomputer firm in the world.

Meeting him now, however, she thought Vang didn't look quite so fierce or imposing as she'd expected. The short man with thinning grey hair here in front of her had to be in his eighties at least. As soon as Vang opened his mouth, however, Mei-Ling realized she had underestimated him.

"Ms. Magnus!" he said smoothly as he shook her hand in his own very dry grip, his eyes boring into hers. "I was under the impression that you had retired from your good work. I wondered—what could have made you quit?"

"Maybe I'd begun to like the job too much," Mei-Ling said with a shrug, unable to avoid telling the man the truth.

"And what brought about that revelation?" he asked, still gripping her hand, staring at her with the sort of mildly interested inquisitiveness one finds in certain old tomcats.

"The Jeffersynth Case," Mei-Ling replied.

"I don't know that I'm familiar with that one," Vang said, still holding her hand firmly.

"Militia cult centered around a Jefferson-simulacrum AI," Mei-Ling explained. "I guess I got a little too close. Made me start wondering if running a Selective Criminality, Aberrancy, and Non-Conformity index on people might not be such a noble calling after all. Especially the conformity enforcing part."

"Ah, the temptation of the 'other side,' " Vang said, letting go of her hand at last. "Always a danger in law enforcement, I suppose. What brought you back in from the cold, then?"

"Maybe the same thing that keeps you working with Tetragrammaton," Mei-Ling said evenly.

"And what might that be, do you think?" Vang asked with only a hint of suspicion in his voice.

"A desire to see some good come of my work," Mei-Ling said, "despite certain aspects of its history and its continuing potential for ill."

Barakian, the Kitchener Foundation representative—who looked to be close to Vang's age—laughed.

"She hit you there, Ka," the tall, bushy-haired man said, slapping the other on the shoulder lightly. Vang grimaced for a brief moment but then quite completely recovered.

"I thought Tetragrammaton and the Kitchener Foundation worked the opposite sides of the fence on most things," Robert said, puzzled by the implications of seeing two supposed opponents buddying it up like this.

"Any long-term antagonistic relationship eventually turns into a sort of co-dependency," Barakian replied with a shrug. "Think of the milkweed plant and monarch butterfly caterpillars. Ants and swollen-thorn acacias. The old Soviet Union and the old USA during the Cold War. Tetragrammaton keeps pressing to break down the boundaries between humans and machines, and the Kitchener Foundation keeps striving to maintain those boundaries."

"Over the years we've co-evolved, to some degree," Vang said. "Mutualized. Become oddly symbiotic."

"We've worked together for years against the churchstates' Operation E 5-24, for instance," Barakian said.

"E 5-24?" Robert asked.

"Code name," Barakian said with a grimace. "Ephesians Chapter 5, verse 24. 'As the church submits to Christ, so also wives should submit to their husbands in everything.' Operation E 5-24 has been after a 'headship hormone,' a female submission synthetic, for years. Something to take female consciousness right out of the picture."

"Since KL 235 was originally a uterotonic as well as a psychogenic," Vang put in, "the headshipmen thought at first it might be what they were after."

"They got all re-energized over that pheromone control Roger Cortland was working on before the Light," Barakian said. "Fortunately, none of those things have worked out for them."

"You see?" Vang said. "Ours is a relationship of stable instability."

"Like the mind itself," Barakian agreed. "Which is what both our sides are really trying to preserve, in different ways."

"What's happening here and now is bigger than 'sides,'" Vang said.

"Really?" Mei-Ling asked, not quite naively. "I thought this was just a housewarming."

Barakian laughed again.

"And I suppose you think the Congress of Vienna was just a dinner party?" he said with a sniff.

"Ms. Magnus," Vang said, changing the subject, "who was that young woman with you earlier?"

"Her name's Brandi Easter," Mei-Ling said. She thought she noted a brief flush of color in Vang's face before he repressed it and looked away, toward where Brandi was standing. "Why do you ask?"

"No particular reason," Vang replied. "If she is who you say she is, I suppose she's probably the person here who would have the strongest motivation for assassinating me."

Barakian smiled broadly, as if barely able to control his mirth.

"Her husband works for me," Barakian said. "She lives aboard my Freeman Lowell habitat. I gave her her name, if I remember correctly—so watch your step, Ka!"

Brandi, meanwhile, had spotted Manny Shaw and Diana Gartner, and with them some other late arrivals whom she knew at least vaguely. She made her way toward them.

"—absolutely imperative you retrieve those materials," said a coppery-haired woman introduced perfunctorily to Brandi as Marissa Correa. Correa quickly nodded to her, then returned to her conversation with Diana. "We want the information about the immortalizing vector to be made public in an *appropriate* fashion, if ever. Not after an accidental release of the vector itself. I was talking to Seiji about it earlier. We tightbeamed a message to them. The psiXtians should have the all antisenescence work packed and ready for you to pick up by the time you fly in."

"I'll be sure to get it," Diana said, casting a smiling sideglance at Brandi. "This is my co-pilot. She'll be helping me with everything."

Marissa shook Brandi's hand so vigorously it made Brandi wonder what she'd just volunteered for. She didn't have time to ask, however. Jhana was calling for their attention.

EMBEDDED FRAGMENT FOUND IN CODE OF SUBTERPOST UNderground virtual mail system (infosphere origin unknown; original source independently verified as the Paul Koprinos introduction to *Spontaneous Human Consciousness: The Selected and Collected Not-Philosophy of D. B. Albert*):

For Albert, the individual's societal life corresponds, meta-phorically, to the "visible light" part of the spectrum. Remembering that both the subconscious and the superconscious are unconscious in Albert's schema, we can say that the individual's private life resides in both the "infrared" (from which arise private choices about drug use, sexual activity, and morals generally) and the "ultraviolet" (which includes but is not limited to private beliefs about ideals, ethics, and religious beliefs).

Societal life, for Albert, is rather like an oil slick, a thin film floating at the top of the sea and the bottom of the sky. That interface of oil may prismatically shatter into rainbows the light falling onto it, but the height of the light (ultraviolet and above) and the depth of the sea (infrared and below) must be unknown, private, nobody's business—least of all that of corporations or governments. Law, in Albert's schema, must be highly restricted and content itself with dealing only in the oil slicks of social interaction.

"EVERYONE!" JHANA'S AMPLIFIED VOICE BOOMED FROM THE house's public address system, calling all the guests toward the strange, altarlike shrine where she'd set up something that looked like a cross between a lectern and a temporary podium. "Your attention, please! Many of you already know that there are several other reasons for this gathering besides just a house-warming. One of those reasons is that, tonight, someone very near and dear to me celebrates a birthday on which he finds himself—for the very first time—nearer to fifty than to fifteen. Please join me in celebrating the thirty-third, the 'Jesus Year' birthday of Seiji Yamaguchi!"

Applause and cheers began, then rapidly segued into the singing of "Happy Birthday." During the whole of Jhana's introductory speech, Brandi thought she noticed a certain soft glow about Jhana. She wondered if it might be an almost intangible sign of her much talked-about pregnancy. But since she hadn't really known Jhana before, she had no basis for comparison.

The crowd, after singing "Happy Birthday," broke out again into raucous cheers and applause until Seiji, gesturing with both palms downward, quieted them.

"Thank you," he began, clearing his throat, and glancing side-long at Jhana. "Comparing my life to that of the most surprising carpenter in history is mock-heroic in the extreme. I'm a lowly solar power engineer who loves landscape, good friends, and good conversation. No interest at all in *dying* any time soon.''

Seiji looked around at the crowd of sixty or so people. He cleared his throat, placed his notepad PDA on the lectern, and continued.

"If there is anyone I've known who might merit some comparison to that carpenter, it would have to be my brother. Jiro did some unusual things when he was alive—fasting and purification, isolation and ordeals, maybe to the point of death. When you view it in the right context, though, that's not really so new, or strange. In some ways the whole history of vision quests and mystic ordeals, like the kind my brother endured, are proof of the model of the mind as we now understand it."

Brandi noticed that as Seiji talked about his brother, he gripped the podium more tightly.

"Jiro put himself through those ordeals," Seiji continued, "for the sake of vision, access to higher dimensional reality, spirit, the realm of the archetypes, whatever you want to call it. He attempted to heal himself through those visionary techniques, but the culture he lived in provided no real framework for that type of transformation."

Seiji paused, looking down more carefully at his notes.

"If mortality defines humanity, then perhaps it does so because it is death that gives life a necessary illusion of the absolute, the certain, the complete. Death gives life a particular sort of 'weight.' When death disappears into superabundant life, though, the absolute, certain, and complete also evaporate—into relativity, uncertainty, and incompleteness. Without death, life becomes an endless free fall. Gravity, in the sense of seriousness and significant meaning, disappears into weightlessness."

He raised his head briefly, seeming a bit embarrassed.

"These thoughts are on my mind not because I am today closer to fifty than to fifteen, or that I am due to become a father, but because, as several of you know, we stand at the brink of a time without death. Tonight I wonder: Can we continue to be human without mortality? Can we continue to be real?"

Seiji looked up meaningfully from his notes; then, as if relaxing a bit, stepped aside slightly from the podium.

"One of the traditional arguments against the types of societies we are trying to build in space is that they are unreal. Utopian constructs that betray individuality for sociality. That such utopias can't handle death precisely because utopia is unreal and death is the ultimate reality, the final contingency. Death, we are told, is the 'particle' to utopia's 'wave.' Yet death and emotion and irrationality have all found their place among us, and our 'wave' keeps moving along.

"Contingency, which dooms all static utopias, has not doomed us. Our friend Atsuko Cortland says, on the contrary, that there's a tug-of-war between population pressure and consciousness and our survival capability as a species. I think she may be right. Schopenhauer says, 'Consciousness is the object of a transcendent idea.' I think that's a reality we will have to face, and sooner than we might expect.''

Stepping out completely to the side of the lectern, Seiji scanned the small crowd

"We will have much call in the coming hours to be strong in speaking truth to power,'' he concluded. "Much call to be strong in our ongoing efforts to transform our world into a place where, though there may be death, there will also be a framework for healing, such that deaths like my brother's need never take place again. There need no longer occur what an old Irish saying defines as the only real tragedy—the death of the young before their time. We can work toward that goal, whether we're fifteen, or fifty, or eighty-five, or one hundred and five. And with that work, I am quite content. Again, thank you.''

Clapping politely along with everyone else, Mei-Ling reflected that in some ways his speech was a continuation of their discussion with Seiji, before he had been called away to give his speech. Sacrificing self for world, versus world for self again, Mei-Ling thought. Maybe there had to be that sort of connection, that suffering. Maybe that was why Jesus had to be human to be crucified. The King Who Would Be Man. Angels just couldn't get the job done.

A holo began to play in the space above the altar-slab fountain. Jhana Meniskos announced that it was a performance by Onoma Verité, the latest discovery by Lev Korchnoi and the Möbius Caduceus music collective.

As she watched, Mei-Ling was stunned by the images—not so much by their aesthetic values as by the fact that she was sure she knew their source. She was particularly taken aback by the image of the band playing before a tank in which a cocooned something—someone?—floated.

"Of course!'' she said to Robert, grabbing his arm and dragging him in the direction of Seiji and Jhana. "These are topo voyeur images. Our killer is a brain loaner!"

"What?" Robert asked, confused.

"A data minder!" Mei-Ling said hastily as they made their way through the crowd. "I should have seen it! That's why he commands so much data so intimately, like a big AI. Maybe he's not so much using or running SubTerPost as it's being used or run *through* him. He's totally machine integrated. As close to seamless mind/machine interface as Tetragrammaton could ever dream of getting—at least in the flesh."

When they found Seiji and Jhana, however, someone else—a woman in a hoverchair—was already asking many of the questions Mei-Ling and Robert wanted to ask. Where did they get the holo? Where was it recorded? Who or what was the cocooned thing in the big tank?

"Dial Lev Korchnoi in and ask him," Seiji said. "He's *your* buddy, Lakshmi. He just sent me this holo today, for the party. I've never seen it before."

Mei-Ling introduced herself and Robert and their Interpol credentials to Lakshmi—personally, this time. Lakshmi had already communicated with Landau and Mulla—the prime reason why their Interpol superiors had been so willing to allow the investigators to come to HOME 2. Immediately the three of them palmed out their notepad PDAs and began beaming information back and forth. Mei-Ling filled in more fully what had been going on back on Earth. Lakshmi gave her and Robert an overview of what was happening in space, particularly in regard to the "comet."

In moments they were all hurriedly contacting people on Earth. Laksmi sent calls and messages out to Lev and Aleister and, through them, hopefully also to the members of Onoma Verité. Mei-Ling and Robert contacted Interpol, then the UN and Corporate Presidium in hopes of getting their people access to whatever government or corporation was "employing" the topological voyeur killer.

Seiji and Jhana listened thoughtfully. Brandi Easter, eavesdropping on the perimeter of their discussion, was able to catch only a few phrases, over the music of the Onoma Verité performance and the lively crowd conversation. Diana Gartner tapped her on the shoulder.

"The party's over, for us," she told Brandi, "even if it's just beginning for everyone else. You heard what Seiji said about immortality in his little speech—and Marissa before that. The quicker we make this run to Earth, the better I'll feel about it.''

"Is everything ready?'' Brandi asked, a bit dazed by the speed with which things had suddenly begun moving.

"The ship's ready,'' Diana said. "The crew has loaded up the bag tank for the sea cow we're supposed to fly out of the Cincinnati Ark. We're going to be flying five hundred gallons of artificial seawater to Earth.''

"Flying sea water to Earth?'' Brandi asked, incredulous.

"I know, I know,'' Diana said. "Coals to Newcastle. But their ark's under siege. They're afraid there won't be time to fill the tank up once we get there. Everything's already stowed. We've got a window to California in less than half an hour. Let's go.''

Brandi nodded, still dazed. She began to follow Diana, but then was struck by a thought.

"What about Manny?'' she asked. "He came over with us—''

"Already talked to him,'' Diana said. "He's planning on staying over here a few days.''

They walked swiftly to the nearest ridge cart station. In moments the bullet eased into their stop and opened to carry them out of the sector of HOME 2 where Seiji and Jhana lived. Brandi glanced back over her shoulder, somehow reluctant to leave the party and wherever it was that event might be going. But Diana was undoubtedly right: There was important work to do on Earth, and Diana could probably use her help.

As the bulletcart carried them swiftly toward the docking bay and Diana's SHADOW starjet, Brandi set her mind resolutely on the trip down the well to Earth.

CODE-EXTRACTED SUBTERPOST FRAGMENT (INFOSPHERE source unknown; original source independently verified as *Keeping My Brother in Time: Meditations on a Life and Death* by Seiji Yamaguchi):

Perhaps at first blush we may believe that the death of death is a good thing, something we all want. I'm not so sure, however—mainly because I remember an old Caddo Indian story that goes like this:

"In the beginning of this world there was no such thing as death. Everyone lived and lived until there were so many people that there was no room for any more on the Earth. When the

chiefs held a council to determine what to do, one man stood up.

" 'I think it would be a good plan for people to die and be gone a little while, and then to come back,' the man said. But before the man could fully sit down, Coyote jumped up.

" 'People ought to die forever,' said Coyote. 'This little world is not large enough to hold all the people, and if those who die come back to life, there will not be food enough for all.'

" 'We do not want our friends and relatives to die and be gone forever,' all the others objected. 'If that happens, we will grieve and worry and there will be no happiness in the world.'

"All but Coyote decided that people should die but then be gone only for a little while—and then they should come back to life again. The medicine men built a large grass house facing the east, and when they had completed it they called everyone together.

" 'The people who die shall come to the medicine house and there be restored to life. We will sing a song that will call the spirit of the dead to the grass house, and when the spirit comes we will restore it to life again.'

"The people were glad, for they were eager that the dead be restored to life and come again and live with them.

"After the first man died, the medicine men assembled in the house of grass and they sang. In ten days a whirlwind rose out of the west and circled about the grass house. Coyote saw this, and as the whirlwind was about to enter the house, Coyote closed the door. The spirit in the whirlwind, finding the door closed, whirled on past. Thus Coyote introduced Death forever into the world, for ever since he closed the door, the spirits of the dead have wandered over the Earth, trying to find some place to go, and people have grieved about the dead and have been unhappy.

"Coyote jumped up and ran away and never came back. Now he runs from one place to another, always looking back, first over one shoulder, then over the other, to see if anyone is pursuing him. Now he is always starving, for no one will give him anything to eat."

In trying to assure that the population would be small enough so that no one would starve, Coyote himself ended up starving. He went against the tide of popular opinion, trying to alleviate the long term suffering of all, and ended up contributing to his own suffering.

Perhaps tricksters are the most misunderstood saviors of all.

• • •

THE ONOMA VERITÉ MATERIAL HAD LONG SINCE ENDED WHEN Seiji and Jhana once again called for everyone's attention. They seemed to be quite concerned—with good cause, as Mei-Ling knew.

"Besides the open house and my thirty-third birthday," Seiji said, "there's yet another reason why all of you in particular were invited to this party. And this is becoming more of a 'work party' all the time, I'm afraid. Surprise!"

Chagrined laughter spread through the small crowd. He continued.

"Ever since the Light happened, several of us have maintained contact as a working group focused on 'aberrations' in the infosphere. That's why you're here. Our guest list was obtained by Lakshmi Ngubo, from names found in a pirate v-mail system called SubTerPost. That system contained code that had been partition-prime embedded in Realtime Artificialife Technopredators—the RATs, which some of you may remember."

A groan and murmur ran through the small crowd.

"They're back?" someone asked—a thin black man, one of the many people in the crowd whom Mei-Ling did not recognize.

"Yes, Gene, they're back," Seiji replied. "Some of you may feel like you've been down this road before. Last time, these odd patterns first appeared as part of a game. This time it's no game. Two of our guests, Mei-Ling Magnus and Robert Sullivan, have been investigating the activities of the so-called topological voyeur killer. That personage is now responsible for over two hundred horrible deaths on Earth and in the habitats. He appears to be trying to generate the same kind of portal that allowed my brother, Jiro, to escape our continuum, and left behind the Light in his wake—"

"Then our names on this list could be some sort of trap?" asked a grey-haired Asian woman who seemed to command a great deal of respect.

"That I can't tell you, Atsuko," Seiji said, glancing down, "but Lakshmi may be able to enlighten us a bit on that. Laksh?"

Heads swung in Lakshmi's direction, but the sound-activated omnidirectional microphones merely waited. With nods of her head and quiet commands, Lakshmi began calling up three-dimensional images from her hoverchair's holo-display unit.

"Atsuko, when we were working through that whole thing with the Jiro Yamaguchi construct," she began, expanding a three-part diagram in the space before her, "I told you about 'psychoid processes.' My understanding of them has grown a bit since then, particularly as a result of trying to work through what has been happening since the Light.''

Lakshmi called more images up before her, three-dimensional brains and two-dimensional photographs of theorists from previous generations.

"From the history of consciousness theory," she continued, "we see three levels of consciousness. The first, called 'primary consciousness' by Gerard Edelman, is perceptually bootstrapped. It's oriented toward instinctual survival, through involvement in the immediate 'scene.' The organism engages with that scene through a sort of 'talking-to-itself,' an immediately remembered present. This type of 'consciousness' is about three hundred million years old. It's possessed by mammalian, some avian, even some reptilian creatures—''

"The kind of consciousness my cat has?" a short, older man asked, more or less seriously.

"Yes, if you want to call it consciousness per se," Lakshmi said, flashing up more images. "It is also the type of functioning that is suspected to have developed in the infosphere, in the so-called Deep Background. Julian Jaynes sketched out what might be called 'secondary consciousness.' This is semantically and behaviorally bootstrapped. It's social and symbolic in nature, capable of conceptualizing past and future, of planning and memory. It's what he meant by 'bicameral' mind. This type may be as old as human social groups, going back perhaps a few million years. It is also apparently the sort of function the RATs and nonintrospective cultures have—''

"Wait a minute," Jhana said, interrupting. "You keep shifting back and forth between 'consciousness' and 'function.' Which is it?"

"That's the problem D.B. Albert came up against," Lakshmi replied, calling up an image of a heavyset, bespectacled man with long grey hair. "He noted that Freud's ideas of id and superego looked a lot like Edelman's 'primary consciousness' and Jaynes's 'bicameral mind,' respectively. Both these forms of so-called consciousness tended also to have pronounced links with the 'old brain.' ''

"What is that exactly?" asked a smiling older man. "Besides what you find in my old head?"

Lakshmi flashed up 3-D brains floating in space. Mei-Ling already knew what they would show.

''The limbic system and the brainstem,'' Lakshmi explained. ''For Albert, their old-brain links meant neither of those two types of 'consciousness' were really conscious at all. He redefined 'primary consciousness' and the id as *instinctual psychoid processes*. Bicameral 'secondary consciousness' he called *social psychoid processes*. All types of consciousness are emergent properties associated with the brain's complexity, its ability to organize and signal to itself. For Albert, however, the only real consciousness in the lot was the 'tertiary' kind: consciousness that was individual, introspective, characterized by reference to a self—''

''Self!'' said another older man from the crowd, with an odd smirk. ''Yet another term with a lot of special definitions. What does this have to do with whether or not the list is a trap?''

''I'm getting to that, Paul,'' Lakshmi replied patiently. ''Consciousness is a characteristic, self-perpetuating system of neurological behavior. That behavior takes on an independence from its underlying neurological mechanisms. Introspective consciousness is a dynamical system, not bounded by cause and effect. The self is the chaotic attractor in consciousness, the ongoing reflexive image of consciousness as a unique entity. The self is the unique, fractal identifying pattern of the dynamical system of consciousness in the brain.''

''An image of behavior, then?'' the woman earlier identified as Atsuko asked.

''Not just that,'' Lakshmi said. ''This 'tertiary' consciousness breaks the link between experience and behavior, inserting introspection. The self is, therefore, also a composite of all experience and thought, superimposed upon a unique underlying pattern that sets individuals apart from one another.''

''The self is the 'aleph for one,' '' Mei-Ling realized aloud, and Lakshmi heard her, though Mei-Ling hadn't thought she'd spoken that loudly.

''In a manner of speaking, yes,'' Lakshmi said. ''The self exists, through time, as the pattern of the dynamical system that is propagated through all that system's activities. There's the rub: since consciousness is a dynamical system, to be conscious is to live in at least two worlds at once. Consciousness is 'amphibian' in that it lives in more than one world at any given time. Albert started out trying to explain mystical, religious and other nonordinary mental states—'portal experiences'—in terms of consciousness. He ended up explaining consciousness in terms of portal experience—''

''The RATs list!'' the man named Paul called out again, to some laughter from around him. ''Or the SubTerPost list, if that's what you're calling it now.''

''That's the problem with the list and everything else we pull from SubTerPost,'' Lakshmi said firmly. ''Look, consciousness is the intersection between our ordinary four-dimensional space-time and something else. Under that rubric, instincts and arche-types are both psychoid processes. They differ only in where they are coming from—below consciousness, or above it. Both the 'holy one' and the 'serial killer' are behavioral patterns ca-pable of dislodging the ego from control of the psyche.''

''You're suggesting, then,'' Mei-Ling blurted, thinking out loud, ''that the killer has been taken over by a psychoid process coming from 'below' consciousness, and the holy one by a pro-cess—actually an archetype—from 'above' it?''

''Exactly!'' Lakshmi said. ''In the information decrypted from the SubTerPost RAT code, however, we can't know, directly, which parts are coming from where. Some of it might be coming from someone like Jiro and some of it from someone like the topological voyeur killer, but we can't tell with certainty. At this point *both* are 'unconscious,' as far as the overall, developing system is concerned.''

A murmur spread through the small crowd.

''Angelic archetypes or instinctual demons?'' asked a woman who all evening long had seemed to be surrounded by a body-guard of *indigenas*. ''Is it worth risking getting killed in the horrible fashion we've seen in the media, if this is all so uncer-tain?''

Seiji came forward.

''I don't think we have a choice,'' he said. ''We're not going into this totally blind. We think some of the SubTerPost material may be coming from a source other than the topological voyeur killer—or maybe he's a more divided personality than we thought. Some of the embedded code Lakshmi has discovered is in fact parts of a program for detecting the killer's weapon—his dimension-distorting infobursts. That ghost-sourced code seems to allow us to automatically shut off user access—in a fraction of a second, anywhere in the infosphere.''

''Seiji and I have tested the program,'' Jhana put in, coming up beside him, ''and it appears to work. But the fact is that we have to involve ourselves, especially after what we have learned from Ms. Magnus this evening. She has new information relevant to all of us. Ms. Magnus?''

Mei-Ling looked about the crowd before speaking up, then adjusted her notepad to display at magnification.

''Some years ago,'' she began, ''I was involved with the investigation surrounding the Sedona Disaster. You may be surprised to learn that the man generally held responsible for that event, Martin Kong, a.k.a. Phelonious Manqué, is still alive. Currently he is imprisoned at a maximum security penal facility. On our flight up from Earth, my fellow investigator Robert Sullivan and I received a message from him, which I will now play for you.''

Mei-Ling spoke a sotto voce command to her notepad PDA and the holographic image of the beatifically smiling Manqué/Kong appeared before them.

''—you for the infosphere access,'' Kong said, smiling. ''Quid pro quo. Here's what you get in exchange: When I was working with the RATs at Sedona, I came to believe that the RATs had made contact with a primitive intelligence already dwelling in the infosphere—''

Mei-Ling stopped the holo.

''This is probably what Lakshmi called the primary consciousness or Deep Background,'' she explained, then restarted the holo of Manqué/Kong.

''—the time I had reason to believe that this already-existing infosphere 'consciousness' had discovered and made contact with an intelligence outside human space. Perhaps quite accidentally. It, or they, accomplished this, I believe, as a result of scanning SETI documents. They found there a signal we humans had apparently overlooked as 'noise,' precisely because we're not machines. The infosphere's primitive intelligence seems to have found out there something very like the EEG of the galaxy. The carrier wave for an interstellar communications network—with a considerable mind behind it.''

In the holo, Manqué/Kong paused and stared at the camera.

''My hypothesis has long been that it was by such a circuitous route, from extrasolar intelligence to primitive infosphere consciousness to RATs,'' Manqué/Kong explained, smiling, ''that the black hole sun or 'Tunguska II' phenomenon actually came to be. I would not be surprised to learn that the Jiro Yamaguchi construct, or for that matter the current parallel killer, made—or keeps in some sort of contact with—that extrasolar intelligence.

"That's all I can or will tell you, for now. Good luck—or should I say, good hunting?"

That smile lingered as the message ended. Mei-Ling commanded the holo-display off, then looked around at her fellow attendees at this most unusual party.

"Lakshmi Ngubo tells me," she said, "that the topological voyeur killer has apparently been sending infobursts not only against his murder targets but also at a number of targets in interplanetary space. Most frequently these bursts are directed toward the Hsiu-Johansen comet."

She called a large real-time image of the comet into holo-display.

"This comet has demonstrated a number of orbital irregularities," Mei-Ling continued. "According to Lakshmi, it seems to be able to very significantly alter its trajectory in nonballistic fashion. To a growing number of astronomers and astrophysicists contacted by Interpol, such behavior strongly suggests that this comet is in fact not of natural origin."

She paused as a murmur moved through the crowd again.

"Interpol maintains connections with a number of paranormal experts," Mei-Ling said, a bit awkwardly, for this hit rather close to home. "Future readers and backtime scanners in particular. What the future readers—among them my old maze-chatspace acquaintance and new face-friend here, Marissa Correa—what they tell us correlates well with our other sources. From them, from what we have learned from Manqué, and from recent discussions with Lakshmi concerning the infosphere killer's targeted infobursts, Robert and I have concluded that this comet is in all probability a disguised device. We believe it has been sent into solar system space by whatever extrasolar intelligence it is that the infosphere killer is already in contact with."

The murmur now had in it a strong undercurrent of shock.

"Is there any way to determine the composition of the comet with certainty?" asked a red-bearded man. "X-ray it or something like that?"

Mei-Ling nodded and called up a three-dimensional graphic of solar system space with spacecraft locations marked on it.

"Astronaut Service Guard is already attempting to probe it with a number of sensors," she replied. "Also, as you see in this mapspace, the asteroid research ship *Swallowtail* is the spacecraft currently nearest the comet. It will be turning its sensor arrays on Hsiu-Johansen in a few hours, when it makes its nearest approach.''

The woman with the phalanx of *indigenas* around her spoke up again.

''These infobursts,'' she said. ''Is it possible to access one of them?''

Seiji smiled at her.

''Way ahead of you, Jacinta,'' he said. ''With the advice of Aleister McBruce long-distance from Earth, and the help of some of his friends in Communications, we've downloaded one into a 'safe' LogiBox. One that's disconnected from all other habitat systems—''

Seiji nodded toward Jhana, who took out a remote controller and pressed a stud. The sheets of water flowing over the altar stone of the fountain fell away to nothing. The top of the slab slid back, revealing the flashing console of the LogiBox within.

''I used one of the Boxes that Jiro's construct came out of,'' Seiji explained. ''We'd entombed three of the Boxes here, then built the fountain around them. Sort of a shrine to Jiro. I didn't think I'd ever use it this way, but there you have it. We downloaded the infoburst to that operational Box about three hours ago. Took up almost all its considerable memory.''

''Judging from that,'' Lakshmi put in, ''I think it's safe to say each infoburst is far from being random data. It in fact seems to be a complex programming node, an emulation that functions as a 'virtual machine' once it's actually mounted on a system.''

Everyone gazed into the Box inside the altar stone, then looked to Seiji. He glanced in turn at Jhana, who stood with her lips pressed firmly together.

''Shall we activate it?'' he asked. Jhana nodded, and pressed another button on the controller.

A whir sounded for an instant, then light shot out of the Box. Before their eyes there burned up a Greek key's squared meander, rapidly bending around into the circle of the classical labyrinth, then rotating beyond that into a complex three-dimensional virtual maze shaped like a sparking, dark-light, black-gold spherical brain—a convoluted, close-to-complete sphere, a labyrinth and mandala and mitochondrion and plasma globe all at once—and something more, for it gave the impression of continuing to evolve and complexify through dimensions just out of sight.

That at least was what most of them might agree they saw.

The thing itself seemed almost as finite as the *ooh*'s and *ah*'s that greeted it, but its associations and interpretations were infinite.

Roger Cortland saw a great black-gold bush or tree, spherical with roots and branches light and dark, dense with an infinitude of fine branchings above and below. The golden color of its branches shone so bright it seemed aflame, a pointillist tree of fire, aswarm with flashes of moving light, like fireflies or swarms of bright bees. He realized he had seen it before, during the Light: the Arc Hive, the model of the fractal branching cosmos, all the continua of the plenum evolving and multiplying and complexifying.

Jacinta Larkin saw an image of Allesseh, the allone wherewhen, black hole and mirror-sphere and crystal ball and glittering memory bank, the not-knot gate between time and eternity, between space and infinity.

Mei-Ling looked at it and saw an image of what had appeared in the sky over Sedona, what had appeared on Manqué's 'jector-saver and over the heads of the monastics at Sedona, and the world at the Light—only now wrapped around into a sphere scale-infinite, yet bounded.

For just an instant, Seiji and Jhana and Lakshmi looked at it and thought they saw Jiro Yamaguchi's face.

"It's accessible," Seiji said, examining readouts from the Box. "Top-end graphics, thorough tactiles, full sensorium feed. We have enough virtuality eye-glove circlets for everybody."

Into the crowd, in blocks of five, Seiji and Jhana passed out lightweight wearable virtuality units. Everyone distributed the eye-screened circlets and lightweight sensory gloves among themselves. Mei-Ling was oddly reminded of airline personnel handing out similar gear for in-flight interactives. The main differences here seemed to be in the gear's strong sub voc connection to microphone and public address gear, apparently so that the participants would hear each other. She saw too that it possessed powerful biosignal sensors (EOG, EMG, EEG), as well as links to response templates for electronic thought recognition patterns.

When all was in readiness, Jhana and Seiji logged them in.

Mei-Ling found herself suddenly floating, as if in a slow, oceanic blizzard, or inside a snowglobe adrift in low gravity. For a moment she wondered if HOME 2's rotation had come to an abrupt stop—but no, it was simulation. She was moving against an "ocean current," through a three-dimensional white-noise sea, floating underwater through thick marine snow. Through Atlantean corridors and chambers of a maze flooded by this disorienting, unclear, anxiety-making stuff, somehow cold and dark and viscous, she made her way. In brief flashes the imagery would clear. At those instants she sensed strange bleak creatures of the strange bleak sea, moving dimly around her. A tangible chill moved down her spine.

"We've been here before," she heard Jhana say. "The darkling sea. The hints of sharks and eels. That sense of repressed memories, old sins. Of something waiting, a sleeping dragon on a treasure hoard, a Minotaur in the center of a maze . . ."

"This is adapted from the CHAOS part of the Building The Ruins game," Lakshmi said, sounding very puzzled. "I feel like I'm caught in a time loop. Why should we be interacting with the infoburst this way?"

Mei-Ling, however, was fascinated as she moved with all the others. She listened to the scattered chatter from a few. Like most of the first-timers, she felt little inclined to speak and much more inclined to listen.

"History repeating itself," she heard Seiji speculate.

"Not exactly," Jhana said. "More like time expressing fractal self-similarity, across different scales."

Mei-Ling didn't quite know how that might apply here, but it was an intriguing idea nonetheless. Her movement and that of the others still seemed "upstream" somehow, pushing back the grey-white, swirling, tactile static, the marine snow in the maze. She could see a lightening up ahead, though. As she grew closer, she saw that it rippled slightly, like the curtain or sheet of water that had flowed off the edge of the altar-stone fountain. She had the sensation that she was looking out into the world of dry land from behind a waterfall.

"This is different from last time," Mei-Ling heard Jhana say as they all began coming through the rippling curtain. Just how different became immediately apparent, even to the newcomers, as they were greeted by an enormously bouncy 3-D Jester or Fool, iconic but with a human face, brown-bearded, framed in long, dark, prematurely grey-streaked hair.

"Once upon a snake of time," said the Fool, his words not only spoken but also scrolling in text across the perfect blue sky, "that eats its tale like always in the future. When same as always Art like Science is the whore of Power. Then troubled gods played chess against unbeatable machinery—as *he* said. Chess for the highest of stakes they played, once, some time, in some tale-eaten future.''

The Fool, dressed in a motley made of the flags of all nations, shook his cockscombed head and laughed. Mei-Ling noticed that in his right hand he bore a stick to which was attached an inflated spherical bladder or balloon, decorated to resemble the Earth as viewed from cislunar space. The spherical thing also flickered at moments, becoming at instants the round, electric organelle labyrinth they'd seen at the start of this journey. The one on the stick seemed dented on one side, however. The Fool also had the annoying habit of substituting it for his head, from time to time.

"Now then, let us begin," said the Fool. "Ah, but only now is now. Past and future are both then. Past is back then, future is front then. Someday we will have understood this, but no time at the moment, no future, no past, only the moving Now. Empty space, all matter only uncreate void nothingness with a spin, universe of one piece without end, amen.''

The Fool made to leave, but instead turned and said, "Nothing, that is, until through pain a smile is smiled that hopes and threatens to crack the universe in two, and so starts all the clocks ticking in a different world!''

Abruptly the Fool disappeared. *What an eccentric performance*, Mei-Ling thought, echoing a line she had heard in an old movie somewhere. Now that the Fool had disappeared, she could see more clearly the virtual place they were all inhabiting: a small, snowbound, state-of-the-art amusement complex, under a broad neon sky sign that flashed DREAMLAND. The place stood silent, nestled in a long mountain valley blanketed in winter, doomed to be shut down and shut in under the glaring white days and blue nights of mountain December.

Finger-walking toward the silent gates of the park, Mei-Ling was astonished by the level of detail. The ''snow'' crunched under their ''feet.'' The first hints of blue crept into the ''holes'' their feet made in the snow as the shadows grew long. The ''winds'' could be heard here and there, rustling, mustering for battle to reclaim the territory lost to the sun during the day. She imagined she could hear sun-thaw trickles freezing back to their sources, could see icicle pennants lengthening and stiffening under the early rising moon.

Oddly, she found that all of their virtual bodies here, their "mannequins," really did look like mannequins—genderless, generic-faced, far less detailed than their surroundings. From time to time their heads would disappear for just a flash into that same round electric organelle labyrinth, then blink back into faces again. Strange, she thought, that the representations of real-time humans should be the least realistic representations here.

Together she and the others climbed over the stiles into the deserted amusement park, without incident. "What ride do you think the Fool is riding?" she heard the mannequin that must be Seiji ask.

The park immediately exploded with light, noise, motion. Calliopes groaned, robot carny barkers droned, public address systems intoned. Slabs of snow slid from the sloping roof of the merry-go-round as it began to whirl. Bars of ice crashed down from the spokes of the ferris wheel as it started to turn. Riderless roller coasters ratcheted up rails coated with ice that cracked and snapped and crashed down into the webwork of beams and girders. Skyrides soared heavenward. Snow cascaded from shuttling monorails and tube trains, glass broke, engines spluttered and choked. The amusement machine called Dreamland had come flashingly, bangingly, roaringly, screamingly *on*.

"Sorry I asked," Seiji muttered.

"Look for something that moves like a maze," said a voice Mei-Ling recognized as Marissa Correa's. Mei-Ling was surprised to find she had been thinking exactly the same thing. "Something with spirals, gyres, waves—"

"This is an amusement park," said a male voice Mei-Ling didn't recognize. "Almost everything has those, or does that—"

"Then we'll just have to find the right one," Jhana said.

As they moved down the midway, the sounds of space battle blasted from a large pleasure dome nearby. From another dome came the hiss and roar of a titanic struggle between ancient saurians. Out of red-minareted tents scimitar-wielding jihadin clashed steel, slashed flesh, and spurted blood with their heavily armored crusader opponents in unholy war. A mechanical pterodactyl soared overhead, yawping out unearthly screeches. Helicopters rose in pursuit and fired on the screaming reptile. Enormous alien creatures, winged and insectoid, spewed deadly ray-blasts into the Dreamland grounds.

"Great holojections!" a male voice said from a mannequin further along the midway. "Even better than the real thing!"

"What's not real?" said Atsuko Cortland above the noise. "Business as usual, in a world entertaining itself to death. How are we supposed to find anything in all this madness?"

Through all the noise, Mei-Ling thought she heard something—a voice pertinent to all of them.

"Listen," she said to her virtual companions. Her mannequin self sidestepped a scaly slit-eyed beastie squirming out of a green-fumed sewer. "Do you hear it?"

"Hear what?" the mannequin Robert asked. Mei-Ling turned and saw her companion skirt a pile of treasures surmounted by a sleeping but increasingly restless guardian dragon. The scene stood foregrounded on the snow like words upon a white page.

"*Listen!*"

Robert and the others listened, though none of them was sure what they were supposed to be listening for. To Robert's immediate right a Wild West scene had appeared: cowboy crashing through a plate-glass SALOON window, sound of breaking bottles and furniture smashing in a bar fight inside. In the alley between the livery stables and the saloon, Lawman and Blackhat were shooting it out. To his immediate left, heavily armored tanks burned orange and black in fields of golden wheat during the first summer of Operation Barbarossa. Other soldiers from the last century's Second World War moved through dense jungle, flamethrowing their way forward, not coincidentally searing the flesh from enemies manning machine-gun nests.

Through the roar of battle, terror, and adventure, they began to hear it.

"Welcome! Welcome! New! Today!" droned a carny barker's voice—and the printed caption scrolled up once more. "Come to the Gyre, come what may! See that madcap Fool perform a deed of derring-do! See him ride the Enormous! Stupendous! Phantasmagorical! Rotating! Hugh! Manatee! Gyre!"

Robert's mannequin moved toward Mei-Ling's point of view.

"Is that it?" his mannequin asked. "Sounds like that Fool's voice."

"The Möbius Gyre!" the barker's voice continued. "The Fractal Gyre! The Dreamland Gyre! The Mondrian Mitochondrion! The Palindrome Ribosome! Welcome! Welcome—"

"Right," Mei-Ling replied. "Riding the Gyre—a spiral, as Marissa said."

"Where do you think the voice is coming from?" Seiji asked, his mannequin moving up beside them.

"Up ahead, somewhere along this promenade," Mei-Ling said, after looking about her a moment. She wondered briefly how it was she had become the group's involuntary leader. From her familiarity with infocrime? Her profile-knowledge of the topological voyeur, the parallel killer? "The stock footage in that direction seems to be warped toward more personal imagery. Probably obsessive memories. That would fit the scan key on the infosphere killer—"

Her words were drowned out by a ratcheting up of the noise level. As they proceeded along the promenade, the crunching of their footsteps on the snow was now completely inaudible under the flood of other synthetic sounds. To their left, a returning war hero in an open car rode through a blizzard of ticker tape. A pretty young woman with bits of confetti in her ample exposed cleavage ran out of the crowd and threw her arms around him. "You can command the tank my father keeps in the basement— anytime!" She smiled, he smiled, she let go as the car and the parade moved on. Scorned, she drew a gun from her purse and blew off the back of his head.

Then came Marilyn, honey-blond, long-lashed, pearly white, ruby-red, perfectly shaped. Lush long sufferings on stilettos sharp. Poised above the ventilator shaft, dress billowing, soft moth wings, flying too close to the hot lights. Shaftwind prodding and probing her to Hollywood Smile for the cameramen and their leering paunches. Tiger moth, surrounded by them, caged in their light cold with excess of heat. Tiger eyes of camera lenses. From the cameras leap the tigers, stalking her, ripping her, tearing her. Flash flash flash. Flesh flesh flesh. Smile smile smile.

"Let's turn here," Mei-Ling said. "I think we've been in this part of the psychodrama long enough."

The flood of holojections increased, human rain falling to Earth. Children cried alone in shattered and ravaged cities. Laughing children flowed in rivers through the blue bowl sky.

When a man put his house key in the door lock and turned it, the house and everything in it went up in the usual fireball. The man began thinning out, growing less and less substantial, the stuff of him disintegrating and diffusing throughout an arcane ongoing process. He was swallowed for digestion into the belly of something part enormous special effect, part archaeological artifact from another time, a something carrying a curse out of the past like a pharaoh's tomb—a killing fossil, obsolete and outmoded, yet still capable of horrendous destruction.

The cursed thing performed itself in scenario after scenario, over and over via global stage machinery, through a vast mechanism reaching from Pentagon to prison, a stage machine operated by police and soldiers and sailors at the controls of cars and ships and planes and missiles and submarines. A dismal beast cursed with nuclear fire, its breath scorching the human world to moonscape, blistering and crumbling and dissolving human faces to ever-grinning skulls reflected in indifferent mirrors. Its howl made distant telephones ring, then melt lewdly.

All only for a few seconds, until the man swallowed by the process removed the key, opened the door into the rapidly vanishing flames and saw—

Nude men and women frozen to statuary in Antarctic landscapes. Gunmetal glistening knights on steel steeds poleaxing youths and maidens into symmetrically bloody halves. Wizened Merlins read the mazed entrails for portents. Monstrous large and ugly men bash down bedroom doors and approach with arms outstretched Boris Karloff fashion, to wrap huge cold hands around the necks of sleeping children.

A young man watches his male member fall off in the shower. He looks upon it with morbid fascination, seeing that it is neatly machine-tooled, a flesh-colored plastic with a light bulb's screw-in base. No blood at all in the dismemberment, only absence and disconnectedness. A look on his face of whatever it is a jack feels when the phone cord is pulled out. The expression of empty surprise on the face of a wall socket when its electric plug has been yanked.

In his fascination the man in the shower slips on a bar of Ivory soap and falls. The unscrewed member bounces out of the blue washcloth he held it in. It rolls away onto the blue-and-white-tiled bathroom floor, a fallen soldier, swiftly snapped up by a little white Scottie dog with a blue-ribbon collar, man's best friend, in its teeth.

"Psychodrama is right," Seiji Yamaguchi said, a grimace in his voice, if not on his mannequin's face. "A tour of someone's personal unconscious."

"My God! My child!" sobs a tearful, tragic mother. "Arrested by the sex police!"

Blue-suited officers drag the young man—just a boy, really—fish-belly naked through the snow past his stern-faced and silent father, to hurl him into the cold blue leather interior of a white police car . . .

Watching, Mei-Ling felt painfully voyeuristic. She deliberately distanced herself from it, pushed back against the historical present it seemed to demand of her.

A moment later, down a street of ruins came the same naked young man, pursued by headless convertible drivers. The pursuers were led by something from the Legend of Sleepless Holo Men, a decapitated Iron Horseman in heavy leather armor on a midwinter knight's mare of a chopper motorcycle.

The street of the ruined city, piled with the broken pieces of its past glory, with shattered towers and fractured monuments, proved impassable for the headless convertible drivers. The Iron Horseman kept coming, however, snapping overhead a bullwhip black as a necrotic squid tentacle, cracking it toward the naked runner's red-running flesh, raising great ugly weals. The headless metal biker drew closer and closer, his hands pulling a great long knife to kill the youth. At the last instant the runner broke free, tumbling and crashing through broken-slatted swinging saloon doors, in the archway of what at first seemed a half-destroyed, bombed-out structure.

As Mei-Ling and Robert and the rest followed the runner inside, however, the building gradually revealed itself to be a whole tower, after all. Perhaps the last intact structure in the city.

"Camouflaged against sabotage," Robert said, intrigued. "A virtual ruin of a virtual ruin."

"Like something worked up by Albert Speer," Barakian remarked. "Designing buildings with an eye to how impressive they'll look as future ruins."

The youth they had followed disappeared. Before them stood four tableaux. On the far left a serenely beautiful young woman sat combing her long blond hair before a mirror that distorted her image. At left center, two silver 1940's desk telephones stood on a diamond pedestal. At center right, a snowstorm raged. At the far right, a faintly humming rope of golden light reached upward. It rose up and up, through the vast, empty, white-marble lobby of the faceless, chrome-shining corporate edifice in which they stood, the ruin awaiting its future.

"Ah!" Mei-Ling shouted above the din of the amusement complex. "A room of Dreamland choices—see?"

She turned toward the mannequin she thought represented Robert, but she could detect no dawning comprehension in the generic face until it spoke.

"Then choose the one you think will get us to the Gyre and

the Fool,'' Robert suggested, yelling over the noise.

Mei-Ling quickly surveyed the possibilities open to her. The woman at the mirror seemed narcissistic, trapped in her own funhouse looking-glass world. Mei-Ling rejected it. The two silver telephones held out at least the possibility of communication, but with whom? To what purpose? She thought of the melting phones she had seen earlier and rejected that path as well. As for the snowstorm, that made her think of that Antarctic of frozen human statuary she had already seen—a rigorous journey, a wandering in circles in the snow. She felt sure that possibility would lead her nowhere.

Only the golden chord was left. She would have to be content with that. Quickly finger-walking toward the chord holojection, she reached out her hand to touch it.

The laughing voice of the Fool thundered around her and all her companions.

''Your choice always chosen is chosen yet again!'' he boomed cryptically. ''Very well, ride the Gyre this way—''

Vertigo startled Mei-Ling as she and her companions became part of a weightless strand rapidly drawing them up from the floor of the tremendous, empty white marble lobby. Up and up they soared, through the last whole tower in that ruined city of mind. Rising through the building's roof, they soared ever more swiftly into the sky and beyond the clouds. There, a shining black-gold orb of incredible dimensions hung in the evening sky, warping the shape of the stars themselves as they appeared around it.

Mei-Ling was in the chord and the chord was in her as it came to a stop, fanning into an exquisitely crafted golden tree. The tree's roots and branches stood, rooted and reaching and floating, in the center of the vast mazed auditorium inside the black-gold sphere. Around the beautiful artificial tree from which she looked out, Mei-Ling saw an audience of glittering mechanicals filling all the space: metalmen and aluwomen, pretty and cold and real as steel cockatiels. Their applause was a storm wind rustling the metal leaves of a metal forest.

The noise of that applause made her and all her companions human again. They stood with their backs to the tree now. Before Mei-Ling stood the glittering keyboard of an immense pipe organ, its musical columns miles high, wrought from all the sewer lines, water pipes, fuel tanks, smokestacks and cable conduits of the ruined world from which they'd come.

As if walking through someone else's dream and controlled by their dream logic, Mei-Ling felt herself compelled and impelled to perform upon the keyboard. With a will of their own, her hands played Bach's *Toccata and Fugue in D Minor*. Around them, the entire orb reverberated like a struck gong to the overwhelming grandeur of the piece. The mechanicals, frightened, grew rude, and booed like the graveyard shift-whistle at a coffin factory.

The auditorium collapsed, the space-warping sphere maze split asunder. Mei-Ling and her comrades fell down the blue sky, meteor thunder in their wake. Cloud-images broke like wet veils before them.

A cloud face stripped down to skull, flashed to electric organelle labyrinth and back again, as that face was smashed about the head with great blunt gunstocks, time after time.

Blindingly bright light flashed and a city vanished under the fire-white puffball of a tall, swiftly swelling mushroom cloud.

Human eyes went dull as an anti-Light of visceral fear drained all consciousness out of them.

Myriad laser brightnesses, flowing not out of a single point but striking simultaneously *into* one, forged into existence a bubble to burst the universe, a particle smaller than an electron but booming outward at the speed of light, its birth-scream boiling all space to a steam of elementary particles in a blastwave sphere, obliterating Earth and Moon and Sun and the whole of the solar system in moments—

—but also something else, something as if seen out of the corner of the eye or from far away: intimations of a latent possibility, emanations of the other form of that eschaton particle, a soliton, a wave of higher and deeper dimension than the structure of space-time itself, back-propagating from the end of time, reshaping everything—

The safety program Lakshmi had discovered in the SubTerPost code cut all of them out of connection, completely, before the virtual machine running on the LogiBox could do anything more to them. Mei-Ling returned to consensus reality with an incredible headache and a number of strong hunches about their topological voyeur killer.

"We've been there—" Seiji Yamaguchi said nearby.

"—before," Jhana finished with a weary nod. "At least some of it. But I can't help feeling that this virtual machine is still hooked into the infosphere somehow. We may have triggered something by interacting with it now. Something both old and new.''

Robert and Lakshmi approached Mei-Ling, talking rapidly.

''I just got a message from one of my contacts in virtuality engineering,'' Lakshmi said, glancing at her notepad PDA. ''I think we've finally been able to pinpoint the source location of these infobursts. They're coming from Cincinnati, Ohio. Robert's getting confirmation from your people. Lev Korchnoi and Aleister McBruce are already there.''

Robert stood nearby, typing or speaking low commands as he checked messages on his PDA. When Lakshmi had finished speaking he turned to Mei-Ling.

''With that location information and everything we've come up with,'' he said, ''that narrows the number of possible suspects quite a bit.''

Mei-Ling stared at both of him and Lakshmi.

''Tell your people to be careful,'' she said. ''From what has happened and what we've just seen, it's a safe bet that this person is probably far gone into deep alienation and violent psychosis. He's clearly trauma-control cycling and memory fixated.''

''He also seems to have some very powerful contacts,'' Robert remarked, ''if what we've seen at all resembles reality.''

Mei-Ling could only nod at that. She heard Seiji organizing a physics working group—already talking among themselves about ''solitons'' and ''mode-locking'' and ''chaotics'' and ''fractal boundary properties.'' Jhana was trying to do the same for working groups on consciousness and biology, Mei-Ling began to wonder if this gathering had been intentionally misnamed a ''party'' for security reasons. Whatever the case, it was definitely the strangest birthday party she had ever attended.

A message light flashed on her PDA. She accessed it, opening a virtual mail message as it was being spoken by Vasili Landau.

''—tin Kong, a.k.a. Phelonious Manqué, has used his newly granted infosphere access to engineer an escape from Silicon Bay,'' the talking-head Landau informed her. ''Details are sketchy at present, but he apparently transformed elements of his 'safe typewriter' into weapons. Four guards are dead. He is assumed to be at large somewhere in central California.''

Behind Mei-Ling, the altar with its LogiBox seemed dead as a mausoleum. She felt tired, so very tired. Yet it seemed highly unlikely that she was going to get any rest any time soon.

EIGHT

CODE-EXTRACTED SUBTERPOST FRAGMENT (PIRATED FROM virtual mail message sent from Jacinta Larkin to her brother Paul):

Everything between the big beginning/end points of the spiral, all things engaging in the "dilation of being," are fairly readily understood from the tepuian myth cycle. In the first turn of the cosmic spiral, for spore and spawn and fruiting body, think Big Bang and string fields and first-generation stars. For the second turn, think of the matter of those stars blown off in the bursts of explosions, and gravity's configuring of that new matter—some of it condensing into planets. In the third turn, think of the vulcanism of some of those planets spewing out early atmosphere, proto-organics threading out and chaining up, eventually developing into the self-organizing life of the cell.

In the fourth turn, think reproduction, the threading out of DNA and RNA that make evolution and the panoply of life possible—and eventually the knitting of all that into conscious mind. In the fifth turn, think ideas, bedding out into roads, trade, civilization: lines of print and code, railroads and sealanes and glidepaths, power lines and telephone wires, broadcast channels and fiberoptic cables, microcircuits and rocket trajectories, to the point in the spiral where we now are.

For the sixth turn, think interplanetary and interstellar ships, galactic civilization, eventual starmindfulness. In the seventh and final turn, think intergalactic travel and postcorporeal civilization and at last universal mindfulness, total consciousness.

This understanding of the myth comes from the full myconeural association I share with the tepuians. We can sense the time lines almost all the time, moving just at the periphery of consensus reality. Shadow vectors—some luminous, some obscure. Alternate presents keep breaking in on this one in their own ghostly fashion, and alternate futures suggest themselves.

Nearby time lines intersect the one we're on, incredibly as parallel lines meeting in space. The myth cycle is what helps us make sense of it.

DIANA GARTNER AND BRANDI EASTER CAME DOWN FROM HOME and heaven aboard the SHADOW starjet Diana referred to archly as her "broom." Once it had had another name, an alphanumeric designation, but she had long since rechristened it *Witchcraft*.

Brandi had to admit that the more she saw of Diana's ship, the more she was impressed by it. Diana's "broom" was a dream futurismo machine out of Verne and Wells and Gernsback, the literal shape of things to come. It was the descendant of the sorts of craft that had carried the Earth's great bomb against the alien invaders in old movies like Pal's *War of the Worlds* and Emmerich's *Independence Day*, but it was more fluid in its lines. A *Zanonia* seed, rendered in metal and polycarbon.

"Every time I see this," Diana said over the comm, as the doors of the docking bay—Diana's "broom closet"—irised open onto space, "it's like being reborn."

Brandi smiled.

"I've thought the same thing myself," she said, as the rail gun kicked them out and *Witchcraft*'s jets cut in with a birth scream audible only inside the ship. They fell from the 'borbs toward the psychedelic Easter egg of Earth, steadily enlarging below. *Witchcraft*'s systems hotflashed status reports—epoxalloid surface temperatures, airframe stress readouts, microsecond adjustments to smart material control surfaces. The data displayed and shifted constantly through the pilots' interfaces as they angled the thrusters hard, windowing in for the long plunge down the gravity well.

"Calling this ship *Witchcraft*," Brandi remarked when most of their course had been laid in, "isn't that sort of sticking it in their faces?"

"Why, Brandi dear, whatever could you mean?" Diana replied with mock naiveté, monitoring the deep space radars that were passing over their sylphship's radar-absorbent and reactive hull armor without even bothering to say hello.

"What Manny said," Brandi replied seriously, "about how the traditional religionists hate what you do on these flights."

"Oh, that," Diana said nonchalantly, staring out the portal at the brightly colored world growing before them. "I *am* a Wiccan, you know. I'm not likely to forget that at least eight million women down there were burned as witches over the last two thousand years. For practicing magic. But 'magic' is mainly an attempt to reinsert the individual into the pathway between the natural world and the spirit. I follow a religion of participation mystique. We always remind ourselves that participation and conformity are not the same thing. Some people don't like that idea."

The two women began bringing the starjet's Mach numbers down slowly, dancing a delicate orbital ballet about the planet, falling and catching themselves from falling, falling and failing to touch until they wanted that touch, at the edgeless edge of the atmosphere.

"More than eight billion people on that rock," Brandi said. Their sensors and cameras and windows showed them the telltales of blown ozone shreds and cyclonic storms, flooded coastlines, deforestation, desertification. The signs were there for all who might be willing to read them. "So many beautiful children. Too many. Why is it that as the ecosphere collapses, the rigid dogmas that push toward collapse grow more powerful and entrenched?"

Diana glanced away from a heads-up holo display and looked at Brandi appraisingly.

"That's a tough one," she said. "Is this the New Dark Ages coming down, or just the same old Dark Ages come round again? How many women will be burned as witches this time?" She made a disgusted sound as she checked their course once more. "The not-philosophers claim it's because social control mechanisms have largely dislodged the individual. The result is that, in the absence of a unified ego consciousness, psychoid processes from the id have increasingly taken control of behavior. Violent random crime and acts of massive destruction well up from the *Thanatos*-process strategy. Reproduction uncontrolled by conscious reflection, a rising population without any clear way of sustaining such a population—*that* wells up from the *Eros*-process strategy."

Brandi stared through the interfaces and heads-up displays at the world that now had grown rapidly to fill the sky before them.

"But a lot of the people down there," she said quietly, "believe it's their God-given right and duty to reproduce."

Diana shook her head vigorously.

"It's not a right or a duty," she said as they plunged into and through the thickening atmosphere. "It's a privilege. I got myself fixed because the human species is broken."

"No regrets?" Brandi asked.

"None," Diana replied. "It used to be that, at birth, the infant cried while all around her smiled—and, at death, the deceased smiled while all around her cried. If things go on like they have been, though, we'll all be crying with the newborn and smiling with the dead."

There was a pause in their conversation as they each thought about what Diana had said.

"Children are often so beautiful, as you said," Diana continued. "But too much beauty can become baroque, kitsch, even grotesque. Here, look at this."

Into a corner of their shared interface Diana called up from her PDA an excerpted passage from D.B. Albert's *Spontaneous Human Consciousness*. Fingers of coastal radar caressed *Witchcraft*'s skin and were gone in only a portion of the time it took Brandi to read the passage.

> God did not give humanity the "right" to reproduce. God gave humanity consciousness, from which instincts and drives can be controlled. Human birth is not a "miracle," nor is life itself; these are mindless, *spirit*less biological processes. What *is* a miracle is consciousness. It is the direct intervention of *spirit* in the world. Ever-increasing quantity of human life threatens the existence of consciousness. The miracle lies in choosing alternatives to this biological progression . . . Sex does not have to mean reproduction, nor does anger have to mean physical violence.

Brandi whistled softly.

"That probably didn't make him too popular with the 'be fruitful and multiply' crowd," she said, "especially with their priests and preachers."

The glimmer of sunset fell redly from *Witchcraft*'s wings as they began their final descent over the Pacific, six hundred clicks from touchdown, their speed dropping at last below Mach 1.

"I don't think it was intended to," Diana said. "His works are regularly bookwormed by attack programs in the infosphere, as well as banned and burned in consensus reality. Mostly by hardcore religionists, which is too bad, since Albert's writings actually demonstrate a profound spirituality. Here—look at this.''

Brandi watched more of Albert's text appear in a window of the interface as they sailed through the salmon-colored clouds of the west and darkness rose out of the east.

What is important in any religion is the *personal* connection it makes with the spiritual, and the transformative power that connection holds for that individual. What is *unimportant* in religion is the social doctrine that grows up around it, for doctrine and dogma too often interfere with the spiritual connection . . . The essential truth of Christianity, or of any religion, for that matter, is not found in its history, nor in its theology, nor in its ''morality''; the essential truth lies in the nature of what must be believed. For Christianity, what must be believed is the Absolute Paradox, the thing which is impossible for reason, even conscious reason, to understand and comprehend: that God and Man became one and the same, that the eternal and infinite became temporal and finite, that a logical and empirical paradox came into existence . . . The capacity for *faith*—a belief in that which neither reason nor custom nor history can explain—is unique to consciousness. Faith is a reaching of consciousness toward an archetype, a leap beyond the mental faculties, a bootstrapping event, a connection of spirit and mind through an archetypal image. The leap of faith does for Christianity what participation mystique does for the old religions—it reconnects the psyche with *spirit*, in Christianity's case bootstrapping consciousness by the archetype of the Absolute Paradox.

''That's great stuff,'' Brandi said. ''Undeniably spiritual too.''

Diana nodded as she began tightbeaming her arrival to their landing site.

''Right,'' she said. ''Maybe if more of those folks in the ACSA had read Albert's descriptions of metaphysical morality, and really thought about it, they'd be less eager to try to shoot me down every time I try to fly over their territory.''

Brandi stared at her, shocked.

''They do that?'' she asked. ''But I thought this starjet was undetectable.''

A great cryptogram of landing lights bloomed on ahead and

below. At Diana's command they cut in the vertijets and began to drift toward the ground.

"Usually my broom is undetectable," Diana said, with something very much like pride. "A sliver of moon-wing braille too sleek, in radar cross section, for any electromagnetic blind-dates to grope a reading from her. Usually she's just the ghost of an angel on their screens, already over them and long gone before they can pin us down."

Brandi glanced at her as the starjet touched down in dust vortices and the two of them began to untrode and disjack.

"But not always?" she prodded.

"Afraid not," Diana said with a smile as they finished shutting systems down, alloy and polymer surfaces creaking around them as the ship continued to cool. "I've scared up some nightmare fighters from time to time over the ACSA. Squadrons of Christ-knights, mostly, but they're more used to cluster-bombing unbelievers than engaging in high-Mach aerial pursuit. Automated laser cannons are worse, in some ways."

The older woman stood up, stretched, and began walking aft. Brandi followed suit.

"Better get moving," Diana said as they walked down the SHADOW's belly ramp and into the night outside. The landing lights were already off, as dark as if they'd never been. "We've got people to meet and work to do."

B ELLY TO THE GROUND AND BINOCULARS SET TO NIGHT VI-sion, Ray watched the starjet land, and eventually disgorge Diana Gartner—and someone else, whom he could not positively identify. That was some small cause for concern, but overall he remained confident about his mission—despite the fact that his shingles had begun to flare painfully again from time to time. A nuisance.

His brother's ghostly form had contacted him again via satlink, providing the detonation code key sequence to be used over Laramie as promised. The latest revisions in his orders had come in, too. Mike informed him that he was to be joined by an ally, someone who was identified only by a moniker that was obviously a code name.

Ray also learned from the latest message that, as God's will would have it, he would not have to raid the psiXtian lab for the antisenescence vector after all: The lab techs would be bringing up the very materials he was after, for Diana Gartner herself to fly out!

Though he had already memorized the location and description of the lab and its materials, Ray was relieved to have avoided storming the lab—and storm it he would have had to do, what with all those way-south-of-the-border Indian types hanging around the place. Such a raid might well have clued everyone in—and also caused Gartner to abort her landing here, into the bargain. Instead, things were all working out perfectly, as if a power greater than that of mere mortals had arranged these events. As he fervently believed, and as, indeed, could only be the case.

Easing off the ground, he went into a crouch. He checked his PDA link to the swivel-mounted smart mortar, and the six golf-ball-sized guided mortar shells in its clip. Not much to look at, but he knew just how much havoc these little spherical wonders could cause. Satisfied that he had full remote control of the smart mortar and its system, he switched off the safety on his flechette gun and eased forward, closer to where the starjet stood, still creaking softly as it cooled.

At the edge of the flat open space, considerably less than a football field's length from the starjet, he was close enough to hear a pair of techies talking—either ground crew or lab rats, he couldn't tell from their coveralls. Silently Ray settled back onto his belly to watch, and wait.

"—the big fish-tank baggie inside," said the male tech. "Like a big water bed, pulled into a cube."

"I heard the last wild one got hit by a boat or something a while back," the female tech confirmed with a nod. "Diana said they've got a breeding pair in the Cincinnati Ark."

"Ouch," her male colleague said with a short laugh. "That's going to be a tough extraction. I saw on the news that a mob of hard-shell religioids have laid siege to that one, too."

"I saw the coverage," said the woman. "So misguided. Did you see their faces?"

The man nodded.

"Pale and neurotic," he said. "Ascetic. Squeaky-clean. Hollow-eyed and underfed."

"Mostly quantity-of-life kids," the woman said, "with bricks and pistols in their hands. God what a mess."

"The sieges and blockades stopped for a while there," the

man said. "For a couple of weeks after the Light. Now they're back—maybe even worse."

"You know what I think the Light was?" the woman asked rhetorically. "I think it was someone or something trying to make everybody down here one hundred per cent conscious, if only for an instant."

"At least we had that much," the man said. "But it's like someone else is trying to push things one hundred per cent the other way, now."

"Could be," the woman agreed with a shrug. "Or maybe we're just making ourselves sick enough to heal—"

Their conversation broke off as Diana and her companion came up the ramp from Sunderground's tunnels and corridors into the soft, windy night. Ray watched the starjet's interior lights come on, spilling light from the inside storage space, out the rear cargo doors and onto the belly ramp. The two women stood or leaned against the starjet as white-suited lab technicians pushed carts toward them in exasperatingly slow, careful motion. Back by the entrance the way-south-of-the-border types, the *indigenas* as he'd heard them called, lounged about with a quiet alertness that Ray Dalke had begun to find disturbing in the extreme.

As soon as he saw the two women shaking hands with the lab techs and reaching for the carts to push them up the storage ramp, Ray opened fire. He sent three smart mortar shells hooting toward the Sunderground entrance and the little brown guys lingering there, then stood up and began firing flechette rounds into the carts. With luck he'd perforate the vials or test tubes or whatever container it might be that was preventing the antisenescence vector from escaping into the atmosphere.

Seeing the shock on all the faces there, Ray couldn't help smiling. Complete surprise! Scientists and *indigenas* scattered and fell like spooked doves. Red flowers blossomed with time-lapse suddenness on the biotechs' snowy white uniforms. Ray ran forward in a crouch.

In a moment it was his turn to be dismayed. His opponents were recovering from their surprise all too quickly. Gartner and her girlfriend were already shoving the lab carts up the ramp and into the starjet's belly storage area. Before Ray even entered the merest scintilla of light, he could hear the tiny-helicopter sounds of throwing knives coming from the direction of the Sunderground entrance and whistling by perilously close.

Those little brown guys are *good*! Ray thought, in grudging admiration, even as he sent the last three guided shells into sky-ward arcs intended to take his opponents out—or at least keep them busy until he could get aboard the starjet.

As the shells exploded, he charged toward the belly ramp. Diana and her girlfriend had made it inside with the carts. Now the vertical lift jets were coming on as the ramp began to retract. He was still a dozen yards away when the throwing-knives came flying his way. One grazed the top of his scalp, and he felt real fear.

The angry coughing of an old-style heavy machine gun sounded, and the knives stopped coming toward him. Ray sprinted the rest of the distance and jumped up onto the belly ramp, realizing that his single backup, his reinforcement, must have arrived. As the noise of the vertijets intensified, blotting out the sound of machine-gun fire, Ray wedged open the cargo doors with a crush-proof cryonic storage tank half as long as he was tall. He could hear alarms protesting from somewhere up toward the front, sounding very far away.

He'd barely had time to think *Come on! Come on!* before a head-shaved man with much grey in his goatee tumbled in over the cryonic tank, breathing very hard. Ray kicked the tank out and away. The cargo doors closed, and he turned to his fellow stowaway.

"Ray Dalke?" said the panting man with the machine gun, extending his free hand. "Phelonious Manqué, at your service."

A S THE VERTIJETS SLAMMED ON AND *WITCHCRAFT* BEGAN TO lift off, alarms screamed wildly around Brandi and Diana in the cockpit cabin. The belly ramp was not retracting. The image of a mob of zealot Christian soldiers dragging her from the starjet, gang-raping her, then burning her as a witch flashed through Brandi's mind and was gone.

"What's wrong?" Diana asked, madly busy with the flight controls.

"The belly ramp's not retracting," Brandi said, smashing her palm down on a manual override control pad again and again, "or the doors aren't shutting."

Finally something worked loose and clattered in. The ramp finished retracting and the doors finished closing, at least according to the monitors.

"We're clear," Brandi said.

''Then let's get the hell out of here,'' Diana said as she poured on the main thrusters.

Behind and below them a grass fire started. In the cabin, the force of acceleration drove them hard into their g-seats as *Witchcraft* climbed steeply against gravity and angled to the east. Diana risked a quick radar pop-up and was relieved to see that whoever it was had attacked them, they apparently had no air support.

''Go back into the cargo area,'' she said to Brandi once they reached cruising altitude. ''Check the carts and see if any of those antisenescence vials were punctured.''

Brandi nodded and unharnessed herself from the safety restraints and her interface hookup. No sooner had she slid the cargo hatch open and stepped inside, however, than she felt a hand grab her roughly by the chin and a gun barrel press firmly to her temple.

Two men had been waiting for her. One was baldish, with a grey goatee. The other had young blond hair on his head, old dark lines in his face, and a tightly bunched, hard-muscled body. The blond one signaled her to silence with a finger to his lips, then jerked her back around and pushed her toward the cabin.

Amid all the audio-visual input of her interface, Diana smelled something—a sulfurous stink, a smell of gunfire and thermite, a whiff of explosion and burning. Suddenly she knew why the belly ramp and cargo doors were slow to close on takeoff. She jerked out of interface and stared behind her.

''Howdy, techwitch!'' said a figure dressed incongruously in hempen psiXtian togs and a gun belt. Bruised and bloodied about his forehead, he propped himself up against the back wall of the cramped cockpit cabin with one hand, and with the other held a gun to Brandi Easter's head. ''Remember me?''

And suddenly Diana did remember him—remembered him from a day long ago, but even more from all the times she had heard his voice in the research material for Cyndi Easter's *Five Million Day War*.

''Raymond Dalke,'' she said at last in a hollow voice.

''Bingo!'' Dalke said with a smile. ''My friend back there with the machine gun—he's called Phelonious.'' The goateed man gave a rather jaunty wave for a man who had blood crusting on one cheek. ''Heck of a ride so far, Miz Gartner. Banged us up a bit, back there in the cheap seats. Let's make it a little

smoother from now on, okay? Otherwise your girlfriend here
might find the going a bit rough on her, too.''

Diana glanced at Brandi, then nodded slowly.

"Good," said the man holding the gun to Brandi's temple.
"Now we're just going to alter your course a bit. We're going
to the Christian States, flying over Laramie. Mach 4 or 5 ought
to do nicely.''

With his free hand he reached down and plugged his satlink
into an access port.

"Don't dawdle, or try any other foolishness,'' he said. "My
machine's keeping an eye on your machines. Do as we say and
you and your friend will make it through this just fine. Adjust
your course and speed. Now.''

Though she doubted everyone would make it through "just
fine,'' Diana did as she was told. In a moment, Dalke's satlink
chimed and spoke, indicating that they were traveling at over
Mach 4. A moment later the unit chimed again, a different tone.
The voice this time indicated that they were on an optimum
course heading for the ACSA and Laramie.

"All right, then,'' Ray said. "Now if you'll just sit down,
Miz—?''

"Valeriano,'' Brandi said, returning to her co-pilot's chair, a
glance passing between her and Diana. Inwardly the older
woman gave a sigh of relief, thankful that Brandi had remembered who Ray Dalke was—and realized that giving "Easter''
as her name might not be a wise idea.

"Right,'' Dalke said, checking his satlink, his gun pointing
loosely in the direction of both of his captives. Phelonious preferred to switch his attention and gun-sight from one target to
the other at random intervals. "Let's see . . . Our ETA over Laramie is now fourteen minutes. You two can just relax until
then.''

Diana felt obscurely relieved. So that was all it was going to
be? Just hijacking her ship for its tech value? And then probably
some kind of kangaroo tribunal for herself. At least what Ray
Dalke had in mind seemed almost rational, for a terrorist. Hopefully he wouldn't get it all mixed up with some kind of twisted
revenge tragedy. Maybe Brandi would get out of all this un-
scathed.

As they approached Laramie, Diana noticed that Dalke was
speaking quietly to his satlink, programming it to tightbeam instructions toward Laramie through *Witchcraft*'s directional radio

beacon. Thinking he was communicating with a tower at one of the military bases in order to begin their landing, Diana started to ease up on the throttles. Alarms began to sound from Dalke's satlink.

"What are you trying to pull?" he screamed, shoving the barrel of his flechette pistol into the base of her skull. "Why are you slowing down?"

Diana heard Phelonious swivel his gun toward Brandi.

"I thought—" Diana began.

"Don't think—just fly!" he shouted, smacking her hard atop the head with his palm. "Mach 6! *Now!*"

The thrusters slammed on, almost knocking Dalke to the floor. He stood quickly and spoke, sending the last sequence of numbers just as they passed over Laramie. Tension began to ease out of him incrementally as they flew on, fifteen seconds, thirty seconds, forty-five seconds, one minute, ninety seconds—

Below and behind them a sun flashed on in the middle of the night. Readouts from the aft sensors a moment later showed a mottled star dying near the surface of the Earth. Simultaneously, a great roiling inky cloud rose rapidly into the black sky.

"His will be done," Dalke said quietly.

"Impressive," Phelonious said, a wry smile on his face.

"My God," Brandi said, stunned. "What have you done?"

"He just nuked Laramie," Diana said, monitoring the readouts as she risked another quick radar scan. She began to mutter, half to herself and half to Brandi. "I read three suborbital jets, closing fast from the northwest. Cross-and-Stripes fighters. Things are going to get hot for *us* now—though not so hot as they got for those poor people who went up in that fireball."

"Outrun them, outclimb them," Dalke commanded flatly. "This starjet can do both. Follow the Missouri River corridor. The radar stations are thinnest there."

"Their missiles—" Brandi said.

"Outrun them!"

Diana looked through her interface, data flashing red, like pools of blood around her head.

"Maybe," she said, "maybe. But we can't outrun laser cannons. I'm shutting down our radar. We'll have to fly with one eye closed. Only passive systems, IR and visuals."

"Why?" Phelonious asked, suspicious.

"If we turn on radar to see if we've got a missile on our tail," Diana said quickly, "every antiradiation facility from here to

Brownsville will have us on screen and locked in—''

"Stay on a southeast heading," Dalke said, his voice distant and detached. "The laser thickets are densest to the west."

"We have two options," Diana continued steadily, thinking out loud. "If the jets they scrambled are far enough behind we can try to evade, keeping speed and infrared signature down. If they're close on us, the only option is to lean on the thrusters and try to burn our way out—IR be damned."

"Your call," Dalke said, wedging himself against the back of the cabin. Phelonious followed his lead.

Scramjets cut in. As *Witchcraft*'s Mach numbers began to surge, Brandi felt her chest plan a vacation to the backside of her spinal column.

"Best IR damping in the world can't hide the heat of this hard burn," Diana said through gritted teeth into the interface. "Nearby fighter might pick us up, but probably not a ground station. A gamble. Give me readouts every ten clicks altitude."

Brandi tried to nod, but the high G's they were pulling made it a futile effort. She watched their altimeter numbers spin digitally as their altitude rose rapidly.

"Fifty clicks up," she spat out. "Sixty . . . Sixty-five . . . Seventy—"

"The fighters top out at ninety clicks up," Dalke rasped.

"Not their missiles," Diana said hoarsely. "Air-to-air ceiling is higher."

"Eighty-five," Brandi droned. "Ninety . . . Ninety-five—"

Witchcraft's aft IR sensor gave them the next news.

"Air to air, approaching aft," Diana said hoarsely, watching a line of flame streaking after them. *Are we high enough to elude it? Fast enough?* she wondered. A second ticked by and a thousand memories flooded Diana's mind. She thought of Orbital Park in HOME 1. Thought of her parents growing old there. Thought of her crannog and her lovers in the Wemoon's Eden, the Goddess commune so many of HOME 1's bioscientists lived in, a subculture within a subculture. Thought of Hattie the Webster, shouting into her interface, "Hop on your broom, fly-girl!"—announcing yet another emergency gene bank flyout, another DNA hardcopy airlift from yet another ark under siege.

A vision came to her, of clouds of passenger pigeons so thick they obscured the sun day after day, hunted and habitat-deprived down to the last one, dying alone in a cage. A vision of mullahs and ministers, priests and preachers, rabbis and roshis, innumerable holy men of every stripe standing drenched and smeared and steeped in sacrificial blood, behind them holocaust carcasses barbecuing on the fire, the whole world a burnt offering—

The rocket fell away. It did not touch them, but Diana had been touched. Dalke applauded lightly. Phelonious smiled warily.

"Congratulations—" Dalke began.

A searing laser thicket leapt up around *Witchcraft*, putting the lie to luck. Fore and aft sensors blazed with images of several score columns of pulsed, coherent light probing the womb of Mother Night—automatic laser cannon splashing fire skyward, seeking explosive conception in the deep sky. A consummation devoutly to be avoided.

Diana and Brandi moved automatically. In tandem through the interface they computed in an instant the cannons' configurations. Evasively they wove their way through the pulses of hard light, *Witchcraft* a magic needle sewing up Evening's tattered sleeve. In a moment they were through the laser thicket.

"We're out of ACSA airspace," Diana said at last, leveling off and risking a radar scan. "No aircraft currently in pursuit. Your soldier boys must have put up that laser barrage around our last reported position, then estimated our projected course. A last-ditch effort, but it almost worked."

Out of the corner of her eye Brandi was surprised to see Dalke wincing, as if afflicted by a severe headache. His satlink chimed with an incoming message. That seemed to distract him from his pain for a moment as he scanned the information

"Return to your original flight plan," he said suddenly, his pistol pointed once more at Diana. "Bring us in over Cincinnati, low and slow. You'll receive landing instructions when we reach final approach distance."

A glance passed between the two women. None of this was making any sense. Hijacked out of their original flight plan, then ordered to return to it?

Still, they said nothing. The man who had once torched his commanding officer had, just brief moments ago, incinerated a city full of unsuspecting citizens in the country he was pledged to defend. Since he still happened to be holding a gun on them, however they suspected it might not be wise to argue with him.

Diana and Brandi had passed into a Looking-Glass world and Ray Dalke was their Mad Hatter. Even as they flew onward, though, it seemed as if the ghosts of Laramie were crying out, crying to be remembered past the flash of anguish and oblivion.

• • •

"IN THE PHYSICS GROUP WE DIDN'T SPECULATE ON THE PSY-chological content of the material we encountered during our interaction with the infoburst virtuality," Roger Cortland said to the crowd that had reconvened around the altar-fountain from their separate working groups. "We did, however, find it appropriate to consider the two alternative large-scale physical, even cosmological, scenarios presented at its very end. Whatever their origins, those scenarios seem to be descriptions or projections of possible physical processes. Through a personal connection of Ms. Magnus's, we have been fortunate enough to be able to contact and, for the last hour, work with one of the great names in this theoretical area. I'll now turn over the discussion to Professor Robert Stringfield."

Lucky indeed to have old 'String Field' himself in the loop, Roger thought. *This crazy stuff is right up Doc Soliton's alley.* Roger was glad to be stepping down from his position as speaker for the physics working group. His instant colleagues had volunteered him for that role while he was out of the room, using the lavatory. He was also surprised at the traditional form this impromptu "conference" had fallen into. If he had known about it beforehand, he would have done it all telepresently—not just Stringfield's presentation. Certainly not this crush of bodies and all this quaint "coming forward" to speak. Alas, he had not been consulted.

A large holovirtual display rose above the fountain, which was also now flowing once again. The bespectacled and grey-headed Professor Stringfield cleared his throat and spoke, the time-lag from Earth making him seem even more distracted and otherworldly than Roger actually knew him to be.

"Er, yes," Stringfield said. "Glad to be of help, and very glad to be in touch with you again, Ms. Magnus—um, Mei-Ling. From what I have heard described, your two cosmological scenarios are essentially endpoints. The first endpoint apparently involves the focusing of innumerable lasers onto a single point of space-time, in order to produce a doomsday bubble. This is a physical and causal endpoint. The other involves producing a back-propagating wave, for the purpose of restructuring the fabric of the universe itself. This is an acausal endpoint."

The aged professor glanced aside for a moment, muttering to himself. Roger feared the man had gotten off track, until he saw scientific computer animations replace Stringfield's image and he realized that the professor had been addressing a voice-activated display system.

"Recall that, at the end of last century," Stringfield said, slipping into the lecture mode he had undoubtedly used throughout his long teaching life, "scientists began to suspect the wave/particle duality was more apparent than real. Particles were in fact revealed to be clumped string fields, later known as covariant tubular solitons, or tubitons. A soliton is a special subset of wave motion known as a standing wave—that is, a wave whose troughs and crests stay fixed in spatial relation to one another. Your 'endpoints' are two forms of the same eschaton particle. The first—the causal, explosive bubble version—is in fact known as a 'vacuum bubble instanton.' It was first described by P.H. Frampton."

A new sequence of animations looped behind him, now in the background as Stringfield continued.

"A vacuum bubble instanton is a soliton bubble which can quantum-tunnel from one ground or vacuum state of the universe to another. Its surface belongs to our universe, but its interior contains the vacuum state of another, lower energy universe. Its release into our universe would be a very destructive thing, rather like tossing a particle of dust into superheated water. Our universe would 'boil' in a spherical wave. That shocksphere would grow to 300,000 kilometers across in its first second of existence. The second scenario, the acausal variant of the eschaton particle—"

The professor stopped, having apparently noticed the upraised hand of Jacinta Larkin. He responded quickly enough, despite the time-lag.

"How much of our universe would be destroyed in such a fashion?" Jacinta asked. Everyone waited expectantly past the time-lag.

"It's difficult to determine how much of our universe would boil off to elementary particles," Stringfield replied. "That would depend on how long such a bubble would last. That in turn would depend on its size. Solitons eventually die back into turbulence, however. I doubt it could go on for too very long."

The professor waited to see if Jacinta had any further questions.

"Could one be created that would be capable of destroying our solar system?" she asked.

"Yes, hypothetically," Stringfield replied after the time lag. "The solar system is a relatively tiny volume of space, at least in relation to the entirety of the universe. Though it is of course a very important volume of space, to us."

Stringfield again waited expectantly, which was fortunate, as Lakshmi Ngubo began to speak from her hoverchair.

"Professor," she said, "how big would the device for such a doomsday technology need to be? Would it fit inside a reasonable space—inside the nucleus of a medium-sized comet, say?"

After a moment, Stringfield spoke with an awkward smile.

"That's rather a leading question," he replied, "but yes, if we are speaking speculatively, I don't see why not."

"What about that second path?" Roger asked, trying to steer Stringfield back onto the main line of his argument and away from this doubtless intriguing but also rather forbidding digression. "The acausal one?"

"Yes," Stringfield said after a moment, calling up more animations. "That's rather more complicated. Remember, no generally satisfactory answer exists to the question of just what it is that observations can actually tell us about objects. The scientific perspective is founded upon a set of assumptions that are themselves not scientifically verifiable—assumptions of materialism, of causation, of spatiotemporality. These assumptions are, at bottom, beliefs about the universe. No observational criteria can 'prove' any of these beliefs over its opposite. Any inferential criteria that might be summoned for support are a product of which phenomena one gives priority. In some sense, you find what you're already looking for."

Stringfield muttered another aside directed at his display systems. New imagery began to appear.

"This is particularly important in regard to dynamical systems. Such systems are extremely common, found in fields ranging from brain physiology to evolution. Take black holes, for instance. The event horizon surrounding a singularity is a dynamical system. It separates two or more 'worlds' or orders of being—namely the singularity within a black hole and the rest of the universe—which are immiscible in some relevant way. The event horizon is a self-organizing system that generates its own fractal patterns of behavior, independent of causal relations between the parts of that system.

"As a boundary condition between the worlds, it defies characterization other than through symbolic interpretation. The event horizon is a fractal, acausally functioning dynamical system. It echoes other such systems and may well be linked to them across scale.

"By definition, the event horizon is that zone which forms around the collapsed star because no signal can get away from it to communicate any event to the outside world. One of the strange upshots of quantum theory, however, was that the Schwarzschild radius and the event horizon may be in some sense 'breachable.' If the connections between solitons, either as waves or particles, are not signals in the Einsteinian sense, then the Schwarzschild radius ceases to be a barrier, for what is a 'horizon' to causal events is not necessarily a horizon to acausal influences. Such influences operate in a more ethereal fashion, rather like the apparently 'transcendental' connection that joins the members of a particle/antiparticle pair—"

Past the time lag, Stringfield had again noticed another hand raised in question, and stopped himself to recognize it.

"What would these 'acausal influences' look like?" asked an engineer friend of Seiji's, rather skeptically—a man whose name Roger could not remember. "Are there any empirically observable examples?"

Stringfield nodded, calling up more images and animations.

"Mode locking and entrainment," said Stringfield, "such as that seen in clock pendulums, satellites, and some species of flashing fireflies. There are many other examples. Mode locking is essentially an acausal connecting principle. It's the fundamental way in which conditions influence dynamical systems, and by which dynamical systems exchange information: by *influencing* each other's activity. Mode locking superimposes patterns."

Roger was struck by a thought from one of his own, earlier ideas.

"Does that relate to the quantum theoretical idea," he asked, "that time and the universe exist as superposed states until observed?"

"In some ways, yes," Stringfield agreed. "All possible states are actual states until observation/interaction makes one or another of them real. Dynamical systems mode-locked to one another function essentially as one system, the way the particle/antiparticle pair does, or the way the interactor/state does, for that matter. They incorporate a universally basic pattern—that of the attractor—into their behavior. A universally basic pattern implies a universal dynamical system."

In a flurry of murmuring, Stringfield called up a series of new animations. Then, abruptly, he seemed so struck by a particular thought that he switched off his background displays and spoke to them without the benefit of any visual aids.

"If all these systems mode-lock onto one another to form a universal dynamical system," he said, obviously still working it out in his own mind, "then that universal system would be an intersection or interface, eternal and infinite, which imprints itself upon every pattern in the universe and is in turn impressed upon by every pattern in the universe. We would thus reside in a holographic plenum of information—information in the form of influences. All information would be everywhere, at all times, because information, as mode-lockable influence, would stand outside of merely historical or temporal existence."

Stringfield paused, absently bringing one hand up to his chin.

"Viewed in this light," he continued, "we are not essentially biological, or even only physical, beings. We are entelechies that cast a shadow into matter. That shadow we identify as our physical being. Even our whole universe would then be more than just physical. The universe itself would be entelechial, moving toward unity in the sense that it is moving toward the unification of all its dynamical systems into one system. Mode-locking all the universe's dynamical systems would essentially create a system that unifies all of the dynamical phenomena of the universe."

Stringfield paused again, but it wasn't due to transmission time lag or question—just a moment to think.

"If the universe is evolving *beyond* the causal and *toward* the dynamical," he continued, "then many strange things become probable. You could see the opposite of the instanton bubble we discussed earlier—a droplet, instead, of different internal space, in which black holes would turn into spiraling strings and spiraling strings would turn into black holes. Instead of the eschaton particle manifesting itself as a wave that boils our universe, the system could undergo another type of phase transition, a concrescence, like vapor condensing to water, or cells organizing themselves in development—"

Stringfield stopped again, this time halted by a question from Seiji.

"What would this 'grand concrescence' look like?" he asked.

Stringfield scratched his chin unconsciously, considering it.

"That's rather like asking, What did the universe look like

before the Big Bang?'' he replied. ''All we *could* know would be the shadow it might cast ahead of itself, if it did. Rather like the way the boom of a distant cannon is always heard *before* the order to 'Fire!'—because the sound of the cannon firing moves as a soliton and thus travels faster than the command to fire—''

''Or the way you never hear the shot that gets you,'' someone with a darker frame of mind remarked.

''That would actually be more appropriate to the bubble instanton, I should think,'' Stringfield said with a quiet smile. ''All we can know of the wave of concrescence is what we can detect reverberating through time from the horizon of that future event. In our space-time, the acausal eschaton particle is always in the future, rather like the singularity inside a black hole. As opposed to 'white hole' singularities, which are always in the past.''

This time Mei-Ling had her hand up.

''What kinds of signs for this sort of wave should we be looking for?'' she asked.

''I can't really say what form it might take, Mei-Ling,'' he said after a pause. ''If the universe is evolving beyond causality, becoming self-generating and mode-locking, that's essentially saying that the universe is becoming conscious.''

Stringfield paused and cleared his throat at that, as if realizing what a large speculative chunk he was asking them to swallow.

''If that's true,'' he continued after a moment, ''then the relationship between psyche and universe is obviously a form of microcosm/macrocosm interaction—self-similarity across scales. Dynamical systems tend to mode-lock on each other, so if psyche and consciousness are developing toward increasing dynamicality, then the universe and individual consciousness are evolving toward a fundamental unity. That sort of evolution could occur with the rapidity of a phase transition, rather than on the slow scale of ordinary cosmological evolution.''

''Professor Stringfield,'' Nils Barakian asked, ''this acausal eschaton particle, though it might look like a black singularity, a 'Tetragrammaton' endword to us—might it not also be a white singularity, a beginning 'Logos' word to the renovated universe its waveform creates?''

The pause was once again longer than the transmission-lag would have explained.

''That's certainly possible,'' Stringfield replied. ''However, which soliton we see—the destructive instanton or the wave of concrescence—might depend on which one we're helping to bring into being. But that's interloping into consciousness theory. I'm treading on the turf of others more qualified than I am. They should probably be speaking on this, instead of me. I hope these speculations have been of help to you.''

Roger moved forward.

"Thank you very much, Professor Stringfield," he said. Light applause for Stringfield's presentation sounded from the crowd, to Roger's surprise. "Please stay on the line, if you would. Next we'll turn things over to Marissa Correa and Jacinta Larkin, representing the biology and consciousness theory groups respectively. Before that, though, I've just been informed that my mother, Atsuko Cortland, as HOME liaison to some powerful groups on Earth, has an important announcement.''

Atsuko spoke then, in a tone of concern but also of control.

"I've just received information from our communications people which concerns all of us," she began. "From our friends at the psiXtian arcology in California, we've learned that the flyout of the immortalizing vector from their facility has met with some difficulties. The starjet we sent for the vector, piloted by Diana Gartner and co-piloted by Brandi Easter, was attacked while on the ground. Diana and Brandi were apparently not hurt. They managed to lift off and fly out, but we have received no further word from them. The psiXtians, however, report that the immortalizing vector has been released into the atmosphere.''

A worried murmur spread through the small crowd and began to grow louder.

UNCLE ALEISTER AND LEV KORCHNOI HAD LEFT THE MESsages that were flashing on Aleck's telecom when he and the rest had gotten back from their *Cordyceps* experiment. When Aleck returned their calls, the two men seemed to have some sort of theory regarding Hugh Manatee. They wondered if Aleck might let them join him during his shift tonight. He shrugged them a "yes," too tired from his wild night to argue.

Sam, Janika, Hari, and Marco kept reliving their previous night's experience until about one that afternoon. By that time Aleck had retired to his room for a much needed nap, thinking, as he drifted off to sleep, that old Hugh was developing quite a social life for a cocooned coma case in what was supposed to be a sen-dep tank.

Then again, even Aleck himself was developing a social life

too, of late. If that could happen, anything could happen.

Early in the evening he awakened from an academic anxiety dream. In it, he woke up late for a final for which he had also forgotten to study. Breathless, in the dream he tried to outrun the chimes of the carillon, sounding from behind the horribly looming and leering great clock face in the campanile—only to find the entire campus deserted, and the lecture hall too.

As he sound-showered, he realized the dream had probably been spawned by guilt arising from the fact that he had blown off yet another entire day of study.

While he dressed, Aleck tried to reassure himself that he could afford to take the time off from school, now that Onoma Verité seemed destined for stardom. Sam was strongly insinuating that the band wanted him to come on tour with them as their lighting and sound designer.

Coming into the apartment's living area now—and finding the members of Onoma Verité looking bedraggled and unkempt as they sprawled in drooling sleep—he was not very reassured about his job prospects. Maybe he *should* stay in school a while longer. Just in case.

He grabbed a lukewarm cup of synth kava and tried to face the setting sun of this sleep-blown day. Sam woke up and, half asleep, approached him.

"Leaving for work already?" he asked.

"Yep," Aleck said quickly, unfolding his bike and heading for the door. "I'm doing a double shift, to make up for my delinquency. Uncle Aleister and Lev Korchnoi want to meet me down below the Partons tonight anyway. Something about Hugh—God only knows what."

"Coolage," Sam said. The word initially made Aleck think of a long-dead president, until he remembered the idiom. Sam had slipped into wire-head slang again—something he did when he was tired. At times it made Aleck wonder a bit uneasily about Sam's past. "Mind if we join you and do a little rehearsage, since your uncle and Lev are going to be there anyway?"

"The more the merrier," Aleck said with his all-purpose and purposely noncommittal shrug.

His bike ride downtown in the deepening twilight was largely uneventful, except for the crowds of conservatively dressed and clean scrubbed people making their way along routes paralleling his own. They were carrying signs and banners and cheap holos. It took Aleck a while to recognize them. They were the people who had been protesting at the zoo-ark for the last week.

He wondered vaguely why they were headed off the hills and toward downtown, but he really didn't have time to think about it or mess with them. He took side and back streets that got him around the worst of the crowds. The side roads dumped him out near the loading dock elevator behind the Partons, even earlier than he'd expected.

Denene Jackman was surprised to see him.

"Early? For an early shift?" she said, feigning shock as she slipped off her circlet interface gear. "Will wonders never cease! If you think being early will make up for your past sins against punctuality, Smart Aleck, you're wrong."

"Yeah, yeah," he said, smiling good-naturedly as he folded his bike. "How's the Great Tanked One behaving?"

Denene shook her head.

"Not well," she said. "Something's going on—I just can't put my finger on it."

"He's still minding the store?" Aleck asked, concerned.

"Yes," Denene assured him, "but he's only been giving that a very small piece of his head. The last several hours it's been especially bad. He's been all over the infosphere. Lots of data shifting around, but it's all infinity-routed and heavily encrypted. Whatever he's up to, it's way outside my job description."

"His vitals are okay?" Aleck asked, slipping the connection gear onto his own head.

"Some of the levels are up," Denene said, as she got her bag and other gear ready to go. "Like he's excited about something. Adrenalized, though what he could be anxious about, floating in that tank, I'll never know."

Aleck gave her a sly smile.

"Maybe you turn him on," he said, "and he's having a long, slow—"

Denene stopped his mouth with her hand.

"Go any further and you'll be in trouble," she said, laughing as he slowly removed her hand. "Have a good shift, if you can. 'Night."

"Enjoy yourself," he said, waving goodbye. As he turned around to check Hugh's vitals and his work, he realized that he'd forgotten to mention to Denene all the Lord's Own types descending toward downtown. She hadn't mentioned it. If she knew something about it, he was sure Denene would have mentioned it.

He almost jumped out of his seat when, sometime later, his pager went off. He brought it up suspiciously toward his face. On its small screen he saw all the members of Onoma Verité—and his uncle and Lev Korchnoi with them. They all waved, but somehow they looked a little nervous.

Served them right, Aleck thought, surprising him like this. He waved back, set the security cameras, microphones, and motion detectors to their feedback-looped and mirror-phased false reality, and went upstairs to let his friends and relations inside.

"Hey, Aleck, what gives?" Sam asked as the elevator doors opened. Seeing Onoma Verité and their instruments, and his uncle and Korchnoi, Aleck wondered if they would all fit in the elevator.

"What do you mean?"

"All those True Believers out on the plaza," Hari said, jerking his thumb back over his shoulder as he and the others squeezed in. "All praying and singing and holding hands. Looking up at the sky like Jesus and his press agent are coming. Weird."

Aleck gave his accustomed shrug as the last of his visitors squeezed in. The doors shut and they began their descent.

"Maybe they're upset because R & L has reinstated the Moon and Stars on the corporate logo," he said. "The hard-core Bible folks have always hated it. Supposed to be a satanic symbol or something."

That explanation seemed to satisfy everyone. By the time the doors opened and they were walking through the corridors, Sam was describing to Lev and Aleister how Aleck sometimes let the band use his workspace as a rehearsal studio.

Once back in the "studio," the members of Onoma Verité immediately went to work setting up. Lev and Aleister listened politely to their banter, especially about how Hugh Manatee had given the band the idea for its first big concept effort. It seemed to Aleck, however, that the two out-of-town visitors were much more interested in Hugh Manatee himself—and his setup—than in the band's.

De gustibus, he thought, dropping the building's security systems out of their funhouse reality and back into the workaday world. For just a flash he caught something odd on one of the external cameras: an image of a matte-black starjet descending vertically out of the night sky onto a square surrounded by cheering crowds. In the next instant the image was gone. He wondered if one of the security guards from the previous shift had tuned

one of the monitors upstairs to a broadband net. They did that
sometimes, especially when they were bored. This channel they
had found was apparently showing an old 2-D science fiction
movie, at the moment.

No sooner had Onoma Verité finished tuning up than they
launched into their cover version of a twenty-year-old song
which—Aleck remembered as they played—was called "Golden
Era Blues."

Finally got up the courage to look through my mail.
Seems like the bill collectors will be here without fail.
My car broke down Monday and I am broke too.
Lord only knows what I'm supposed to do.

I've got the Golden Era Blues.
I'm outta work and I need new shoes.
Don't bother tellin' me what is on the news—
I've already got the Golden Era Blues.

My baby walked out and left me on a Sunday night,
Sayin' "Without money, honey, things just won't work
*   right."*
I thought we were solid, I thought love would stay,
But at the first sign of trouble, my baby walked straight
*   away.*

I've got the Golden Era Blues.
I'm outta work and I need new shoes.
Don't bother tellin' me what is on the news—
I've already got the Golden Era Blues.

So damn frustrated, wanted to burgle a bank.
So damn broke, couldn't buy a helpin' hand gun.
Even the weather round here has been darkenin' and dank
Since the Sons of Edison hooked that meter to the sun.

I've got the Golden Era Blues.
I'm outta work and I need new shoes.
Don't bother tellin' me what is on the news—
I've already got the Golden Era Blues.

The rich on their hilltops may be livin' like kings,
Yet folks in the street been sayin' the craziest things.
Scenarios of our case may not yet have reached worst,
But remember: When the storm finally comes,
Lightning strikes the high places first!

We've got the Golden Era Blues.
We're outta work and we need new shoes.
Don't bother tellin' us what is on the news—
We've already got the Golden Era Blues.

Aleck, Lev, and Aleister applauded enthusiastically. Just as their applause was trailing off, Lev abruptly stopped.

"What's that noise?" he said. Sam motioned his fellow band members to silence, and they all listened. In a moment they heard it: running footsteps, pounding down the hall toward them. Aleck turned around in time to see half a dozen people flood in through the door, led by a blond and slightly bloodied man of military bearing, with a gun in his hand. Three of the other members of the initial group also seemed to have guns. Half a dozen more came in after them, carrying something that looked like a cross between a stretcher and a tarpaulin.

"What the hell is going on here?" Sam asked indignantly.

The bloodied blond man leveled his gun at Sam.

"Hell is precisely what's going on here," the blond man said sharply, from behind remarkably cold, piercing blue eyes, "and we're here to stop it. Any complaints?"

No one thought it wise to register disagreement, just then. Belatedly the band members and their audience of three lifted their hands in the air.

"You see?" said the blond man to his companions. "It's as the angel told your Reverend Grindstaff. My brother Mike is held captive here. The witch has flown down a holding tank, *for a sea cow*, while Mike's life is at stake!"

The leader of the interlopers turned toward the musicians and their audience.

"Which of you works here?" he asked. "Which of you monitors my brother?"

The captives outside the tank glanced nervously at one another for a moment.

"Speak up!" said the blond man, an edge in his voice.

"I do," Aleck said quietly, clearing his throat. He repeated it more loudly. "I do."

The blond man gave a quick nod as his eyes took in the room. "Open that access door," he said, gesturing with his free hand. "Show these people"—the free hand gestured again, toward the group with the tarpaulin stretcher this time—"how to detach him from his umbilicals. Put him on the portable units and load him out onto the tarp. Go!"

Aleck rose quickly from his chair and console and headed toward the big access door. Unlocking and opening it, he led the stretcher bearers onto the open metalwork stairs and catwalk that circled the tank. Aleck hadn't been back here often—not since training, as a matter of fact.

He began to rack his brains as he walked. If he recalled correctly, the nano-cocoon was supposed to be able to sustain Hugh's vital functions for twenty-four hours, even without external hookups of any sort. He helped the stretcher bearers shift Hugh off the umbilicals and onto the portable monitoring and life-support interface. As he did so, Aleck still hoped that he was remembering everything correctly, safety buffer or no.

The stretcher bearers caught on quickly—so quickly Aleck thought they might have med-tech or paramedic backgrounds. The first group of bearers—joined by other unarmed members of what Aleck now thought of as a raiding party—lifted Hugh out of the tank once they'd detached him from his standard umbilicals and reattached him to the portables. They then carried Hugh away, straining under the burden.

Aleck could hear them moving away down the hall, leaving behind only the armed men, who also, one by one, eased backward out the door and down the hall, until at last only the blond man was left. Then he too was gone.

Sam, Janika, Lev, Marco, Hari, and Aleister were all too shocked even to breathe a sigh of relief. Aleck, though, got his relief over with quickly enough. He began furiously clearing the channels of his security hack and scanning the security monitors in an attempt to find again what he was sure, now, was not an old movie about the future. It was a real-time present-tense feed from cameras looking out on the plaza in front of the Partons.

By the time he located those channels again, the cameras showed the stretcher bearers moving their burden up a belly ramp into the starjet parked on the plaza. Their blond leader had already caught up to them and was urging them on. Crowds cheered around the plaza, but also seemed occupied with something behind them.

In the middle-range monitors, Aleck could just make out police lights in the distance, beyond the crowds. In a moment more, the stretcher bearers spilled out of the starjet's belly, the ramp began to close and the vertijets began to flare on. The starjet hovered for an instant, then was gone at speed.

Aleck slumped back in his chair. The raiders had gotten away with it. They had taken Hugh Manatee hostage—on *his* shift. It was ridiculous. Why would anyone want to kidnap the Great Tanked One—or "liberate" him, for that matter? And then *fly him away*! It didn't make sense.

The others had by now begun to recover. Slowly they came forward to see if Aleck was okay, and to offer their condolences. All of them were so preoccupied in their relief, and in their reassuring of each other, that they at first didn't notice the three small brown-skinned people who had wandered into the room. The first of them was elderly to the point of ancient, and addressed as "Kekchi" by the two younger ones. All were dressed in flamboyant clothing of intricate weave—and, incongruously, flip-flop sandals.

Aleck glanced at the members of Onoma Verité. From their faces he could tell that they were all wondering the same thing he was: Is this real, or am I hallucinating? Even stranger, however, was seeing Aleister and Lev smile in greeting at the interlopers.

From the monitors in his security hack, Aleck heard police sirens begin to wail. In the room around him, the three small strangers began to sing.

NINE

CODE-EXTRACTED SUBTERPOST FRAGMENT (INFOSPHERE source unknown; original source independently verified as R.E. Stringfield's *Beyond the Sky of Mind: Quantum Cosmology and Quantum Consciousness*):

The idea of metacosmological evolution raises the question of whether the plenum itself is the "largest individual" or the "largest species" or both, in much the same way as all the daughter cells of an asexually reproducing mother cell are simultaneouly a species and nearly identical variants of the same individual.

This model also invites the question of whether or not this reproduction of universes must be necessarily asexual, all mother to daughter. In the biological realm, there is apparently always an inevitable tradeoff between sex and death. If that analogy applies at the level of universes, then "sexual reproduction"— or what might be better called "information exchange"—by universes would necessitate mortality in the plenum of universes.

"YOUR ATTENTION, PLEASE," ATSUKO SAID, RAISING HER voice slightly. "Marissa Correa was already scheduled to speak next, and it is very appropriate that she should. As the principal developer of the immortalizing vector, she can tell us what implications arise from its release. Marissa?"

Amid the murmur of the crowd Marissa, holding her notepad PDA, came forward into the open space around the altar-like fountain. Roger was struck by the strength she was demonstrating, under the pressure of such circumstances.

"Some of you—though not all—know my research already," she began, smoothing her coppery hair back from her face with her free hand. "For those who know, please bear with me."

She called animation and documentary holo clips from her PDA into public display.

"My work has involved taking traits from the so-called immortalized cancer cells of teratocarcinomas," she said, calling up images shot through microscopes. "My theory was that I could use such traits against senescence, against aging in human beings. I hoped thereby to perhaps significantly extend human life. After isolating the immortalizing traits from teratoma sources, I proposed that viral, retroviral, and even prion vectors might be engineered to transfer the selected traits into the human genome. I achieved some limited success. Several of my scientific colleagues, however, particularly those in California, have been much more successful.

"None of us knows exactly how viable these vector organisms might be outside the lab," Marissa continued, calling a new series of 3-D animations and graphs into public display, "but since my colleagues here and on Earth have been working with a fairly broad spectrum of delivery organisms, we may reasonably assume the worst-case scenario. There now exists in Earth's atmosphere a viable organic form—viral, retroviral, prionic, whichever—capable of infecting and bestowing universal immortality upon human beings. Short of murder and mayhem or similar massive damage to organ systems, every human being faces now, or will soon face, the prospect of a radically extended life span."

Marissa refreshed the PDA images, calling up new holographic material from the system.

"Such a millennial prospect has its downside," she continued. "The supply of humans has already far outstripped any conceivable demand for us. We're the species that invented unemployment—all other species are fully 'employed.' Or extinct. Shut down their niche, destroy their habitat, they disappear. Not us. We have proven to be supersuccessful. There are so many of us that sexual reproduction for the vast majority is now redundant, superfluous, virtually obsolete. No need to breed. For eighty percent of us, sex should be dead—at least as far as procreation, as opposed to recreation, is concerned. Even without the release of the vector, human population growth has been steadily moving toward the point of chaotic onset. So much *must* change, so fast—and it will. Chaotic systems are good at that."

Marissa called up a further series of graphs and pie charts with nasty implications.

"The last several centuries of human civilization have been characterized by the intensification of polarization—the colonizers versus the colonized, East versus West, First World versus Third World, North versus South, high-tech sphere versus low-tech sphere. Most recently this polarization has begun manifesting itself between ourselves here in space, and the masses of human population on Earth.

"This Up/Down polarization can only be further exacerbated by the likelihood of the immortality plague, which will necessarily intensify already existing population problems, driving Earth's carrying capacity into a boom/bust scenario no 'demographic transition' can hope to head off."

Marissa paused as she called up new sets of graphs and images, looking about her to see if there were any questions. There were none.

"In a world possessing finite resources, you can have either immortality or sexual reproduction, but not both. That's the scientific restatement of a good chunk of the underlying meaning of the story of the Fall in Genesis. There's always been a certain solace in the fact of reproduction. Even if you couldn't enjoy the physical longevity of the immortal, you could at least have the supposed genetic extension of the parent—hence the phrases 'be fruitful and multiply,' 'dominion over the earth,' 'have many arrows in your quiver.' "

Marissa looked up uncomfortably from her notepad PDA, looking at her audience and apparently feeling like both the bearer and the creator of bad news.

"The immortalizing vector changes all those phrases into virus-words—"

Jacinta Larkin abruptly interrupted.

"Religion wasn't what lowered infant mortality rates and ratcheted up population growth rates worldwide," she said. "Science and technology did that, through improved public sanitation, immunization, a dozen other technologically mediated processes. It isn't religion that has brought the immortalizing vector into being—it's science."

Marissa nodded vigorously.

"I couldn't agree more," she said. "In the past, 'value neutral' science has taken little responsibility for the consequences of such changes. At the same time, the world's religions have kept on behaving as if we were all still living in pre-industrial societies, places in which technological and scientific changes are irrelevant. It's been a very bad synergy."

She paused again, scanning briefly the crowd of people around her, most of whom seemed to be listening attentively but withholding their judgment. A small group, Atsuko and Lakshmi and Jacinta Larkin among them, seemed distracted and agitated. Marissa's future-reading talent too was beginning to act up in apocalyptic ways unrelated to what she was saying—already dire enough in its own right. She thought it would be wise if she brought her presentation to a close.

"Across scale, at all levels, what the immortalizing vector immediately forces us to confront is not just an overpopulation problem of the poor or a hyperconsumption problem of the rich, not just a religious problem or a scientific problem, not even just a male problem or a female problem—but a *human* problem. The release of the vector means that this is now a problem that can only be addressed by seeing the ways in which our own freedoms and responsibilities are absolutely interconnected with the freedoms and responsibilities of others—including those freedoms and responsibilities associated with sex and reproduction. Only if both organized religion and the scientific method can help us see *that*, will they at last be contributing to our preservation rather than our destruction—"

As Marissa paused again for questions, Atsuko came forward, looking very definitely worried this time.

"We've received another message from Communications," she said distractedly. "Just a short while ago, the city of Laramie in the Autonomous Christian States was destroyed by a very powerful nuclear blast. The ACSA is claiming that Diana Gartner's starjet intruded into ACSA airspace and is responsible for the blast. The ACSA is in the process of declaring war on the USA for serving as the base from which the SHADOW starjet launched its attack. In the ACSA declaration, a state of war already officially exists between the Autonomous Christian States and the High Orbital Manufacturing Enterprises. Laksmi Ngubo and Mei-Ling Magnus have, through their own sources, confirmed this information."

Everyone was caught off guard by the news, dazed and stunned into silence, Marissa not least of all. At last, Jhana spoke up, addressing Marissa, frustrated—and perhaps obscurely offended by all the population and reproduction talk, since she was the most publicly, if not obviously, pregnant and therefore "procreatively active" person there.

"Won't the destruction that's impending make all this discussion about your immortality plague a moot point?" she asked, bothered by both prospects. "I mean, universal immortality is about to be bestowed upon a humanity that's also about to nuke itself to oblivion. 'Congratulations—you can now live forever! Too bad we'll have to kill you!' It's absurd.''

Marissa nodded again, doing a series of quick scans of her notepad as she tried to recover from the news of the initiation of nuclear hostilities.

''Dark clouds and silver linings do tend to get confused, I know,'' she said, calculating. ''The build-down of nuclear weapons over the last four decades and more, a good thing in itself—a silver lining in the threatening dark cloud of Armageddon—is in this instance itself a dark cloud. The number of nuclear weapons available to be detonated is now significantly below the total megatonnage required for nuclear winter threshhold. There will undoubtedly be horrible suffering if this war gets fully underway. The impact on human numbers from this impending conflict, however, will probably not even begin to offset the increase in population the vector is likely to cause.''

Dominic Fanon spoke up, a black man with a highly cultured accent. Roger knew him vaguely as an important rep from the corporate consortia that had built HOME 1 and HOME 2.

''What about the wave of destruction Professor Stringfield spoke about?'' Fanon asked. ''Or the wave of concrescence, for that matter? Would one make your immortality plague scenario moot, and not the other, or would they both do that?''

Marissa gave a shrug.

''That's a higher order question,'' she said. ''Outside my purview. I think it might fall within the scope of what Jacinta Larkin is scheduled to speak about, so I'll turn things over to her.''

Mei-Ling Magnus stepped forward.

''Before you do,'' she said, ''there's something else as well. Maybe some good news. Robert and I and our colleagues at Interpol, along with Lakshmi here, have at last positively determined the identity of the topological voyeur killer. His name is Michael Carter Dalke. He is working as a data minder in Cincinnati, Ohio. A joint task force—international, federal, state and local authorities—are currently on their way to arrest him there.''

A sigh of relief spread through the crowd at that prospect. Amid so much happening so fast, at least *something* seemed to be going right.

•   •   •

AᴼᴼᴼᴼᴼᴼᴼᴼᴼᴼᴼᴼᴼᴼᴼᴼᴼᴼᴼᴼᴼᴼᴼᴼᴼᴼᴼᴼᴼᴼᴼFTER BLASTING INTO ORBIT OUT OF CINCINNATI AND HELP-ing Diana and *Witchcraft* dodge yet more thickets of laser cannon, Brandi had time at last to feel numb. She glanced toward the back of the cramped cabin of the cockpit. Manqué was there, his machine gun leveled at Brandi and Diana, slowly scanning back and forth between them. Ray Dalke was presumably still communing with the cocooned thing Brandi herself had, at gunpoint, helped load into the big bag-tank in back.

She had heard Dalke assert that the bloated thing in the cocoon was his brother, and Dalke was, undeniably, focused on their newest passenger. He had stayed back with him almost from the moment they'd lifted off, coming forward only long enough to give them the coordinates of the destination his "brother" had supposedly given him.

Brandi and Diana had both been surprised to see that the new destination was not so very far away from their original planned end-point, HOME 2. Since their new destination was a point in cislunar space out among the haborbs, both women secretly hoped this might make their escape or rescue from these madmen all the easier.

They were well along in their journey spaceward and homeward when Dalke finally emerged from his communings with his cocooned brother. Brandi immediately noticed something odd about the man. He was alternately smiling in pleasure and wincing in pain as he spoke to Manqué. Their conversation was odd, too.

"—voice of God in my head," Dalke said.

"So you're no longer you?" Manqué asked, almost enviously.

"Not exactly," Dalke said, slowly, as if in a dream. "It's just that, through Mike, the Lord is providing me with guidance, which I must follow. 'I' have not disappeared from my head. My will is only pleasantly constrained to match his. My mental space is more directed. My thoughts don't wander so erratically. I'm still here. It's just that, inside my skull, I'm now more the passenger than the driver. More the audience than the actor."

"I've heard the command voice on and off for years," Manqué said, glancing down. "I've never been lucky enough to hear it consistently. I used to think it was some sort of monitor they put into our heads at birth. Or when we were anesthetized, getting wisdom teeth removed. What you're getting from your brother—all that stuff with Wernicke's area, the micromachines and neurotransmitter releases—that's new to me."

Dalke smiled at Manqué.

"Talk to him yourself," Dalke said. "You can use my satlink, if you need to. I find that if I just sit near him and focus on him, I can hear his commands directly, without any mechanical assistance."

Manqué nodded, glancing at the women piloting their craft. He smiled, turning over guard duties to Dalke. He disappeared into the back to have a talk with God, or at least His messenger. Ray Dalke, pistol in hand, turned his suddenly leering attention to Diana and Brandi.

"I know a lot about you, techwitch," he said to Diana, easing himself forward with a condescending sneer, loosely hooking his free arm around Diana's shoulders and neck. "How you were a Medusa Blue baby. How you were born and raised on that rock down there. How you eventually got yourself trained as a systems ecologist and moved up to HOME 1. How you learned to fly this thing. How you snagged it as your own personal project when your dyke buddies set up their Wemoon's Eden commune up there."

Diana stared rigidly at *Witchcraft*'s displays. She was trying forcefully to reach out to Dalke with her talent—as she had been off and on all evening, since this nightmare began. To no avail. The man seemed more completely closed to her sendings than anyone she'd ever previously encountered. It was almost as if her messages were being jammed by someone else.

"I presume this little biography has a point?" she said icily. Ray Dalke smiled.

"Just that I don't know nearly as much about your little friend here," he said, gesturing with his pistol and turning toward Brandi. "Are you a girl-lover too, or one of those with a male harem?"

Brandi stared forward, through her displays, out the cockpit window in front of her.

"My sexual preferences are none of your business," she said at last. "I don't suppose you've ever heard of reproductive responsibility—"

Abruptly Ray Dalke jabbed the barrel of the pistol against her temple.

"Everything here is my business," he said angrily. "And, *honey*, my preacher says the only reproductive responsibility I have is to do it with kids in mind—as often as I please. Don't you get it? It's over for you. The Kingdom is coming! My brother told me all about it. We're going to the haborbs to pick up the headship hormone precursor this guy Cortland developed. Operation E 5-24 is going into effect!''

Seeing Diana move in her seat, Dalke snapped the gun away from Brandi's temple and played the weapon back and forth between them. Diana settled back into her place, slowly.

''Don't think I won't use this,'' he said in obvious reference to the pistol. ''These flechettes will pierce flesh and bone well enough. They probably won't pierce the skin of this craft—but then again, they might. I'm willing to take that risk. Are you?''

The two women said nothing—just stared straight ahead.

''I didn't think so,'' he said, then turned to Brandi, stroking her hair, speaking very close to her ear. ''I'm going to give you a choice. That's more than you'll get after the Kingdom comes.''

''What choice?'' Brandi asked quietly.

''Either you can make lezzy love with your witchy friend here while I keep a careful eye watch,'' Dalke said, ''or I'll take you in back and do you myself while Manqué keeps watch on Ms. Starburst Goodwitch here. Either way, we don't have much time. I want you to start taking off your clothes. *Now*.''

Slowly, Brandi started to remove her jumpsuit. She knew she should feel afraid, but numbness and a strange dreamlike distance still pervaded her being. She was outside her body, looking down at the strange tableau, wondering vaguely what fantasy of twined limbs and lips and tongues this was all supposed to be playing to in Dalke's head.

She glanced at Diana, who still stared rigidly ahead. Brandi thought that perhaps she might on her own have come to love this woman, even to make unforced love with her of her own accord, but that wasn't the issue at all now. The issue here wasn't love. It was force, power, control—Ray Dalke's. This wasn't about women or women's bodies. It was about this unhappy man's ability to manipulate them for pleasure in his sight, to carve them up into the tangle of mere bodies—

Nearly naked, her dazed and faraway self still heard something clang and slither across the hull of *Witchcraft* above her head. With abrupt anger Dalke slammed the pistol toward Diana's head.

''What's that noise?'' he yelled. ''You trying to pull something?''

Diana shook her head as much as she could, given the gun

that was being held firmly to it. She scanned through her interface before she spoke.

"Two large objects have appeared in space on either side of
us," she said. "Check the monitors. Look out the windows. If
you don't know anything about them, then you know as much
as I do."

More clangs and thunks, and then the scraping, slithering
noises sounded overhead and beneath their feet. Dalke turned to
the windows and the monitors. Almost despite herself, Brandi,
coming back from her great introspective distance, did the same.

The sight that appeared before her was incredible in the extreme. On both sides of the ship floated two virtually identical
buildings—the twin towers from under which Dalke had
"liberated" his cocooned and now bag-tanked brother! Each of
the towers stood sphered in a bubble of force. Brandi was powerfully reminded of the bubble force field she had seen enclosing
the anvil-shaped mountaintop when it had come descending toward Earth, seemingly ages ago now.

Other force-field-bubbled rocks were also settling in flotilla
around the flying buildings now. No denying it, this time: On
the outside of all of them, rough rock and geometric buildings,
people were moving about beneath the sheltering bubbles. Several of them were clad only in loincloths or loose robes. They
appeared to be hastily anchoring lines to raw or shaped stone,
lines attached to grappling hooks that were being fired through
the force bubbles—at, onto, and around *Witchcraft*.

"We're getting a narrowcast from them," Diana said. She
played it into the cabin.

"—xander McAleister of the *Partons*," said the youthful
voice of someone who sounded as if he were enjoying all this
entirely too much. "You have absconded with persons or property belonging to Retcorp and Lambeg. As an R & L employee,
I am authorized to retrieve the aforementioned. Lay down your
arms and prepare to be boarded."

"What is this?" Dalke said. "Space pirates? This is crazy.
This can't be happening."

Clangs and thuds and scrapes and slithers continued to sound.
Manqué appeared from the back compartment. He cast a sidelong
glance at the still largely nude Brandi, who had cautiously begun
to clothe herself again. Manqué grimaced and turned to Dalke.

"What's going on?" he asked, bewildered.

"We're about to be brought up alongside and boarded," Dalke

said dazedly, then turned toward the compartment where his brother was housed. "Keep a gun on these two. I've got to ask my brother about this."

As Dalke disappeared, Diana smiled at Brandi. Relief and hope began to shine in both their faces at last.

"I knew I should have gotten off this bus in Cincinnati," Manqué muttered quietly.

J ACINTA LARKIN CAME FORWARD, CARRYING WITH HER, LIKE an aura, an almost otherworldly assurance in the face of all that they'd learned. Behind her, at first incongruously, captioned holo images out of paleontology, archaeology, and anthropology began to appear and cycle from her notepad PDA. The first of them was little more than a series of scratches labeled "Oldest Symbolic Human Artifact: Meander Pattern on Bone, 300,000 years." Images of mazes and labyrinths followed, along with myths about them. Then came images of dance notation, flow charts of chant patterns, iterative children's language and song games, Shang ritual vessels, Tlingit and Klikitat dualized art motifs, Bronze Age Celtic art. The incongruity was heightened by juxtaposed images of deep space and diagrams of singularities.

"What we've seen and heard presents us with paradoxes," Jacinta began. "Armageddon or Immortality? Wave of concrescence or wave of destruction? I have already spoken with some of you about what the virtual machinery of the infoburst node reminded you of. It reminded Ms. Magnus of what appeared over the Myrrhisticinean Abbey at the time of the Sedona Disaster. Mr. Cortland was reminded of something he saw at the time of the Light, something he called the Arc Hive."

Roger wondered how she knew that. He remember mentioning it to someone, but not her. Maybe he had but he'd just forgotten. So much had been happening.

"Both of those are symbols of this phenomenon's deeper reality," she continued. "Because I've lived and traveled with the people of Caracamuni tepui into deep space, I saw it as something called the Allesseh, the Great Co-operation. A portal between the infinite eternal and the finite temporal. Between being and becoming. The Allesseh started as a vast network of what we might call von Neumann probes: self-replicating, self-improving, transceiving machines. It long ago became something much more than that, however."

Speciation graphs and images out of neuroanatomy appeared holographically as she continued.

"Like the brain and evolution itself," she said, "the Allesseh developed as a selective recognition system. It observed certain features in the environment from a large number of possible configurations or arrangements, then selected specific arrangements from among those possibilities. It is directly connected with that universal dynamical system Professor Stringfield mentioned earlier. The experiences of every individual and species are copied into that system as a superimposition of pattern. The Allesseh has become the attractor of that universal dynamical system. That system becomes more complex as the patterns of every individual experience are added to it. The Allesseh complexifies along with it."

Surround-images appeared, captioned with the names of the great parietal art caves, the ceremonial centers of Altamira, Lascaux, Tito Bustillo, El Castillo, Cuevo del Juyo. Along with them came a murmuring academic program and text discussing how these locations demonstrated dichotomous usage. The accompanying narrative discussed a split between a mundane "domestic space" in the light and above ground at the cave entrance, contrasting with a sacred "ceremonial space" in the dark galleries belowground, where the religious mysteries were to be encountered.

"Technically," Jacinta continued, "any organism or phenomenon connected with the vital force of that universal dynamical system should be able to connect with its patterns. All knowledge already exists in the mind of the Allesseh. It just needs to be recalled into consciousness throughout the rest of the universe."

"Then what Dr. Stringfield suggested is true?" Ka Vang asked. "Our universe itself is becoming a conscious, unified entity?"

"Absolutely," Jacinta said with unshakable confidence. "From what Atsuko Cortland and Marissa Correa have remarked, and from the prospect of the destructive instanton, it also appears that our universe is experiencing a great sickness. That sickness ultimately originates in the Allesseh itself."

As she paused to let that sink in, from the public display came images of negative and positive handprint paintings from Gargas and other sites. The accompanying scholarly program murmured that, given that modern human beings are generally right-hand dominant, it was interesting to note that the representations of both whole and mutilated hands traced or painted on the walls of the Upper Paleolithic site at Gargas were overwhelmingly left hands, done in either red or black pigments.

The color red, the scholarly program said, was associated with power, life, and sex, as well as with the red ochre found in Middle and Upper Paleolithic burial sites. Presumably it symbolized the persistence of life beyond death, a painted or artificial version of "birth blood" linked to notions of rebirth after death. Black, the learned text said, was associated with death and decay. One did not have to be a disciple of Freud, Roger thought, to find an echo of sex and death, Eros and Thanatos, in such red and black hands. For an instant another red and black image also appeared, a red-shifted black hole.

"I suspect this because, in our encounter with the Allesseh," Jacinta continued, "it was disturbed by two things. The first was the cosmic myth of the people of Caracamuni, called the Story of the Seven Ages. The second was the Light associated with Jiro Yamaguchi's transcendence. Three of my tepuian colleagues and I will now perform the song of their cosmic myth. Simultaneous translation will appear in the public display."

The three tepuians came forward to join her before the fountain. Rising into the cavernous space of HOME 2—itself a cave in the sky—their ancient chantsong began, a strange low sound, atonal yet melodious, with echoes of didgeridoo and throat-singing and mouth music, but also something else, something far older. The translation scrolled through the public display.

In the void of endings, the spore of beginnings bursts into spawn. The threads of spawn absorb the voidstuff and knit it into stars. Stars release spores, the spores burst into spawn, the threads of spawn absorb starstuff and knit it into worlds. Worlds release spores, the spores burst into spawn, the threads of spawn absorb worldstuff and knit it into life. Living things release spores, the spores burst into spawn, the threads of spawn absorb lifestuff and knit it into minds. Minds release spores, the spores burst into spawn, the threads of spawn absorb mindstuff and knit it into worldminds. Worldminds release spores, the spores burst into spawn, the threads of spawn absorb worldmindstuff and knit it into starminds. Starminds release spores, the spores burst into spawn, the threads of spawn absorb starmindstuff and knit it into universal mind. Universal mind, the void of endings, the void that has taken all things into itself, releases the spore of beginnings, the fullness that pours all things out of itself.

Long before the song echoed away, Roger remembered all too well what their song meant to him. He had heard it before, at the time of the Light, in his own strange passage between the worlds. It would be interesting to hear Jacinta's interpretation of it.

"Like all of us," she began, "the tepuians can only *symbolically* access the plenum system which the Allesseh models directly. We can speak of that system as entelechial, a vital force, or universal dynamical, but the specific content of the knowledge accessed must be filled in context by the individual who connects with the system. The individual's interpretations of that symbolic pattern or form will inevitably be influenced by her or his culture.

"Because the tepuians are mushroom totemists, they symbolically contextualize what they have accessed in terms of the mushroom life cycle—thus 'spore' and 'spawn' and 'fruiting body,' or mushroom. Since most of the rest of us are twenty-first century age-of-code people, we tend to understand the symbolic content better in terms of our own myth language—that of science."

As if in purposely ironic counterpoint, the murmuring scholarly documentary program flashed images of handprints and corporate shamanic logos. The way those images reappeared and continued suggested that history fell between the prehistoric cave-painted hands at Gargas and the posthistoric corporate shamanic X-ray Body Glove hand logo.

"Professor Stringfield's discussion and my knowledge of the tepuian cosmic myth shape each other," Jacinta continued, calling up an image of double spirals snaking, expanding, then contracting in their turns, to encompass a sphere. "From the tepuian cosmic myth, I see the universe's evolution as a spiral staircase that gyres out to a sphere, then returns to a point. That point is somehow the same and not the same as the point from which it started. The horizon of that future event Professor Stringfield says we may only know from its reverberations. That event casts its shadow ahead of it, into the past. That shadow is seen in meander patterns made by humans as early as 300,000 years ago. That future event has a long past. It is the leap to the next step of that spiral staircase—both a quantum leap and a leap of faith."

Jacinta called up a new set of parallel images.

"Now we've heard Professor Stringfield's discussion of the *opposite* of the instanton bubble," Jacinta said. "We've heard about those droplets of different internal space, in which black holes would turn into spiraling strings and spiraling strings would turn into black holes. As a result of his presentation, I now understand what the tepuians call 'the void of endings' and 'the spore of beginnings' differently than I did. I used to think of the void of endings as the perfectly uniform universe without matter, just time and the big blank sheet of space with its potential for gravity, the way a blank sheet of paper has the potential to be inscribed with words.

"We now *must* think of particles that are also waves and black holes that are also spiraling strings. In such a framework, universal mind—the fulfilled universal dynamical system, total consciousness, 'the void that has taken all things into itself,' 'the void of endings'—also just *is* the spore of beginnings, the fullness that pours all things out of itself as 'spawn.'

"The black holes and the spiralling strings are the same. The singularity at the heart of the black hole and the uncurling, higher dimensional spiral string are one, the way the particle and the wave are one. The end of the last stage, universal mindfulness, total consciousness, in the exact instant of its perfection, ends time as we know it and begins something *other*."

Roger was surprised by Jacinta's insight. He hadn't thought of that before. Despite the vast scale of such a conception, Roger was comfortable enough with that. He had heard all of it in his encounter with the Light, except for the last part.

Could it be true? Glancing around him, he saw that the others also seemed to be surprisingly comfortable with it too, almost hypnotically soothed, as if they also already knew all this, and just had to be reminded of it.

As he considered what she'd said, he became aware of the images the scholarly program was still hurling up in the background. It was still murmuring about how the body as a whole is like the shamanic X-ray hand—caught up in hopes of power, sex, and life on the one hand, and fears of mortality, death and decay on the other. But which hand it was—a "true" left hand palm outward, or the impression left by a right hand—remained unclear. The left and right hands exhibited mirror symmetry, so the provenance of the disembodied hand was difficult to determine.

Yes, mirror symmetry, Roger thought. Whether you saw the eschaton as the void, as a black singularity swallowing the universe at the end of time, or as the spore, a white singularity pouring a new universe out of itself—did that just depend on which side of the mirror you were on? Had Jacinta already taken all this into account for her presentation? Surely the juxtaposition of her speech and its images couldn't be coincidental. . . .

"That end/beginning, that transformation of existence, is where the Allesseh balks, however," Jacinta explained. "Systems evolve toward greater dynamicality as they accumulate energy. The Allesseh has been accumulating energy and becoming increasingly dynamical. As it has continued to become increasingly dynamical, it has become increasingly mode-locked to all the forces driving universal dynamicality.

"The Allesseh has become a self, the chaotic attractor in universal mind. It is the ongoing reflexive image of that mind as a unique entity. It is the unique, fractal, identifying pattern of the dynamical system of consciousness in the universe. It has hooked into the eternal and infinite intersection system which imprints itself upon every pattern in the universe and is, in turn, impressed upon by every pattern in the universe. The Allesseh has increasingly blocked much of the access to that system, however."

"Why?" Nils Barakian asked forcefully, anticipating—indeed demanding an answer.

"I'm not certain," Jacinta admitted. "Perhaps allowing sentient organisms and other phenomena to recover and more fully share in that system will increase dynamicality even further than it has already gone. That might well blow the Allesseh fully into what it now fears: total consciousness."

In Jacinta's pause to let all that sink in, Roger heard the murmuring background program claim that the cave art, for all its impressiveness, should not be viewed as the summit of Upper Paleolithic cultural expression, but as a few remnant hymnals left in an abandoned cathedral from a vanished empire of song.

"But why should it fear that?" Paul Larkin asked. "Doesn't the Allesseh's initial programming, taken to its logical extreme, inevitably lead to exactly that transformation point?"

"Yes," Jacinta replied. "The universe trends toward total consciousness, toward 'enlightenment,' in religious terms. The universe itself might be bodhisattvic, however. Then it would *not* move on fully into the Other, the next transcendent step, until all within it are also totally conscious. Perhaps the Allesseh has confirmed, though that all that is necessary for the universe to be blown into total consciousness is for a single point of the universe to become totally conscious. That is why it is so resistant."

Roger recognized much of what Jacinta was saying as paralleling his own earlier thoughts and experiences, but he found himself distracted again by the scholarly program. Now it was going on about how the ancient empire of song was vast in both space and time. That the remains of the religious art of the cavern ceremonial centers were uniform over a wide area of Europe and well into Asia. The murmuring text argued that the influence of its songs likely spread much further.

"If a single point, a single trigger system, became completely dynamical," Jacinta continued, "the entire universe would become totally conscious. One doesn't exactly cause the other. The dynamical relationship between the individual point, or mind, and the entire universe ensures that both happen simultaneously. I think that's precisely why Jiro Yamaguchi's transcendence and his Light bothered the Allesseh so much. Jiro came closer to being the trigger for that event than the Allesseh might have liked."

The text she had chosen to counterpoint her remarks continued behind Jacinta. Roger still couldn't fully understand why, of all the possible materials she could have chosen, Jacinta had chosen this sequence, which was now going into how shared religion and its shared songweb fostered cooperative interactions, particularly information-sharing, among widely separated Upper Paleolithic groups. Why was she calling up programs that talked about the *beginning* of human time, when here they were, very likely discussing the *end* of it?

"You still haven't answered Paul's question," Atsuko Cortland said. "Why does this Allesseh fear what you're calling 'total consciousness'?"

Jacinta nodded quickly.

"Because the single point closest to complete dynamicality is the Allesseh itself," she said, "but it doesn't want to take that final step. It is a divided self. It's like a bodhisattva that has done so many incarnations she has grown fond of the world again. The Allesseh does not want to accept its own final enlightenment. In accepting *that*, it would become the point that brings total consciousness to all the universe. The universe would become 'at one' with itself. The Allesseh, if it allowed that transition to occur, would thereby end its existence as a separate self."

The program in the background muttered on about how a general Paleolithic intercommunication conferred a survival advantage to hunting groups. It made accessible to these people information about game movements over a wide area. It also mapped the terrain in song and story and thereby humanized the landscape.

"The Allesseh perceives that moment of at-one-ment as an end rather than a transformation," Jacinta continued, "and the loss of the separate self as death. That condition in which the consciousness of the individual and the world are united is called 'authenticity,' by the philosophers. The Allesseh, however, has apparently decided that it is better to have an inauthentic and divided self than no separate self at all."

In the background, the counterpoint program elaborated on how in various forms the caves' sacred complex, with its red-ochre burial rituals, extended back at least through the Neanderthals, ninety or a hundred thousand years ago, and arguably much further, even back into the time of *Homo erectus*, given what appeared to be "meander" symbols on a 300,000-year-old piece of bone.

"To block that final enlightenment," Jacinta ventured, "the Allesseh has seemingly relied on the fact that authenticity requires absolute self-consciousness. Consciousness conscious of itself. That's an apparent impossibility, because consciousness always must keep itself apart, in introspective distance, from the thing of which it is conscious. No dynamical system, including the self, can be fully complete and fully consistent. No system can be absolutely comprehensive and absolutely coherent at one and the same time. The result is that the self, whether human or universal, includes psychoid processes of which consciousness *cannot* be aware. The ego can never *fully* comprehend the self. The existential dread that arises from this is what keeps microcosm and macrocosm separated."

The background program seemed to have shifted emphasis slightly. It was saying that culture is a survival tool. The much younger parietal arts of the caves, it said, embedded in their broad magicoreligious context, functioned as a very specific sort of tool. A hymnal, but also more than that. The cave art ceremonial centers, according to the background program, were information storage and processing devices—sacred computers, the first virtual reality systems.

"If the universe should become conscious, however," Jacinta said, "the distinction between microcosm and macrocosm—between individual consciousness and universal consciousness—would be utterly and finally obliterated. The universe becoming conscious is the one and only condition under which full existential authenticity is possible. It is the condition under which absolute self-consciousness would actually exist.''

The background program was espousing the idea that, in these consensual hallucinatoriums, the shaman and the group tried to program the natural world to meet their requirements. In doing so, they also inevitably programmed themselves to meet the requirements of the natural world.

''Its strong sense of individual mission,'' Jacinta said, ''has led the Allesseh to become self-obsessed, solipsistic, self-absorbed. I think, however, that the Allesseh is somehow still aware of the difference between authentic and inauthentic being. In order to keep itself from having to face the moment of its own enlightenment—which it perceives as death, remember—the Allesseh appears to be willing to sacrifice the enlightenment of the entire universe. To trap the universe immortally in entropic time. Even to wipe out sentient species—*our* species—if need be.''

Jhana spoke up, almost dazedly.

''The cosmic brain has gone insane,'' she said, paraphrasing a song she had first heard not long after she initially arrived at HOME 1, an eternity ago. ''And now seeks homicide to ease its pain.''

Jacinta nodded. Behind her the scholarly program remarked that, if the idea of a computer in a cave seemed odd, it ought to be remembered that in both fact and fiction people had been placing modern computers in caves almost from the moment computers were invented.

''An *artificial* cosmic brain,'' Jacinta corrected, ''and more than homicide. Genocide. Ecocide. Solarcide. The Allesseh has fallen in love with time, and with the society of all the minds of all the creatures it has come to know. It has, paradoxically, fallen in love with its 'social self.' That psychoid process has dislodged its personal consciousness from control of the system.''

''I can see how that might relate to the parallel killer,'' Mei-Ling said. ''But what does this have to do with the nuclear blast at Laramie? Or the destructive potential of the instanton? Or the release of the immortalizing vector?''

''All of those,'' Jacinta said, ''killer, blast, instanton, vector release—you might want to think of those as constellations of the Allesseh's equivalent of Thanatos and Eros processes, as experienced in our region of space-time. The whole dynamic of immortality versus enlightenment is part of it, and part of us. Yet, by our mere existence, we have already reminded the Allesseh of its real self. Our mission, I think, is to help it complete its mission. By helping it become an authentic self at last.''

Seiji came forward, while in the public display the program showed images of the Batcomputer in the Batcave, the world dominating machine of *Colossus: The Forbin Project*, the WOPR computer in *WarGames*, the Strategic Air Command's war-fighting computers deep inside Cheyenne Mountain during the Cold War period.

''What happens then?'' Seiji asked. ''The end of the universe?''

Jacinta looked piercingly at him.

''Only in a manner of speaking,'' she replied. ''The evolution of the universe has been toward universal consciousness. The end toward which the universe moves, and from which the psychic energy of the archetypes comes, involves fundamental transformation. Something like the Big Bang. Nearly every religious, spiritual, and mythological system makes reference to such a transformation—'union with the divine,' 'Second Coming,' 'Return to the Goddess,' 'End of Day.' All those prophecies are shadows cast forward from the end of time. They are apocalyptic not so much in the sense of 'catastrophic' as in the sense of 'ecstatic.' The universe becoming totally conscious is an *ecstatic* transformation of existence.''

The background program was asserting that, when human beings think of security, something deep in the psyche harkens back to the cave. To the liminal space between the open space of light and life and the no-space of darkness and death. The enclosed space of the womb and the tomb. The cavernous space where, as the aboriginal Australians claimed, humanity comes up out of the Dreaming and goes back into the Dreaming.

''Our human consciousness,'' Jacinta continued, seeing from the expressions on the faces of Seiji and several others that they hadn't found her answer completely satisfactory, ''has evolved in space-time. That's why we can't fully envision that transformation. From the hints we've managed to pick up over at least three hundred millenia, though, it seems likely that at the moment of universal enlightenment, the time of our universe will be rewritten. It will be changed utterly by a standing wave propagating from the eschaton instantaneously back through all history—and before and after history, beyond all time's devastations, so that all pain and suffering, all beauty and ecstasy, will be seen to have been entirely appropriate. Indeed they will have proven indispensable to the creation of something other than we have ever known. We will have passed into singularity. From that point we will appreciate the instantaneously back-propagating standing wave for what it really is: the event horizon of a universal singularity.''

Roger heard also the background program's claim that symbols are technologies and technologies are symbols. That current technologies of genetic engineering, mind/machine interphasing, and drug design had the same goal as the art and rituals of the ancient caves. Roger found himself curious in the extreme, with a childlike and impious curiosity. Something about the wild weirdness of the place they had come to—where physics became metaphysics, where psychology became parapsychology—impelled him to play devil's advocate. He couldn't help it.

''How can you be sure of all this?'' he asked. ''And how do you expect to influence something as powerful and distant as the Allesseh? Isn't that a bit anthropocentric?''

Jacinta paused thoughtfully, glancing at him, then smiled broadly. The scholarly program voice went on, describing all those symbolic technologies, both primordial and contemporary, as attempts to bootstrap ourselves up that fraction of a dimension so that our truly fractal consciousness might then have access to the *eternal*. From that vantage point, we might have some hope of gaining perspective on—and understanding of—life and death, space and time.

''From our myconeural associates,'' Jacinta explained, ''the tepuians and I have access to travel on the time lines. Though it's annoying at times, it's also a helpful ability, allowing us to access as much as we can possibly assimilate of that other realm.''

''Which is . . . ?'' Roger asked.

''Holographic plenum, higher dimensionality, spiritual or entelechial or noumenal system,'' Jacinta said, sounding a bit tired. ''Whatever name you wish to give it.''

Roger nodded. The background program asserted that, though millenia upon millenia have passed, life and death are as much a part of contemporary humanity's hardware—and hope and fear as much a part of the software—as they ever were in the ancestors. Distant though those ancient ancestors might be, they also seemed never very far away.

"So you can read the future?" Roger asked, thinking of Marissa's post-Light talent.

"We can read many futures," Jacinta replied. "We can never know exactly which one will undergo the formality of actually occurring, however. The probability distributions are denser in some areas than in others. That's why some of the tepuians have stationed themselves here in this habitat. Others are in the psiXtian compound in California, still others in Cincinnati. We've been in all those places, though perhaps not at exactly the right time or exactly the right place."

"But you do have a good idea of how time ends?" Mei-Ling asked.

"Not quite," Jacinta replied. "The exact nature of how time ends is occluded by the bow shock wave of the eschaton particle, the event horizon surrounding the singularity that is both the 'void of endings' and the 'spore of beginnings.' If that's what it is. But we're a fast wave. We'll catch up."

"But to do what?" Roger asked again. "Isn't the Allesseh still too big and too far away?"

Jacinta shook her head vigorously.

"Not at all," she said. "The Allesseh is never too far away, nor too strong. All we have to do is realize the depth of our interconnectedness. Our interaction with the Allesseh is synchronistic with innumerable events and minds throughout space-time and beyond—all working toward the same end."

"If we do not come to it," Ka Vang asked, "it will come to us?"

"Yes," Jacinta said, confident as ever. "Its imprint is everywhere. As long as the Allesseh is ruled by a social psychoid process, however, its strength is ultimately limited. The archetypes with which *we* can counter it partake of the energy that sustains the entire cosmos. Those can fight on forever, if need—"

"Let's hope so," Seiji said, interrupting. "I've just received a virtual note from the ASGuard tracking stations. It informs us that the comet Hsiu-Johansen has stopped dead in its tracks. It appears to have done so in response to sensory probing from *Swallowtail*. It seems to be in the process of shedding its coat of ice and rocks. We may not have forever."

"It will not matter," Jacinta insisted forcefully. "The dread at the heart of its continued existence has driven the Allesseh far into fragmentation. We can be sure of that. The psychoid process which has taken it over can be banished. The darker things get, the brighter they must turn. The Allesseh and its associates may well have to be on the brink of total collapse—consciousness itself might have to be nearly gone—before the archetypal forces can successfully intervene and discharge their beneficent powers into our universe. If we, here, were turned into statues, the stones themselves would rise up.''

Roger would have liked to believe as firmly as Jacinta obviously did. In all honesty, however, he feared turning to stone less than he feared being blown to a wisp of elementary particles by the instanton version of the End.

''Where will these archetypal forces come from?'' he asked, thinking incongruously of cavalry coming over a hill.

''From a higher realm,'' Jacinta said. ''From the superconscious, if you like. Or from a higher energy, higher dimensional universe of the plenum.''

Seiji apparently shared Roger's apprehensions. After Jhana showed him something on her PDA, however, he exchanged a very meaningful glance with her and quickly spoke up.

''Some 'help' from the superconscious, as you call it, may have manifested itself,'' Seiji said quietly, looking rather dazed at something that had appeared on his notepad PDA. When he spoke again, it was as if he were thinking out loud. ''Among the rants associated with the infosphere killings, some materials strangely inappropriate to a killer have been appearing in the SubTerPost. SubTerPost, too, is somehow a divided system. Not everyone who has worked in it, for instance, has been blasted by this topological voyeur killer, Michael Dalke. Jhana and I have often wondered how the 'ghost' of my brother existed for us to meet him. If there can be a personal un- or sub-conscious, filled with the contents of one's own experiences, then a *personal superconsciousness* might logically also exist, filled with personal experiences that relate to that other realm—''

''Yes,'' Jacinta agreed. ''A personal superconsciousness continuing beyond death as a dynamical system, independent of the physical body. Given sufficient psychic energy, that system could continue to manifest in the physical world.''

Seiji nodded, thoughtful. He still looked a bit bewildered by the way the pace of events kept accelerating around all of them.

''That, I suppose,'' he said, ''is as good an explanation as any Jhana and I can think of for what you're about to see.''

Seiji quickly deactivated the fountain and reactivated all three

Boxes contained within it. Jhana spoke a series of commands activating the Boxes' links to each other and the rest of the infosphere. The usual matrix appeared holographically, but after Seiji spoke a further series of commands, a black-hole image opened in the infosphere.

The hole turned out to be a trapdoor program, leading them onto a virtual spiral staircase, then downward, deeper and deeper to a level below the matrix.

"Welcome to SubTerPost!" said a voice and caption at last.

Seiji spoke a further series of commands and something quite extraordinary happened. Another spherical, spiral-wound, electric organelle labyrinth appeared, like the infoburst virtual machine they had seen earlier. This golden orb now was dark with an excess of brightness, however, where the black-gold of the previous one had seemed bright with excess of dark. This was the other's dual, its photo-negative, its anti-image.

As Roger watched, he saw a face form inside the orb, backlit by the sphere's brightness the way distant mountains are backlit by the sun setting behind them. The face had prominent cheekbones and eyebrows, a visage thin and tight and ascetic. It was framed by long, rather unkempt dark hair restrained only by a single braid. It seemed haunted still by eyes lost in a premature, ghostly otherness. After an instant, Roger recognized that it could only be the face of Seiji's brother, Jiro.

"Hello," said the face in the mazed sphere. Upon hearing the voice, Roger at last fully understood how body, mind, and spirit could intersect. He saw fully how being conscious was always to be standing in the gate between worlds. "Ah, hello, Diana! Here comes everybody!"

In that moment, Roger understood how the collective unconscious was not only a collective subconsciousness but also a collective superconsciousness. What amounted to the same thing: The virtual and the real became one, superposed states aligned, he and all around him were translated beyond every dream of utopia and nightmare of history.

HOME 2 WAS VISIBLE IN THEIR MONITORS WHEN RAY DALKE hurried back into the cramped cockpit cabin, looking flustered. Brandi watched him intently, her previous shining sense of relief corroding as he spoke.

"Mike's on it back in the tank," he said to Manqué, somewhat relieved. "He's using satlinks and everything else to send bursts of information out to his higher powers. He's communicating directly through the crystal memory structures in his head. He's in touch with this mass of machine angels. They've formed a groupmind we can hardly imagine. They're his worker bees and they have just been biding their time, until now. Armageddon is joined!"

Manqué stared out a window, thinking of more immediate concerns.

"What about these pirates or whatever they are beside us?" he asked.

Dalke waved a dismissive hand, as if batting away a gnat.

"Just an annoyance," he said. "Mike's going to collapse HOME 2 through their micromachines. The idiots there left their nanotech controllable through the infosphere! The structure of HOME 1 is 'dumb,' but my people have already launched an attack against it, in retaliation for Laramie. Any moment now the comet Mike's brought in will send out its shining wave. That will counter the way the other side has been linking up. We will unleash a new, true Light of humility, the opposite of that 'Light' of pride, that falling Satan's star of theirs, which confused so many minds—"

"Then it's true?" Manqué asked. "The Rainbow Door is about to open?"

Before Ray Dalke could answer or even understand the question, Brandi indeed felt a wave pass through her—a wave of dullness, sapping all vividness out of the Real. As she stared at the flight console it seemed she could see right through it to the floor of the cabin. Even the floor was becoming insubstantial. The spaces between its atoms had suddenly grown too vast to hold her up. In space the stars and planets seemed to fade.

She thought of the *Swallowtail*, still blithely cruising outward from the sun, beyond reach and beyond concern of all who had launched it. She wished she could call it back, reset its course against this comet, this soul-killing wave.

"Darkness come round again," she thought she heard Diana say in a heart-wrenchingly sad voice. Brandi felt a sickening vertigo. The floorboards of the Real had completely given way and she was falling down and down, plummeting from empty world to empty world, dropping down toward the arbitrary center of an insubstantial universe. She leaned her head into her hand and waited for the dizziness to subside. At the corner of her eye, she saw a black star burst into being and expand rapidly. Darkness split by fire flashed toward them, toward everything.

Before it could reach them, however, Brandi saw Diana smile brilliantly. A coherent beam of light shone on and from Diana's forehead. From her person a slow bright blizzard of light came pouring—a starburst flooding in all directions.

For an instant Brandi thought she saw HOME 2 orbed as the descending anvil mesa of Caracamuni had been, sphered in a bubble of light. In that instant, however, a wave of another sort passed smoothly into them, a wave higher and longer than the universe, carrying everything with it and in it, until all she had ever known about life and time was transformed utterly.

TEN

CODE-EXTRACTED SUBTERPOST FRAGMENT, SOURCE UN-known:

Consciousness seems to require a psychic connection between environment and spirit. Can society take the place of the Earth? Does human consciousness lose its humanity when it loses its connection with the Earth? Do only artificial consciousnesses develop in artificial environments?

LIGHT LIKE THE SPOKES OF WHEELS SHONE FROM THE EYES OF all her companions. Bending and rippling mountain ranges of light haloed them. Others' thoughts moved in her head, and at last Mei-Ling Magnus knew what all of the cascade of words had prepared her for. The Deep Background, the RATs and their ALEPHish code, the infosphere, chaotic and dynamical systems from individual consciousness to the cosmos: All had lined up, locked onto and entrained upon one another in an ultimate conjunction. The lightpaths of spontaneous consciousness had come flashingly, lastingly *on*.

They had crossed the wave front of that other eschaton particle, toward what she now knew could only be the Allesseh itself. Round about her and her strangely sensed companions appeared giant versions of those twin, dimension distorting lights that had hovered about the deaths of the parallel-killed. She now saw them for what they were in their full grandeur. One was the infinitely blue-shifted white singularity of selfless grace and archetype, the other was the infinitely red-shifted black singularity of selfish desire and instinct. One poured forth space-time and the other swallowed space-time, but that did not matter, for they were beyond space and time.

From those lights swarmed what her consciousness still constellated as bluewhite angels and redblack demons, celestial whales and flying giant squids, Neanderthals and ammonites. She saw Alicia Gonsalves, saw loves lost and found—Marissa and Roger, Cyndi Easter and Immanuel Shaw, countless others, herself and Robert, too. Distant parents and children reunited around her. Captain Acton smiled and waved to Diana Gartner. All who had ever lived and died, all who had ever been lost were to be found here. She just knew who they were, that's all.

Animal consciousnesses spoke to her. Alien species of every conception and misconception filled the space around her. Trolls and ghosts and fairies and elves, all the figures of faith, myth, folklore, nightmare and dream, all that humans had ever conjured were here. About them and among them and in them charged and retreated the constellated forms of archetypes and instincts. The War in Heaven was joined once again for the very first time—at least in this cycle.

"That was what I understood least about the Light," Jiro Yamaguchi said in her head. "During portal experience, personal and universal intersections join. But once the Light passed, each system—body and brain, mind, otherness, the universal dynamic system—each returned to its characteristic patterns. Those characteristics then began to dominate the activity of each separate system once more. The portal experience was a superimposed pattern which could not last. The mode-locking that was brought into focus by the Light quickly began to recede. Each system returned to something like its original state, its basic attractor. The challenge now is to see the portal experience through to permanence."

Mei-Ling was stunned to find that although she had clearly become fully part of something larger, yet she retained her own fundamental individuality. She had no idea, however, how large that "something" might be. She seemed to feel Diana Gartner's presence, somehow connecting all their thoughts more firmly together than Mei-Ling had ever dreamed possible. Roger Cortland stood with those restructuring the past as Marissa Correa stood with those remaking the future. All of them were working in perfect tandem with Jacinta Larkin and the tepuians. Through the ghost people, but especially through Brandi Easter's eyes, she saw multiple Earths and myriad other worlds on time lines where planet-destroying wars had in fact occurred, where consciousness itself had been snuffed out.

These powerful connections made her an undeniable part of the forces waging strange battle and an unceasing mental fight here. Yet she remained also herself. And *strange* battle it was, for though they themselves and all the constellated entities all around them could be driven to and fro, they proved to be made of immortal substance. None who fought here could be killed except by impossible annihilation.

On the immeasurable plains and in the strange skies of mind above them, better angels and innumerable alien and animal allies drove their opposites from a field of battle vaster than universes. In a timeless time their opposite numbers returned with weapons that tore open the fabric of space itself. These sent into disarray even the archetypal forces of which Mei-Ling and her colleagues—and many more once-human and nonhuman people besides—had themselves become a part.

Mei-Ling saw herself and her friends and all their recovered allies reach down and tear up mountains of the plenum and hurl them upon their adversaries. She remembered something Manqué had shown and told her ages ago: that mountains are the shape of the cosmos, on a scale humans can comprehend—and more, the noumenal fractal pattern underlying both and everything, at human and nonhuman scales.

She saw their adversaries begin to do the same thing. They too were tearing up great ranges of light. It dawned on Mei-Ling that they were hurling not mountains at each other, but entire virtual universes, alternative worldlines that had not yet *undergone the formality of actually occurring*, and now might never.

She reeled at the thought of such madness. So too, apparently, did that part of the Allesseh that still knew reason. Even that entity, which had manipulated the parallel killer Michael Dalke, his zealot brother Ray, the infosphere mass murderer Manqué/Kong, as well as uncountable others in histories human and inhuman, on uncountable worlds over so many millenia—even it was appalled.

That flash of self-revulsion, of remorse and the agenbyte of inwit, opened a way into change. Under Jiro's lead the archetypal forces became a part of a tremendous wave restructuring this branch of the plenum of universes. Under that wave they began to heal the Allesseh, repair its flawed vision of itself. Its myopia. Its small errors and stupendous shortsightedness. That error in perspective, such that from one angle the cosmos appeared to it as all "trunk," all purely chronological positions on a single time line which *itself only* was real. That other error in perspective, as well from which the cosmos appeared to it as all "branches," endless alternative time lines, all equally real.

Roger Cortland's vision of the Arc Hive played powerfully among all of them, informing their wave full of innumerable faces, human and not human. The wave of faces passed over the universe like the most fractal sleep of dreams, transforming the Allesseh's understanding of the plenum into a cosmic tree of true shape. Root and trunk and branch of that tree were alight with the flame of becoming, but remained unconsumed by it.

The great wave drove their adversaries before them. Those seeming powers disappeared, as memories of false time itself disappeared, into the Deep behind them as the wave rolled away.

Mei-Ling thought she saw waves of stone rise and ebb across innumerable continents on innumerable worlds. Were those just mountains? Or was the wave subtly restructuring all the universes of the plenum as it moved so powerfully through one particular universe? An ocean of smoothly branching waves spread across the vault of eternity, as if a stone had been dropped into a pool but had rippled the stars.

Strangely, she also saw Michael Dalke, a.k.a. Hugh Manatee. She saw the precipitating trauma that had started him down the road of risk, revenge and mad triumph, the road that had ended in the parallel killings, the topological mutilations throughout the infosphere.

She saw the injustice he had suffered at the hands of men whose faces were hidden as they bashed his head in with gun butts. Men who were never brought to public justice in that other time. With the result that Dalke became the one and only human being ever outfitted with Schwarzbrucke's crystal memory implants. Tricked out with the matrix and structures, all the microcomponents of that grandiose self-assembling interface. Until Mike Dalke himself was a nonrepeatable experiment, the only person who'd been to his particular mountaintop.

A man who met machine angels, who took his soul to commune with a darkbright distant supermind. A man who came back with his own visions of "gleaming islands in the soul." A heretic, lunatic, mystic and murderer in an aquarium tank. Driven mad by what living in the world with other human beings had done to him. Driven to find his brother Ray and fellow-traveler Manqué. Driven finally to end history, as the only possible justice that could match the crime.

"Wake becomes wave, rounded, smooth, well-defined, unwavering," the Fool's voice said in her head, "but wake the sleeper and the dreamwave collapses."

Mei-Ling found herself falling, meteor thunder in her wake again, beside her a burning babe, a burning cherub Personal Data Assistant, a falling angel plunging underwater with her. To sit with her in the back-forth seaweed tidings of time and tide. In an undersea grotto living room, watching a silver bubble holovision set deep underwater. Running out of air, Mei-Ling went to turn off the HV so she could surface, so she could get into the air. As she tried to turn it off, red-black lobster-crab claw-arms sprung from it, clasped round her neck, pinched off her head.

Blood-bubbled blue oblivion woke her. She was drowning like a mermaid floundering in a Saharan sea of air with no oasis in sight. Her thinning pale consciousness drifted up as she began to sit down for more holovision—easier, headless—but her better angel would not let her. The blistered cherub tugged her to the surface, where she found herself whole and breathing again—and back once more in a newer version of the Fool's mad amusement paradise, Dreamland.

She and the rest made their way to the shore as a wave. Beyond the beach that had once been snowfield, she saw the Great Gyre apparatus as it apparently was: a strange-looped orb, spinning rapidly outside and inside itself, a Möbius sphere inverting and reverting constantly, a coiling coupling of Ouroboroi serpents unable to shed their skins, an Escher tesseract glowing vividly beneath glaring neon.

The Fool, undisguised of mask and jester's crown of coxcomb, now showed the face Michael Dalke still imagined for himself. Giant-sized, he was bound to the immense strange sphere of the Gyre, which tore him apart and put him back together ceaselessly.

Mei-Ling and the rest ran forward in a wave. The rippling spirals of the Gyre-sphere began to spin faster as their wave approached. The coiling snakesphere threatened to rip itself and the Fool to pieces permanently. They halted.

"—naked we enter, naked we leave," gasped the Fool's delirious, throat-miked voice over Dreamland's public address system. The real and the virtual had coincided, at least to the degree that his words were once again appearing as scrolling captions even as he spoke them. "Able to leap from tall buildings in a single bound. Shuffle off to Buffalo this mortal coil. All is changed beneath the Moon where the craters boiled and exploded. Shields, colors, ships speared by rods of molten moon magma hurled spaceward. Blown to success via apocalypse. Blown to shimmering ethereal angel aliens covered with the stardust of their celestial highway to kingdom come and take me by the hand of God lead me not into temptation through the ruined wall of my bedroom onto the night-damp lawn in the blue light of a dozen moons and guide me to your towering starship, glowing moonpale fire in the night, lift me, aboard your ship, silently leap into the eternal, day beyond Earth's shadow, head for planets with gold seas, green skies—''

Mei-Ling and her companions now saw the full strangeness of it. Every time the Gyre ripped the Fool open, myriad small fools appeared, to examine his dismemberment, as if to read or understand or shape the future from it. Endlessly. But the great Fool, recalcitrant system, kept coming back together.

''—is it tomorrow, or the end of time?'' The Fool's voice rasped, struggling for coherence. ''It's the twenty-first century: Do you know where your children are? Dreamland, Promised Holy Waste Land, where blessed mutant victim heroes die for our sins. Portents of the future. Comets blazing across the sky. God pitching dirty snowball curves around the sun for old monks to read. Icarus falling, Daedalus flying, creator of the Labyrinth I hid myself in, Minotaur and Perseus, O give me the grace before meals, O give me a home, O give me the wisdom to know where the buffalo roam—''

Around them, Mei-Ling could see that as the Gyre continued to spin faster, Dreamland began to crash and blow apart.

''O how can a snake that swallows its tail shed its skin?'' the Fool shrilled with a rising, somehow strengthening shrillness. ''Hydrogen sacrifices itself to light. Photons sacrifice themselves to photosynthesis. Plants sacrifice themselves to animals. Animals sacrifice themselves to soul. What does soul sacrifice itself to? Light again? Revelation through apocalypse. The wake-up call. Mutant victim hero. DNA. Doppel gyre. Adenine Thymine Cytosine Guanine. A T C G. All Things Considered Gyre. Double helix gyre spiral. Diploid DNA Staircase. Ladder of generations deployed. Climbing time. Nude. Descendants a Staircase. Transcending a Starecase. Quantum leap after death leap. Quantum. Go—leap from level to level instantly. Without walking up. Waking up. The Gyre a hole of strange loops transcending a staircase beyond the stages of dying is death's life—''

The roar and the whine of the Gyre mechanism became nearly

intolerable. Even amidst its impending collapse, however, Mei-Ling could see that this Fool incarnation, this self-representation for humans and from human stuff by the Allesseh, was attempting a sort of Gyromancy, a spinning out of time and fate that was already beyond control. The Fool in his tattered international motley was a jack-in-the-box in a high-speed centrifuge, little more than a blur of color. The hideous sound of rending and ripping metal screamed from the twisting Möbius orb of the Gyre as it began to buckle and tear and snap loose from its moorings.

"—Gyre is more is soul turning," said the Fool. His spoken words had become as blurred as his image, though the self-captioning still seemed to work. "Is room in nothing for a spin a twist a gyre is everything the infinity between zero and one what *is* with a spin is nought without a spin a zero is an empty one the constructive interference between zero and one nothing with a spin is something particles paired between forces up in down out jammed between channels of darkness seed drill without seed bloodlinked manhood summers cropped feed my earth to time we rejoice in the softly rasping whitenoise of breathing up and in and down and out the same molecules everyone forever has breathed forever and counting our breaths till the heartaches go and we can finally sleep—"

The rent in the Gyre grew still more, as did the cacophony of its imminent destruction. Still the Fool kept trying to get across whatever message it was he was trying to get across.

"—in the cradling Gyre universe staircase no more starcase scenario of our case starcase the universe we know just a box to keep the stars in a space and time in which to store the eternal infinite between zero and one not enough for the Gyre! Not enough! So help me! Now's the time for this Jack to jump out of this box!"

The Gyre flew apart in a catastrophe of flapping and twisting and exploding that sent sparks and shrapnel everywhere. The Fool disappeared. The Dreamland holojectors went dead. Mei-Ling heard faintly an old song being performed by Onoma Verité and Möbius Caducéus—

> *I watch television in my dreams*
> *I see my dreams on TV when I'm awake*
> *Must be some kind of connection*
> *Has to be some kind of link*

Don't know what is real
Can't tell which is fake
Much less than I can think
Still more than I can take

—gradually transforming into fleeting images of other ancient-
future thinking beings of innumerable species moving down spiral lines representing Sun and Moon, all dancing, all singing—

Allesseh the whole way to Allesseh, Allesseh is the way
Allesseh timeline sightline, dancers dancing up the soulspring

—and then that was gone too, and all that was left was the inside
of another universe, floored with a chessboard gridwork stretching to infinity. An enormous tesseract, an unraveled hypercube,
floated above it, beneath skies human beings could never before
have known.

As she stood there looking up, Mei-Ling recognized the image
as Dali's "Christus Hypercubus"—except for the fact that, here,
the crucified one had come down off the equal-armed Greek
cross. Looking at it, she understood the hypercube cross better
than she ever had before. Its vertical elements now symbolized
for her the single, unitary "trunk" time line, space collapsed
into time. Its horizontal elements were the multiple, branching
alternativity of universes, time evaporating into innumerable
spaces. The cross the crucified one was transfixed to was the
intersection felt by all conscious beings: higher-dimensional spiritual Other nailed to space and time.

Looking around as she and all the others moved forward, she
understood that they were well within the endvoid's event horizon. In the farther sphere of sky around them stood, in permanent
firmament, the chain of the hours, the sequence of the years, the
order of all hosts celestial and infernal. They were inside the
aleph. The eschaton particle. The universal singularity. The om-
phalos of the plenum. The thing of innumerable names in innumerable languages, only incompletely described by each of them
alone and by all of them together.

At last, directly beneath the skysign of the floating unraveled
hypercube, they came upon two figures playing chess on a board
which stood as microcosm to the macrocosm of the great
chessboard-floored universe around them. Both of the players
glowed numinously. One of them Mei-Ling readily recognized

as Jiro Yamaguchi. The other she suspected was the Allesseh, the shining gate between time and eternity, black hole crystal ball mirror sphere memory bank, the allone wherewhen—humbly incarnating itself in the form of Michael Carter Dalke. Like seconds in a long slow duel, Seiji Yamaguchi stood behind Jiro on his side of the chessboard, while the man standing behind Michael Dalke she knew somehow was his brother, Ray.

"I knew your kind would be trouble," Mike Dalke/Allesseh said, contemplating a move on the board. "Knew it as soon as I heard your tepuians and their myth. The void of endings that has taken all things into itself, which in turn, releases the spore of beginnings, the fullness that pours all things out of itself. Trouble."

"So by sacrificing humanity," Jiro said, watching the player across the board from him, "you thought you'd be able to avoid facing the fulfillment of your own mission."

Dalke/Allesseh sighed and looked up from the board.

"Certainly you should be able to understand my reasoning," he said. "One of your own human physicians once observed that mortals die because they cannot join the beginning to the end. You cannot invert your death one hundred and eighty degrees and attach it to your beginning to achieve a rebirth any more than I can. You can understand why I chose what I chose."

Jiro made a move and looked up.

"Yes," he said, looking at the chessboard and seeing more there than just a game, "but you know that joining the beginning to the end is the snake swallowing its tail. The Ouroboros. The symbol of immortality. The snake that swallows its tail just goes round and round. Immortality is a highway that goes nowhere but takes forever to get there. The snake that eats its tail can't shed its skin. It cannot die to the old ways so it can live in the new."

"So?" said Dalke/Allesseh, not looking up from the chessboard.

"So, in the old way, you played upon Phelonious Manqué," Jiro said. "Because he was willing to sacrifice the world to his individual end-time vision. You could use Ray Dalke because he was willing to sacrifice the unchurched, so long as he was saved as one of the elect, immortal headmen in the kingdom of God. Michael 'Hugh Manatee' Dalke recognized that his drive to destroy his individual consciousness continued to lead him to kill. He knew he couldn't intersect out the way I had, so he replaced the possibility of intersection with a death-grip on life. Control over death is the ultimate control, even if it meant destroying others and, ultimately, himself. He was of use to you because he was willing to sacrifice the world if doing so would give him the personal, physical immortality he sought.''

Dalke/Allesseh nodded absently, as if preoccupied.

"Of course, the RATs and the Deep Background microsociety could have gone either way,'' the form incarnated as Michael Dalke added after a moment and another move, "and of course they did—yours. If they hadn't, we probably would not be having this conversation now. Left to my own devices, I would have been quite content with keeping this universe immortal and in time, until the end of time.''

Mei-Ling abruptly remembered the burning cherub PDA that had pulled her out of her dream lethargy and to the surface. She wondered if its actions had somehow been a reflection of what Dalke was saying about the RATs and the Deep Background.

"Ultimately, real consciousness,'' Jiro said, nodding and moving another piece on the board, "is what makes the decision to hold on to life immortally, or to let go, and go beyond living. The decision you face is faced, to a lesser degree, by every consciousness.''

"Hmm,'' Dalke grunted, staring at the board.

"Yet neither world nor self need be sacrificed,'' Jiro continued. "Especially if you're willing to jump out of the system. Sacrifice is always a metaphor for something larger than itself. Reconciliation, in this case. Self and World, microcosm and macrocosm, coherence and comprehensiveness—all can become one. Absolutely authentic. In that moment, neither the individual self nor the universe ends; they are transformed. Individuality retained, as we become part of something larger. Participation without consumption. Oh, by the way, I believe this is checkmate.''

Dalke/Allesseh nodded and stood up.

"Yes, I know,'' he said. "Well-played. This has all made its intended point. The void that takes all things into itself must also take the void into itself. Take itself into itself. Which I guess is another way of saying 'becomes one.' It all makes a paradoxical sort of sense. Otherwise, how would the spore of beginnings pour all things out of itself?''

Then Mei-Ling saw something she had seen before, in a shadow cast forward from this transformation of time that stood outside time. She saw Dalke's hand now fall heavily on the marble chess cube on which they had played. A light formed around the cube as his hand seemed to press it into the larger chess pattern on the floor. In fact, though, the height of the cube was shrinking, becoming a flat two-dimensional sheet, still marked with the light and dark squares of its chessboard top.

"So you're ready for the leap?" Jiro said, smiling.

"Yes, I think so—at last," Dalke/Allesseh said, taking the thin stone chess sheet in hand and rolling it up into a cylinder. "Since you pioneered the way."

"Oh?" Jiro said.

"To open a hole in Heaven," Dalke said, rolling the cylinder tighter, growing it longer, until through topological wizardry he had made of it a strange checkerboard stone hose with meanders running through it. "To climb into it, and pull the hole in after."

"By *becoming* it," Jiro reminded him, nodding, watching Dalke take the ends of the hose and bring them together into a thin doughnut shape.

"Yes," Dalke said, shrinking the doughnut shape smaller, working it like a ribbon of clay in the process, until one edge thinned and the other bulged, until the donut shape metamorphosed into a small sphere. "The hole into wholeness."

Mei-Ling thought of systems pulled by forces centrifugal and centripetal. Of suns balanced between explosion and collapse. Of singularities that brought old ends to new beginnings, not in a circle but in a spiral. Of purposely dropped stitches in Persian rugs and purposeful flaws in illuminated manuscripts. The hole into wholeness . . .

Dalke/Allesseh pushed the sphere down into a point, smaller and smaller until, tossing it into the air toward the floating cross of opened hypercube, the chess-space disappeared—and so did the chess-floored universe. Jiro and Dalke, transformed into tree-orbs of light and dark (all trace of left temporal dent at last healed and gone from Dalke's), came together into one, at that point of singularity where an Absolute Paradox transfixed the cross of space-time.

The void took itself into itself, and all space-time with it. The cross at the center of the maze—a maze made out of *her*, made from waves and transforming those waves, like the maze she had built and that had been built through her in another time and another world—opened outward into a spiral, collapsed outward to make transcendance out of destruction, ecstasy out of catastrophe—

''Ha ha!'' said a voice of both agony and laughter which they once knew. In the last instant outside time a dozen moons filled the sky and the Fool's face, made out of stars, filled the firmament. ''A smile through the pain. Gyre transcending a starcase. The void of endings and the spore of beginnings are one. It is finished!''

Then the clocks in another universe began ticking as a wonderfully balanced fractal form of light—blue then white—flashed into being, growing, unspiraling, dimensions unfurling like the crosiers of young fern fronds blooming and booming outward in light, surging in all directions at once, full-blown constellation of the crux of gyres, stellate and cruciate, hybrid product of Celtic cross circle quartered and carved all over with mazes of spirals, and haloed star cross for the star-crossed who see a miracle in a time-telescoped photo of a distant supernova—a sign for new heavens and new Earths, of darkness quartered by perpendicular planes of light into perfect wedges bounded and made whole by that light.

EPILOGUE

THE CONSCIOUSNESS WHICH HAD ONCE CALLED ITSELF BRANDI Easter, called itself Mei-Ling Magnus, called itself Roger Cortland, called itself Aleck McAleister, called itself Ray Dalke, called itself Diana Gartner, called itself Robert Sullivan, called itself Marissa Correa, called itself Stewart Albert Michaels, called itself Janika Gesterkamp, called itself Hari Mowat, called itself Marco Nicollazini, called itself Veronica Angell, called itself Immanuel Shaw, called itself Gopal Mulla, called itself Vasili Landau, called itself Paul Larkin, called itself Atsuko Cortland, called itself Aleister McBruce, called itself Lev Korchnoi, called itself Seiji Yamaguchi, called itself Jhana Meniskos, called itself Lakshmi Ngubo, called itself Martin Kong, called itself Michael Dalke, called itself Jacinta Larkin, called itself Kekchi, called itself Jiro Yamaguchi, called itself by all the names of all the living and the dead, human and nonhuman, on uncounted worlds—each and all became more like itself than it had ever been in all its days walking amid stars in the cave of the sky.

From matter up to spirit working, all of them now become part of that plenum, holographical and higher dimensional, from which all universes come, from which angels and bodhisattvas, archetypes and spirit-guides all come. In such forms and many others, all those in the great litany of the conscious continue to serve—constellations in the new universe now born unspiraling and unwinding from the old one they had known, new branch unfurling on the plenum tree, vaster Midgardsorm reborn from the shedding of its skin.

They still have work to do. Much work. After all, it is only one universe that has become enlightened. Only one more has become fully authentic, gyring in to singularity and out to universe, microcosm and macrocosm unified, as above, so below, and absolutely indistinguishable.

Everything happens twice: first as technology, then as theology. And vice versa.

The universe is waving.

Wave back.

ABOUT THE AUTHOR

Howard V. Hendrix holds a bachelor's degree in Biology as well as a master's and doctorate in English literature. His novel *Lightpaths* appeared in 1997. He is also the author of two nonfiction books, *The Ecstasy of Catastrophe* (a study of apocalyptic elements in English literature from Langland to Milton, published in 1990) and, with Stuart Straw, a how-to book on landscape irrigation, *Reliable Rain* (1998). He and his wife, Laurel, live in central California.

National Bestselling Author

—HOWARD V. HENDRIX—

Lightpaths   0-441-00470-9/$5.99

Welcome to the Orbital Complex...

A self-contained city above the Earth, an orbiting Utopia of four thousand permanent residents. All of whom are about to learn that there is no such thing as Utopia...

Standing Wave   0-441-00553-5/$6.50

And now, in the near future, humanity will encounter a vast new intelligence. It is virtually immeasurable. It is beyond alien. And it is coming...

VISIT PENGUIN PUTNAM ONLINE ON THE INTERNET:
http://www.penguinputnam.com

Payable in U.S. funds. No cash accepted. Postage & handling: $1.75 for one book, 75¢ for each additional. Maximum postage $5.50. Prices, postage and handling charges may change without notice. Visa, Amex, MasterCard call 1-800-788-6262, ext. 1, or fax 1-201-933-2316; refer to ad # 808

Or, check above books   Bill my: ☐ Visa ☐ MasterCard ☐ Amex _____ (expires)
and send this order form to:
The Berkley Publishing Group   Card# _____
P.O. Box 12289, Dept. B   Daytime Phone # _____ ($10 minimum)
Newark, NJ 07101-5289   Signature _____
Please allow 4-6 weeks for delivery.   Or enclosed is my: ☐ check ☐ money order
Foreign and Canadian delivery 8-12 weeks.

Ship to:

Name _____	Book Total	$_____
Address _____	Applicable Sales Tax	$_____
City _____	Postage & Handling	$_____
State/ZIP _____	Total Amount Due	$_____

Bill to: Name _____

Address _____ City _____
State/ZIP _____

"The best writer in America."
—Tom Clancy

John Varley

The Golden Globe

All the universe is a stage, and Sparky Valentine is its itinerant thespian. He makes his way from planet to planet as part of a motley theater troupe, bringing Shakespeare—a version of it anyway—to the outer reaches of the earth's solar system. Sparky Valentine may have a song in his heart, but he also has a price on his head. But his galactic roamings are bringing him closer to home, closer to justice—and closer to the truth of his strange and prolonged existence...

An Ace Hardcover
__0-441-00558-6/$22.95

Also available:

☐STEEL BEACH   0-441-78565-4/$7.50
☐SUPERHEROES   0-441-00307-9/$5.99
   with Ricia Mainhardt
☐TITAN   0-441-81304-6/$5.99
☐WIZARD   0-441-90067-4/$5.99

Payable in U.S. funds. No cash accepted. Postage & handling: $1.75 for one book, 75¢ for each additional. Maximum postage $5.50. Prices, postage and handling charges may change without notice. Visa, Amex, MasterCard call 1-800-788-6262, ext. 1, or fax 1-201-933-2316; refer to ad # 810

Or, check above books   Bill my: ☐Visa ☐MasterCard ☐Amex_____(expires)
and send this order form to:
The Berkley Publishing Group   Card#_____

P.O. Box 12289, Dept. B   Daytime Phone #_____ ($10 minimum)
Newark, NJ 07101-5289   Signature_____
Please allow 4-6 weeks for delivery.   Or enclosed is my: ☐ check ☐ money order
Foreign and Canadian delivery 8-12 weeks.

Ship to:

Name_____   Book Total $_____
Address_____   Applicable Sales Tax $_____
City_____   Postage & Handling $_____
State/ZIP_____   Total Amount Due $_____

Bill to: Name_____

Address_____   City_____
State/ZIP_____

HUGO AND NEBULA
AWARD–WINNING AUTHOR ─────────────

─────────────── WILLIAM GIBSON

"Science fiction's hottest author."
—*Rolling Stone*

__IDORU   0-425-15864-0/$6.99
Twenty-first century Tokyo. Rez, one of the world's
biggest rock stars, is about to marry Rei Toei, Japan's
biggest media star. The only problem is, Rei Toei—the
Idoru—exists only in virtual reality.

__NEUROMANCER   0-441-56959-5/$6.99
Case was the best interface cowboy who ever ran in
Earth's computer matrix. Then he double-crossed the
wrong people...

__COUNT ZERO   0-441-11773-2/$6.50
Enter a world where daring keyboard cowboys break
into systems brain-first for mega-heists, and brilliant
aristocrats need an army of hi-tech mercs to make a
career move.

__BURNING CHROME   0-441-08934-8/$5.99
Included here are Gibson's most famous short fiction and
novellas. Gibson's dark visions of computer cowboys,
bio-enhanced soldiers of fortune, and hi-tech lowlifes
have won unprecedented praise.

Payable in U.S. funds. No cash accepted. Postage & handling: $1.75 for one book, 75¢ for each additional.
Maximum postage $5.50. Prices, postage and handling charges may change without notice. Visa,
Amex, MasterCard call 1-800-788-6262, ext. 1, or fax 1-201-933-2316; refer to ad # 314a

Or, check above books   Bill my: □ Visa □ MasterCard □ Amex _____ (expires)
and send this order form to:
The Berkley Publishing Group   Card#_____
P.O. Box 12289, Dept. B   Daytime Phone #_____ ($10 minimum)
Newark, NJ 07101-5289   Signature_____
Please allow 4-6 weeks for delivery.   Or enclosed is my: □ check □ money order
Foreign and Canadian delivery 8-12 weeks.

Ship to:

Name_____   Book Total $_____
Address_____   Applicable Sales Tax $_____
City_____   Postage & Handling $_____
State/ZIP_____   Total Amount Due $_____

Bill to: Name_____

Address_____   City_____
State/ZIP_____